THE GATE
TO WOMEN'S
COUNTRY

THE GATE
TO WOMEN'S
COUNTRY

SHERI S. TEPPER

FOUNDATION BOOKS

Doubleday

NEW YORK   LONDON   TORONTO   SYDNEY   AUCKLAND

A Foundation Book
Published by Doubleday, a division of
Bantam Doubleday Dell Publishing Group, Inc.,
666 Fifth Avenue, New York, New York 10103

Foundation, Doubleday and the portrayal of the letter F are trademarks of Doubleday, a division of Bantam Doubleday Dell Publishing Group, Inc.

Library of Congress Cataloging-in-Publication Data

Tepper, Sheri S.
The gate to women's country.

I. Title.
PS3570.E673G38   1988   813'.54   88-387
ISBN 0-385-24709-5

THE GATE
TO WOMEN'S
COUNTRY

STAVIA SAW HERSELF as in a picture, from the outside, a darkly cloaked figure moving along a cobbled street, the stones sheened with a soft, early spring rain. On either side the gutters ran with an infant chuckle and gurgle, baby streams being amused with themselves. The corniced buildings smiled candlelit windows across at one another, their shoulders huddled protectively inward—though not enough to keep the rain from streaking the windows and making the candlelight seem the least bit weepy, a luxurious weepiness, as after a two-hanky drama of love lost or unrequited.

As usually happened on occasions like this one, Stavia felt herself become an actor in an unfamiliar play, uncertain of the lines or the plot, apprehensive of the ending. If there was to be an ending at all. In the face of the surprising and unforeseen, her accustomed daily self was often thrown all at a loss and could do nothing but stand aside upon its stage, one hand slightly extended toward the wings to cue the entry of some other character—a Stavia more capable, more endowed with the extemporaneous force or grace these events required. When the appropriate character entered, her daily self was left to watch from behind the scenes, bemused by the unfamiliar intricacy of the dialogue and settings which this other, this actor Stavia, seemed able somehow to negotiate. So, when this evening the unexpected summons had arrived from Dawid, the daily Stavia had bowed her way backstage to leave the boards to this other persona, this dimly cloaked figure making its way with sure and unhesitating tread past the lighted apartments and through the fish and fruiterers markets toward Battle Gate.

Stavia the observer noted particularly the quality of the light. Dusk. Gray of cloud and shadowed green of leaf. It was apt, this light—well done for the mood of the piece. Nostalgic. Melancholy without being utterly depressing. A few crepuscular rays broke through the western cloud cover in long, mysterious beams, as though they were searchlights from a celestial realm, seeking a lost angel, perhaps, or some escaped soul from Hades trying desperately to find the road to heaven. Or perhaps they were casting about to find a fishing boat, out there on the darkling sea, though she could not immediately think of a reason that the heavenly ones should need a fishing boat.

Near the Well of Surcease, its carved coping gleaming with liquid runnels and its music subsumed into the general drip and gurgle, the street began its downhill slope from the Temple of the Lady to the ceremonial plaza and the northern city wall. At street level on the right a long row of craftswomen's shops stared blindly at the cobbles through darkened windows: candle makers, soap makers, quilters, knitters. On the left the park opened toward the northwest in extended vistas of green and dark, down past the scooped bowl of the summer theater where Stavia would play the part of Iphigenia this summer. Not play, she thought. Do. Do the part. As someone had to do it. In the summer theater. In the park.

A skipping seawind brought scents of early spring flowers and pine and she stopped for a moment, wondering what the set designer had in mind. Was this to remind her of something? All the cosiness of candle flame and gurgling gutters leading toward this sweet sadness of green light and softly scented mist? Too early to know, really. Perhaps it was only misdirection, though it might be intended as a leitmotif.

The street leveled at the bottom of the hill where it entered the Warrior's Plaza, unrelenting pavement surrounded on three sides by stories of stolid and vacant colonnades. The arched stone porches were old, preconvulsion structures. Nothing like that was built today. Nothing so dignified, so imposing, so unnecessary. The ceremonial space seemed far emptier than the streets behind her. The arches wept for spectators; the polished stones of the plaza cried for marching feet, the rat-a-bam of drums, the toss of plumes, and the crash of lances snapped down in the salute, ker-bam! The plaza sniffled in abandonment, like a deserted lover.

Oh yes, the journey had been meant as a leitmotif, she could tell. The plaza made it clear.

On three sides of the plaza, the colonnades. On the fourth side, the towering wall, high-braced with buttresses, glimmering with mosaics, pierced by the Defenders' Gate, the Battle Gate, and the Gate of the Warriors' Sons, which comprised a triptych of carved timbers and contorted bronze depicting scenes of triumph and slaughter. The Defender's Gate was at the left of this lofty arrangement, and she stood close to it for a long time—perceiving herself before it as though from a front-row-center seat, the compliant lines of her cloak melting before the obdurate metal—before reaching out with her staff to knock the requisite three times, not loudly. They would be waiting for her.

The small door at the base of the great portal swung open; she walked with every appearance of calm down the short corridor beyond. In the assembly room she found an honor guard. And Dawid, of course.

How could she have forgotten he was fifteen? Well, she hadn't. She was thirty-seven, so he was fifteen. She had been twenty-two when . . . when everything. All this pretense that the summons was unexpected was really so much playacting, a futile attempt to convince herself that something unforeseen might happen despite her knowing very well what the plot required. Despite Dawid's ritual visits on holidays, his twice-yearly home-comings—during which the initial shyness of the original separation had turned to fondness, then to shyness again, finally becoming the expected, though no less wounding, alienation—despite all that, she had chosen to go on thinking of him as she had when he was five and had gone into the hands of the warriors.

So, now, she must guard against speaking to that child, for this was no child confronting her in his polished breastplate and high helmet, with pouted lips outthrust. No child anymore.

"Dawid," she said formally, bowing a little to indicate the respect she bore him. And "Gentlemen," for the respect she bore these others, also. One had to grant them that; one could grant so little else. She risked one raking glance across the ranked faces above the shining armor, subconsciously thinking to see faces that she knew could not be there. Those that were there were young. No old faces. No old faces at all.

"Madam," intoned one member of the host. Marcus, she thought, examining what she could see of his visage between the cheek and nose guards of his helmet; Marcus, probably, though it might have been another of her sister Myra's sons—all three looked disconcertingly alike and had, even as babies. "Madam," he said, "your warrior son greets you."

"I greet my warrior son," the actor Stavia said while the observer Stavia annoyed herself by weeping, though inwardly and silently, as befitted the occasion.

"I challenge you, madam," said Dawid. His voice was light, very light, almost a child's voice, still, and she knew he had been practicing that phrase in the shower room and in corners of the refectory, no doubt listening with heartbreaking attention for the vibrant echo of command. Still, it quavered with a child's uncertainty.

"Oh?" she questioned, cocking her head. "How have I offended?"

"During my last homecoming"—he gave the word the aversive twist she had believed only a mature warrior could give it, "homecoming," as though it were something dirty; well, perhaps it was—"you made a suggestion to me which was unworthy of my honor."

"Did I, indeed?" The actor Stavia was properly puzzled. "I cannot remember any such."

"You said," his voice quavered. "You said I would be welcome to return to my mother's house through the Gate to Women's Country."

"Well, and so you would be," she said calmly, wishing this farce were done with so she might go home and weep. "So are any of our sons."

"Madam, I summoned you here to tell you that such a suggestion offends my honor! I am no longer your son. I am proud to name myself a son of the warriors. I have become a Defender!"

So, and well, and what had she expected? Still, for a moment she could not respond. The observer Stavia held the actor in thrall, just for this moment, seeking in that face the face of the five-year-old Dawid, mighty hunter of grasshoppers, thunderer on the toy drum, singer of nursery rhymes, leading contender in the skipping race from home to candy shop. That level-browed, serious-eyed, gentle-lipped child. No more. No more.

No, it was all bronze and leather now. The Marthatown garrison tattoo was on his upper arm. He had a cut on his chin where he had shaved himself, though his skin looked like a baby's. Still the arms and chest were muscular and almost adult, almost a man's body. Fit for love. Fit for slaughter.

Get on with it, wept the observer Stavia.

"Then I relinquish all claim to you, Dawid, son of the warriors. You need not visit us again." A pause for the words which were not obligatory but which she was determined upon. Let him know, even now, that it cut both ways. "You are not my son." She bowed, believing for a moment that the dizziness which struck her would prevent her getting her head up, but then the actor had her up and wheeling about, finding her way almost by instinct. Women could not return through the Defender's Gate. There was a corridor here to the left, she told herself, remembering what she had been told and managing to get into it with level tread, not breaking stride, not hurrying or slowing. Even the hiss behind her did not hurry her steps. A serpent's hiss, but by only a few, possibly only one set of lips, and those not Dawid's. Stavia had played by the rules since Dawid was born, and all those metal-clad automatons knew it. They could not hiss her in good conscience, and only zealots would do it. Despite them, she would not hurry. No, no, and no, the thing must be done properly if it had to be done at all.

And then, ahead of her at the end of the narrow corridor she saw it for the first time, the gate that all the fuss was about, narrow and quite unprepossessing. The Gate to Women's Country, as described: a simple sheet of polished wood, with a bronze plaque upon it showing the ghost of Iphigenia holding a child before the walls of Troy. On the right was a bronze latch in the shape of a pomegranate, set low, so that even a small woman could reach it easily. Her eyes sought it, her thumb pressed it down, and the door swung open smoothly, as though well used, well oiled.

In the plaza arcade, where the gate opened, old Septemius Bird was waiting for her with his nieces, Kostia and Tonia, their twinned exoticism long since become familiar and dear. Though not friends of her childhood, they were neighbors now, and Morgot must have told them the summons had come. Beneda was there as well, even though Stavia didn't really want to see her, not right now. But Beneda was a neighbor, too, and she had found out about Dawid somehow. Well, she had a right, in a sense. Besides, Beneda always found out about such things.

"Alone?" she now asked. Beneda had become fond of rhetorical questions and purely exclamatory phrases, needing to fill all silences with little explosions of sound, like a string of firecrackers which once lit could not keep itself from popping, set off no doubt to keep her own demons away. So she repeated herself, "Ah well, Stavia, so you return alone, as I have done, as we all have done. We grieve, Stavia. We grieve."

Stavia, who had loved her dearly once and still did, wanted to tell her to be quiet for heaven's sake, but instead merely smiled and reached for her hand, hoping Beneda would silence herself for lack of anything to say. What was there to say? Hadn't they all said it to one another, over and over again.

Septemius, on the other hand, knew how to be comforting. "Come on along, Doctor. I'm sure it's no more than you expected, and these girls of mine have been to the Well of Surcease for a kettleful. There's a nice cup of tea waiting." His arm around her shoulders was firm and wiry, as though it belonged to someone half his age. Next to Corrig, who as a servitor could not appear in the plaza with her, Septemius was the one she found most comfort in.

As they returned through the empty streets, the observer Stavia, now in command of herself once more, noted the quality of light. What she had thought was nostalgic and sweetly melancholic was now livid and bruised. The light was a wound, and like a wound it throbbed and pulsed. If it had not been for the old man's arm about her shoulders, Stavia might not have managed the last few steps into her own house where Morgot and Corrig waited with the tea, where Stavia's daughters, Susannah and Spring waited with questions.

"So Dawid chose to stay with the warriors, Mother." Susannah was thirteen now, her face already firming into a woman's face, with serious dark eyes and a strong jaw.

"Yes, Susannah. As we thought he would," said Stavia, telling them the truth she had refused to tell herself. She had not really let herself think he would stay with the warriors, even though both Joshua and Corrig had known that it was certain.

"I wish for your sake he'd come home to us," Spring said, repeating some adult comment she had overheard. Spring was only eleven, still a little girl. She would be slenderer than Susannah, and prettier. For Stavia, looking at Spring was like looking into the mirror of her own past. Now the girl added her own perceptive comment. "I knew he wouldn't come back. He never really cared about us."

She knew more than I, Stavia thought, looking deep into Spring's eyes.

"What are you thinking?" Corrig murmured into her ear as he warmed her tea.

"Of me when I was almost Spring's age," she said. "Long before I knew you. Of my first trip to the Warrior's Gate when we took my little brother, Jerby, to his warrior father." She turned to her mother, murmuring, "Remember, Morgot. When you and Beneda and Sylvia and I took Jerby to the plaza."

"Oh, so long ago," Beneda, overhearing, interrupted with a little explosion of breath. "I remember it well. So very long ago."

"I remember," said Morgot, her face turning inward with a kind of intent concentration. "Oh yes, Stavia. Of course I remember."

STAVIA HAD BEEN TEN. She remembered kneeling in the kitchen, picking at her bootlace to make it lie absolutely flat. It was a bargain that she had made with the Lady. If she learned the whole Iphigenia play, word for word, and if she cleaned up her room and did the dishes by herself and then dressed perfectly, without one dangling button or wrinkled bootlace, then they wouldn't have to give Jerby away. Not ever. Not even though her older sister, Myra, was already standing in the doorway, impatiently brushing the five-year-old's hair to get him ready.

"Stavia, if you don't hurry up with those boots, Myra and I are going to leave you behind." Morgot had arranged the blue woolen veil over her head for the tenth time and had stood before the mirror, running her fingers over her cheeks, looking for lines. She hadn't found any lines in her beautiful face, but she had looked for them every day, just in case. Then she had stood up and begun buttoning her long, padded ceremonial coat. Time to go.

"I'm hurrying," ten-year-old Stavia had said.

"Stand still," Myra commanded the little boy she was brushing. "Stop fidgeting." She sounded as though she were about to cry, and this took Stavia's attention away from her boots.

"Myra?" she said. "Myra?"

"Mother said hurry up," Myra commanded in an unpleasant voice, fixing her cold eye on Stavia's left foot. "We're all waiting on you."

Stavia stood up. The arrangement she had made wasn't going to work. She could tell. Not if Myra was almost crying, because Myra almost never cried except for effect. If something was bad enough to make Myra cry for no discernible advantage, then Stavia couldn't stop it, no matter what she did. If she were older, then she could have tried a bigger promise, and maybe Great Mother would have paid attention. At age ten one didn't have much bargaining power. Of course, Morgot and Myra would tell her there wasn't any reason to make promises or seek changes because the Great Mother didn't bargain. The deity didn't change her mind for women's convenience. Her way was immutable. As the temple servers said, "No sentimentality, no romance, no false hopes, no self-petting lies, merely that which is!" Which left very little room, Stavia thought, for womanly initiative.

This depressing fatalism swelled into a mood of general sadness as they went down the stairs and into the street. Her mother's friend Sylvia was there with her daughter Beneda, both of them very serious-looking and pink-cheeked from the cold. Sylvia's servitor Minsning stood to one side, chewing his braid and wringing his hands. Minsning always wrung his hands, and sometimes he cried so that his bulbous nose turned red as an apple. There were other neighbors, too, gathered outside their houses, including several serving men. Joshua, Morgot's servitor, had gone away on business, so he wasn't able to tell Jerby good-bye. That was sad, too, because Joshua and Jerby had been best friends, almost like Stavia and Beneda were.

"Our condolences go with you," a neighbor called, dabbing at the inside corners of her eyes with a crumpled handkerchief.

Morgot bowed, receiving the words with dignity.

Sylvia said, "Morgot, are you going to be all right?"

Stavia's mother nodded, then whispered, "As long as I don't try to talk."

"Well don't. Just bow and keep your veil straight. Here, let me carry Jerby."

"No!" Morgot stepped away, hugging the little boy through his quilted coat. "Sorry, Syl. I just . . . want to hold on to him as long as I can."

"Stupid of me," Sylvia dithered, turning red. "Of course."

The six of them went down the hill in a quiet procession: Morgot carrying Jerby, with Sylvia alongside, then Myra by herself, then Beneda and

Stavia—who was trying not to cry and to look dignified at the same time, and failing at both. Beneda giggled, and Myra cast them an angry red-eyed glare over one shoulder.

"You little girls behave yourselves."

"I am behaving myself," Stavia said, then more softly, "Beneda, you stop getting me in trouble." Beneda often said things or did things suddenly that got them both in trouble, though she never meant to. Stavia was more self-conscious. When Stavia got into trouble, it was generally over something she had thought about for a very long time.

"I wasn't getting you in trouble. I was just laughing."

"Well, it's not funny."

"You look funny. Your face is all twisted up." Beneda mimicked Stavia, screwing up her eyes and mouth.

"Your face would get twisted up, too, if you had to give your little brother away."

"I don't have a little brother. Besides, everybody has to. It isn't just you."

"Jerby's not everybody. Joshua will really miss him."

"Joshua's nice." Beneda thought about this for half a block. "Joshua's nicer than Minsning. I wish our family had a servitor like Joshua. Joshua can find things when you lose them. He found my bracelet that Mother gave me. He found Jerby that time he was lost, too."

Stavia remembered hysteria and weeping and Joshua calmly concentrating then going to the empty cistern and finding Jerby curled up in it asleep. "Maybe we can do something to make it up to him."

"Maybe Mother will have another baby boy," said Myra, not looking back.

"She's had three already," said Stavia. "She says that's enough."

"I didn't know that," Beneda said, looking curiously at the women. "My mom only had one. And then there's me and Susan and Liza."

"Mother had Myra first, then Habby, then Byram, then me, then Jerby," Stavia confided. "Myra's seventeen, and that means Habby and Byram are thirteen and twelve, because they're four years and five years younger than Myra, and that's how we keep track. How old is your brother? What's his name?"

Beneda shook her head. "About the same age as your brothers, I think. His name is Chernon. He's the oldest. He went to the warriors when I was real little, but I don't think he's fifteen yet. Something happened and he doesn't visit us anymore. He goes to Aunt Erica's house. Mom doesn't talk about him."

"Some families don't," Myra offered. "Some families just try to forget about them unless they come home."

"I won't forget Jerby," Stavia announced. "I won't." Despite all her good resolutions, she heard the tears in her voice and knew her eyes would spill over.

Myra came back to them abruptly. "I didn't say you would," she said angrily. "Jerby will be home twice every year, for visits, during the carnival holidays. Nobody's going to forget him. I just said some families do, that's all. I didn't mean us." She turned and stamped back to her place ahead of them.

"Besides, maybe he'll return when he's fifteen," comforted Beneda. "Then you can visit him, whatever house he's assigned to. You can even travel to visit him if he goes to some other town. Lots of boys do come back."

"Some," amended Myra, turning to glare at them with a peculiar twist to her mouth. "Some do."

They had walked all the way past the Market District to the Well of Surcease. Sylvia and Morgot each took a cup from the attendant and filled it, spilling some toward the Lady's Chapel for the Lady, then sipping at it, drawing the time out. Myra took their offering to the poor box outside the chapel door, then sat on the well coping, looking sulky. Stavia knew that Myra just wanted to get it over with. There was no necessity for stopping at the well. The water was purely symbolic—at least when drunk directly from the well like this—and offered no real consolation except a reminder that surcease would come if one didn't fight it. "Accept grief," the priestess said at services for the lost ones. "Accept grief, but do not nurse it. In time it will go." At the moment, that was hard to remember, much less understand.

"We all have to do things we don't want to do," Morgot had said. "All of us here in Women's Country. Sometimes they are things that hurt us to do. We accept the hurt because the alternative would be worse. We have many reminders to keep us aware of that. The Council ceremonies. The play before summer carnival. The desolations are there to remind us of pain, and the well is there to remind us that the pain will pass. . . ."

Stavia wasn't sure she could ever learn to find comfort in the thought, though Morgot said she would if she tried. Now she merely took off her boiled wool mittens and dabbled her fingers in the water, pretending there were fishes in the fountain. The water came from high up in the mountains where the snow lay deep almost all year long, and there were fishes up there, people said. The hatchers were putting more of them in every year. Troutfishes. And some other kind Stavia couldn't remember.

"There could be fishes," she told Beneda.

"There are fishes in the big marsh, too," said Beneda. "Teacher Linda told me."

"Vain hope," sniffed Sylvia, overhearing her. "They've been telling us there are fishes in the marsh for twenty years now, but nobody's caught any. Still too contaminated."

"It might take several more decades before they've multiplied enough to be harvestable," Morgot said. "But there are some new things living there. When I was by there last, I saw a crawfish."

"A crawfish!"

"I'm pretty sure it was a crawfish. I've seen them in some of the other marshes. With armor on the outside. With lots of legs and two bigger claws in front?"

"A crawfish," Sylvia marveled. "My grandmother used to tell me a funny story about one of her grandmother line eating crawfishes."

"The thing I saw didn't look good to eat," Morgot remarked, making a face. "Very hard on the outside, it was."

"I think the meat's inside."

Deliberately, Morgot rinsed the cup from the overflow spout and set it down. The fountain attendant came forward politely to take it, replacing it with a clean one. "Condolences, matron."

"Thank you, servitor. We can always hope, can't we?"

"Certainly one can, matron. I will pray to the Lady for your son." The man turned away and busied himself with his cups. He was very old, perhaps seventy or more, a grandsir with white hair and a little tuft of beard. He winked at Stavia, and she smiled at him. Stavia liked grandsirs. They had interesting stories to tell about garrison country and warrior sagas and how the warriors lived.

"Best get along," said Morgot, looking at the sun. The dial above the fountain said almost noon. She picked Jerby up once more.

"I want to walk!" he announced, struggling in her arms. "I'm not a baby."

"Of course you aren't," she said lamely, putting him down once more. "You're a big boy going to join his warrior father."

His thickly clad little form led them down the long hill and into the ceremonial plaza. Once there, Morgot knelt to wipe Jerby's face with a handkerchief and set the earflaps of his hat straight. She gave Myra a look, then Stavia. "Stavia, don't disgrace me," she said.

Stavia shivered. It felt as though Morgot had slapped her, even though she knew that wasn't what her mother meant. Disgrace Mother? On an occasion like this? Of course not! Never! She wouldn't be able to stand the shame of doing something like that. She reached down inside herself and gave herself a shake, waking up that other part of her, making it come forward to take over—that other Stavia who could remember lines and get up on stage without dying of embarrassment. Real Stavia, observer Stavia, who was often embarrassed and stuttery and worried about appearing wicked or stupid, watched the whole thing as from a shocked dream state, feeling it all, but not making a single move. It was the first time she could remember purposely making her everyday self step aside, though it had happened occasionally before, in emergencies, all by itself.

"Morgot! What an unkind thing to say to the child!" Sylvia objected. "Even now!"

"Stavia knows what I mean," Morgot replied. "She knows I want no tantrums."

Observer Stavia reflected gloomily that she hadn't had a tantrum for at least a year. Well, part of a year. She had been so guiltily miserable after the last one, she might never have one again, even though sometimes she desperately felt like screaming and rolling around and saying, no, she wouldn't do whatever it was they expected her to do because they were always expecting her to do something more or be something more until it didn't feel like there was enough of her left to go around. Still, it wasn't really fair of Mother to bring that up now, and she longed to say so.

Actor Stavia, however, kept her role in mind and merely held her face still as she moved at Morgot's side. Myra was on the other side, holding one of Jerby's hands as the little boy stalked sturdily along, taking two steps to Myra's one. They stopped before the Gate of Warriors' Sons, and Morgot went forward to strike its swollen surface with the flat of her hand to make a drum-gong sound, a flat, ugly thum-hump.

A trumpet blew somewhere beyond the gate. Morgot swept Jerby up into her arms and retreated to the center of the plaza as the gate swung open, Myra and Stavia running at either side. Then there were drums and banners and the crash of hundreds of feet hitting the stones all at the same time, blimmety blam, blam, blam. Stavia blinked but held her place. Warriors. Lines of them. High plumes on their helmets and bright woolen skirts coming almost to their knees. Bronze plates over their chests, and more glistening metal covering their legs. To either side, groups of boys in white tunics and leggings, short-hooded cloaks flapping. One tall man out in front. Tall. And big, with shoulders and arms like great, stout tree branches.

Everything became still. Only the plumes whipping in the wind made any sound at all. Mother walked forward, Jerby's hand in hers.

"Warrior," she said, so softly Stavia could barely hear her.

"Madam," he thundered.

His name was Michael, and he was one of the Vice-Commanders of the Marthatown garrison. First came Commander Sandom, and under him were Jander and Thales, then came Michael—Michael, Stephon, and Patras commanding the centuries. Stavia had met Michael two or three times during carnivals. He was one of the handsomest men she had ever seen, just as Morgot was one of the most beautiful women. When Stavia's older brothers, Habby and Byram, had been five years old, each of them, too, had been brought to Michael. Beneda had said once that this meant Michael was probably Stavia's father also, but Stavia had never asked Morgot about it. It wasn't a thing one asked about. It wasn't a thing one was even supposed to think about.

"Warrior, I bring you your son," Morgot said, pushing Jerby a step or two in front of her. Jerby stood there with his legs apart and his lower lip protruding, the way he did when he wanted to cry but wouldn't. His little coat was bright with embroidered panels down the front. His boots were worked with beads of shell and turquoise. Morgot had spent evening after evening on those boots, working away in the candlelight, with Joshua threading the beads on the needle for her and saying soft words to comfort her.

The warrior stared down at Jerby and Jerby stared back, his mouth open. The warrior knelt down, put his finger to the flask of honey at his waist and then to Jerby's lips. "I offer you the sweetness of honor," he whispered, even his whisper penetrating the silence of the plaza like a sword, so sharp it did not hurt, even as it cut you to pieces.

Jerby licked his lips, then grinned, and Michael laid his hand on the little boy's shoulder.

"I give him into your keeping until his fifteenth year," Morgot went on. "Except that he shall return to his home in Women's Country during the carnival holidays, twice each year until that time."

"A warrior chooses his way at fifteen." Michael was thundering once more. He had a voice that would bellow across a noisy battlefield.

"In that year he shall choose," said Morgot, stepping back and leaving Jerby there all alone.

The little boy started to turn, started to say, "Mommy," but Michael had seized him up, lifted him high, high above his head, high above his dark eyes and laughing mouth, high above his white gleaming teeth and cruelly curving lips as he cried, "Warriors! Behold my son!"

Then there was a wild outcry from the warriors, a hullabaloo of shouts and cries, slowing at last into a steady, bottomless chant, "Telemachus, Telemachus, Telemachus," so deep it made your teeth shiver. Telemachus was the ancient one, the ideal son, who defended the honor of his father, or so Joshua said. The warriors always invoked Telemachus on occasions like this.

Stavia scarcely noticed the uproar. One of the tunic-clad boys was watching her, a boy about thirteen years old. It was an eager, impatiently sulky look with something in it that stirred her, making her feel uncertain and uncomfortable. Somehow the boy looked familiar to her, as though she had seen him before, but she couldn't remember where. Modestly, as befitted anyone under fifteen, she dropped her eyes. When she peeked at him from beneath her brows, however, he was still looking at her.

There was another rat-a-blam from the drums and a rattle of shouted commands. The warriors moved. Suddenly the white-tunicked boy was beside her, staring intently into her face as the plaza filled with wheeling warriors, plumes high, guidons flapping in the breeze, feet hammering on the stones.

"What's your name?" he asked.

"Stavia," she murmured.

"Is Morgot your mother?"

She nodded, wondering at this.

"I'm her friend Sylvia's son," he said. "Chernon."

Then someone took him by the arm, he was pulled back into the general melee, and the marching men hammered their way through the gate, drowning out Jerby's cries. Stavia could see her brother's tearful little face over Michael's shoulder. The white-clad boys boiled through the opening like surf, and the Gate of Warriors' Sons closed behind them with a ring of finality.

Chernon had eyes the color of honey, she thought. And hair that matched, only a little darker. He had looked familiar because he looked like Beneda, except around the mouth. The mouth looked swollen, somehow. Pouty. As though someone had hurt him. His hair and eyes just like Beneda's, though. And his jawline, too. This was the brother Beneda had mentioned! Why did he never visit his family during carnival? Why had Stavia never seen him before?

Morgot and Sylvia had turned away from the plaza to move up the stairs that led to the top of the wall. Stavia climbed behind them to find a low place where she could look over the parapet into the parade ground outside the city. The ceremony of the Warrior's Son was continuing there.

Michael's century came marching out through the armory doors, Jerby high on Michael's shoulder while the men cheered. As they came through, the trumpets began a long series of fanfares and flourishes, the drums thundered, the great bells near the parade ground monument began to peal. At the foot of the monument was a statue of two warriors in armor, large and small, father and son. Before this monument Michael went down on one knee, pushing Jerby down before him so that the little boy knelt also. There was a moment's silence, all the warriors pulling off their helms and bowing their heads, then the drums and trumpets and bells began once more as the procession swept away toward the barracks.

From the tail of the procession, one of the white-clad boys looked back and raised a hand toward Stavia.

"Who are those statues?" asked Beneda.

"Ulysses and Telemachus," said Sylvia abstractedly.

"Who's Ulysses?"

"Odysseus," murmured Morgot. "It's just another name for Odysseus. Telemachus was his son."

"Oh," said Beneda. "The same Odysseus that Iphigenia talks about in our play? The one at Troy?"

"The same one."

The women went down the stairs, across the plaza to the street, the way they had come. Myra was walking beside them now, her arm around her mother's waist. Both Morgot and Sylvia were weeping. Beneda ran to catch up, but Stavia dawdled, looking back over her shoulder. Chernon. She would remember the name.

3

S ITTING IN THE FIRELIT ROOM with Corrig and the others, thirty-seven-year-old Stavia reflected that she might have been better off now if she had not remembered Chernon's name then. Better for everyone if she hadn't remembered him or seen him again. She caught Corrig's gaze upon her and flushed. He went on staring at her and she said, "I was remembering the day we took Jerby down. It was the first time I saw Chernon. That day." He gripped her arm for a moment, then went to get more tea as she gazed around the room. It was a combination of common room and kitchen. Everything in it had memories attached to it. The thick rag rug before the stove was where Dawid had curled up while she read him bedtime stories. When he was home at carnival time. Before he grew up. His napkin ring was still in the cupboard. Joshua had carved it for him. Every shadowed corner of the place was full of things that said Dawid, or Habby, or Byram, or Jerby.

Corrig came back with the teapot. He put his hand on her shoulder and squeezed, very gently, as he filled her cup.

Beneda looked up, saying, "What did you say, Stavvy?"

"Nothing, Beneda. I was just thanking Corrig for the tea."

"Well, no more for me, thanks. I've got to be getting back to the children. Mother has an early morning meeting with the weavers' guild over
the linen quota, so she needs to get to bed."

"How is your mother?" asked Morgot. "And your grandchild?"

"Sylvia's fine. The baby's teething and cross as two sticks, but the girls
are all well. We want you both to come over for supper sometime soon.
Now, where did I put my shawl?" She was halfway to the door, still bubbling with words and short phrases.

When she had gone, Stavia sighed. "We used to be best friends."

Both the twins, Kostia and Tonia, looked up, but it was Tonia who said,
"So far as Beneda's concerned, you still are, love."

Stavia caught her breath. "It's true. I feel like such a hypocrite. It hurts."

"I know. Are you going to be all right now?"

"Yes," she said. "I'm going to be all right." She was going to be all
right. Almost everyone went through this. Everyone was all right. But now
that Dawid was really gone, now that he wouldn't be coming home anymore, she was remembering things she hadn't really thought of in years—
not memories of Dawid so much as memories of Chernon, of Beneda, of
her own family. "Things not so much lost as unremembered," she murmured to herself. Things from childhood.

FOR SEVERAL DAYS after Jerby had been taken to his warrior father, Morgot had grieved a lot. Young Stavia was very aware of it, not so much because she was alert to her mother's moods, though she was, but because she had wanted to ask Morgot about the boy in the plaza. Chernon. Stavia didn't want to remind Morgot of anything to do with that day while Morgot was still grieving so much. Each time Stavia had delayed asking, she had congratulated herself on being sensitive and compassionate, giving herself little love pats, contrasting her own behavior with that of Myra, who never tried to be sensitive about anything. Stavia kept assuring herself she was behaving in a properly adult manner. That business about the tantrums still rankled, and she was trying to get over it.

A week went by while Morgot moped and Stavia watched. Then they were in the kitchen one night, and Stavia realized that Morgot hadn't cried all day.

She kept her voice carefully casual as she said, "Sylvia's son, Chernon, came up to me in the plaza, Mother. He asked me who I was, and he told me who he was. Why hasn't he ever come home on holidays?"

Morgot stepped back from the iron-topped brick stove, the long fork dangling from her hand as she pushed hair back from her forehead with her wrist. In the pan, bits of chicken sputtered in a spoonful of fat. Morgot put down the fork and dumped a bowl of vegetables into the pan, covering it with a high-domed lid, before turning to give Stavia a long, measuring look. It was an expression she had whenever she was deciding whether something should be said or not said, and there was no hurrying it. The pan sizzled and hissed. Morgot uncovered it and stirred, saying, "Sylvia thought it was best. When Chernon was about nine or ten, he came home for carnival and said some ugly, terrible things to Sylvia. Things no boy of that age could possibly have thought up."

"But you said boys do that. You said that's just warriors' ritual, Mother."

"Yes, there is some ritual insult that goes on, though most warriors are honorable enough not to suggest it and some boys are courteous enough not to be part of it. This stuff was far worse than that, Stavia. Sick, perverted filth. We learned that one of the warriors had instructed Chernon to make these vile accusations and demands of Sylvia. The warrior's name was Vinsas, and the things he wanted Chernon to say were . . . degenerate. Very personal, and utterly mad. Sylvia was taken totally by surprise. Hearing them from a child, her own child . . . well, it was unnerving. Disgusting.

"It turned out that Vinsas had told the boy he had to come back to the garrison and swear he had followed instructions on threat of cruel punishment."

"Well then, Chernon didn't mean it."

"We knew that, love. It wasn't Chernon's fault. But Chernon was being used in a very unhealthy way, don't you see? These weren't things a ten-year-old boy should even think of, and yet by the rules and discipline of the garrison, he was obliged to obey a senior warrior. It was unfair to Chernon to put him in that position." She lifted the pan onto the tiled table and left it there, steam escaping gently from around the lid.

"What happened?"

"Sylvia suggested that since the warrior was obviously mad, Chernon just put him off by saying, yes, he'd told Sylvia and she didn't respond. Somehow, Chernon didn't feel he could do that. His visit turned into an interminable argument about what he could and couldn't say, about what the warrior would want to know, and what Chernon would have to tell him. It was almost as though Chernon himself had been infected by this madness and was using it to whip himself up into a kind of prurient tantrum." Morgot frowned. "I was there once when Chernon was doing this crazy thing. It was like hysteria. Sylvia asked my advice. I told her there were

only two things she could do: speak to the Commander of Vinsas's century
—Michael as it happened—or refuse to have Chernon come home thereafter. She couldn't go on with every carnival becoming a frenzy of frantic,
ugly confrontation with her own son. So, she spoke to Michael, and he
chose to do nothing.''

"I thought he was nicer than that."

Morgot considered this, wrinkling her forehead. "No. Charming on occasion, yes. Sometimes witty and sometimes sexy, but I don't think anyone
could call Michael 'nice.' Well, at any rate, Sylvia sent word that Chernon
should go to his aunt's house during carnival. Sylvia has a sister, Erica, who
lives over in Weaver's Street. Chernon has been going there for carnival
ever since. Since Vinsas has no obsession about Erica, he now lets Chernon
alone. I took the trouble to find that out from Michael, though he was
snippy about it." She stirred the mixed grains in the other pot. "This seems
to be done. As soon as I've cut some bread, I think we can call the family."

"Poor Chernon."

"Why did he speak to you?" Morgot wanted to know.

"I don't know." Stavia was honestly puzzled by the whole thing. "I really
don't know."

"Perhaps he misses his mother," Morgot said, her mouth shaking a little,
the way it sometimes did when she was thinking about the boys, down
there in the garrison.

"Are you going to have any more babies?" Stavia asked, assessing her
mother's mood to be one which allowed exchange of confidences.

Morgot shook her head in time with her slicing knife. "I don't think so,
love. Five of you is enough. Three boys. It's been seven, eight years since
we gave Byram to his warrior father. I'd forgotten how much it hurts."

Myra came into the kitchen, walking in a new slithery way she'd been
practicing a lot lately. "Don't have any more boys. Have a girl. A baby
sister for me."

"Now that's an idea." Morgot laughed. "If one could just be sure it
would be a girl!"

Maybe Morgot would try for another girl, but not this coming carnival,
Stavia could tell. Morgot might decide sometime to have another baby—
she was only thirty-five—but it wouldn't be soon.

And even the next carnival was a long time away. There would be weeks
of studies first. Stavia was doing drama in her Arts division, where the
current project was to learn about *Iphigenia at Ilium,* the traditional play that
the Council put on every year before summer carnival. All the drama students had to learn how to make costumes and do makeup and build sets, in
addition to learning the part of at least one character in the play. Since the

play wasn't very long, Stavia had decided it was really easier just to memo-rize the whole thing. Then in Sciences division she'd be studying physiol-ogy, which she was good at, and in Crafts division there'd be some kind of practical gardening project which would be fun. There was always a new section of the Women's Country Ordinances to memorize or an old one to review. And in addition to all that, because she had turned ten, women's studies would start this year: management, administration, sexual skills. Plus special electives in any outstanding talent areas. Stavia mentioned this in puzzlement, wondering what she would choose.

"So far as I can see, Stavvy, you have no talent area." Myra picked into the dish of stewed dried fruit to pull out a chunk of apple between two fingers. Morgot slapped her fingers away.

"She's very good in biological sciences," Morgot corrected, spooning the hot grain into a bowl. "Her potential as a physician is high."

"Oh, doctoring," poohed Myra. "Dull."

"We can't all be great choreographers," said Morgot, mentioning Myra's current ambition. "Or even weavers."

Myra flushed angrily. The director at the weaving shop had threatened to drop Myra from the junior staff for lack of application. All Myra wanted to do was dance, and she had no patience for anything else. She started to say something, then thought better of it.

Morgot observed this reaction and went on calmly, "Stavia will do very well with the talents she has. Myra, will you tell Joshua that supper's ready, please?"

"He knows when we eat," Myra said sarcastically.

"Myra!" Morgot turned on her, a face full of furious embarrassment. "That was unbearably rude!"

Myra had the grace to flush again, and the sense to keep quiet. When she had left the room, Stavia asked, in wonderment, "Why would she say something like that?"

"Your sister's getting rather focused on a particular young warrior. Joshua tells me they've been exchanging notes from the wall walk. I expect they'll have an assignation next carnival."

"Why does that make her be rude about Joshua?"

"The young warrior is probably rude about Joshua—or rather about all the men who have returned. You know the warriors' attitude toward servi-tors."

"I know they've got this sort of sneeriness, but I didn't know it was communicable." Score one off Myra, she thought.

Morgot's mouth quirked a little. "Well, seemingly it is. Though the course of the disease is usually brief. Perhaps Myra will get over it." She put the tallow lamp in the center of the table, adjusting the wick to minimize the smoke. The soft colors of the glazed tiles gleamed in the lamplight, bringing highlights from the glaze of the soft clay plates and cups, the oiled wood of the spoons and two-tined forks. "Napkins, Stavvy."

Stavia reached them down from the shelf beside the window, each in its own carved ring. Joshua had whittled the rings himself—a dancing lamb for Myra; an owl for Morgot; a wreath of flowers and herbs for Stavia; and a funny goat for Joshua himself. At the back of the shelf were three other rings; a curled-up fish, a crowing rooster, a grasshopper. They belonged to Habby, and Byram, and Jerby. No one used them now except during carnival time when the boys were home.

Joshua joined them for supper, taking his place at the foot of the table with a sigh. "I was glad to see evening come. Everyone in Marthatown either cut themselves or fell down and broke something today. The hospital hasn't had this much business in months! On top of everything we had returnees."

"Returnees?"

"Among many other crises, yes. Two of them. One of whom was beaten rather badly, I'm afraid."

Morgot put down the fork she had raised halfway to her mouth. "That's not allowed!"

"Oh, the boy said the attack wasn't sanctioned by the officers. Just some of his peers, he said, acting out their hostility at him."

"Nonetheless. . . ."

"You should probably mention it to the Council." He nodded in a particular, meaningful way which Stavia had always interpreted as a reminder to Morgot of something she was in danger of forgetting. A kind of "My dear, not before the children" expression.

"You're quite right," Morgot agreed. "Is he staying in Marthatown or moving on?"

"He's chosen to move on. In about a week, I think. He'll be well enough then to move to Susantown."

"I don't blame them for beating up on him," Myra said. "You wouldn't catch my warrior friend acting like that!"

"Myra," Morgot said in a dangerously quiet voice. "Let us suppose it had been Jerby."

Myra flushed, started to say something, then subsided, looking both rebellious and confused. "It isn't the same. Jerby's only five!"

"He's only five now. Do you mean you would not be glad to see him if he returned at fifteen? Think of Habby. He's almost fifteen. Do you mean you would enjoy seeing him beaten by those who chose otherwise?"

"Well, I wouldn't expect him to act like a baby anymore!" she said unreasonably, her face red.

Morgot shook her head, staring at the girl until she dropped her eyes. "I'll mention the attack to the Council, Joshua. They meet tomorrow night, so it's fortuitous timing. More vegetables, Stavia?"

"Please."

"Myra, more vegetables?"

"I'm getting too fat," she mumbled.

"Where did you get that idea."

"Oh, I just think I am."

"Well, greens will hardly make you any fatter. It will make your skin smooth and your hair shiny, however, which young warriors are said to admire. More?"

"Winter food is boring. Cabbage is particularly boring."

"Yes, it is. It is also just about the only leaf vegetable we can keep all winter. When the town finishes work on the new sunpits this summer, we should be able to have fresh things a little oftener. Do you want more or don't you?"

"A little, I guess."

Joshua shared "the look" with Morgot once more, and the conversation became suddenly very general and amusing, the way it did when Joshua or Morgot didn't want to talk about something in particular.

CORRIG FOUND STAVIA in the kitchen, looking ill and middle aged, her eyes puffy from lack of sleep, the text of *Iphigenia at Ilium* open on the table before her.

"I heard you moving around during the night," he said as he stroked her hair. "You look dreadful, dear one."

"I thank you," she said laconically.

"Well, let's say then that you look less lovely than usual." He filled a pan with water and grain and set it upon the stove.

"I couldn't sleep. I kept thinking about Dawid. Wondering what's going to happen to him."

"That's normal. It will take a while to accept the fact that he's gone." He poured hot tea into the empty cup before her, glancing down at the text. "That's hardly the most cheerful reading in the world."

"I know," she said. "I'm doing it mostly for distraction. I knew it by heart once, all the parts. I've seen it every summer, but I haven't actually thought about it in years. Morgot's done Iphigenia as long as I can remember. I have to learn it all over again if I'm going to do the part in this year's production."

"You're not doing it until summer. Spring isn't even really here yet." His dark brows rose, making perfect arcs over his tilted eyes and long, straight nose, deep furrows curling up from below his chin to bracket his wide, mobile mouth. He licked his lower lip, head cocked, examining her as he chopped up dried apples to add them to the grain.

"I thought it might be easier if I just read it over a dozen or so times," she said listlessly. "Then it might all come back to me without my trying very hard."

"You'd have been better off getting another hour's sleep."

"I couldn't sleep. Besides, it should cheer me up. The play's a comedy."

"Comedy!"

"Well it is, Corrig. The audience laughs."

He made a face at her, trying to make her smile. "There are some things about Women's Country I still find difficult to understand. How old were you when you first did that play?"

"Oh, about ten or eleven, I suppose. We did it every year in school, taking different parts, building sets, making costumes."

"So you've been doing it for at least twenty-seven years. I should think you'd pick something else to do for a while, but Joshua says you Councilwomen never get tired of it."

"It isn't that we don't get tired of it. It's that the play is part of the . . . part of the reminders. You know that!" She ran her fingers through her hair, fingering the roughness of scar tissue at the top of her head, wincing at a little tenderness there which had never gone away. "When's Joshua coming back?"

"Soon, I hope," he said. "There's more to do around here than I can keep up with. Tell you what. If you're determined to review this play now, I'll read the lines to you and you see if you can remember Iphigenia's part."

"She doesn't come in until about page six. . . ."

"Then while I'm reading the first six pages, you'll have time to drink another cup of tea and have some breakfast." He took the text from her, leaned his chair back on two legs, and began to read in his furry, deep voice, beginning with the "notes."

Stavia, too tired to complain at hearing all the unnecessary detail, merely listened, letting his voice wash over her.

"Iphigenia at Ilium," read Corrig. "Note to students: The play is based upon a millennia-old preconvulsion story concerning a conflict between two garrisons, the *Greeks* and the *Trojans,* brought about when a Trojan

warrior abducted a Greek woman named *Helen*. The *Greek* garrison pursued the couple to the city of *Troy* (also called *Ilium*) and laid siege to the city. This siege iasted for ten years, largely because of mismanagement among the Greek forces, but in the end the Greeks succeeded in conquering the Trojans and in destroying the city. The action of the play takes place after this destruction, outside the broken walls of Troy. Appendix A at the end of your drama book lists the names and attributes of some of the Greek and Trojan warriors such as Agamemnon, Menelaus, Odysseus, Hector, etc., who are referred to in the drama. Appendix B contains an outline of the original book upon which this play is based. Appendix C gives the history of the play together with comments on its significance to Women's Country.''

"Did you ever read the Appendices?'' Corrig asked, flipping rapidly to the back of the book.

"I think I had to read them once for school. I really don't remember.''

"Persons of the Drama," read Corrig.

Trojans

HECUBA: Widow of King Priam of Troy and mother of Hector.

ANDROMACHE: Widow of Hector.

The infant, ASTYANAX: Hector's son.

The Ghost of POLYXENA: Hecuba's daughter.

CASSANDRA: Hecuba's daughter.

Greeks

TALTHYBIUS: A messenger.

The Ghost of IPHIGENIA: Agamemnon's daughter.

The Ghost of ACHILLES: A Greek warrior.

HELEN, seen upon the battlements.

Several soldiers and serving women.

Scene: At the foot of the broken walls of Troy. To the right the stones of the wall have tumbled into a rough stairway which permits ascent to the top of the battlements. On the left a few warriors, who were detailed to stand guard on the women, are playing dice. Huddled together are Hecuba and Andromache, with their serving women asleep around them. In Andromache's lap is her infant son, Astyanax, whom she is comforting.

ANDROMACHE There, baby, there. Take the nipple. Suck. Oh see, Mother Hecuba, he's too tired to suck. Poor baby. All the smoke and noise. . . .

HECUBA And howling. We've all been doing that. It's the crying's kept him awake, daughter. Well, I'm through crying. I cried for Hector, my son, and I cried for King Priam, my husband, and I cried for the city of Troy, and then I cried for me, and that's enough of it.

ANDROMACHE   I'm dry of weeping, too. *(She looks up at the walls above her where a group of people have paused to gawk)* Bitch!

HECUBA   *(Looking up)* You mean Helen.

ANDROMACHE   Well, she's not down here in the dirt with us, is she? She's not trying to find food for a baby or worrying whose slave she's going to be.

HECUBA   That one is no man's slave. Still, Menelaus vows he'll kill her.

ANDROMACHE   He'll not kill her. Kill the source of so much glory? Kill the topic of ten thousand poets' songs? She'll go back to being wife and honored queen, shown off like a prize cow. She'll sit in a carved chair with a silver sewing box and spin purple wool when all of us are dead. *(Looks up at Helen laughing on the battlement)* May her womb be closed forever. May she never bear another child. May she have boils in her. . . .

HECUBA   Shhh, shhh. Your curses may bear fruit, and if they do you'll bring Erinyes down upon yourself. All those who curse their kin bring down the three avengers on themselves. . . .

"Stop for footnote," said Corrig, flipping to the back of the book. "What are Erinyes? I can never remember."

"Furies," Stavia replied, taking another sip of tea.

"Ah yes. 'Anger, Vengeance, and Jealousy, who return from the underworld to earth to punish certain acts, particularly the murder of relatives, et cetera.' Was Helen a relative? Were the Greeks?"

"She was sort of married to one of their countrymen. I don't know, Corrig. I think in school they said it means all women are kin, sort of."

"Hmm," he mused. "Well. Back to text. . . ."

ANDROMACHE   I wasn't cursing kin. I cursed at her and at those Greeks who brought my Hector down. They are no kin of mine.

HECUBA   She's a woman, Andromache. A sister of ours. Perhaps she even thinks herself a Trojan. Long years she's walked the torchlit halls of Troy.

ANDROMACHE   One day was too long.

HECUBA   Even one hour's too long, Andromache, but do not risk what little we have left on her behalf.

ANDROMACHE   What little's that?

HECUBA   You are my son's loved wife, and you're alive. Your baby Astyanax is alive. And even I'm alive, though that may be sparse comfort for us both.

ANDROMACHE   Your daughters, Polyxema and Cassandra, are alive. Such as they are.

HECUBA   That's true, so let's not tempt the Furies down for the sake of mere cursing. *(She takes the baby from Andromache)* Oh, baby, baby. Little Astyanax. He's trying so hard to fall asleep.

ANDROMACHE   Speak of reasons for cursing. Here comes Talthybius.

(Talthybius enters left)

HECUBA   *(Fumbling in her skirt)* Do you come like the raven, messenger, to croak dishonor in my aged ears?

TALTHYBIUS   I bring such messages as I am sent with.

HECUBA   They do not ever send you with good tidings, do they, Talthybius?

TALTHYBIUS   Priam's wife, if they had good to say, they'd come themselves with joy salving their lips.

ANDROMACHE   But you they send with vomit in your mouth and Hector's blood still warm upon your tongue.

HECUBA   Shh, shh, daughter. The messenger brings only what he's given. What are you given now, Talthybius?

TALTHYBIUS   Some word about your children, Priam's Queen. *(He casts about for some acceptable part of the message)* Cassandra. I bring word of Cassandra.

HECUBA   *(Nodding)* She went quite mad, you know. She ran throughout the palace, up and down, dancing with Hymen's torches in her hands, whirling until she'd set fire to her hair. We threw wet blankets on her, holding her until the flame was out. Her nuptials shall light a funeral pyre, or so she says. What else is there to know about Cassandra?

TALTHYBIUS   Agamemnon will take her home with him. She pleases him.

ANDROMACHE   One can account so little for some things. He's pleased with her? Then he is likely pleased to taunt the Gods and court his own destruction. What will he do with her?

TALTHYBIUS   He will bed her, I think, madam.

ANDROMACHE   He'll bed the virgin priestess of Athena! When he is done, then will he curse at Zeus and piss upon the image of Apollo? Or is he turned by madness that he seeks a mate most like himself. . . ?

HECUBA   Shh, shh, daughter. Do not curse the Greeks who seem well able to proscribe themselves. So, Talthybius. Agamemnon will take Cassandra. What of Polyxena?

TALTHYBIUS   *(After an uncomfortable pause)* She was assigned by lot, as were you all.

HECUBA   Where? To whom? What Greek takes Polyxena?

TALTHYBIUS   She has been assigned to serve the tomb of Achilles.

HECUBA   Slave to a graven tomb! How dreadful for her. She loves the lively arts, Talthybius. Dancing. Eating. To think that she must serve Achilles' tomb.

TALTHYBIUS   Count her as happy, Queen. Her fate frees her from troubles that still follow you. . . .

HECUBA   What troubles have I? So, I'll be a slave. When thousands lie unburied on the field, when blood runs down to feed the summer trees, does slavery count for much?

TALTHYBIUS   You will be slave to Odysseus.

HECUBA   His ownership will be as short as my subservience, Talthybius. I am an old woman. See. My hair is white.

TALTHYBIUS   *(Leaning down to look at her closely)* You have years yet.

HECUBA   *(She fumbles in her skirt again, then removes her hands and clenches them in front of her, staring at them. There is a pause)* My daughter Cassandra says not.

TALTHYBIUS   No one believes Cassandra. As for Andromache. . . .

ANDROMACHE   I'll be a slave. I know it already. I say with my husband's mother that my slavery will be brief.

TALTHYBIUS   But you are young yet.

ANDROMACHE   So I am.

HECUBA   Enough, Talthybius. You have told us enough for one visit. Croak somewhere else for a time.

TALTHYBIUS   Queen, I cannot.

ANDROMACHE   Oh? Do you bear some vomit yet?

HECUBA   Shh, shh.

TALTHYBIUS   Your son, Andromache. . . .

ANDROMACHE   Do not tell me of any wickedness which would wrest a suckling from his mother's arms. Don't tell me he'll be taken from my care to grow to manhood in some other house.

TALTHYBIUS   I will not tell you that.

ANDROMACHE   He'll go with me? You would not leave him here?

TALTHYBIUS   *(Sadly)* Here, yes. On his father's soil. In his father's place.

ANDROMACHE   Whose words are these?

TALTHYBIUS   Odysseus spoke before the Achaeans, extolling Hector's glory. He said that they could ill afford to rear a hero's son lest he rise up when he is grown and venge him for his father's death.

ANDROMACHE   They *will* leave him here? With some shepherd, some potter, some lowly family?

TALTHYBIUS   Here among these stones. Thrown to his death from Troy's new-riven walls. So they have said.

ANDROMACHE   *(Screams and clings to her child. Talthybius summons the guards who help him wrest the child from her. He then ascends the stair of tumbled stone, she crying after him)* I call doom upon you, Talthybius, and those who sent you here. I call doom upon their ships and on their men. I call the Furies down. Oh do not, do not. Give him to me. He is only a little child. My milk is still warm on his lips. Gods, Talthybius, they'll curse you—don't. *(She screams and weeps)*

HECUBA   *(Holding her)* Andromache. Love. Daughter. Sweet girl. Oh why didn't I, when I had the chance—oh why didn't I? Oh here, hold on to me. How can they do this to a baby . . . ?

(There is a cry from the top of the wall, a high, piercing sound, like a bird. They look up. Talthybius has thrown the child from the walls. The guards are all looking down. The ghostly figure of Iphigenia wanders near them. . . .)

"I think this is my entrance coming up," said Stavia, filling grain bowls for them. "Aren't you tired of reading, Corrig?"

"I love the sound of my own voice. Now, get ready, you're almost on." He went on reading.

HECUBA   Who's that? Who walks on these walls among the warriors?

"The cry comes again," quoted Stavia from memory, "and the ghost of Iphigenia is seen. In her arms, she carries the ghost of the child, as she descends the stair."

ANDROMACHE   Do warriors have no pity that they do these things? What stomachs them? Are men made up of iron? What do they use for hearts? Do they not see we are the same as they, our children like their children, and our flesh like that of women whom they left behind.

IPHIGENIA   *(Crying like a seabird)* What difference would it make? They do the same to their own.

ANDROMACHE   Who calls? Is that my child?

IPHIGENIA   *(Holding out the baby)* Your child? Or some other's child? Two children dead. One virgin girl, one suckling boy. See, here we are, wandering together. *(She dances)*

HECUBA   *(Frightened)* Who are you?

IPHIGENIA   Agamemnon's daughter, come from Hades' realm to seek revenge on him who killed her.

HECUBA   Daughter of Agamemnon? The man who says he'll take Cassandra?

IPHIGENIA   Ah well, we know the truth of that, old woman. He will not take her far nor keep her long. And you need not curse him. I've cursed him quite enough without your curses.

ANDROMACHE   Is that my child?

IPHIGENIA   If I am my father's child, this is your child. No, this is a better child to you than I to my father, for this babe does not curse you. See, he smiles.

HECUBA   You curse your father?

IPHIGENIA   I curse him who killed me. And him who tricked my mother into letting him.

ANDROMACHE   Give me my child. *(She reaches for him but cannot hold him)*

IPHIGENIA   He is beyond your grasp, unhappy queen. But see, he smiles again. Be glad he's come to me. He has kinfolk who walk among us ghosts. Polyxena will rock him in her arms and give him buds of asphodel to suck.

HECUBA   Polyxena dead! But Talthybius said she served Achilles' tomb.

IPHIGENIA   She was slain on Achilles' tomb, if that is service.

HECUBA   Oh, false Talthybius, to riddle me these serpent's words. My daughter dead.

IPHIGENIA   Her throat was slit above Achilles' corpse as mine was cut above Artemis's. They like the smell of virgin blood, these men.

HECUBA   They tell us that the Gods are pleased with blood.

IPHIGENIA   Oh shhh, shhh, don't curse the Gods, old woman. It's man who puts the blood-stink in their noses and clotted gore upon their divine lips. Would you drink human blood instead of meat? Do not the Gods have cows? Don't they have cooks?

(Enter, upon the battlement, the ghost of Achilles)

ACHILLES   I seek my servant, Polyxena!

Starid's eyes were closed as though she might be asleep.

Corrig watched her for a moment, then asked gently, "Who's going to play Achilles?"

"Joshua, I think. He has several times before." She blinked.

"Good old Joshua."

"Good indeed," said Stavia. "You know, Corrig, I remember once when I was about eleven, Myra was reading the play for me, cuing me, just the way you were. . . ." Her voice trailed off as she thought of Myra.

Corrig didn't speak for a time. Then he asked, "Have you seen Myra lately?"

Stavia came to herself with a start. "Not for months. I only see her if I happen to run into her at the market or somewhere. I guess she's never really forgiven Morgot for asking her to move out."

Corrig shook his head slowly. "No, she's never forgiven you, Stavia. Because you stayed."

Myra's LEAVING Morgot's house had been inevitable from the moment Myra met Barten. Not that Barten had intended it or Myra foreseen it or Morgot known it would happen. No one knew, but it was inevitable just the same.

On the day the rift between Myra and Morgot began, Stavia had just turned eleven. She and Myra were in Stavia's room, going over the opening lines of the play, both of them already more than a little bored with it.

"You know, Stavia," Myra said in her dramatically fed up older-sister voice. "You've got most of the lines all right, but you seem to keep forgetting this is a comedy!"

"I don't forget," Stavia objected, rolling over on her bed to stare at the low ceiling. Last winter the rain had come in through the roof tiles and left a long, swirling stain that sometimes looked like a man with a long beard and sometimes looked like something else. "I do fine until they get to that bit about throwing the baby over the wall, then I think of Jerby and it doesn't seem funny."

"Well you've *seen* it every year, for heaven's sake. You go with the rest of us, just before summer carnival. They use that crazy clown-faced doll for the baby. It doesn't even look like a real child. It isn't supposed to be a real baby. The old women aren't real old women. The virgins aren't really virgins. It's supposed to be a satire, you know?" She frowned, trying to remember something an instructor had said. "A commentary on particular attitudes of preconvulsion society."

"I know." Stavia knew it was a commentary, but knowing and feeling were two separate things. She felt the play in ways she didn't know it.

Myra went on, "Hecuba and Andromache are all tarted up, like a pair of river Gypsies, with red on their cheeks and their lips as bloody as Talthybius's are supposed to be. And where he says Andromache's young yet, he puts his hand on her, you know? Then Achilles comes down the stairs with that great dong on him, sticking way out and bobbing around like anything, looking for Polyxena. . . ."

"I *know,* Myra! I just keep thinking of Jerby, that's all."

"He'll be all right," Myra had said, not sounding as though she believed it. She no longer talked very much about Jerby. His being down at the garrison confused her. She did want him to come home, and yet men who did come home were cowards and tit-suckers, according to Barten, the young warrior she'd been spending a lot of time talking to from the top of the wall. Cowards and tit-suckers and impotent, too. Or else gelded when they came back. All the warriors said so. Until recently she had not thought of Joshua as a coward and a tit-sucker, and she wasn't sure what gelding really did to a man, but she supposed he must be if Barten said so. "Jerby'll be coming for a visit soon."

"It's only two months to midsummer carnival."

"I know." Myra got up off the floor where she had been sitting to cue Stavia in her part. "Oh, I know." She looked at herself in the mirror, turning her head from side to side, striking a dance pose with her arms.

"You're going to have an assignation, aren't you?"

"Maybe." She tossed her light red hair. "One of the warriors has been courting me."

"Is he good-looking?"

"Mmmm." Myra rolled her eyes and made fainting motions. "Shoulders out to here, with the cutest bottom, and blue, blue eyes and his hair and eyebrows are black, and he has these lips that curve down in the middle. . . ."

"What's his name?"

"Barten. He's in Michael's command. Tally's fit to be quarantined, she's so mad at me. He was courting her until he met me." She preened, throwing her head back, looking for an instant as beautiful and mysterious as Morgot sometimes did.

"How old is he?"

"He belongs to the twenty-two, I think. He's not twenty-five, at any rate. He doesn't have any scars yet."

"What's the real reason they don't let them fight until they're twenty-five?"

"You know. They told you in women's studies."

"I know what they told me. They're strongest and healthiest and most virile between the ages of eighteen to twenty-five, and if they're going to father babies, that's the time to do it. So, they aren't risked in battle until they're older. But is that the real reason?"

"What else?"

"I thought it was maybe to give them a few more years to decide if they want to come back or not."

"Not very many come back after they're twenty," Myra said definitely, her lightly freckled face drawn into a frown. "Hardly any at all."

"I'll bet you were hoping. . . ."

"I wasn't hoping anything!" she said angrily. "Don't be silly. Barten is proud to be a warrior. He'd never do that. Morgot says it's better if they don't get talked into it, either, or you end up with someone coming back who's just miserable. 'A warrior home against his will remains at heart a warrior still.' Do you want to do your lines anymore?"

"No. I'm only second understudy, anyhow. I won't get to play a part until next year or the year after." Stavia found herself slightly annoyed about this, mostly because the young woman playing the lead was, in Stavia's opinion, very bad at it. "Michy's doing Iphigenia this year."

"*Michy?*" she asked incredulously. "You're having a *fat ghost?*"

"Well, I suppose Iphigenia could have been fat. Who knows? Maybe that's why they wanted to sacrifice her. I suppose if you sacrificed a goat or a sheep, you'd pick a nice fat one."

"A *fat ghost!*"

"Who's a fat ghost," Joshua asked from the door.

Seeing Myra's lips set into a stubborn line, Stavia explained, hastily. Myra was continuing to be unpleasant around Joshua, not answering direct questions, pretending not to see him. If this was the effect Barten was having on her, Stavia didn't look forward to meeting Barten, blue-blue eyes or not. Not that she'd probably have a chance to meet him. During carnival the warriors stayed near the plaza where the assignation houses and carnival taverns and amusements were; they weren't allowed in the residential sections of town, and Stavia was too young to go tavern-hopping.

"Michy will probably be dressed in floating draperies and you won't be able to tell what shape she is," Joshua commented. "Myra, Morgot wants to see you, please, as soon as possible. And Stavia, I ran into your physiology instructress at the hospital. She sent a message that she wants to talk to you and Morgot about your going to the basic medical institute at Abbyville."

"The institute?"

"At Abbyville. Oh, she doesn't expect you'd want to go for a few years yet. It's a nine-year course if you do the whole thing, seven years' study plus two years internship, with not much opportunity to come home. She wants to know how you feel about it, and how Morgot feels about your going, of course. . . ."

"Why would she have told you that?" Myra asked in a dangerously unpleasant voice. "What business is it of yours?"

Joshua looked at her, a long, rather quiet look, as he sometimes looked at weeds in the garden, deciding whether to pull them out or not. "Perhaps she values my opinion of Stavia's talents, Myra. I am asked from time to time to offer opinions concerning both of you."

He turned and left.

Myra took a quick breath, as though she had been slapped.

"Well, you had it coming," muttered Stavia.

"Shut up."

"I will. But if a few soppy looks from the walls make people as rude as you, Myra, I hope I never go near the walls again."

"It's none of his business!"

"It wasn't about *you*. It was about me! And I'm willing to have Joshua talk about me, so it was his business. Who the hell are you, all of a sudden?"

"It was about me! He said he gave opinions about me, and if you want to know who I am, I'm someone who's sick and tired of having a . . . a *serving man* sticking his nose in my business."

"Oh, you'd rather some *warrior* stuck his nose somewhere else, huh?"

"Stavia!" Morgot's voice snapped like a whip. "Myra! Will you come with me, please?"

Stavia shrunk into herself, wishing she were invisible. Fighting with Myra was something she'd promised herself not to do. Myra flounced out of the room, and Stavia heard her voice through the closed door. "None of his business. . . . Don't know why you . . . ? Barten says. . . ." then the crack of her mother's voice.

"Never say to me 'Barten says.' Never. This is Women's Country, and if you cannot hold to its courtesies you can leave it."

Silence. Oh, Great Mother.

Weeping.

The door opened. "Stavia?"

"Yes, ma'am."

"Myra would be less likely to forget herself if you didn't argue with her. Her current state of mind should be obvious to you."

"Yes, ma'am."

"You've learned something about it."

"Yes, ma'am."

"You know what it's called."

"Infatuation."

"You know what it does?"

" 'Infatuation makes otherwise reasonable women behave in unreasonable and illogical ways. It is a result of biological forces incident to racial survival.' "

"And?"

"And, 'Infatuation should be regarded with forbearance. Though episodic, it is almost invariably self-limiting.' "

"Stavvy. . . ."

"Mom."

"She upset you, didn't she?"

"She was so . . . she was nasty to Joshua."

"I know. Remember it. That way, if you ever go through what Myra's going through, you won't be as foolish as she is."

"She won't just give up on the ordinances, will she? She won't just leave?"

"Become a Gypsy?" Morgot chewed her lip, as though she had had a sudden thought. "I doubt it. But if she does, well, almost all of them who try it come back in a few months." Morgot looked even more thoughtful.

"I know. But there's quarantine."

"Only for as long as necessary to be sure they're not sick. Well, we'll do what we can to forestall that. Speaking of Gypsies, I'm making the weekly health inspection at the camp this afternoon. I think it would be a good idea if you came along."

"I . . . I didn't like it the last time."

"Good! That's a very appropriate reaction." Morgot started out the door, then turned back. "As a matter of fact, I think we'll take Myra along."

"Myra! She'll puke."

"Well, that won't kill her." She went out, leaving Stavia with very mixed feelings. It was good to be included, but not always. Not in everything.

THE SOUTH WALLS of Marthatown rose up out of sheep pens and pig pens and hay barns, a bucolic clutter wedged between the walls and the patchwork of pasture and stubble field, green and yellow and ashy white, dotted with huddles of dirty-gray sheep and scattered flocks of spotted goats to the place the fences ended. Beyond that open meadows ran off to the foot of the mountains where the woodcutters worked.

The north walls of the city were girded by warriors' territory. Armory and ceremonial rooms stood at the foot of the walls facing the parade grounds. North of the parade ground were rows of long wooden barracks, their carved gables and doors fronting on the exercise yards and the playing fields. East of these lay the pleasantly shaded walls of the officers' residence. To the north, at some distance from the city, the virtually empty hulk of the Old Warriors' Home huddled in a screening grove of trees. All this was garrison country—surrounded by a low fence—off limits to women and a more or less well-observed boundary for the men except when in search of what they were pleased to call "recreation."

Beyond the Old Warriors' Home the river ran westward toward the sea. It came from the eastern hills, through the marsh, then over a series of little dams and weirs which irrigated farmland from the foot of the hills almost to the shoreland in the west. There, near the shore, a road came down from the northwest to cross the river at a shallow ford, and near this ford the Gypsies had their perennial though not continuous encampment, a ragged and fluid collection of shacks on wheels, some brightly painted and others the faded gray of sun-dried wood, a sprawl of messy domesticity around the blackened stones of a central cooking fire.

Morgot, in her role as chief medical officer of Marthatown, went out each week to inspect the Gypsies, or sent a delegate. True to her word, she had brought both Myra and Stavia with her on this particular occasion.

During the medical visits, there were seldom any men around—except one.

This man, who called himself Jik, met them as they pulled off the road. "Back too soon, Doctor. You women just got done with them yesterday." He had a narrow face with a lopsided jaw. His teeth pointed in various directions, some filling in for others which were missing. One shoulder was lower than the other, and his laugh was a sneer made large. "Just yesterday I got them working."

"You had all of them but one, Jik. A sick one."

"Off the whole week, and not a coin out of her."

"She's cured now, Jik. You've probably already got her flat on her back milking the warriors for their amusement money." Though this wasn't Jik's only source of income, Morgot knew. The man dealt in beer and scarce commodities and information and rumor, as well, all of which the Council was well aware of and used for their own purposes from time to time. Morgot got down from the wagon and pulled her bag from beneath the seat. "It'll go quicker if you line them up for me."

Jik made a rude gesture, but started his circuit through the wagons. Women climbed from the wheeled huts, lining up around the fire, hoisting their skirts, some wagging bottoms while others thrust pudendas in the general direction of Morgot's wagon, laughing and catcalling, "Want some, Doctor? Want a little puss-puss, girlies? Hey?"

Morgot stared down the row, looking at each woman deeply and calmly, and in a moment the catcalls stopped. "Just in case you've forgotten, ladies," she called, "I've got the seal, and there won't be another doctor out until next week. No seal, no business."

The mockery became muted.

"Swabs," Morgot said to Stavia. "And remember to keep the vials labeled."

"What shall I do?" whispered Myra, her face very pale.

"Just sit there," her mother told her. "And watch."

Stavia kept telling herself it was never as bad as she remembered that it was. They smelled, sure, but it was mostly just dirt and smoke. Morgot took two swabs from each of them, one vaginal, one rectal, dropping them into the vial that Stavia held ready before she sealed the woman on the forehead with indelible ink. Last week's seal was still there, too, a faded circle on the left side. This week's went on the right. The date and the medical officer's initials. MRTM. Morgot Rentesdaughter Thalia Marthatown. No one else in Women's Country had those initials. No one else had Stavia's, either. SMRM. Stavia Morgotsdaughter Rentes Marthatown. Thalia was her great-grandmother's line.

Plop, the swabs went into the vial.

"Is it labeled?"

"Yes, ma'am."

Over in the wagon, Myra was looking at everything except the line of flabby buttocks and bushy vulvas on display.

Morgot had it down to a kind of chant, "Left leg up. Thank you. Bend over, please. Thank you. You're Vonella, aren't you?" she asked. "I thought so. Go climb into the wagon, Vonny. You'll have a week in the quarantine house. You can be thinking up the names of all the warriors you've fucked since your last clean seal, too. I'll need them all." The women were supposed to keep a contact book, but few of them were accurate about it.

When they had finished, Morgot asked, "All right, Jik. Are you harboring any elopers? Any silly little girl some handsome warrior has talked out here for his pleasure?"

He shifted from foot to foot. "The warrior paid me. . . ."

"He could have paid you and gone to bed with you," Morgot snapped. "He might have told you she'd never had sex with anyone but him, and him only once, I'd still need to see her."

"In there," he said, pointing. The wagon looked cleaner than some of the others.

"Get her out here."

"Can't you go . . . ?"

"You know the rules, Jik. Examination is done in public, with everybody knowing all about it. No secrets. No girly saying she didn't know old Rosy had the plup. This way everybody knows who's got what and whether they're curable or not."

"She's only a kid."

"Weren't they all kids once?"

Jik had some trouble getting the girl out, and when Stavia saw who it was, her mouth dropped open and she felt her face turning bright red. It was one of Myra's friends. Tally. Seventeen, just like Myra. From the wagon behind her came a muffled exclamation. Myra had seen her, too.

"You're Tally," Morgot said, as impersonally as if she'd never seen her before. "I'll make up a page for you in my Gypsy book. . . ."

"I'm not. . . ." the girl protested. "I didn't. . . ."

"Stand up straight and lift your skirts."

"I . . . Morgot, please."

"Lift—your—skirts."

"Might as well, honey," cried one of the Gypsies. "She'll get that swab up your ass one way or another."

The girl started crying, her hands before her eyes and her mouth twisted up. "Do you want to go home?" Morgot asked. "You can come back to Women's Country, you know. Or you can stay here. If you stay here too long, however, we won't take you back. Once disease is chronic, we don't take people back or allow them to stay near the city."

"Barten said he'd take me away. . . ."

Stavia heard the sound from behind her in the wagon, the intake of breath, the creaking of that breath, like aching wood, stressed in wind.

"Oh? Really! I think he probably told my daughter Myra the same thing. Where did you think he'd take you? Into the wilds? Did he plan to join the

Gypsies with you? He's already taken you as far as he intended to, girl. What's the matter, couldn't he wait two months until carnival? Or did he have other plans for carnival and want to get some fun out of you in the meantime?"

The girl broke and ran toward the wagon, weeping.

Stavia whispered, shocked, "You were mean."

"I was, wasn't I."

"Did you know she was here?"

"I'd heard rumors to that effect."

Stavia said nothing in a combination of furious embarrassment for Myra and anger for herself. Morgot had *planned* this!

"If you make it embarrassing enough, they usually don't repeat," Morgot said in a low voice. "I really don't want to come out here next time and find Myra in that wagon. Barten has quite a history of getting girls from Women's Country out here. Dishonoring them is part of the fun for him. I think Tally is his third or fourth. It's as though the girls were some kind of spoils of battle. They keep score, you know—some of the warriors in the garrison. How many women they've taken. It's a kind of game with them."

"I didn't know," Stavia mumbled, abashed. She still felt angry but she couldn't be angry at Morgot. This wasn't one of the things she had learned in women's studies. It wasn't one of the things Habby had talked about, or Byram.

"Not all of them do it, Stavvy. I don't think Habby would. Or Byram."

"How did you know I was thinking about them?"

"I think about them. All the time."

IN THE WAGON, Myra rode with her scarlet face straight forward, her mouth clamped in a grim, voiceless line. Tally lay in the back of the wagon, crying noisily, with many gulps and sniffles. The other woman, Vonella, chatted as though a week in quarantine was a treat for her.

"It probably is," Stavia thought. "Showers and a clean bed and cooked food and too much of our precious antibiotics."

"I've got a daughter in Marthatown somewhere," Vonella said. "And a son in the garrison at Susan."

"Then what are you doing out there?" Stavia demanded, forgetting for the moment that she was a child and not supposed to ask personal questions.

"Stavia!" Morgot warned.

"Oh, it's all right, Doctor," the woman said. "I don't mind the kid askin' and I don't mind sayin'. I just wasn't suited for town, you know? Too clean.

Too neat. Too much expected of you all the time. Studies and work and crafty things—no more time to yourself than a dog with the itch. Somebody after you all the time to cook better or weave better or be responsible for somethin'. I'd rather be out here, travelin' around. Jik's an old villain, but he's not bad to us, really. Some of the men are all right. We have some times."

Morgot sighed. "Have you been pregnant since you've been with Jik?"

The woman didn't answer.

"Did your baby disappear? Did Jik kill it? Or did it die?"

"It died," the woman said sullenly."

"How much of what Jik collects from your . . . your clients do you get? Half? Less than that?"

The woman didn't answer.

"How many times have you had a disease? You know, you keep passing these diseases around, and they lead to cancer. We can't cure cancer. People got close to a cure once, so it's said, but that's all lost now. Since the convulsions, we can't treat a lot of things that were curable before." Morgot said it as though she didn't really care, but Stavia knew she did. "You're no better than a slave, Vonella. You've been taken captive, and you don't even know it."

The woman threw up her hands, exclaiming angrily, "Oh I know. I do know. Likely I'll kill myself well before my three score and ten. I smoke willow, too, and that's no good for the lungs. And we all drink a bit there in camp. Jik makes good beer. . . ."

"From stolen grain," Morgot remarked.

"Well, he gets it where he gets it. Smoking and drinking and fucking. One or the other will probably kill me, right enough, but who wants to live to be old, anyhow. I've never wanted to be old." Vonella waved her hands again, exorcising age and infirmity.

"You'll probably have your wish," Morgot agreed. "Slaves mostly died young, even in ancient times. It's your life, but we can't let you infect Women's Country."

They stopped at the quarantine gate to drop both Tally and Vonella. "Stavia, go in with her and get the names of all the warriors and Gypsies she had contact with, will you please?"

"Oh God, lady, don't send your little girl in that pesthouse just for that. There was only one, this whole week. That mad old white-headed one with just the one eye. He always comes to me."

Stavia hesitated, waiting for the order to be rescinded. After a moment, Morgot nodded to her. "Unless you'd like to keep Tally company."

It was one of those maternal "unlesses" which could be understood a dozen ways. Did it mean, "Unless you're curious about the quarantine house and would like to see the inside?" or "Unless you think it would be womanly to help Tally regain her equanimity?" or "Unless it would be a good idea to rub Myra's nose in this just a little more?"

"I'll go in with Tally," Stavia said. "I have to do a report for my community medicine course, anyhow, and I can do it on the quarantine center."

Morgot nodded and drove the wagon away in such a manner as to suggest still another unless: "Unless you think it might be a good idea for Myra and me to have a private talk."

7

Aᴀ FTER ANOTHER SLEEPLESS NIGHT spent grieving over Dawid, Stavia dragged herself to the hospital, to work. Morgot came out of her office, took one look at her, and told her to go home. "Stavvy, you usually look about twenty-five, but today you look fifty. I heard you tossing and turning, up all night, wandering around. Go home and get some sleep."

Stavia, who was conscious of the imminence of her thirty-eighth birthday, was peculiarly annoyed by this repetition of Corrig's comment concerning her appearance. "I was checking the windows."

"Against what? Ghosts?"

"I thought it might rain in."

"It quit raining yesterday about noon. Go on home, Stavvy. This place is almost empty. Everyone in Marthatown is disgustingly healthy, it seems. A lot healthier than you look. I'm not surprised, mind you. I don't think there's a woman in Marthatown who really believes her son will be lost to her until he reaches fifteen and repudiates her. You try to get ready for it,

43

but you can't. It's like losing an arm or leg. Go ahead—take a little conva-
lescent time."

"Oh, Morgot, I did so hope. . . ."

"I know, love. We all told you not to, but you wouldn't be human if you
hadn't. Say the ordinances over to yourself; that'll put you to sleep. If you
can't sleep, at least rest. There's a Council meeting tonight."

"I'd forgotten!" She bit her lip, annoyed with herself. What a thing to
forget.

Stavia buttoned her padded coat and left the hospital, unbuttoning the
collar again as soon as she got outside into the sun. The chill rains of early
spring had passed for the moment and a mock summer had come, a tran-
sient warmth to stir false optimism. Cold would return inevitably before
there could be true spring, no matter what the sun and sea conspired to
suggest. It was too early for lunch. There was no one at home—the girls
were at school and Corrig had gone to the servitors' fraternity, where he
was teaching a class in the mysteries. She would have the house to herself if
she wanted to nap, but she didn't want to do that, not just yet.

She wound her way through the market, not realizing until she came to
the candle makers shops at the edge of the plaza that she had intended all
along to come to the wall.

"Stupid, sentimental sop," she told herself as she climbed the stairs.
"What do you think you're going to see down there?"

What Stavia saw was the empty parade ground with its tower and its
monument to Telemachus, behind that the carved gables of the barracks
buildings sweltering in the sun, and beyond them black specks racing about
on the playing fields. The garrison was only half the size it had been when
she was a child, and every member of it seemed to be either playing or
watching, mostly from low bleachers along the field. Three or four men
were looking on from the terrace of the officers' residence. Shaking her
head at herself, she found a sheltered corner hidden from the plaza and
fished in a pocket for the book. It was warm here in the sun. She would
spend an hour or two reviewing *Iphigenia,* then buy herself some lunch at a
tea shop before going home to the promised nap. By then she'd be tired
enough to sleep, she told herself, leafing through the pages to find the
place where she and Corrig had left off that morning.

"THE GHOST OF ACHILLES appears upon the battlement," she read, wondering how Joshua could bear to play Achilles. One would expect some
servitor with a broad sense of humor and not much dignity, not someone
like Joshua.

ACHILLES   I seek my servant, Polyxena!

IPHIGENIA   *(Calling from ground level)* Oh, mighty warrior, she is not here.

ACHILLES   *(Petulantly)* She's supposed to be here. They spilt her maiden blood upon my tomb so she would be here.

IPHIGENIA   But they didn't ask her if she would serve you, Achilles. Now that the warrants of warriors no longer run, she is her own ghost.

ACHILLES   She is my slave! It's all been arranged. Spill a maiden's blood, heart's blood or maidenhead, and she's yours. Everyone knows!

IPHIGENIA   She is no one's slave, Achilles. In the place of shades, we are all equal. . . .

HECUBA   Oh, maiden spirit, what is this mouthing?

IPHIGENIA   Achilles' shade stands on the battlement, his member turgid with the fever of his passing, calling for Polyxena.

HECUBA   Poor Polyxena.

IPHIGENIA   She may do as she likes, Priam's Queen. Nothing here constrains her.

ANDROMACHE   What will Polyxena do if nothing constrains her? Mother, what will she do?

HECUBA   I think she'll sleep. Polyxena was ever fond of sleep. Do they sup in Hades? Do they dance? Perhaps she'll eat, or dance. She liked to dance.

If it were me, I'd sleep, thought Stavia. Not dance or eat. Just sleep. She yawned, turning the page.

ACHILLES   *(Descending the stair)* If Polyxena won't attend on me, I'll set myself some other likely game. Are you Iphigenia, maiden child of mighty Agamemnon?

IPHIGENIA   Well I was.

ACHILLES   Why then, we are betrothed!

IPHIGENIA   *(Laughing)* Don't play the fool, Achilles!

ACHILLES   Odysseus bid you come to Aulis to wed me, did he not?

IPHIGENIA   Pure trickery to get me there, Achilles. They didn't call Odysseus the fox for nothing! I curse him as I curse my father. You knew nothing of betrothal then. When my mother greeted you as my betrothed, you thought her daft!

ACHILLES   That's true, but later on I agreed it was not a bad match. You were Agamemnon's daughter, after all. I offered to defend you.

IPHIGENIA   *(With shrill laughter, which echoes from the battlements as though from a horde of female spirits)* Oh, Achilles, Achilles. . . . *(Declaims)*

After I died, you said that you admired
my courage, though courage it was not!
Anger it was, at all you murderous men.
Anger which steeled me not to shame myself!
   Some poet, hearing of your fatuous words
composed a song about the bloody deed,
and not content with truth, embroidered it
with fulsome lies and patent sentiments.
What really happened was, you hid yourself,
and stayed in hiding until I was dead.

ACHILLES   It wasn't you who died. Artemis sent a hind to take your place.
Everyone knows. . . .

IPHIGENIA   What people know is what they want to know.
That was a late-come hind, great warrior,
for I was there and never saw it come!
Artemis sent no hind. Artemis had
more urgent business in some other place.
It was my blood spurting upon the stones
each time my heart's fist clenched, it was my brain
afire with pain, my voice gone dumb, my eyes
turned into dimming orbs of sand-worn glass,
their youthful luster lost forevermore.
Iphigenia, Agamemnon's child,
died on that bloody stone, not some poor hind.

ANDROMACHE   Oh pity. Pity.

IPHIGENIA   And though by now all poets gloss it o'er
to make it seem a different, kinder thing,
there was no great Achilles at my side,
no goddess-given hind to take my place.
I made no offer of myself as sacrifice,
though all the songs in Hellas say I did.

HECUBA   What are you saying, spirit?

IPHIGENIA   I am attempting to explain to the warrior that those who took
my life murdered me, though every poet in Hellas sings it otherwise.

"Halloo there," said a voice in Stavia's ear.

"Hah!" Stavia grunted, jolted out of a half doze. "Who . . . what . . .
what's it?"

"Joshua, Stavvy. What are you doing up here, falling asleep, getting
yourself sunburned?"

"Josh? I didn't mean to fall asleep, though every poet in Hellas says I did. . . ." Her voice trailed away, not yet awake. "When did you get back?"

"An hour or so ago. Nobody was home. I went to the hospital and your mother said you were having lunch or a nap, but I thought I'd find you here. Though, from the looks of you, you ought to be in bed." He sat down on the parapet and gave her a hard stare, the light behind him making his gray braid shine like a silver rope across his shoulder. The lines around his eyes were squeezed deep in concentration. "It was really bad, Stavvy?"

"Well, I knew how it would feel, but then I lied to myself a lot," she confessed, as she would have confessed to no one except Joshua or Corrig. "I couldn't sleep last night, thinking about Dawid, wondering what I might have done differently. Remembering when I was a kid, when things started. You know. How did you find me? You couldn't see me from down there." The words were out before she thought, then she flushed. Of course he had known where she would be.

Joshua took the book from her lap, scanning the section of the play she had been marking with her finger. "Stavvy, you knew there wasn't a chance in hell that boy would do anything but what he did. Think of Achilles. That's Dawid. 'I can't offend my friends, but you won't really die, mommy. Athena will send a hind.' Warriors all think like that or they wouldn't stay in the garrison. The trouble is with you, you've been creating playlets in your head. 'Dawid's change of heart.' 'Dawid overcoming his heritage and environment.' 'Dawid being blinded by the holy light.' Come on, Stavvy." He turned away from her, and she, seeing the muscles of his jaw clenching and unclenching, realized that he was trying to keep her from seeing the broken expression on his face. So. Despite his harsh words, he had loved Dawid, too, just as he had loved Jerby and Habby and Byram. He had hoped, too.

"I wish you'd been here to talk some sense into me before I went down there," she said softly. "Or after."

"I wasn't here for very good reason, as you know. Now quit breaking yourself up over Dawid. He may be half yours, girl, but it's the wrong half. Come on, I'll take you to lunch."

He half dragged her to the sausage shop, settling his face into a cheerful expression, giving evidence of enjoyment at a plate of mutton links heavy with basil and garlic and a dish of rare, wonderful rice. Around mouthfuls of sausage he told her stories, making her almost laugh. When he had eaten half of what was before him, he asked, "Why are you studying old Iphi?"

Stavia, who was only playing with a salad of early lettuce, looked down at the dog-eared book. "I'm doing the lead this summer. Morgot has refused to do it again, and they're all very flattering. They tell me I'm the only Council member who can look convincingly girlish. Don't laugh. I know what I look like today. Morgot told me."

"Summer's quite a time away. I'm doing Achilles, but I don't intend to look at it for weeks yet."

"I'd be surprised if you had to look at it at all! You've been playing the part for ages. I thought if I read it over every week or so, I'd pretty much learn it again without having to labor over it." Sudden tears filled her eyes and she gasped at a remembered pain so intimate it was like childbirth.

"Stavvy?"

"I'm all right, Josh. It's just . . . I was really reading it to distract myself, but I keep finding things in it that apply to me. Like Iphigenia being tricked to come down to Aulis. To get married, they said, when all they wanted to do was use her. You know that, you know all about it, and yet you let yourself. . . ."

"They wouldn't be acting it out every year in every city of Women's Country if it weren't applicable to something."

Stavia picked at her salad, the tears drying in the corners of her eyes, wondering at herself once more. "Things happen to you when you're young. And you think you know what it was that happened, but you really don't. Then later, sometimes years later, you suddenly understand what was really going on. And you feel such a fool because it's too late to do anything about the mistakes you made. I keep thinking of examples. Like the day Beneda and I were on the wall, and Chernon came up on the armory roof to see us. I was so excited. I thought he liked me. It seemed so casual, so fortuitous. I hadn't any idea what was really happening."

He put his hand over hers. "Do you want me to come home with you?"

"No. I'll just cry, and I don't need anyone to help me do that."

"You're sure? Just for company?"

"I'm sure. Go help Corrig. He's teaching a class in the mysteries. At breakfast yesterday he said he needed you to keep up with things. I'll be better by suppertime." She kissed him and left him in the shop, still polishing the plate the sausages had been on, staring after her with a reflection of her own pain.

At home in the quiet of her own room she lay on her bed, propped on pillows, the book facedown on her lap. She didn't need to read it. She remembered it.

ANDROMACHE   If it is not as poets say it was, why did they kill you, maiden?

IPHIGENIA   *(Sighing with impatience)*
  Upon the shore the hosts of Hellas stood,
  ranked by their thousands near their bird-winged ships,
  come full of martial fervor to the aid
  of Menelaus whose wife was raped away.
ANDROMACHE   So much we know. Helen was here. We did not want
  her, but she was here.
IPHIGENIA   Don't interrupt. If I lose the rhythm, I forget what I'm saying. Upon the shore, etc., etc.,
  whose wife was raped away. Ah, let's see—
  They stayed in Aulis where contending winds
  gave them no passage forth to Ilium
  and waiting, felt their blood begin to cool.
    Some spoke of Helen as a stolen cow,
  unwilling to risk lives for such a cow.
  Some thought of harvests waiting them at home.
  Some thought of wives and babes, though but a few.
    Until at last the host was discontent,
  no longer single-mindedly intent
  upon the course of warlike righteousness.
  Yet still, each man was shamed he should appear
  a laggard 'fore his peers. So some of them
  conspiring to the benefit of all,
  gave Calchas minted gold to act as seer
  and prophesy that there would be no wind
  to bear them forth to topless Ilium
  until the hour my father kept a vow
  he'd made long since—a vow to kill his child,
  as sacrifice to maiden Artemis.
HECUBA   *(Horrified)* Which he would never do!
ANDROMACHE   No father would do that!
IPHIGENIA   Well, so they thought. They thought that Agamemnon would
  refuse, then they could all go home.
HECUBA   Surely he offered other sacrifice.
IPHIGENIA   Which did not suit their purposes at all.
HECUBA   And when they would not take a substitute. . . .
IPHIGENIA   He sent Odysseus, full of trickery, to bid my mother bring
  me to be wed—to Achilles, if you can believe that—then gave me to the
  priests, who cut my throat.
HECUBA   And none of what the poets say is true?

IPHIGENIA   Oh, Hecuba, Hecuba! You're a woman! Can a woman believe such nonsense? Think! I was a maiden girl! Scarce more than a
child! My head was full of new gowns and festivals and wondering
whether I should ever have a lover or not. The words the poets poured
into my mouth were the prideful boasts of Argive battalions! They say I
offered to die for Hellas! What did I know of Hellas?!

HECUBA   It's true. When I was thirteen, I wouldn't have died for Troy.

ACHILLES   *(Irritably scratching his crotch)* I don't understand why they said
all those things if they weren't true. I thought you were my betrothed
whom I defended.

IPHIGENIA   My father used me as he would a slave or a sheep from his
flock. I think that many fathers do the same. Then, having done, he
claimed I'd wanted it. Perhaps it made him feel less vile. Men like to
think well of themselves, and poets help them do it.

ACHILLES   *(Petulantly)* Apollo save me from a clever woman. *(He looks her
over, head to toe)* Still, it is *said* we were betrothed.

IPHIGENIA   You may as well forget it, Achilles. There is no fucking in
Hades.

8

"THERE IS NO FUCKING IN HADES," eleven-year-old Stavia had declaimed, striking a dramatic pose for Beneda as she did so. The two girls had been sitting in the sun on top of the city wall. Stavia had agreed to help Beneda with her math—though Beneda was almost totally impervious to math—if Beneda would cue Stavia in Iphigenia's part. The test on the play was to be given the following week. "I like that line. It has a ring to it."

"I watched rehearsal yesterday," Beneda commented. "Michy won't say 'fucking.' She says it isn't womanly."

"Michy's mother is a very strange person. Morgot says she almost never takes part in carnival. She doesn't like sex at all!"

"Some women are like that. You know what I heard? I heard some men are like that, too. Do you believe that?"

"Not like sex?"

"Can't do it or something."

"Oh well, sure. That's physiological. Or sometimes psychological. There's stuff about it in one of my medical books."

"Can I read it?"

"If you want to. It's kind of dull, though. All about hormones and the prostate gland."

"Oh. I thought it was about penises."

"Well it is. Except the penis is just a protrusion of everything else, you know. It doesn't exist independently."

"Except to warriors."

"What do you mean?"

"They must think it exists independently," Beneda pointed at the barren field below them. "Look at that great thing they have out at the end of the parade ground. It's four times as high as the Warrior and Son statues. It's like a tower!"

"They call it a victory monument," objected Stavia, really looking at the pillar for the first time. It did look rather like a phallus.

"Oh for heaven's sake, Stavvy. It's even got a prepuce."

Stavia yawned. "I don't care if it's got an epididymis or what it is. All I care is that studies will be over for a whole month and we get to have carnival, and the boys will be home. I miss Jerby."

"What's Myra going to do?"

"Oh, she'll probably go ahead and have a liaison with Barten," Stavia said in a disapproving voice. "She's decided all that business between Barten and Tally was probably Tally's fault, if you can believe that. According to Myra, Tally seduced Barten and offered to come out to the Gypsy camp. Every time Barten does something dishonorable, Myra puts frosting on it and eats it. She is so dumb. Morgot just shakes her head and hopes a liaison will help Myra get him out of her system."

"You make it sound like an infection!"

"I was quoting Morgot. Well, it is how Myra acts, all feverish and delirious. She's talking about having a baby by him, just because he's so good-looking."

"There's nothing wrong with that," said Beneda, doubtfully. "Is there?"

"She's physically mature enough, so I guess not. There ought to be something wrong with it, though, you know what I mean?"

"Because he's the way he is?"

"Well, don't you think so? I mean, some of the warriors are perfectly honorable, aren't they? Some of them are smart, too. But Barten isn't. So, it doesn't seem right he should get to father a baby when he's that way."

"Except he's so good-looking. If you're going to raise a child, wouldn't you rather it was good-looking?"

"I guess. But suppose it's a daughter, and it grows up to be like him?"

"Yech. A crowing hen! Cock-a-doodle-doo!" Beneda spread her right hand above her head like a comb and flapped the left arm like a wing.

"That's what I thought. Since Myra's thinking of it, though, Morgot's got her on all kinds of dietary supplements." She twiddled her fingers, then stretched, like a cat. "Myra will do what she wants, regardless."

Beneda put down the book she had been pretending to study and said, "Stavvy, talking about chickens reminded me. Mom asked me to go to market to pick up some eggs for the house."

"Go ahead," Stavia said idly. "I'll wait for you here."

"Come on with me."

"I don't want to. You go on. You always get to talking and take an hour when it should only take ten minutes. If I wait for you here, I won't be impatient."

"What will you do here by yourself?"

"Read." She looked at the scattered books around them. "Preconvulsion societies. I'll read your anthropology book, then quiz you on it."

"It's dull. All about islands and tropical places and Laplanders."

"What are Laplanders?"

"You want to read it, you find out." Beneda stood up and brushed herself off. "I'll be back."

She went off, looking not too displeased to be going alone. Beneda liked to talk to people in the market and Stavia didn't. But then Beneda's mother wasn't on the Council and Stavia's was. Beneda could say anything that came into her head—and usually did—and no one thought anything of it, but if Stavia said, "It looks like rain," everyone wondered if it had significance because of something Morgot had said at home. As though Morgot ever said anything at home! She was as closemouthed as a vinegar shaker.

Left behind, Stavia picked up the red book Beneda had been reading. Preconvulsion societies. Tropical island tribes. Tribes based on trade. Migratory tribes—the Laplanders.

Stavia read, entering the world of the Laplanders in their padded coats and tall boots (not unlike the winter wear in Women's Country), picking the most docile reindeer to breed so they could lead their great herds from pasture to pasture without losing them. She could almost smell the huge rivers of animals moving north and south with the seasons, almost hear the lowing of the beasts, feel the bite of the snow, the weight of felted coats and boots, the tug of the leashed bull being led along so that all that river of beasts would follow. She lost herself in the words, becoming one of the migrants, feeling it. . . .

When Beneda came back, Stavia was sitting on the wall, the book open in her lap, tears running down her face.

"Stavvy! What happened?"

"Reindeer," she said, half strangled by her own teary laughter.

"What do you mean 'reindeer'?"

"Just . . . we don't have them anymore."

Beneda's mouth dropped open. "Stavvy, honestly. There's lots of things we don't have anymore. We don't have . . . clothes-drying machines and mechanical transportation and furnaces that heat your whole house, and cotton and silk and . . . and cows and horses and . . . and all kinds of other animals and birds and—oh, lots of things."

"I miss them."

"You've never *had* them!"

"Yes, but I know about them. That makes it different."

"You're weird." Beneda threw her arms around Stavia and squeezed tight, half laughing. "I love you best, Stavvy, because you're weird! Will you always be my best friend?"

Stavia laughed at herself, drying her eyes on the hem of her shirt. "I'll always be your best friend, Beneda. Forever. And I know I'm weird. That's what Morgot says, too."

"I wish we were sisters."

"Why? Sisters aren't so much." Stavia made a face, thinking of Myra.

"Oh, it's just I wish you were my own family. I wish you belonged to me." Beneda flushed, embarrassed at this declaration. "That sounds silly."

"No, it doesn't. It sounds nice. But I don't have to be your sister to belong to you, Beneda. We'll belong to each other, all right?" She put the book she had been reading down and hugged Beneda back, suddenly full of joyous warmth to replace the vacancy the book had evoked. "I wasn't really grieving, I guess. I just hate those people who made the desolations, that's all. They robbed us."

"Which is why we must obey the ordinances, so we don't rob our own descendants," quoted Beneda primly, waiting for Stavia to recover herself. "Do you want to quiz me about the Laplanders?"

"Tell me about the Laplanders," Stavia asked obediently, still wet-eyed, taking hold of Beneda's hand.

"They lived way up in the north where it was cold and snowy most of the time. They made clothes out of felt, like we do. Way back they followed these wild deer around, and it was hard to keep the animals together, so they picked the bulls that didn't run off and bred from those. And they milked them, too, the females, I mean, the cows. And they used deer hides to dress in. And the Lady knows what they did for fresh vegetables, because the book doesn't say. . . ."

"I wonder if they're still there."

"Where?"

"In Lapland. I wonder if they still exist. They might, you know."

"Well, we'll never know. That was on the other side of the world. But the book says they guaranteed both their own survival and the animals' by domesticating them, so maybe they still exist."

"Maybe one of these days, when the Women's Country exploration team goes out, they'll find a way through! Or maybe they'll decide to send a ship all the way across the ocean!"

"They did that hundreds of years ago, Stavia! The ship never came back!"

"Maybe they'll decide it's time to try it again. Things could have changed. Anyhow, when the next team goes in ten years, maybe I'll go along as medical officer."

"Small chance." Beneda made a teasing face.

"No, big chance. I think I'm going to Abbyville to the medical academy. Maybe in a couple of years. There could be a chance." She stopped, her eye caught by movement on the parade ground below them. "Someone's waving at us." Stavia jumped to her feet, surprised.

Someone was crossing the parade ground toward the stairs which led to the roof of the armory. From the armory roof to the wall top was only about twelve feet, which made the armory roof a favorite spot for the arrangement of assignations. "Is that Chernon?" Stavia asked. She had seen Chernon only in his white ceremonial tunic. This boy wore dull tan sheepskin work clothes.

"Stavia?" he called as he came up the stairs. "Remember me?"

"Chernon?"

"Right. Is that Beneda with you?"

"Are you my brother?" Beneda leaned across the wall, and Stavia caught her around the waist, afraid she would tip herself over.

"I haven't seen you since you were about six or seven years old." Chernon smiled up at her from under heavy eyelids, a measuring smile.

"Mother told me what happened. I'm so sorry, Chernon."

"Me, too. That warrior, the crazy one, the one who was bothering me, well, he's dead now. He got killed during a bandit sweep. Would you tell Mother? Please. I'd like to come home this carnival. Or at least visit. Aunt Erica is fine, but I'd like to see you. And Mother." His eyes were frankly pleading now, his lips quivering, ever so slightly.

"And the girls."

"And the girls." He cast a watchful look at the garrison grounds. "I can't stay here. Boys aren't supposed to be up here, only warriors. Besides, I'm on sleeper-in duty. I've got one quarter of the eight century to look after. Listen, there's a storeroom in the wall down past the west end of the parade ground. It's got some junk in it, but if you come to the outside wall there's a hole you can talk through or shove stuff through. Some of the warriors use it to make assignations. Bring me word there, will you? I can be there at noon, tomorrow. . . ."

His voice trailed away as he heard a trumpet calling from behind the barracks. "The fourteens! My section," he said, then called softly as he raced down the stairs and away, "Remember."

The two girls stared at one another, scarcely believing the brief encounter. "Chernon," breathed Beneda. "Oh, Stavvy, that's wonderful. I think he likes you, you know? The way he looked at you."

"Let's find this place he spoke about," Stavia suggested in a practical voice. Her insides did not feel at all practical. They felt liquified. It was a strange, almost indecent feeling, and she did not want to deal with it, or even consider it. "If you're going to be there at noon tomorrow to give him the message, then you'll need to know where it is."

There were stairs from the wall down into a street slightly east of the plaza. From there they crossed the plaza, speckled with lunchtime sunsearchers, and found a twisting alley leading between the wall and a two-storied row of assignation houses, their doors and windows open for a semiannual cleaning prior to carnival. Along the alley were several locked doors and, at the end, an unlocked one. The room within was spider-veiled and full of rubbish, but someone had made a path through the trash to the far wall. The hole was at shoulder level, an opening the size of a hand, broken through a four-foot width of wall. Light came in from the far end, a pale spot marbled by wavering shadows.

"It's behind a tree," mused Stavia. "That's why no one has reported it."

"You won't report it, will you, Stavvy?"

"No. At least not until you've told Chernon whatever your Mom says."

"I don't think you ought to report it at all," Beneda said, examining the almost dust-free path among the rubbish, made by the prints of many feet of different sizes. "Somebody comes here a lot."

CHERNON WENT DIRECTLY from the armory roof to report to Vice-Commander Michael who was sitting with Stephon and Patras under a spreading tree near the officers' residence. The slatted chairs and low tables under this tree were part of officers' country, and when they beckoned Chernon over, he hoped that some of his century were watching. It wasn't often that century Commanders were seen talking with a boy who was not even a warrior yet.

"You saw her?" Michael asked.

"Yes, sir."

"And?"

"And . . . and what, sir?"

"How did she react?"

"Fine. I mean, she seemed interested."

"Your sister?"

"No, sir. I mean, yes, sir, Beneda was interested, too, but I thought you meant Stavia."

"He did mean Stavia, grub," smiled Stephon, a tall, angular centurion with a tight, narrow face, heavily lined around the eyes. "Your commander wants to know if you'll be able to get into her . . . good graces." The smile turned chill, like a knife, and his smooth black eyebrows joined forces above his nose.

"Yes, sir. I will, sir."

"You know what this is all about, don't you?"

"Yes, sir. Michael told me."

"What did he tell you?" This with a confiding, easy glance at Michael, who lay back in his chair regarding Chernon under eyelids so heavy they looked almost swollen. When Chernon sought guidance from those eyes, they did not blink.

"He told me. . . ."

"Spit it out, grub."

"He told me the women know something. Something they're keeping from us."

"All the women?" This was the third man, bulky, bearlike Patras.

"No. No, sir. That is, probably not. But the Councilwomen do. And Stavia's mother is on the Council. And Michael said maybe I can find out something if I get Stavia to visit me at home during carnival, or if I get to visit her. . . ."

"Very good, Chernon," murmured Michael. "And of course you'll tell us everything you find out?"

"Of course, sir."

They waved him away, and he went, his head spinning with the honor and glory of it all. Most boys his age didn't even get to talk to the officers, much less do a special job for them.

"Not much chance of getting anything from that, is there?" bearlike Patras, furry Patras murmured to the other men as the boy went out of sight. Patras had hair where other men had skin, and even his voice sounded soft and growlly, as though there was fur in his throat as well.

"You never know," said Michael. "We keep detailing enough of our best-looking men to court the Councilwomen and their daughters, we're bound to find out something. They can't all be as tight-mouthed as Morgot is. The kid might pick up on something, or one of the others might."

"And it might all be for nothing. Jik could be lying through his teeth, just to keep you from killing him."

"That's possible. Likely, even." Michael stretched, smiling his lazy smile. "Next time the fool cheats me on a woman, he'll lose some vital anatomy over it. Meantime, though, we won't disbelieve him just because he's a thief. He's been to Emmaburg and Annville. He's been to Tabithatown, which is a damn long way north of here. Jik hears things. If he says he's heard that the women are hiding something, he's probably heard just that. Secrets, he says."

"What kind of secrets, did he say?" Stephon asked.

"Just something going on that we don't know about. Something to do with the servitors and the Councils," Michael replied.

"I don't know why we care what little secrets they have. Why do we put up with them?" Stephon's lips twisted in a grimace of distaste as he sneered, "Stupid, baaing ewe sheep! Why don't we just take over the city? We could. Any garrison could. Why don't we?"

Michael laughed, a burst of genuine amusement. "Oh, what an ambitious warrior he is! There is the little matter of Commander Sandom. Commander Sandom is perfectly comfortable, right where he is."

"I've heard him," muttered Stephon. "One of the twenty-two asked him the other day why we let the women run things, and old Sandom said, 'I'm sitting here at my leisure, boy, wearing fabric I got from Women's Country, drinking beer made from Women's Country grain. Tonight little Bilby will fix my dinner and he'll do it with Women's Country meat and beans and cheese. You want to get out in those fields and dig? Get yourself all muddy and cold? You want to be a shepherd, boy? Let the women run things. They like it, and why should I bother?' "

"He has a point," said Michael mildly.

"From a lazy man's point of view, yes," sneered Stephon. "The trouble is with Sandom, he's got no ambition."

"Well, say we did take over. Do you want to get out there and grub in the dirt?"

"Don't be stupid. I wouldn't have to. The women do that."

"Of course they do that," Michael said. "You think they'd go on doing that if we 'take over the city'? We 'take over the city' and we might have to take over what goes with it. We might find we had to work like women. No amusements except during carnival? You want that? Short rations when the harvest isn't good? The city takes the cut, you know; we don't."

"In the first place, if we were running things, we'd take our amusements when we liked. And we'd set the rations to suit ourselves, too."

"And you think the women would go on doing all the work?"

Stephon replied, "I think there are ways the women could be encouraged to do what they do now even if we did take over."

"You're saying you've got it all figured out."

"I'm saying nothing right now. Except I don't see why we should stay out here in garrison country when it would be so comfortable inside the walls. Why be satisfied with Gypsies, when Women's Country is full of prettier things."

Michael smiled, narrowing his eyes. "The problem with you, Stephon, is you don't sit around the fire at night listening to the old men. Men who remember things that happened thirty or forty years ago. You ought to listen more, Steph. Take what happened in Annville, for example."

"When?"

"Oh, twenty years ago at least. While you were still listening to your sleeper-in tell bedtime stories."

"I was not!"

Michael laughed, a long, lazy laugh as he rubbed his belly. "The garrison in Annville decided to take over the city. They did it, too. One night they just moved in through the gate and put a warrior in every house. Well, almost every house. And three days later they had the whole Tabithatown garrison camped outside the walls. A day after that, they had the Abbyville garrison. Anybody went out, they stayed out. Women went out to farm, they stayed out. Food ran out in the town. Pretty soon, the men started drifting out. Last thing was, the officers got hanged on the parade ground and the garrison got split up between Abbyville and Tabithatown."

"I never heard that!"

"You think it's something they want you to hear? Let me tell you something, Steph. I could take Marthatown. You could, too. I've thought about it. I might do it. But anytime I figure on taking over the town, I'd better have two or three things ready ahead of time. The first thing, I'd have to have all the other garrisons set to go along. Either that or they agree to look the other way."

"And what else?"

"There'd have to be plenty of food. There'd have to be a huge harvest. The fall trading among cities would have to be over so there'd be a lot of surplus food in the warehouses."

"I don't see. . . ."

"Right now we're living from harvest to harvest, Steph. Use your eyes and ears. Listen to women talk. You may think the women would work if us warriors took over the city, and eventually they probably would. But it might take a good long while to convince them. Your men get hungry, they start drifting away. You're not going to hold a city without men, and you can't hold men without food!"

"Hell," snorted Stephon. "All that might take forever."

"Well, we're only talking," Michael replied with a slow smile. "I'm like old Sandom. I'm comfortable now. I'm young. I've got time. If I ever get involved, I say 'if,' in anything like—oh, call it taking our rightful place in the world—if I ever do, I'll have everything planned out first. Talk about ambition all you like. If ambition means doing something stupid when the time isn't right, then I haven't got any more ambition than old Sandom has." He watched Stephon's face, seeing the slow agreement build in his eyes. Stephon was clever. He was a good tactician, one of the best Marthatown had. If Stephon was willing to relax and let things happen, well then, Michael might be able to use him. Michael was not as lazy or as unambitious as he appeared, but he had no intention of risking his life or position, either.

"Something unfortunate would have to happen to Commander Sandom," said Stephon. "That's sure."

"Well, yes. And not only to Sandom. To his cronies, too. Armory-master Jander. The head provisioner, Genner. Vice-Commander Thales. Maybe a few others. They're all popular, Stephon. And they're all senior to us."

"They're all a lot senior to us. They won't live forever."

"No. We could almost bet on that, couldn't we? Meantime," he yawned, "Chernon and the other pretty grubs'll see what they can find out. I've told them all to keep their ears open. Listen in on conversations, that kind of thing. Long term, I want Chernon in tight with that younger daughter of Morgot's. . . ."

"Morgot's daughter? She's your daughter, too, isn't she? Morgot never has carnival with anyone but you, does she?"

Michael laughed. "Warriors don't have daughters. They may beget an occasional girl, my friend, but we don't have daughters. You ought to know that! No, you've got to use girls for what they're good for. Forget daughters. Stavia's nothing to me. Or Myra, either. Barten's courted Myra until she's eating out of his hand. He's done well, Barten."

"With some protest," laughed Stephon.

"Well, Myra wasn't his first choice. Let's put it that way," Michael agreed. "A bit screechy and bony, he thought. He had a lust for the juicy little Tally. It took some fatherly instruction, but Barten will do his duty to the garrison."

"If you think Morgot knows so much, I don't understand why you can't get it out of her," Stephon said maliciously. "According to you, she can't leave you alone."

"Morgot's good at some things, but she doesn't talk," said Michael. "But little girls with their first assignation . . ." He laughed, knowingly. "Oh, they talk, don't they? They chirp like crickets. You can't shut them up."

"Has Barten found anything out?"

"Not much, but he's got Myra all steamed up about how foolish the ordinances are. Stuff like that. If it runs in the family, Stavia might be another one. That's all we want, two lovesick little chickens, mad at their mama and cheeping their heads off to our young cocks!"

"Maybe you should have gotten rid of Vinsas earlier, Michael. It would have made it easier for the boy to stay close to his family."

"I don't take action against warriors because some woman asks me," he replied angrily. "I don't do anything because some woman asks me."

"Of course not," said Stephon soothingly. "But killing that bastard Vinsas was a damn good idea, no matter what the reason."

STAVIA TOLD MORGOT about Chernon's request to come home while they were fixing supper that same night. "He says that warrior, Vinsas, is dead."

"That's odd," said Morgot. "I hadn't heard of any warrior deaths recently."

"Chernon said it was during a bandit sweep?"

"I would have heard of it. . . ." Morgot looked both puzzled and troubled, but seeing the concern on Stavia's face, she smoothed her own and went on. "Well. At least that's good for Chernon. Sylvia will probably agree to have him come home."

"Is there some reason she might not?"

"There's every reason, but I think she will. It's hard to take a son back and maybe have to grieve over him again when you've already done it and gotten over it."

"I don't understand."

Morgot got a faraway look on her face, her eyes sad. "You bear a son. When he's still a baby, you think of losing him when he's five. You grieve. You get over it. Then the day comes that your son is five and goes to his warrior father. You grieve. You heal. Then, every time he comes home for carnival, it's like ripping the wound open again. Each time you heal. And then, when he's fifteen, maybe he chooses to stay in the garrison, and you grieve again. You lie awake at night with your eyes burning and your pillow wet. You choke on tears and they burn. You worry about his going into battle, being wounded, dying. Every battle means . . . every battle means someone dies. Maybe your son, or your friend's son. Some women can't go on doing it over and over. Some women try to forget; they never speak of their sons again after the boys turn fifteen. Other women go on watching them, waving to them from the wall, sending them gifts." Her voice broke and she turned away.

"Don't you think Habby and Byram will come back?" Morgot's distress was unexpected and frightening, and Stavia asked for reassurance, even though she already knew the answer.

"I don't know, Stavvy. I hope so. But we just don't know." Morgot's eyes were wet as she sought a way to change the subject. "Why don't you go tell Myra to come peel these potatoes?"

"I'd just as soon not. She's been pretty awful ever since that day," Stavia said in a glow of self-righteousness.

"I think that's mostly just drama."

"Well, whatever it is." She sneaked a look at her mother who looked more herself now.

"Go get her anyhow."

Stavia went, taking her time about it, giving Morgot time to get herself together. Myra came to the kitchen and peeled potatoes with a look of remote distaste. Stavia and Morgot talked about nothing much, their conversation swirling around Myra's silence like water around a half-submerged rock. Stavia thought their familiar babble might eat Myra away in a thousand years. Myra was blaming them for what Barten had done to Tally, blaming both Morgot and Stavia for being there when she found out about it. Not blaming Barten, though, which Stavia found aggravating.

"Did you get down to the medical center today?" Morgot asked the silent girl.

"No." A curt monosyllable.

"Will you please go tomorrow?"

"I haven't decided."

"Myra, we've talked this over and over. If you don't want to be in detention during carnival, you've got to get down to the med center for a checkup and get yourself stamped."

"You're not stamped!"

"No, because I have no intention of putting on skirts and taking part in carnival. Not this year. But you probably do."

"I haven't decided."

"You can't leave it until the day of carnival, Myra. You have to make the decision well in advance. That's just the way it's done."

"And what if I don't?"

"You know very well what if you don't. If you don't, you can stay in the house during carnival as you chose to do last year and the year before. That was fine then. You weren't interested in anyone particularly, and I'm not about to suggest that you should have played catch-as-catch-can in the taverns at age fifteen or sixteen. However, you're seventeen now, and you are interested in someone. I don't want you being angry at me because you won't obey the ordinances and then you want to have an assignation with Barten and can't!"

"I'll stay in the house. The rules are stupid, anyhow."

Stavia, who agreed that some of the ordinances were stupid but who never would have said so, was aghast at Myra's comment.

"Fine. If that's your decision. If you go onto the street, you'll be picked up and taken to detention, and they'll probably assign you to a supervised labor team to clean the assignation houses."

Myra slammed down the bowl of peeled potatoes and stalked down the hall to the sanitary closet.

"She's hiding in there," said Stavia.

"I know. Poor thing. She's all mixed up between what her body wants to do and all the romantic, dramatic notions Barten had helped her work up for herself. Deathless love. Undying promises."

"That's just Myra," she said uncertainly.

"Well, it's any of us, Stavvy. I've heard a few of those same promises from young warriors. I've had a few romantic or sentimental notions myself, from time to time. We all like to invent worlds that are better than this one, better for lovers, better for mothers. . . . For all I know, Barten believes it himself. Many warriors do."

"Like the poets."

"What poets?"

"In *Iphigenia at Ilium*. Making what really happened to Iphigenia into something else. Really she was murdered, but that made the men feel guilty, so they pretended she had sacrificed her own life. Barten knows what would really happen to Myra if she went out to the Gypsy camp, but he makes it into something else in the stories he tells her."

"Mmm. Yes. As a matter of fact, that's a very good comparison. It's one of the things we on the Council try to keep in mind, the need to keep sentimentality and romance out of our deliberations. Leave romance to the warriors: We can't afford it in Women's Country."

"You could tell Myra she'd better get it while she can. There's no fucking in Hades."

"Stavia!"

Stavia flushed, then turned guilty white. The phrase was more literary than womanly. She heard a choking sound and turned to find her mother bent across the kitchen table, eyes flowing with tears, lost in silent laughter.

ON THE LAST DAY POSSIBLE, Myra went to the medical center and was given an implant in her upper arm—vitamins, Morgot said, because she hadn't been eating properly. At the same visit she was sealed for carnival. The red ink of the stamp was hidden by a fall of auburn hair at one side of her forehead and was thus scarcely a visible matter. However, once she had it, she seemed to come to terms with herself and almost stopped flouncing about. She did stop twitting Joshua, though she didn't treat him with her old, affectionate respect. Still, it made life pleasanter for both Morgot and Stavia, as well, no doubt, as for Joshua himself. Carnival was never a comfortable time for the servitors. They stayed mostly in the residential or private areas in order to avoid any confrontations between servitors and the warriors they might once have known rather well. Not that any of Marthatown's garrison except Habby and Byram would know Joshua. Joshua had come from Susantown when he was only eighteen. Men who returned through the Women's Gate often chose to go to different cities from the ones they were born in, just to avoid seeing old acquaintances. If Habby returned through the Women's Gate, he could choose to be sent to Susantown or Mollyburg or to one of a dozen other cities. Morgot or Stavia could always visit him there.

Beneda had delivered a message to Chernon, telling him he would be welcomed at home. Stavia passed her examinations in women's studies and physiology, and was commended for her gardening project. Her sketch for a setting of *Iphigenia at Ilium* was acceptable, as was her rendition of her assigned part. She managed to write from memory the assigned section of the ordinances, making only a few mistakes in punctuation. Then all studies and projects were terminated for one month to allow the instructors time to make their own carnival arrangements. Except for these semiannual holidays, school went on year after year, all year around. No matter how old they were, almost all the women in the city were studying something.

"After the convulsions," Morgot said, "a lot of knowledge was lost because people didn't know anything outside their own narrow areas, and the books were gone. Even if you're seventy, you should be learning something more in case it's needed."

The thought of still having to study when she was seventy made Stavia's head ache.

Chernon's arrival at his mother's house coincided with Stavia's having more time than usual to visit Beneda—and visit Chernon, too, of course, since he was there. Since he had made a point of asking Beneda to invite her.

"Why did you speak to me the day we brought Jerby to his warrior father?" she asked him. They were on the upper porch of Sylvia's house, hanging the washing out above the courtyard. Beneda had taken the wash-wagon to fetch the full baskets from the sector wash-house, and Stavia had offered to hang the load if Chernon would carry the basket up the stairs for her.

He thought carefully for a moment, deciding what to say. He certainly didn't want to tell Stavia that he had spoken to her because Michael had suggested it. "I didn't dare go up to Mother, or Beneda," he temporized. "I didn't know if I'd be welcome, and besides, they were standing too far back. I was going to give you a message for them, but there just wasn't time." He shook out a wet sheet and handed her one corner of it.

She pegged the sheet to the line and hauled the line on its pulley out over the courtyard. "You're allowed to send written messages, aren't you?"

"Oh yeah, if you have to. If you're willing to explain everything all the time and argue with the officers. If I'd been eight or nine, no one would have thought anything of it. I do sleeper-in duty for kids that age, and they're always homesick. But when you're thirteen or fourteen, you're expected to go home just because it's a duty. You're not supposed to want to."

"I suppose they say it's womanish." She finished hanging the last of the wash—Beneda's undershift—and wiped her wet hands on her trousers.

"That, yes. And worse things. It's all right to miss your mother's cooking, though."

"Beneda says you eat a lot of it!" What Beneda had said, actually, was that he gulped and didn't even bother to taste what he was eating.

He flushed, and she changed the subject. "Why did that warrior make you insult your mother?"

There was an odd expression on Chernon's face, half hungry, half furious.

Stavia blurted, "Oh, I'm sorry. Morgot tells me my mouth will be the death of me. I didn't mean to be personal."

"It's all right. I don't think he ever knew her. Mother said she might have met him once. And she said she was never—you know—with him. He claimed he got her pregnant but she didn't name him as the father out of spite. . . ."

"That's silly, Chernon."

He gave her a quick glance from the corner of his eye, intercepted an unexpectedly sceptical glance, then laughed unconvincingly. "Oh, it was all crazy. Sometimes he claimed I was really his son, but I'm not. I asked Mother and she says no, I'm not. He probably never even had a son. Probably no woman ever sent a boy to him."

"Then why make such a fuss over it?"

He seemed angry at the question. "You women don't understand! Mother wanted me just to lie to him, but I told her that was dishonorable. She said telling the truth to a madman was fruitless, and your mother said the same thing, but he was my superior, my senior, anyhow, and I had to do what was honorable. Warriors don't lie to each other. I tried to tell you women that."

" 'You women'?"

He flushed. "My mother. Your mother. I tried to explain I had to do what Vinsas wanted, even if it was crazy, because that's what we do in the garrison. We obey orders, and we don't ask whether the officer is crazy or not!"

"You knew he was crazy?"

"During carnival . . . one of the warriors said that during carnival there were always six big women with clubs near him, wherever he went, and if he even looked at one of the women, they landed all over him. I heard—I heard he even forced one of the boys."

"Chernon! That's absolutely forbidden." Stavia bit her lip. Even in preconvulsion times it had been known that the so-called "gay syndrome" was caused by aberrant hormone levels during pregnancy. The women doctors now identified the condition as "hormonal reproductive maladaption," and corrected it before birth. There were very few actual HNRMs— called HenRams—either male or female, born in Women's Country, though there was still the occasional unsexed person or the omnisexed who would, so the instructors said, mate with a grasshopper if it would hold still long enough. If the warrior had indeed "forced one of the boys," it had almost surely been done out of viciousness and dominance, not from any libidinal need. Libidinal need was fully accepted as a normal and useful fact of life. Viciousness was not; rape wasn't tolerated in Women's Country. "He could have been executed for that," she said soberly. "I can't imagine why he wasn't."

"No one could prove anything," he said uncomfortably. "Anyhow, it was just a rumor."

"Couldn't they control him?"

"They? You mean the officers? Vinsas was in Michael's command, and I suppose Michael could have done something, if he'd wanted to. But when Mother came to Michael it just made him stubborn, and he wouldn't do anything. Vinsas was out of his helmet, really. Mostly they let him alone. And then he died. I think someone killed him."

"Murdered him?"

"Just killed him. I think it was during a raid his century did on the bandits. Except we all suspected it wasn't the bandits that did for him. Everybody was glad he was gone."

Stavia bit her lip as she picked up the empty basket to carry it downstairs. Even though Chernon was unreasonably bitter toward his family, she excused it because of what he had gone through. The thought brought hot moisture to her eyes. She shook her head furiously, letting the nearest wet sheet flap in her face to hide her tears. "Do you think about coming home?"

"You mean like now, for carnival?"

"I mean for always. Through the gate. . . ." She caught a glimpse of his face, suddenly remote and faintly contemptuous.

"Don't say it, Stavia. Of course I think about it, but I don't want to talk about it. It's not something we talk about, that's all."

This withdrawal surprised and frightened her. He had not refused to talk about anything else. "All right. Let's talk about something else. Do you know Barten?"

He relaxed, now on safe ground. "Oh, everyone knows Barten. You were talking about your mouth getting you in trouble. Barten's mouth is a lot bigger than yours. He brags all the time. We're going to be so glad when he gets to be twenty-five and can actually fight instead of just talk about how great he's going to be. Maybe somebody will wound him around the mouth and make us all happy."

"You don't like him much, do you?" She thrust an extra clothespin over the corner of the nearest sheet, watching it belly into the wind.

"Barten likes Barten enough for all of us. Mostly because of who his warrior father is."

"Who's that?"

"Michael. They've always got their heads together. Didn't you know that?"

Stavia shook her head, not trusting her tongue. So, in point of fact, Barten might be her half brother. Myra's half brother? No. No, if that were the case, Morgot would have said something about it. Not that a liaison with a half brother was necessarily a bad thing. Depending. She sat down on the railing, staring out over the back courtyard wall toward the sea.

"What are you thinking about?" he asked her.

"Genetics."

"What's that?"

"The science of how things pass on their characteristics to their offspring."

There was a long silence. He sat down on the railing beside her, his head turned away. If she could have seen his face, she would have seen it concentrated in thought, in sudden inspiration.

"What's the matter?" she asked him.

"You make me feel . . . you make me feel ignorant," he said in a wounded voice. "I don't know about things like that."

She gave him an astonished look. "It's all in books! The garrison has a library."

"Romances, Stavia. Tales of battle. Sagas. Designs for armor. Hygiene. Maintenance of garrison property. You know! Nothing about real things. Nothing about medicine, or engineering, or management."

"Those are women's studies."

"I know what they are. I just said you made me feel ignorant, that's all." He looked hurt again. "It isn't a nice feeling."

"I could lend you some books, while you're home. I'll even give you some old ones to take back with you if you want." She made the offer before she had time to think, and a part of her stood aside, aghast, as it realized what she had said. Giving Women's Country books to a warrior was absolutely forbidden!

"I couldn't do that." His lips said it, but his eyes were looking at her from their corners, as though weighing the offer. "They'd have me up on charges."

She almost sighed with relief. "You're not allowed to read?"

"Not things like that. Not womanish things."

"Ah." She sought some compromise. "Beneda's got books you can read while you're home, though."

"Hers don't have the kinds of things I'd like to know," he said with calculated sadness, eyes falling away from her own to contemplate something distantly chill, an attitude which had always brought Sylvia to him, begging him to tell her what was wrong, what she could do to make it better.

It had a similar effect on Stavia. She found herself wondering what harm it would do. After all, there was no ordinance against reading to him, or talking to him about anything she had read. What was the difference? It just showed how stupid some of the ordinances were. "I just never thought of a warrior wanting books. But, if you're that interested."

He turned back to her, flushing, face as eager as Jerby's would have been at the promise of candies, and her reluctance seemed arbitrary and unkind. And yet . . . it was against the ordinances.

She put on a deliberate gayety. "In return for which you can do me a favor."

"Name it!"

"Tell me what the warriors call that monument you've got at the end of the parade ground."

"The Ulysses Statue?"

"No. The tall one."

He turned red. "We call it the reviewing stand."

She shook her head in exasperation. "That's silly. You can't stand on it."

He blushed again.

"Come on, Chernon. Why do you call it that?"

"It's an erection suitable for a parade ground," he muttered.

It took her a moment. "I see. What is it, really?"

"Just what it looks like," he muttered again. "Blooded warriors take their oaths of honor on it. It's a symbol of shared manhood."

"Penis worship?"

"It's symbolic," he said resentfully.

"Yes," she agreed in amazement. "It certainly is."

CARNIVAL TIME gathered momentum. Habby and Byram and Jerby all home, with Joshua and Morgot fixing special meals and giving presents. Popcorn by the stove, holiday pies, the whole family off to see the magicians or the fireworks together. Except for Myra. She went flitting out every morning with flushed cheeks and a giddy laugh, her usual trousers changed for short, colorful gowns—for which Habby and Byram had learned a short and very vulgar name—going twice a day to the assignation house, drinking beer and wine and dancing with Barten in the carnival taverns until all hours of the night.

There was no time to miss her or worry about her with the dozens of itinerant clowns and magicians; the rockets screaming into the evening sky; the acrobats; jugglers; jongleurs; the city full of the sound of music and drums and choirs. There were song contests between the warriors and the women—which the warriors almost always won. Warriors had a lot of time to practice, all the time they weren't fighting or practicing fighting, or engaged in their interminable sports contests. They sang battle epics, mostly, though they did do some amusing songs and some of the old folk songs and love songs that everyone knew: "Gone Away, Oh, Gone Away," and "The Lost Century," and "What the Warrior Wears Beneath His Kilts," and "I Lost My Love at Carnival," a lament. The women didn't have nearly as much time to practice, but they sang nonetheless, and the town resounded with voices.

After five or six days of it, Stavia got the impression that Myra might be tired.

"Just because I yawned," Myra snarled. "It doesn't mean I'm tired.

"You can miss a day if you like," Morgot said.

"I don't like."

"Well, maybe skip some of the drinking tonight and get a night's sleep."

"Barten doesn't want to drink alone."

"He wouldn't be alone, Myra," Habby yawned, echoing the gaping jaw on Myra's face. "He'd find somebody."

"Habby!" Myra, red in the face, really angry. Or hurt.

"Yes, Habby," Morgot remarked. "I'd keep my helpful suggestions to myself, if I were you."

The eighth day, Myra didn't go out at all. Sodden sounds from her bedroom, gulpings and howls.

"They had a fight," Morgot explained.

"He had a fight," said Stavia. "Chernon told me all about it. All of the young warriors planned to have a fight with their sweethearts after seven or eight days. That's so they can try some of the others."

"A basically self-defeating proposition," sighed Morgot. "Since the 'others' are all at home crying, too."

There seemed to be some logic in that. A messenger brought a plea from Barten for Myra to join him.

She went out, giddy-eyed.

"Oh shit," said Stavia. "She doesn't have any sense at all."

"No," yawned Morgot. "None of them do. Neither did I, when I was that age."

"I refuse to be that age."

"I wish you luck."

THEN CARNIVAL ENDED. Chernon went back to the garrison. So did Habby and Byram and Jerby—Habby and Byram resignedly, Jerby in tears. It was easy to know how they felt, but Chernon? Who knew what Chernon was feeling?

"He likes you, doesn't he?" begged Beneda, her eyes shining. "When you're older, maybe you can be lovers."

"Beneeda," Stavia protested.

"Well maybe you can. And maybe you can have Chernon's baby, and we really will be like sisters."

"Beneeda! I won't talk about that." Her face burned. She couldn't talk about that. It was too close to feelings she was having that she couldn't understand or control.

The great central gate through which warriors had been coming and going for two weeks was slammed shut on the plaza once more. Bemused women set about cleaning the littered streets. The shedlike carnival taverns were closed, the drink barrels drained until next brewing time. In the houses of assignation, sheets were thrown over the furniture, the plumbing was drained, and the doors were closed again.

There was an almost silence in the city, a funeral quiet. Doors shut quietly. Voices murmured. Even the Well of Surcease seemed to have muted its music, and bird song came as a puzzled question rather than an affirmation. It seemed a time of mourning. "Severance," murmured Morgot, quoting a Women's Country poet. " 'The silence of severance, a vessel of quiet to hold mourning, for those who have said welcome, and farewell; a time to summon once again those things not so much lost as unremembered.' "

"I think everybody's just tired," said Stavia practically. She knew she was tired. Not being with Chernon was unthinkable, but being with him made her weary in strange ways. "Just tired." Preoccupied with her own confused feelings, she did not see the appraising look that Morgot gave her.

The week after that, Stavia went back to her studies.

Not before she gave Chernon a book, however, against her better judgment, against her common sense, the observer Stavia pleading with the actor Stavia to be sensible. Actor Stavia did it anyhow, asserting that the ordinances were stupid, arbitrary, and that Chernon was different.

"And you'll bring me more, won't you?" Chernon pled through the hole in the wall, their fingers touching deep within that recess, quivering like tiny animals, smelling one another out. "Please, Stavia. To the hole in the wall. Anything. Anything I can read!"

"You'll get caught," she said, halfheartedly hoping he wouldn't press it. It would get them both in trouble, probably . . . perhaps. And yet it tied them together, probably. . . .

"I won't get caught. I'll come there during my free time, I'll stay right there and read, then I'll leave the things there, pushed down behind the tree. Oh, I know you will. Please, Stavvy."

"All right, Chernon," she promised him, giddy from that liquid, furtive feeling he gave her, a feeling which she assumed was "infatuation." She had no other name for it. Lending him a few books seemed such a small thing to do to keep that stricken, wounded look away from his face. She couldn't bear to see him looking like that.

SEVERAL DAYS after carnival, Myra went to the medical center, taking Stavia with her for company. After an hour, Myra came out looking angry and ill used, and they walked toward home together.

"Have you got something?" Stavia asked.

"No, I have not got something. I'm healthy."

"What's the matter."

"Just—they're so rude. Always the same questions. When was my last period? She knew. It was just before carnival, and she gave me an exam then. Was I taking my supplements? Did I have any sexual problems?"

"That doesn't sound too rude."

"It was something else. She had me up on the table all spread out like a split fish with that metal gadget in me, squirting me with syringes and stuff, and then they called her out for an emergency and she left me there!"

"There are emergencies, My. There really are."

"Well, somebody could have come and let me loose. I was there for half an hour, flat on my back."

"Does she think you're pregnant?"

"She says she can tell in six weeks or so."

"Do you want to be pregnant?"

"Sure. I mean, I have to start sometime, right?"

"But do you really want to be pregnant? By Barten?"

"It would be the prettiest baby, Stavvy. I have always hated this hair. And freckles. I hate freckles. Barten's baby will have dark hair and blue eyes and skin the color of spun wool."

"You can't be sure of that, Myra."

"Well, it's a good chance."

"I'm just saying, don't count on it. The baby may have hair and freckles just like you, and it wouldn't be a good idea to let it know you were disappointed."

"Oh, for heaven's sake, Stavia, you are not the only person in this family ever to have taken childrearing courses! I swear to God, some days you sound just like Morgot. You're only eleven and I wish to God you'd act like it!"

Stavia was so astonished that she stopped short, letting Myra walk on by herself. It was true. She did sound like Morgot. It struck her for the first time that she even thought of herself as a kind of Morgot. A smaller version. It seemed unfair that Myra had reminded her she was only eleven. It was true, but it didn't mean anything, except physiologically. She had no breasts. She had no menses as yet. Presumably these would come. When she lay in her bed at night, touching herself for her own pleasure, she thought of Chernon, longing for the years to pass until. . . . She flushed, aware of the heat in her body. That meant she was quite normally sexual. And she did have a womanly mind.

Her thoughts flowed on: If it was true that Morgot and Stavia were much alike, then Morgot would understand Stavia's giving Chernon the books, understand and approve of it. . . .

The thought abruptly drained out of her, like irrigation water flowing down through some hidden gopher hole, all her easy, consoling rationales pouring away to leave only a soggy certainty behind. She, Stavia, might be as like Morgot as one twin to another or as mother and daughter could be, but Morgot would not approve giving books to Chernon. Morgot would quote the ordinances. Morgot would say, "If he wants books, let him return to Women's Country and he may have all the books he likes. . . ."

It was true. Joshua had books. Many. And so did little Minsning, and so did any other servitor who wanted them.

But not the warriors. A man who chose the warrior's lot chose to fight for his garrison and his city. A warrior needed all his powers of concentration. Having other, irrelevant thoughts in his head could be risky. Also, it could be dangerous for a warrior to know too much about certain things. Metallurgy, for instance. A warrior might obtain an unfair advantage if he had learning that other warriors didn't. Out of loyalty to his garrison, a warrior might make some device which could return them to the time of convulsions. Only equal match between equal warriors at arm's length could decide things fairly without imperiling others, without threatening devastation. . . .

She could hear Morgot's voice. But she could also hear Chernon's. "Please, Stavia. I want them so bad! There's things I need to know. . . ."

When he pleaded with her like that, he melted her. As though she were no better than Myra, turning to mush when some man begged her. "Please, Stavvy." His eyes were as clear as Jerby's, childlike still. His hair was soft gold, like Beneda's. He looked so much like Beneda, too, with that lovely, bony face, all planes and angles.

No. She could not say anything to Morgot. And Chernon must be told firmly that he could have all the books he wanted if he would only come back.

Except that he wouldn't let her talk about that. He had begged for books where he was, not where he might someday be.

She stamped her foot angrily, biting her cheek on one side and bearing down until it hurt. She couldn't stop giving Chernon books now. Not now. But it wasn't really wrong, not yet. He wasn't really a warrior yet. Not until he was fifteen. . . .

"Shit," she murmured at the stones beneath her feet. "Oh shit."

THOUGH EVERY SCHOOLGIRL in Women's Country learned *Iphigenia at Ilium,* it was actually produced and acted by the Councilwomen of each city. Thus it was Councilwoman Stavia who stood on the stage of the winter theater at Marthatown's center with half a dozen of her fellow Council member–players, working their way through the first rehearsal of this year's production. The evenings were still too cold to rehearse outdoors in the summer theater, so here they all were in the wide, low-ceilinged room which had been designed to be warmed by bodies alone. With only the cast and stage crew present, there weren't enough people to raise the temperature noticeably, and Stavia shivered under her coat.

They had tried Cassandra's entrance three different ways, none of which pleased the director.

"Enter Cassandra from stage left," the director said plaintively. She was an old Council member but a new director, and she had not yet come to terms with the job.

CASSANDRA Mother! Andromache! I've come to say good-bye.

HECUBA Cassandra! You? Still here? Oh, girl, I am so weary of farewells —saying good-bye to living and to dead! Long, sad farewells when there's no good to come. There is not sleep enough to heal farewells, and now you're here when I had thought you'd gone.

CASSANDRA Others have gone, but Agamemnon stays. He says he has some trouble with the sails, so long left furled upon this Trojan shore they're full of rot.

ANDROMACHE Any housewife could have told him that. All seaside towns hold mildew like a sponge.

HECUBA Such a humble thing to thwart a tyrant's purpose.

IPHIGENIA Strength often comes from unexpected sources, perhaps most often from the humble things. . . .

ACHILLES Is that Polyxena?

IPHIGENIA That is Cassandra, great Achilles. Look closely. That one is still alive.

CASSANDRA Ghosts! Who are these ghosts?

ANDROMACHE You see them too?

CASSANDRA Is that Achilles? And the child—Andromache, is that your son?

ANDROMACHE It was my son. Odysseus had him slain.

CASSANDRA (Weeping) Alas. Such is the fate of warriors' sons. . . .

10

VERY FEW MOTHERS in Women's Country ever spoke of their boy
children as "warriors' sons." Myra had been an exception. When her first
baby had been born, Myra had used the phrase on every possible occasion.
She never spoke of him as "my little Marky," or even just as "Marcus." He
was always, "My little warrior son. . . ."

He had been born with a full head of dark hair and deep blue eyes.
These resemblances to Barten had been mentioned to everyone at least ten
times a day. When within a month all the dark hair fell out and the eyes
turned hazel, Myra had considered the change a personal affront, arranged
by some human agency.

Morgot seldom lost her patience as completely as she did over this issue.
In such chilly weather as they were having at the time, the family spent
long hours together in the big, warm kitchen, listening to Myra's continuous complaints. When Margot could bear it no longer, she said, "Myra, if
you say one more word about that baby's hair or eyes, I'm going to go to
the Council and suggest it be given in fosterage. If you're going to go on

and on like this, the poor child will grow up self-conscious and unhappy and it will be your fault." Morgot was pale and thin lipped with anger.

"I only said. . . ."

"You only said that the midwife committed some kind of scientific indecency by modifying the child's heritage—though that is utterly impossible —or that the birthing center mixed up the babies. Which you know is ridiculous, because Marcus never left the room where you were from the moment he was born, and you brought him home yourself a day later!" Morgot opened the iron door on the front of the tile cookstove and put two split logs inside, positioning them carefully, obviously trying to gain control of herself.

"Besides," Stavia offered, "Marcus is a very cute baby." She picked up the broom and swept bits of bark from the tile hearth, turning to warm herself at the exposed coals before Morgot shut the door and narrowed the air supply. The kettle on top of the stove had begun to steam and the air in the room was almost summery with moisture and the scent of herbs. "The baby looks a lot like Jerby. There's a definite family resemblance."

"*This* family," snorted Myra in disgust.

"Yes, *our* family. The Margotsdaughters! And what's the matter with that? Barten is good-looking, but he's a rattlesnake. I'm sure he's fun to have sex with, but otherwise he's a serpent. Everyone says so. . . ." She burrowed into a cupboard among the herb-tea cannisters, looking for the one with fruit peel in it.

"Chernon says so, you mean," Myra sneered.

Stavia felt herself turning red, heat rising inside her as though she had a furnace in her belly. "Chernon says everyone in the garrison says so. What I mean is, if Marcus doesn't look like Barten, maybe Marcus won't act like him, and you should be happy over that." With shaking fingers, Stavia measured tea into the pot and poured boiling water over it.

Myra subsided into outraged and sulky silence. Her romantic dream of motherhood had been riven into sharp-edged fragments by late-night feedings, constant diaper washing, and a baby who persisted in looking and acting like a baby, not like a young hero. She had more than half convinced herself that when she took this child to his warrior father at age five, Barten would probably reject it.

Morgot shook her head and went back to packing food into a heavy canvas sack. She and Stavia were to leave on the following morning for a short trip in the direction of Susantown. "Stavia, are your clothes and necessaries packed?"

"Yes, ma'am."

"Then Joshua said he'd like your company while he does the shopping."

"Is Joshua going with us tomorrow?"

"I think it's a good idea, yes. There have been a few Gypsy attacks on the road to Susantown within the last few months."

"Fine lot of help he'd be," snorted Myra. "A servitor!"

"Are you quoting Barten again?" her mother asked dangerously.

"Well, when I took the baby to the wall walk to show to his warrior father, Barten said. . . ."

Morgot took a deep breath. "Myra. Almost a year ago I told you never to repeat to me Barten's opinions about our ways here in Women's Country. We do not assert the opinions of warriors in Women's Country, particularly opinions on matters about which they know nothing. It's not merely bad manners, it shows a fundamental lack of respect—for me, for the Council, for our ordinances. You have done it twice. Once more and it will go to the Council."

"You wouldn't!" Myra was white with anger. "You wouldn't!"

"Because you are my daughter? It is precisely because you are my daughter that I would. If you cannot accept admonition from me, then it is time others tried with you. Young women often do not get along with their mothers. Adolescence is a time for establishing separations and independence. Sometimes daughters need to change houses. It is acceptable to do so, not in the least frowned upon, scarcely a matter for comment. But it does require Council notice." Morgot sounded as though she were delivering a rehearsed speech, and Stavia realized with a pang that she was doing exactly that. This was something Morgot had planned to say, something she had probably lain awake in bed as she practiced saying it.

"You'd throw me out!" Myra howled.

"Oh, for heaven's sake, Myra, she didn't say anything about throwing you out!" Stavia exploded. "She just said if you won't take correcting from her, maybe you'd be happier somewhere else."

"I'll thank you to keep out of this, you little bitch."

Stavia started to explode once more, but her mother's hand on her shoulder stopped her. "No, Stavia. Don't dignify that with an answer."

The speech making had stopped. Now Morgot was herself again, a very angry self, speaking with a dangerous calm. "Myra, if you are fond of Barten, which you seem to be, think on this. You are drawing unkind attention to him by your rather consistent failure of courtesy. At some point, someone may blame him for what you are doing and saying. Do you want that?"

"I don't care! You can't discipline him the way you're trying to get at me. You can't touch him. He's a warrior, and he's out of Women's Country, and I wish to hell I was, too."

"I see." Morgot's face was perfectly blank, perfectly quiet. Seeing it, Stavia wanted to scream. Myra had just said something unforgivable, and Stavia didn't even know what it was. She shuddered as Morgot went on, "Well, I'll consider that, Myra. We may talk about it again when I get back." Morgot turned and left the room.

Myra turned a furious face at Stavia, obviously trying to think of something cutting to say.

Stavia didn't give her a chance; she snatched up the teapot and two cups and fled. Joshua would be in his own warm room at the corner of the courtyard, and Stavia badly wanted to be there, or anywhere else, rather than in a room with Myra.

"I don't understand her," she mumbled while Joshua shaved himself, wielding the ancient straight-edged razor with much practiced skill. Only warriors wore beards. Servitors were clean shaven. Razors, like anything else made of good steel, were treasured possessions. Most of Women's Country's tiny steel production went into things like razors and scalpels and other medical equipment. The warriors did very well with bronze manufactured by their own garrison foundry.

"I'd overlook a lot of what she says," Joshua advised, taking a sip from the cup she had brought him. In the mirror his wide, hazel eyes gave her a kindly glare. His face had high, strong cheekbones and a wedge-shaped jaw. His long, brown hair swung from side to side in its servitor's plait as he turned his face before the mirror, searching for unshaven patches. "She's just had a baby. She's probably having postpartum depression. Then, you've got to keep in mind what kind of person that little bastard Barten is. One of his worst qualities is that he likes to whip people around emotionally. He's jerking Myra this way and that every time he sees her. It's an expression of power for him, I think. Either that or someone's put him up to it, and that thought does keep coming into my mind. Myra's trying to nurse the baby and keep up her studies, too. She's up two and three times a night, and we both know she was never much of a scholar. Give her six months, and I think she'll level off."

"Not if Barten keeps after her the way he is."

Joshua got a peculiar expression on his face and began to rub his brow as though it hurt. "Is there something particular he's agitating her about?"

"He wants her to espouse warrior values. He wants her to leave Women's Country."

"And become a whore?" Joshua put down the razor and turned to face her, two tall wrinkles between his eyes, one hand still rubbing.

"He tells her he can keep her, her and the baby. Somewhere off in the wilds."

Joshua's mouth turned down, angrily. "You told Morgot this."

"I promised Myra I wouldn't."

"But you're telling me?"

"I didn't promise I wouldn't tell you."

"You know I'll tell Morgot."

"What you do is what you do," she said uncertainly. Why did she feel she had laid some kind of spell on Barten. Or cursed him, like Iphigenia had cursed her father. "I kept my promise."

"Oh, Stavia," he laughed ruefully. "Really." He wiped his face with a towel and then thrust his long arms into the sleeves of his long sheepskin coat with the bright yarn embroidery down the front. "Let's go see what the market has to offer."

They left the house, Joshua with the large shopping sack over one shoulder and Stavia with a flat basket for things that shouldn't be crushed. It was late April, a sunny day chilled by small sea winds that came down from the Arctic, gusting with intermittent ice. Stavia tucked her trousers into her boottops and buttoned her padded coat tight at the neck.

"It's cold!" she complained, tucking her hair under her earflaps and tying them under her chin. "We've done nothing but burn stove wood for months, and it's supposed to be spring!"

"It's just a little delayed, is all. We still have plenty of our wood allotment left."

"For another month, maybe," she remarked in a dismal tone.

"That'll be enough," he said comfortingly. "Relax, Stavia."

They strode along a street lined with house walls, broken only by high kitchen windows—whose evening candles served to light the street after dusk—and double doorways with wooden grills. There were no windows at all in the higher stories, no openings from which heat could be lost. Inside the houses, grilled openings in the upper floors let heat rise from stoves in the lower rooms. All the windows were of double glass. There were insulated shutters to close across them in the coldest weather. Each pair of houses shared a common wall between them to further reduce the heat loss, and the courtyards shared a common wall as well.

Some of the doors stood open and one could look along the sides of the houses to the courts where reflecting pools gleamed in summer, where vegetable gardens burgeoned and potted flowers glowed with fresh color. Now they looked desolate, littered with winter's windblown trash.

"I thought we'd stop at the garden-craft shop," Joshua told her. "We haven't planned a thing for the courtyard yet this spring. We can start some things in the kitchen now. We need vegetable seeds, and flowers. Wella's shop always has flower sets. . . ."

"I'd like some lobelia," Stavia said. "And nasturtiums, trailing out of those baskets along the back wall."

"Morgot said she wanted a pot of pink geraniums. She said Jemina Birds-daughter would give us some cuttings."

"Put that on the other side, where it won't clash," Stavia sighed. The vegetable garden was always given over to what they could eat or preserve and it tended to be pretty much the same, year after year, but Morgot and Stavia usually planned the courtyard flowerpots to look interesting and gay. This year Morgot had been preoccupied with Myra's baby and other things.

"Joshua, is Mother worried about something?"

"Not more than usual, why?"

"She's seemed . . . different."

He paused before answering. "She's upset about Myra. Barten is the last person we would have wanted Myra to become infatuated with. However, I've told Morgot just what I've told you. Give the girl six months and see if she doesn't settle down. Some of her age mates have had babies; they'll all get together and share experiences, and before you know it, she'll be a dignified matron."

"Myra?"

"It could happen," he shrugged, then turned very pale and clutched at his head as though it hurt him. "Damn."

"Joshua! What's the matter?"

He laughed unconvincingly. "I should never tell a lie. Tell a lie and it makes your head ache."

"You mean Myra. . . ."

"I think . . ." he gasped. "I think that twenty years from now there's very little chance that Myra will be any different from the way she is right now," he said, straightening up and massaging the skin over his eyes.

"Then Mother's right. Myra ought to live somewhere else."

"Your mother is very impatient. She always wants everything to have happened yesterday."

"Myra was too young to have a baby."

"Women have been having babies at Myra's age for most of human history," he said, dropping his hand and wiggling his eyebrows as though to test for pain. "You're right, though. Myra was too young, but Barten went after her like a coyote after a lamb. . . . I do have this feeling that someone put him up to it. He was very serious about Tally, and then suddenly . . ."

"Are you all right?"

"Yes, Stavvy, I'm all right. Just a twinge I get sometimes when I think too much about something."

The street curved and climbed as it followed the gentle upsweep of the city wall, made up of the back walls of houses and joined to the public thoroughfare by twisting flights of narrow stairs. Behind them, down the hill and through the western wall, the Processional Road ran out to the shore where the fishing boats bobbed in rocking clusters along zigzagging piers. On the first day of summer the entire populace, led by the Council, paraded down from the hill to the shore to beg the kindly regard of the Lady on the honest effort of the fisherwomen and farmers and herds-women. Shepherds led rams with ribbons on their horns and the farmers had bells on their wagons.

From the top of the hill the straight, downhill street that ran to the plaza and the garrison went off to their left. Straight ahead were the market streets, a tangle of narrow ways crowning the height, crowded with booths and shops and with awning-covered stands in summer. Through the marketplace ran the Itinerants Road, which led down past the Spinners and Weavers streets and through the eastern gate to the huddled itinerants' quarters outside the wall. There were only a few dozen people living in the intinerants' town now: a score of oldsters existing on the charity of the Lady, part of an acrobat's troupe, staying near Marthatown so the girls could attend Women's Country schools, a wagoner or two making a lengthy stop at the wheelwright's or the farrier's, and a water-witcher hired to locate a well for the billy-goat keeper who lived in an isolated valley five miles east of town. It was said that the servitor who kept the billy goats smelled as bad as his charges. In any case, the distance from Marthatown had been carefully calculated to avoid smelling either, even when the wind was from the east. Itinerants' town was always fascinating, though off limits to young girls who might, it was thought, be tempted by the romance of travel to leave the city and become mere wanderers.

To the right ran the Farm Road, winding down past grain and wood and wool warehouses to farmers' housing and the southern city wall, outside of which the goat dairy and poultry farms stood among sheep pens and barns along the lanes leading to the tannery and then to pastures and fields. Where the four roads came together at the top of the hill, the Chapel of the Lady stood with the Well of Surcease out in front, right at the center of everything.

"A fresh chicken," Stavia said with enthusiasm, spilling some well water for the Lady and dropping a coin for the poor into the box outside the Lady's door, as she mumbled, "Food and shelter for those who have none, amen." Then, "With dumplings. Could we?"

"There will be fresh chickens, yes," Joshua mused. "We need to pick up our grain allotment, too. And there are fresh leaf vegetables at Cheviot's stall. She has that protected area south of Rial's Ridge. She'll have lettuces two weeks earlier than anyone else will."

Stavia did not ask him how he knew. Servitors, some of them, the good ones, simply knew things. They knew when visitors were coming before they arrived, knew when people were in trouble, knew when something bad was going to happen. This facility of certain servitors was never mentioned, however. Stavia had said something about it only once, and Morgot had shushed her in a way that let it be known the subject was taboo. The servitors certainly weren't ostentatious about it. Some people, Myra for instance, never even noticed, but then Myra didn't notice much outside of herself and Barten.

They wandered among the stalls and shops, stopping for the chicken at one, for the lettuces at another. The grain co-op was uncrowded, and they drew against their allotment in half the usual time. Joshua shook the sack, looking thoughtful.

"Not much there, is there?" The servitor who asked was a lean-bellied man with a thin, mobile mouth. "Not since they cut the allotment."

"No, not much," Joshua agreed.

"We hear the Council plans to cut it again this year. Not for the garrison, of course. Just for us. Would that be so, do you suppose?"

Joshua shrugged. Servingmen of Council members were often queried as to what was going on, but they, like family members, were encouraged to be closemouthed. "I couldn't say."

The lean man moved off, and Stavia whispered. "If they cut the grain allotment, people will go hungry this winter. We can't live on dried fruit and fish and what vegetables we can put up, not unless the glass factory can make more jars."

"So Morgot says," Joshua agreed. "It's the old question of power, Stavia. They could make more jars if they had more power. With only the one hydroelectric plant, it's a question of priorities. Glass for windows or jars or lenses. Or drugs to heal people. Or steel for kitchen knives or a million other things. We're doing everything with watermills that we can."

"Maybe the grain harvest will be better this year."

"That's always possible."

"Don't we get more since Myra had the baby?"

Joshua shook his head. "No. Our allotment stays the same. Jerby went away and Myra got pregnant in the same year."

It didn't seem possible that over a year had passed since Jerby had gone to his warrior father. He had come home at midsummer, and Myra had gotten pregnant. Then at midwinter holiday, Jerby was home again. And so was Chernon, with his demand that she bring him another book because the books he had already had weren't the right ones, and she must give him more because she had already given him so much. She couldn't refuse him, but. . . . Stavia set that thought aside. And then baby Marcus was born, and it was almost time for midsummer carnival again.

"Myra won't take part in carnival this time, will she?"

"What do you think?" he asked.

Stavia sighed. "She will if Barten wants her. She did last time, big as a melon. It really surprised me that he had the carnival with her. With her pregnant I thought he'd . . . well, you know."

"You know why he did?"

She shook her head. "I don't. Well, maybe. Maybe he was showing everybody that he could father offspring."

"That may have been it," Joshua replied, shaking his head doubtfully.

"Joshua, any male rabbit can make babies!"

"I know that and you know that, Stavvy, but Barten may be confused about it. He may think it proves something."

"She will go to carnival with him if he'll have her. Just to keep him from having carnival with someone else."

"I think so, yes."

"She shouldn't get pregnant again so soon."

"That's probably right." Joshua felt a winter-stored apple. "These would be good with the chicken—applesauce."

"If we don't have dumplings, I'd like mashed potatoes."

"We've got potatoes left, but we're short on flour."

"Who'll do the cooking while you and Morgot and I are gone?"

"Sylvia has invited Myra to stay with her family."

"Poor Sylvia. Myra probably won't be good company."

"No. Not very."

"Joshua. I know I'm not supposed to ask, but I really want to know. What was it like to come back?"

"It was probably the most difficult thing I've ever done," he said. "Do you want to stop at the tea shop?"

"Could we? Do we have tea-shop chits left? Will you tell me about it? I don't want to pry, if it's none of my business."

"I won't take it as prying, Stavvy. No. I'll tell you, if you promise not to repeat what I say to anyone else—except Morgot, of course." They crossed the street and went down a twisting alley which ended in a miniature plaza protected from the wind by high side walls and decked with tables. They occupied one of these, piling basket and shopping bag in an empty chair.

When the steaming pot had been delivered, along with a saucer of sweet, jam-filled biscuits, Joshua poured for each of them then leaned on the table, hands curved around the steaming cup. "I came back partly because of the war between Annville and Abbyville."

"I don't know about that."

"No reason you should. It was twenty years ago. I was eighteen. I was in the Abbyville garrison, but too young to fight, of course, and when the centuries marched out, I was on the side, watching. . . . I had a special friend among the warriors. His name was Cornus. We called him Corny. A jokester. A clown. The funniest man I've ever known. He'd keep us laughing half the night, sometimes. I used to wish I had a writer's talent, just to write down some of the things he said.

"Well, he was killed in the battle. I knew he was wounded, the moment it happened, though he was miles away. I could feel his pain, and I knew when he died because the pain stopped. You're not asking about that, Stavvy. I can see you biting your lips. Morgot told you not to ask, but I'll tell you. It's something some of us servitors have. We call it the long-feel or the time-feel. Not all of us have it, not even most. But some of us do."

"Just servitors?" she whispered. "Not warriors?"

"Let's put it this way. I don't know of anyone who has this—this whatever it is—who stays in the garrison. If the rank and file notice it, and sometimes it's hard not to let them notice, they don't like it. And the officers don't trust it. Well, at any rate, Cornus's death weighed on me. I hadn't thought to ask before, but I asked then what the war was about. Why had we gone to battle with Annville. And the officers told me something about the Abbyville garrison having insulted our garrison, or our town, or maybe our garrison monument."

"Insulted how?"

"I don't know. There was some talk about some of our men being ambushed and killed, but nothing sure. So far as I could tell, no woman's life was ever in danger. Abbyville wasn't in danger, and neither was Annville. But we went to war, and a lot of the garrison got killed."

"And that made you decide to come back?"

"No, not just that. You know, in garrison you spend about a quarter of your time doing drill or mock battle, then some time is spent on maintenance of equipment and grounds, but most of it goes to games. In Abbyville it wasn't body-ball, the way it is here. Battle-ball was our game. Every century had a team, then the winning centuries played off against each other. Twelve men to a team, goals at each end of the field with a gate at the center, the idea is to get the ball through the gate and the opposing guards and into the goal."

"I know more or less what it is."

"Well, it was just like war. People didn't usually get killed playing battle-ball, but they did get hurt, and the winning team had all kind of honor and recognition. Let me tell you, if you were a great battle-ball player and a war came along, depend on it, your Commander would put you right in the rear of the battle—or find something else for you to do entirely. No Commander wanted his star players wounded or killed. And at the end of the year, when it came down to two teams, there wasn't a man in garrison who didn't wear the colors of one or the other team. And there'd be drinking and fights. It was just like war, all over again, only more so because the men cared more about how it came out. I mean, wars didn't happen that often, but there was the battle-ball series every year!"

"Did you play it?"

"Play it? Hell, Stavia, I was a star gatesman. I was so good my centurion put me on messenger duty just so I wouldn't get hurt in arms practice. I was good at the game because I always knew just who was going to do what, and where the ball was coming from. I just knew. . . ."

She stared at him, trying to understand.

"Don't you see, Stavia? When all the games were played, nothing had changed. If my team won or lost, nothing was better or worse. If I won, I got ribbons to wear and everybody drank to me and we all got drunk. If I lost, nobody drank to me but we still all got drunk. Either way, nothing was different. The sun came up the next day, same as always. The river went on running. The rain came down, just like always. Night came, stars came out, men went up on the armory roof courting, women made assignations, babies were born, little boys came to their warrior fathers, and nothing changed. Corny died and nothing changed. Oh, he got a hero's burial. They gave his honors to one of the boys to carry when his century paraded. The trumpets cried and people wept, the whole thing, but he was dead. It wasn't until they put me on messenger duty I really figured it all out, but once I'd figured that out, I came back to Women's Country."

"Did they hiss at you?"

"Oh yes. They did indeed. They hissed and somebody threw rocks, but I just kept walking. Then, after I got here, I moped around for about a month while they were testing me to see what I might be good at. They said there was an opening here, so I chose to come to Marthatown."

"And you began to study?"

"That's right. Began at the beginning, as they say. In the servitors' school. All warriors learn is how to read and write and sing and do a bit of arithmetic. Servitors have to start over. Though we do have it a little easier than you women. Since we get a late start, we're allowed to specialize."

"And you specialized in medicine."

"I had to learn something that would change things. I became a medical assistant, and met Morgot, and ended up in her house. Because of Corny."

"Returners don't have to learn a craft, do they? Or an art?"

"Oh, we can, if we like. I have an art, you know? One of the mysteries." He made a comic face.

"I've never heard of it."

"It's mostly a servitors' study," he grimaced, "though not entirely. And please don't repeat what I've said. I shouldn't have mentioned it." Though the look in his eye told her he had mentioned it just to see what she would say, and do.

MORGOT, JOSHUA, AND STAVIA started out early the following morning in the donkey cart, the four little animals pulling strongly as they trotted eastward toward the hills. Joshua drove. Morgot lay in the bottom of the cart on a folded quilt, her head propped on their sack of provisions, her eyes shut. She had been getting up at least half the time with baby Marcus, changing him and bringing him to Myra to be fed. Now she lay in the gently jostling wagon bed, rocked to sleep as in a cradle, catching up on many interrupted nights. Stavia read until her eyes got tired, then slumped on the wagon seat, staring out at the changing scenery. The nearer hills were softly green, some bright with early grain, others dotted with low, dark shrubs, like crouching bears. Behind them the wooded mountains folded, ridge and valley, and over all the sky spread in eastward banners of streaming cloud. The previous day's chill wind had given way to warmth. Wildflowers bloomed along the road, splashing flares of gold and white and orange. Stavia sat up and began to notice their surroundings.

"How far are we going?"

"Two days' travel. About halfway to Susantown."

"What's there? At halfway?"

"A hotel for travelers. It's halfway between Mollyburg and Abbyville, too. Kind of a crossroads."

"We're meeting someone?"

"Morgot is meeting someone," he said softly. "Something to do with a trade agreement. Grain supplies, I think."

"She's been really worried about the allotments. I guess the harvest wasn't good last year."

"Well, actually, it was about the same as usual."

"Then why was our ration cut?"

"Because there are more of us. There were about two hundred babies born in Marthatown last year, and the year before that."

"People must have died to balance it out!"

"Not many. No contagious diseases this year. No raids or battles."

"What's Morgot going to do?"

"I think there's some move afoot to trade Marthatown's dried fish for inland grain."

The road began to coil up into the hills. Morgot drove while Joshua and Stavia walked beside the cart to save the animals. Not far down the slope from the road a reforestation crew was working in a cleared area, dropping feathery tree seedlings into shovel slits, pressing them closed. Morgot called out to them and walked down, inspecting the soft tufts of new growth among the stumpy roots of old trees. At the edge of the clearing something moved and fled with a flash of white.

"A deer?" Morgot asked, incredulously.

"We've seen several," the crew leader told her.

"I thought the project released them far north of here."

"They did, Morgot. But it's been ten years."

"That long!"

"They could even be wild ones. Survivors from before the convulsion."

Stavia was still gazing at the place in the forest the thing had vanished. A brown flow of incredible grace and speed. Deer. She had seen pictures, of course, but they had not been seen in the wild for generations. After the convulsion, a few deer had been found in a park or zoo somewhere north, and a breeding program had been started with annual releases into the wild. But, to think of actually seeing one! They were certainly different-looking from sheep or donkeys, or even from those pictured reindeer in Beneda's book.

They went on, over the first range of hills. A strangeness at the edge of the landscape caught Stavia's eye. Below them, to the south, was a place where the green of field and tree ended and a carpet of black and gray extended to the south and east, losing itself in distances. "Look at that! What is that?"

"A bleak devastation," remarked Morgot from the back of the wagon, sitting up to get a look at it. "You haven't seen one before, have you? There are only a few them up here in and around Women's Country, but if you went far enough south of the sheep camps past Emmaburg, there wouldn't be room to drive a wagon between them. Down there, south and east of the mountains, there's nothing but bleak desolations, as far as you can travel. The whole continent is gone. Here, use my glasses."

Stavia twiddled with the precious glasses, bringing the cancerous gray up close. "But there's nothing growing there!" The land looked ashen. Even the rocks were twisted and melted.

"Nothing at all," Morgot agreed. "Remember Cassandra's lines in *Iphigenia at Ilium,* 'I have seen the land laid waste and burned with brands, and desolation born from fiery wombs.' Well, that's one of the places she was talking about."

"Is it dangerous?"

Morgot flapped her hand in front of her mouth in a cooling gesture. "Hot. Not with fire, with radiation. You walk across that place, a few days later all your hair will fall out and you'll start dying. Still, a bleak desolation isn't as dangerous as some of them, because you can see it. Some of them, you can't see. The rock looks all right, and the plants, but it will kill you just as surely as this one. The one south of Marthatown is like that. We call them masked desolations when they're like that."

"How do you know it's there?"

"We've still got some preconvulsion radiation detectors. Whenever we send an exploration team, we send a detector with them. Or a good map."

"A desolation," repeated Stavia, staring at the bare, black place until it was hidden behind a hill, lost in the tree-specked ranges. "How did they make it?"

"With their evil weapons. You know that."

"Yes. I guess I did know that."

That night they camped in a grove of eucalyptus trees, the air redolent with the medicinal tang of the leaves. The donkeys were tethered in a meadow, the wagon half hidden among junipers.

"We won't let the fire linger," Morgot said. "There really have been some Gypsy-bandit attacks up this way, and I don't want to attract their attention with a blaze."

"What do they want?"

Morgot paused before answering, as though to choose among possible answers. "Oh, the usual thing seems to be a little rape and abuse, steal the wagons and the animals, take any food, sometimes kill whoever's along."

"Where do they come from?"

"Garrisons, mostly. Men who won't return to Women's Country because it's considered dishonorable but who can't stand the discipline of the garrison either. They're mad at everyone, but maybe a little angrier at women than at anyone else. And they feel guilty for having left the garrisons, which makes a dangerous combination. They link up with one another, maybe with some Gypsy women, and create a gang."

"Why didn't we bring an escort of warriors?" Stavia looked from face to face in the firelight. They seemed not to have heard her. "Morgot?"

"Don't worry about it, Stavvy. I'm sure we'll be fine."

Stavia was sure she would not sleep, but when her eyes opened, it was on morning light. Joshua was brewing tea. "Get yourself up, girl. Take those little beasties down to water so they won't have a cold bellyful when we start off."

Morgot was sitting at the edge of the stream looking little older than Stavia, her skin gleaming like ivory as she rubbed it with a rough cloth and ladled water over herself. "Good, daughter," she said approvingly. "Let's get a quick start and be at the Travelers' Rest before dark."

They breakfasted quickly, then drowned the fire and departed. Looking back, Stavia could see the haze of their smoke still hanging in the grove, like fog. Far down the valley was another foggy plume, dust stirred up on the roadway. Gypsies? A band of itinerant metal scavengers? Or a traveling show? Both Morgot and Joshua looked at it, without comment.

They went between bare hills and down long slopes, coming at evening to a grove almost like the one they had camped in the night before, tall, untidy trees with bark and leaves hanging in shredded curtains of aromatic gray. Here, however, was a long, low building half of stone and half of timbers, steep-roofed and heavy-doored. Outside the wall were half a dozen wagons: a couple of brightly painted ones—show people; three laden with bits of metal and lopsided ingots from the hermit mines and smelters in the mountains; plus one wagon very much like their own.

Over the gate the words were spelled out in twisted twigs. TRAVELERS' REST. The gate opened on a courtyard with stables; the door upon a huge common room floored in wide boards and full of suppertime smells. From across the broad, low room two women came toward Morgot, greeting her with sober looks, casting quick glances at Stavia.

"My daughter," Morgot announced. "This is Joshua. They were company for me on the trip."

The women nodded, introduced themselves. "Melanie Hangessdaughter Triptor Susantown. Jessica Hangessdaughter Triptor Susantown. Sisters of Susantown. We've ordered supper. If you'll join us?"

Joshua excused himself to go unhitch and stable the donkeys, saying he would dine in the servitors' quarters. Stavia wavered. She could go with him or stay, opting finally to stay, regretting later that she had. The talk was all of trade, of grain quotas, of the movement of dried fish and root crops. Individually, parsnips could be interesting. By the ton they were not. Once her hunger was assuaged, she curled into the inglenook beside the fire, drifting off into quiet as their voices went on and on.

". . . we can manage if it's reduced by one third, at least," she heard Morgot say.

"Agreed," one of the sisters said.

"We'll send our agents."

"And we ours."

"Done then. Thank you, sisters."

Then Morgot was shaking her. "Come, Stavia. It's time we went to our beds."

She sounded so tired, Stavia thought, so very tired. When they were side by side in their bed upstairs, she put her arm comfortingly over Morgot's side, hearing a murmur in return.

"Sleep well, Stavvy."

"Sleep well, Morgot."

THEY RETURNED by a different road. About noon, Joshua halted the donkeys and sat as though listening, rubbing his forehead between fingers and thumb of one hand.

"What?" asked Morgot.

"Something happened. Something changed. Somebody headed this way. . . ."

"Shall we go back?"

"No. I don't feel so." He clucked to the donkeys and they set off once more. Toward evening, when it came near time to make camp, Joshua leaned back into the wagon and said softly, "Morgot!"

"Hmm."

"I think we've bought trouble."

"I thought you felt this road would be clear?"

"I think it was. Perhaps this morning someone had decided to go somewhere else and then during the day, they decided to come here. I don't know. I wouldn't feel it until they decided to do it. Things change sometimes. Besides, there's been much movement among the trees along the ridge this last mile or two. No birds. A very great and unusual silence."

"Oh, Lady."

"Well, we are interested in finding out, are we not?"

"What do you think?"

He shut his eyes, as though concentrating, his forehead wrinkled. "I'd say half a dozen of them. No more than that."

"What shall we be? Bait or fleeing prey?"

"What are you two talking about?" Stavia begged. "Who decided to do what? Are we going to be attacked?"

"Likely, yes. We're discussing whether to flee and hope they can't catch us or camp and let them come find us. Bait them in."

"Bait them in!" Stavia's voice squeaked, a treble peep, like a terrified mouse.

"It rather depends on Stavia, doesn't it?" Joshua said.

Morgot nodded. "Stavvy, I want your oath."

Stavia gulped and trembled, going into one of those fits of self-consciousness which required that the actor Stavia take over before the usual Stavia did or said something hideously gauche. Oaths were given only on the most important occasions. Oaths were not daily activities. "Why? What?" She blurted.

"Whatever happens, you are to say nothing about it afterward."

"You don't need the oath for that. If you don't want me to say anything, I won't."

"No. That's not good enough. Your oath on it."

She shivered. The actor Stavia said calmly, "Oh, all right, Morgot. By my citizenship in Women's Country, I swear. I haven't any idea what's going on!"

"Perhaps better so." Morgot nodded. "We bait them, Joshua. And we pray you've seen rightly that there are no more than six."

They drove the donkeys into a thick grove of trees, and Stavia watched in amazement as Joshua opened a panel in the side of the wagon and removed several lengths of chain. With these, he chained the donkeys to the wagon and the wagon to several of the trees, making the fastenings tight with many tight turns of tough wire.

"They might try to cut the animals loose in the dark," he said. "Or make off with the wagon. They can't. They won't be able to get any part of it loose and go running off with it."

Then Morgot moved around the wagon, laying fires. She laid five of them, getting Stavia to bring sticks, and piling them thickly above thin, shaved kindling. When this was done, she sprinkled each pile of sticks with powder and laid a trail of the powder to a point close to the wagon. It had the sharp, interesting smell of fireworks.

"Now, we eat," said Joshua, building a small fire at some distance from this arrangement. "We'll have tea, and munch our supper, and lay our blankets out over there, where we're in plain sight, and then, as soon as it's dark, we'll go back in there where the wagon is. Got that?"

"Stavia goes up a tree," Morgot remarked. "I've got it all picked out."

Stavia opened her mouth to protest, then shut it again. There was no point in protesting. She had no idea what she was protesting against. There were a number of things going on that she could not understand.

Nor did she have any better idea when the star-pricked dark came down like a heavy curtain and she found herself tied to a thick branch twenty feet above the wagon, a folded blanket cushioning her from the ragged bark.

"Not a word," Morgot had said. "Not a sound. If you are in pain, suffer silently and not a squeak."

The only sound from beneath her was small talk, the mumbled exchange of people readying themselves for sleep. Nothing at all interesting. Darkness. Discomfort. A sky full of glaring stars. Somewhere something moving in the underbrush.

Stavia tensed.

A birdcall, like a signal. Not Joshua, not Morgot. Then people, moving.

A cry. A flare of light, darting off in different directions like a starfish of fire, then leaping flames from the fires Morgot had laid. Stavia saw people beneath her, scurrying figures near the donkeys, near the wagon, several other strangers staring around themselves, taken by surprise, one starting to turn his head when his head came off and bounced away down the hill. A silver wheel was turning where his head had been. The wheel whipped away. Stavia opened her mouth to scream, then decided to bite down hard on her tongue instead.

Someone else screamed and then stood there, staring at the place where his arm had been. He had been leaning over Morgot's blankets with a knife raised in the hand which was no longer there. Other cries, shrieks, something silver whirling like a great platter, around and around. Stavia couldn't help it. She gasped.

Beneath her, someone looked up, saw her, grimaced through discolored teeth, and started up the tree. The silver platter came out of the fire-lit shadows and plucked him away, in halves.

There was a great quiet. Only the firesounds. A light wind. Joshua was beside the wagon, putting something beneath the wagon floor. A short handle and a chain with a curved knife at its end. Morgot handed him another, then took a pair of wood-handled pliers and began unwiring the chain that tied the donkeys.

"Alas," said Morgot. "Alas, such is the fate of warriors' sons." Her voice was soft, flat, unemotional, and yet there was an undercurrent of exhaustion in it, as it sometimes sounded when she came home from a long Council meeting or when Stavia came upon her in the middle of the night, in the kitchen, brooding silently over a cup of cooling tea. "Stavia. You can come down now."

"I'm coming."

"Step directly into the wagon, daughter. There's a good deal of gore around."

"How . . . how many of them were there?"

"Joshua?"

"I counted seven. I felt one going away." His voice was weary and depressed.

"I'll get our blankets." Morgot was gone, stepping over and around

misshapen objects which littered her way. In a moment she returned.
"These will have to be laundered. Josh, look at the shoulder on that body
over there."

He went to lean over it. "Melissaville tattoo," he said. "The one down in
the hollow had a Mollyburg label on him."

"I saw one Annville and one Tabithatown. I think the other two were
Gypsies."

"Almost as though they'd been detailed here, wasn't it?" Joshua asked.
"Picked out, one from here, one from there."

"What do you think?"

"I think the one that got away would have had a Marthatown tattoo.
Aside from that, there's nothing much. Fuzzy. Confused. No real intentions
yet."

"Someone may come looking for them."

Joshua sighed. "I remember there being a ravine about two miles back."

Morgot sighed as well. "Stavia, go over beside that rock, spread out your
blankets, and stay there until I call you."

"Mother, what does . . . ?"

"Your oath, Stavia."

"Was not to say anything about it afterward."

"It is now afterward. Not a word."

Stavia bit her already somewhat mangled tongue. They weren't going to
tell her. They weren't going to explain. They were going to leave it just as
it was. She stepped down into the wagon. One of the boards of the wagon
bed was not quite flat. She kicked it and it dropped into place. There was
something under it. Obviously. Some kind of weapon. Weapons. But
Joshua was not a warrior. And Morgot . . .

And she had given her oath not to ask.

She looked up to find Joshua's eyes upon her, his head cocked warningly.

She took her blankets to the rock Morgot had indicated and lay there,
wide awake, while Morgot and Joshua gathered up the remains in the
wagon. After a time, Joshua drove away east, toward the gray light of a
gibbous moon, whistling thinly between his teeth. Morgot lit the lantern
and wandered around their campsite with the little camp spade, burying the
burned remains of all the fires but one, raking all the footprints away,
shoveling dirt over bloodstained soil and raking it smooth with a branch
before littering it with small rocks and bits of wood. After a time she came
near Stavia's blankets, spread out her own and went to sleep.

Shortly after dawn, Joshua came back in the empty wagon. Morgot and
Stavia got up beside him, and they set out again.

"Do you think we'll be home in time for supper?" Stavia asked, folding the bloody blankets into a neat pile at the rear of the wagon and carefully not looking at her mother or at Joshua. Whoever and whatever he really was.

All she could think of was Myra's saying, "Fine lot of help he'd be. A servitor."

AT THE SUMMER CARNIVAL when Stavia was twelve there was a new and highly touted magician who came all the way from Tabithatown. There were the usual two shows a day at the summer theater as well, plus street dancing and rowdy roistering in the taverns. Before carnival Myra had gone off to the medical center and returned with a scarlet stamp on her forehead and an implant in her upper arm. She had looked pale and worn, but was strangely hectic, or so Stavia had thought, though Morgot had said nothing about it.

"The doctor says my hormonal balance is all screwed up since Marcus came," she complained to Stavia. "This gadget is supposed to keep me ticking."

"They're very effective devices," Morgot murmured. "I'm glad Doctor Charlotte thought of it."

Stavia had scarcely listened. Midsummer carnival was starting, and Chernon would be home.

"Stavia, you ought to get some new clothes," Myra complained. "She should, Morgot. She's twelve now, but she dresses like a child. All long undershifts and plain shirts. Nothing pretty."

"Whatever Stavia wants," Morgot said. "If she's comfortable the way she is, that's all right."

Stavia did not want any new clothes. Her well-worn trousers and thigh-long undershifts were smooth from many washings and as familiar as her own skin. Her shirts, linen for summer and wool or leather for winter, were comfortable and still large enough. She didn't want to be different or wear anything different. Nothing should change or be changed. Chernon was coming home and if he liked her at all, he liked her the way she was.

But the Chernon who came home for carnival had become strangely secretive and shy. He was a Chernon with a deeper voice, with a sprinkling of beard on his face, a Chernon who looked at Stavia with a new intentness, as though she had something he wanted. She felt it. She told Beneda his intensity made her uncomfortable.

"It's because he'll be fifteen soon," said Beneda. "Mother counted up."

Oh, Chernon. Fifteen! Time to choose whether to become a warrior or return to Women's Country. What would he choose? She hadn't even thought about his being fifteen. Now all the easy apologies she had been making to herself for breaking the ordinances, all her complicated excuses were suddenly invalid. How could she rationalize giving books to a warrior? What justification could there be?

But he wasn't a warrior yet. Not yet. There was still time for him to decide to come home, and she must use that time, what little there was.

He would ask. Being Chernon, he would ask. She had to be ready when he did.

And it took him only until the second day. "That last book you brought me had something in it I'd like to know more about, Stavvy. I've written it down." His voice was cool and preemptory.

She gulped, clenching her jaw until her ears hurt. There would be no later, it had to be now. The words she had rehearsed came out in a spate. If she had waited even a moment, she would not have been able to say them at all. "I can't bring you any more books, Chernon."

His expression was of surprise, perhaps of shock. Later she thought it was shock. As though he had not thought her capable of saying it. "No . . . no more books?"

"You're going to be fifteen. You choose at fifteen. If you choose . . . if you choose one way, you choose to do without this kind of books. If you choose the other, well, you can have all the books you want. I mustn't mess up your choice for you." She had practiced it, over and over. It had come out cleanly and simply, just the way she had planned it.

Then why this agony?

His face. So white. Then pink, then red, then white again. He turned his face away. Finally, he said, "That's not fair."

She writhed. How could he say it wasn't fair? Yes, she had broken the rules for him, but it wasn't fair for him to think she would always do so. He had to make his own choice. "Chernon?"

"Leave me alone." Hard and obdurate.

"Chernon!" Hurt and horror.

"Just go home and leave me alone." In that moment he did not even think what Michael would say. In that moment, he did not care. What had just happened should not have happened. He had not liked it.

She was too paralyzed by confusion to argue. She went. The residential streets were quiet, separated from the carnival throngs by street barricades and watchful groups of older women, but she could hear the sounds of music and laughter from over the hill. It was Chernon who wasn't fair! Did he think that because she had broken the ordinances once for him she would go on doing so forever? Didn't he care what happened to her?

She was in the kitchen, huddled over the ache in her middle, when Myra came in.

"Where's Morgot?" she asked

"Upstairs," Stavia mumbled.

"Stavia, Barten says there may be a war!"

Stavia jerked, splashing the tea onto the table. The terrible word was nonsense. "War! What do you mean, war?"

"With Susantown. The garrison at Susantown plans to attack us."

"That's ridiculous. We have a trade agreement with Susantown."

"But the garrison thinks the agreement is a ruse, or something. Our garrison has spies there, and they told Barten's Commander."

"Michael? Vice-Commander Michael? Jerby's father?"

"Stavia. Are you paying any attention? I'm telling you there may be a war."

Morgot's voice came from the doorway, calm and calming. "I'd heard something about that, yes."

"But we have a *trade agreement,*" Stavia asserted again, telling them both how nonsensical the idea was. "An agreement!"

"Sometimes these things happen," said Morgot in a weary voice. "We make agreements, treaties, we do our best, and somehow, everything goes wrong. I suppose the Commanders had spies in Susantown?"

"Barten told me that his centurion, Stephon, did."

"Most of the garrisons do maintain their own intelligence systems. Well, just be thankful we have strong men to defend us. We are thankful, aren't we, Stavia?"

Stavia nodded, scarcely aware she had moved. Oh yes. She was thankful they had warriors to defend them. Before her, on the table, she moved the cup of cooling tea, stretching the spilled liquid into a long, curved shape, like a knife. Chernon. And war. Except that Chernon was too young. They wouldn't make him fight. Not yet. He had ten years yet before he would have to fight. Or he could come home. . . .

"When," Morgot was asking, "do they anticipate an attack?"

"No one knows exactly. Sometime within the next few months. Whenever they find out, they'll march on Susantown at once. Before the Susantown warriors can get here and threaten us."

"Very wise. The garrison Commanders are excellent tacticians, Michael and Stephon, particularly. Well, I suppose Barten can hardly wait for his first action."

"Why . . . why Barten won't go," Myra faltered. "He's not . . . he's not twenty-five yet."

Morgot nodded briskly. "Oh yes. Twenty-five last month. I know because we were straightening out some garrison records a week or two ago, and it came up then. There were more than a hundred boys born in the year Barten was, too many for a century, so a few of them were put over into the year following. Some of the twenty-fours are actually twenty-five and eligible for battle. No one pays any attention unless there is a threat of war, but then, of course, the Commanders want every available man."

"But he's too young," cried Myra in a panicky voice.

"Myra, you're not listening. Surely you realize that there are not precisely one hundred little boys born every year. One year in my mother's time we even had two centuries with the same number, we had so many. Barten is twenty-five, even though he's with the twenty-four century. Come now. You don't want to spoil his pleasure by being negative. You'll need to find out from him what device you should make for him to wear into battle."

"Device?"

"Hasn't he asked you to sew him some device to wear over his breastplate? I thought all lovers did that. Ah well, maybe things have changed since my youth. I remember making one for Michael. Three wasps on a field of gold. For speed, you know. And endurance." She shook her head and wandered out of the kitchen.

"You'll need to ask him what device he'd like to have," Stavia said, breaking the silence, breaking the frozen concentration on Myra's face, breaking her own pain and preoccupation.

"I don't think he realized he'd be going with them," faltered Myra. "He said how much he wanted to, of course."

"Of course!" Of course.

"I must go to find Barten. He was going to meet me later, but I must find him. Now. . . ." She was gone, half running, her hands dangling in front of her helplessly, like flippers.

Stavia went to find her mother. "Did you really sew a shirt for Michael?" It was not the question she wanted to ask. It wasn't even what she wanted to talk about, but the thing she needed to know was too close, too dangerous even to mention.

"I did. I was seventeen years old, and he was the most beautiful man I had ever seen in my life. He was just twenty-five. He told me I was his love and his heart's delight."

"Michael did?" Stavia was disbelieving.

Morgot laughed. "He did. Of course, he was younger then. More given to romantic excess."

"Is he Myra's father?"

"Oh, my dear, no. No, I didn't get pregnant with Myra until a year or two later, and Michael wasn't her father."

"Who was her father?"

"Stavia!"

"I'm sorry. I just. . . ."

"You're curious, I know. However, we don't consider it good manners to discuss our fathers, Stavvy. It has no relevance in Women's Country. You know that. We don't ask. It was decided a long, long time ago that we'd all get along better here in Women's Country if we just didn't talk about that. Who Myra's male biological progenitor was doesn't matter at all unless she gets involved with some warrior who's too closely related to her. If that were the case, of course I would tell her." Morgot sounded stilted and rehearsed, and Stavia realized that this, too, was a speech she had planned to give, if not to Stavia, then to Myra. "Or, if I didn't, the assignation mistress would tell her. We do keep records."

"Myra's gone to find Barten." But she, Stavia, could not go to Chernon because he had told her to go away. Though he would not make her go away if she brought books, if she did what he wanted. He would be nice to her if she always did what he wanted.

"Well, of course Myra's gone to Barten. She'll want to spend every possible minute with him." Morgot's voice became suddenly strange, shut up, as though there were an almost closed door between them.

The last two nights of carnival Myra stayed up all night sewing Barten a shirt. It had two green trees and a mountain on it—symbolic of the wilds, Myra said. Where there was no Women's Country, though with rare tact she didn't say that.

For days after carnival, Stavia went to the wall, hoping to see Chernon, hoping to hear from him that he hadn't meant what he said, but she did not find him there.

CHERNON WAS SPENDING a lot of his time at the Gypsy camp with Michael and Stephon, loafing with them as they sat around the open fire, ready to run to Jik for another pitcher of beer or to fetch a burning splinter to light a pipe of willow, listening as they planned the possible battle with Susantown and harkening to their advice about women.

"Let her sweat a little," Michael lectured. "She'll come around. You act kind of like you're aloof and hurt and a woman just can't stand it. Every woman in the world is ready to believe anything is her fault if you just tell her it is. She'll have to make it up to you. Just wait, you'll see. . . ."

It was late, and the fire was burned down to coals so that the men's faces glowed red in the dim light. The beer made them logy and disinclined to move, and they turned slowly as Michael was hailed by someone just entering the encampment, a cadaverous man disfigured by sword cuts across both cheeks and brows. Chernon had never seen him before, but he greeted Michael and Stephon familiarly.

"So, Besset," murmured Stephon, "we wondered when you'd be back."

"I damn near didn't get back," the man complained, seating himself beside them and giving Chernon a significant glance.

"That's Chernon," Michael told him. "Very useful lad, Chernon. He knows Commanders have to have information, so you can say what you need to say. He's all right. What do you mean you almost didn't get back?" He offered the three-quarters-empty pitcher of beer and a mug.

The man addressed as Besset drank deeply, sighed, wiping his mouth on his arm. "After you arranged for me to get killed off, and that, I joined up with that Gypsy bunch the way we talked about."

"Hell, Besset, that was over two years ago we said you'd died."

"Well, I haven't been anyplace close. The bunch I got in with moved around. We went up to Tabithatown and that, and then down the coast and cut back over to Annville. We picked up a man here, a man there. More'n half the men wanderin' around with those bunches are from the garrisons, you know? And some of 'em are just gone without leave and that, and some of 'em are like me, keepin' in touch to let their Commanders know what's goin' on and that, so everywhere we went it was them tryin' to find out what I know and me tryin' to find out what they know."

"And what did you all know?" drawled Stephon in a bored tone. "Not much, from the sound of it."

"Not much," Besset assented. "That's true enough. All the men I talked to feel pretty much the same way. They all think the women've got some secret or other they're not tellin' and that. Most of 'em think it's somethin' religious. Like the Brotherhood of the Ram, you know? Only for women."

"We don't talk about the Brotherhood, Besset. Chernon here may be useful, but he's not a warrior yet."

"I was just comparin'."

"Well don't."

"All right. That's just what some of 'em say, anyhow. There's talk here and there about takin' over and that, but nobody's doin' anything about it. Up north, toward Annville, they don't even talk about it, because of that other time and that."

"So? Where have you been?"

"Well, then we worked back east for a while, and it was pretty much the same thing."

"You don't look like you've been eating all that well," observed Michael.

"We're not exactly welcome in itinerants' town, are we? On the road it's what we can take, not what they give us. We had a couple of lucky bits, took over a wagoneer's family for a while, but he tried to get away and then she acted up and that, so we did them, and then one night their kids run off with the animals. Well."

"So!" said Michael again, impatiently.

"So, I'm tellin' you. We were east of here. It was sometime back, before the Marthatown carnival and that, and we saw this wagon makin' for Marthatown. We thought it was some wagoneer family. One man and one woman and a kid."

"Yes."

"There was seven of us, so Challer—he's the one from Melissaville called himself the boss—Challer decides we should have a few games and that with the woman and kid, then take the animals over and sell them at the donkey market in Mollyburg. We followed along until it got dark, then waited while they made camp and settled down." The man called Besset drank deeply from his mug, the foam making a white ring around his dirty mouth.

"You didn't see who it was?"

"No, just that at least one of 'em was a woman. We heard her talkin', but it was too dark to see anything. Then we rushed the camp, or I should say they did, because I hung back. I thought maybe if they was from around here, they might recognize me, you know?"

"What difference would that have made?" Stephon asked in an interested tone. "You didn't intend to leave them alive, did you?"

Chernon flushed red, unnoticed in the fireglow. They were talking about murder! And Michael wasn't even surprised!

"I guess I wasn't thinkin', to tell you the truth. Well, so the men rushed the camp, and all of a sudden there was fire all over the place and that and this silver thing whirlin' around, and I heard Challer scream and then his head came bouncin' down the hill where I was, and I took off."

"A silver thing?" Stephon asked in an ominous tone. "That's all you can tell us is some wagoneer had a silver thing?"

"I couldn't see any more than that. Just this silver thing, like a wheel, and the men screamin', and not a sound otherwise." Besset took another pull at the beer, his hand trembling.

"Damn," said Stephon, disgustedly.

"Wait, I'm not done yet. So I went away about half a mile and hid out in this kind of gully there was down there, and waited until morning. Long about first light, here went the wagon out of there and that, still three people in it, no sign of anybody else, but it wasn't no wagoneer. Least they wasn't dressed like wagoneer people. It was a servitor and a woman and a girl from Women's Country. I couldn't see who, but it was Women's Country people. And somethin' else. I swear there was nothin' in that wagon but them. No bodies, nothin'. But when I went over where they'd been camped, all there was there was ashes from one campfire and that's all. Challer's head was gone. So were the rest of 'em, gone.''

There was a lengthy silence, during which Chernon made himself small and inconspicuous, hoping they would not notice him again. He did not know what to think about what he had heard. It occurred to him that Michael might prefer that he hadn't heard it. The Commanders didn't even look at him, however, and he thought they had forgotten he was there. So, probably Besset wasn't even telling the truth, and that's why Michael didn't seem surprised. Besset was lying, or had been drunk, or had been eating mushrooms the way some of the Gypsies did to make them see visions. Maybe. Though, if he was telling the truth or something like the truth, it could mean the women had some kind of weapon nobody knew about. Or some kind of power nobody knew about.

Chernon wanted to believe it was some kind of power they had, something he could learn about and use. Later, when he listened outside the officers' quarters window, however, he learned that Stephon and Michael thought it must be a weapon.

"That's probably it," Michael rumbled. "The thing they're hiding. The thing the women know that they're not talking about. Something left over from old preconvulsion times, most likely. Isn't that like them! Tell us we have to do without any preconvulsion stuff and then use it themselves! Hypocrites! We need to find out about that. We'll get this war with Susantown out of the way, then we'll concentrate on finding out what this is. Maybe send out some of the younger men. Maybe fix some of them up like itinerants. . . ."

"How?"

"Oh, teach 'em to do some kind of act. Acrobats or something. Juggling, maybe. We've got a few young ones who are good at that."

Chernon had not stayed under the window to hear any more. If they sent anyone, he wanted to be that one.

FALL CAME with chilly winds and the leaves turning gold when the word swept through Women's Country like another kind of wind. The evil intentions of the Susantown garrison had been confirmed. War was declared.

Every woman and child in the town was on the wall when the garrison marched out, staring down at the parade ground where the warriors assembled, banners flying, armor glittering like ten thousand sun-shattered mirrors, throwing shards of glory into their eyes. Barten was not wearing the device Myra had sewn for him, but he pointed to his pack when he saw her, indicating to her that he had it. Stavia thought he was very pale.

"He thought he had another year to make up his mind," she surprised herself by saying to Morgot. "Then, all of a sudden, he didn't have any time at all."

"Barten?" her mother asked. "That's true, Stavia. I spoke to Michael during carnival this summer, and he told me Barten did seem quite surprised when he was told he was a year older than he thought."

The warrior drum and buglemen began their blammety blam, ta-ra ta-ra; the ranks wheeled into an endless line and began the march, di-da-rum di-da-rum di-da-rum. Before it seemed possible they could be gone, there was only the flutter of guidons down the road and a haze of dust to the east, showing which way they went. Then the wagons pulled out, full of food and blankets and extra boots, driven by old one-eyed, lack-armed, lost-footed warriors who hadn't died while the glory was still around them as they probably wished they had done.

The women's band struck up, "Gone Away, Oh, Gone Away," and Stavia found herself singing.

"Where's my lovely warrior gone,
the one who made me sigh,
He's gone to fight for pretty girls,
for Mom and apple pie.
Gone away, oh gone away,
I'll never see him more,
he's found another lover
on some far distant shore."

Though Susantown wasn't some far-distant shore but merely sixty miles east, and the warriors wouldn't go more than half that distance, probably, before meeting the Susantown garrison coming west. Perhaps there would be a treaty and no one would be killed.

One of the Council members came up to Morgot and asked a question.

"Bandits?" Morgot said. "Yes. I did speak to the garrison Commanders about that, Councilor."

The Councilor, an elderly woman whom Stavia had met half a dozen times but never really come to know at all well, mumbled something which Stavia could not hear.

Morgot answered, softly but clearly. "Oh, we all agree that's likely, ma'am, but there's no proof as yet." Then she turned, letting Stavia surprise a look on both their faces, a shut-in, secret look which she had seen before on her mother's face, though rarely. Not for the first time, she felt the wheels of Women's Country turning beneath the city, turning silently, without her help.

As on that night on the road from Susantown.

"Which never happened," Stavia reminded herself. "Which never happened." For a long time after that night, she had caught herself imagining what might be going on. Men with tattoos from different garrisons, all together, almost as if they'd been selected to make up some kind of inter-garrison team. For what? She had driven herself crazy wondering for what, finally deciding that if she couldn't talk about it, it was better to pretend the thing had never occurred at all. The actor part of her was able to do this easily. To the actor part, none of it had happened. The observer, however, found this selective memory difficult.

With all the men over twenty-five gone except for a few armorers and cooks, the younger warriors and boys left behind were more or less free to wander about the garrison territory as they liked, and Stavia found Chernon waiting for her on the armory roof the next time she and Beneda went to the wall. Her heart slowed, then hammered, and she felt terrified.

"Benny, let me talk to Stavvy alone, will you?"

"Stavia's too young for assignations, brother," said Beneda, pretending that she had not brought Stavia to the wall at his request.

"I'm not talking assignations, now get lost, will you?"

Beneda flounced off, pretending to be annoyed. All her hopes for Chernon revolved around Stavia's influence on him. Or so, at least, she thought.

"Stavvy." His eyes were so clear. The skin on the hand he reached up to her was as clean and soft as a child's.

She wanted him to touch her. Hold her. "I've missed you," she faltered. "I wish you hadn't gotten mad at me."

"I . . . I wasn't mad at you. Not really. I know what you were trying to do, Stavvy, and that's why I came today. I have to explain, you know?"

"Let her know you're not going to do what she wants you to, boy," Michael had said. *"Make it clear that she's not that important to you. Then she'll break her neck trying to become that important. Women are like that."*

"Stavia's pretty . . . well, she's independent," Chernon had objected.

"I don't care how independent," Michael had laughed. *"They're all the same."*

"You have to explain what?" asked Stavia, trembling.

"The fifteens have to choose in a few months. I have to explain to you why I'm going to stay with the garrison."

Stavia heard him without real surprise. Well, there it was. What was the point of standing here listening to anything else. She might as well leave now, go home, get her grieving over with. Morgot said one had to do that, over and over. No sense drawing it out.

"Stavvy!" There was something withdrawn in her face which frightened him. Michael could be wrong. He could be. He didn't know everything. Michael couldn't get Morgot to talk, so he didn't know everything. "Stavvy!"

"Yes."

"Don't look like that." He temporized, trying to make it sound less bare and incontrovertible. Michael would not have played it this way, but Chernon thought it necessary. "Don't you see, if it wasn't for the war, I could have done it? But I can't do it *now!* Not with the war. Not with so many probably getting killed, not with men coming back wounded who'll need our help. I've got ten years left to make up my mind, Stavvy. I can return to Women's County later. After the war, when everything's settled down."

"I don't understand what it is you can't do."

"I can't let my friends down," he said in a dedicated voice, as though he were taking the oath of a defender. "Not now."

"But you think you will later?"

"Well . . . I wouldn't even then, Stavvy, except for the books. There are so many things I want to find out. Things you know. I know I have to come to Women's Country to do that. But I can't be selfish, either."

"I see." Her tone made it clear she did not.

"You don't see. But I hope you will. And respect me for it."

"We respect the warriors," she answered formally, a faint far ringing in her voice, like a knell. "Are you going to do that terrible thing to your mother? Tell her she's insulted your manhood?"

The question caught him off guard. With a good deal of anticipatory satisfaction, he had planned to do exactly that. "N-n-no," he stuttered. "It's not obligatory. I wouldn't do that."

"Well, that's something."

"But you will go on bringing me books, please. Please, Stavvy. I can't make it without. I really can't!" His eyes were full of tears, his lips trembled. He really couldn't. He meant it.

Though every part of her longed to tell him yes, she shook her head. She didn't know. She would have to ask someone. Maybe Joshua.

"I don't know," she said. "I'm not sure. I'm not sure the war should make any difference. There are always wars."

11

"THE GHOST of Polyxena appears on the battlement," called the director. "Slowly, she descends the stairs."

Councilwoman Stavia, in her character as Iphigenia, with the doll representing Astyanax cuddled in her arms, turned and looked up the stepladder that was doing duty as a battlement. The woman playing Polyxena was crouched at the top. For a moment Stavia couldn't remember the line, then just as the prompter began, she recalled it.

IPHIGENIA So, you have come at last, Polyxena. Please take this child from me.
POLYXENA I am not fond of children. Girls perhaps, who have some hope of life, but not of boys. Boys play with death as though it were a game, cutting their teeth on daggers. No. I am not fond of children.
IPHIGENIA Be fond of this one. It is your brother's child.
POLYXENA Hector's son? Well, and so they killed him, too.

Stavia tried the next speech, but something caught her just below the ribs, as though a knife had been inserted. "Well, so, they killed him, too," she said, repeating Polyxena's line. She heard her voice with dismay, a rising, unconscious keening.

The director gave her a look, then called the rehearsal to a halt, waiting until the others got out of earshot before asking, "What is it, Stavia?"

"It's just . . . just that line is the same thing my sister said a long time ago. Lately I've been all muddled up. Too many memories." She tried to laugh, unsuccessfully.

The director sighed. "You're tired, that's all. I'm making you all do it over too many times. My fault. I don't know what I want until I see it, and you all do it over and over until I see it. We've been at it long enough for today. Get some rest. Tomorrow we'll try again."

STAVIA HAD JUST TURNED THIRTEEN when heralds had come
from the battlefield to bring word that the armies of Marthatown and
Susantown were arranging themselves for honorable battle. The herald had
entered Women's Country through the Battlefield Gate after much blatting
of trumpets and thunder of drums, and a deputation of the Council had
gone down to the plaza to hear the word.

From a space on the second level of the colonnade, Stavia had seen
Morgot come into the plaza from the east, where the Council Chambers
were, her hastily donned ceremonial robe swaying around her and the dark
blue matron's veil blowing in the light wind. Even at that distance, Stavia
could see the whiteness of Morgot's eyes, so pale that they appeared to
look blindly at the world. How strange, to appear so blind and see so
much.

"But, I look like that, too," Stavia told herself. "I have eyes just like
that."

Chernon told her he liked her eyes, but Stavia wasn't sure she liked them herself. "Cassandra eyes," her drama teacher had called them when she asked if Stavia wanted to play the part of the luckless prophetess.

"It's a small part, but it would give you some performance experience. Then next year, perhaps you'll be ready for the part of Iphigenia."

"Just because of my eyes?" Stavia objected.

"No. Not just because of your eyes. Because you seem to understand what the play is about."

That had come as a surprise to Stavia, though she hadn't said anything to contradict it. There was no question what the play was about. It was about . . . well, it was about what it was about. Troy. The women.

"I'll do Cassandra, if you want me to."

"Suit yourself, Stavia." Her teacher had seemed somewhat disappointed, as though she had expected some other response. "There are never enough parts to go around."

Morgot had said performance experience was important.

"When you are grown, you may be asked to serve on the Council," she told Stavia. "Half of what we do is performance. Ritual. Observances. If we are seen to be in control, the people are calm and life moves smoothly. Nothing upsets the citizenry more than to believe its administrators are uncertain or faltering. Doing nothing with an appearance of calm may be more important than doing the right thing in a frantic manner. Learn to perform, Stavia. I have."

So now in the plaza, Morgot moved calmly. She seemed to feel Stavia's eyes upon her, for she turned, searching the colonnades, lifting her hand in a gesture of recognition. Stavia lifted her own in response, then dropped it again as the trumpet blatted once more and the herald stood forward to deliver his message. The armies had met one another halfway between the two cities. The garrisons were arrayed so, facing one another. Challenges had been uttered. Single combat had taken place. This one of Marthatown was wounded. That one of Susantown was dead. Single combat did not satisfy the garrison of Susantown. The rituals of combat were proceeding.

Soon the general battle would commence. The safety of the Marthatown women was assured. Susantown garrison would have no opportunity to attack Marthatown.

The head of the Council replied, an old voice, but strong, tolling among the plaza walls. "Honor of the city . . . protection of the women . . . protection of the children . . . glory awaiting . . ." Morgot stepped forward to present the honor ribbons which the women of the city had prepared. Oh, they glowed, those honors. Ribbons of purple for single combat. Ribbons of crimson for wounds suffered. Ribbons of gold for meritorious conduct in the face of the enemy. The herald bowed. The

Councilwomen bowed. The Battle Gate opened wide and the herald departed, honors bearers behind him, musicians behind them, blametty blam, ta-ra ta-ra.

Morgot turned and looked up once more, finding Stavia among the watchers, beckoning. Meet me. Stavia went down the steps among the cluck and mutter of the crowd. Women, girls, little boys, no serving men. Serving men were never present when garrison matters were under review. Never when warriors were present, in order to show the warriors proper respect. Though the herald was not, strictly speaking, a warrior. There were a number of men beyond the wall who were not, strictly speaking, warriors.

"Morgot, what about the musicians? And the cooks?"

Morgot turned a tired face on her, the lines around her eyes seeming deeper than usual, and the pale, slightly protuberant orbs touched with a pinkness, an irritation, as though she had not been sleeping well or had been weeping. "What musicians, daughter?"

"The ones with the trumpets and drums. They aren't warriors, are they?"

"They are in one sense, in that they chose to remain outside the wall. They aren't in that they've made themselves useful in some noncombatant way, and are thus likely to have a long and unthreatened life. Why do you ask?"

Stavia hesitated.

Morgot sighed. "You're thinking about Chernon. What has he told you?"

"That he will stay. That he can't let his fellows down now, because of the war."

Morgot looked stricken. "Because of . . . Oh, Lady! Poor Sylvia. Oh, Stavia, he really said that? But there are always wars."

"He says perhaps later. He still has time."

"But if Chernon . . . Habby is fifteen, you know, next month. He's the same age as Chernon, almost exactly. Sylvia and I got pregnant at the same time. My second, her first. Lady, if Chernon is influenced in that way, perhaps Habby could be, too."

"Why did there have to be a war just now?!"

Morgot shook her head, swallowed, then did it again, as though something were stuck in her throat. "I don't know, Stavia. Things happen. Populations get edgy. Particularly when food gets short. Ever so often, they just happen. I suppose it was time."

"What if Chernon . . . or Habby . . . what if they made themselves useful in some noncombatant role? Like . . . doctors, for instance?"

"Doctors? Warriors don't have doctors."

"I know they don't. But. . . ."

"No buts, Stavia. It's part of the ordinances. Warriors can't have doctors. And they must fight at close range, not at a distance. And they must see their own blood and the blood of their fellows, and they must care for their own dying and see their pain. It's part of the choice they have to make. You know all that."

"Chernon . . ." she started to say, then turned away, choking.

"I know. You see him in your mind, suffering, maimed. You see him dying. You feel his pain as though it were your own. I know, Stavia, for the sake of the Lady, you think I don't *know!* Every mother of sons knows! Every lover knows!"

"Why!"

"So that they know what they choose and know what they risk when they choose. It's their choice. They can return through the Gate to Women's Country or they can stay there, but they have to know what staying there means! They can't be asked to choose without knowing what they're doing! It can't be covered up or gilded or glossed over! Stavia, you know why!"

"And no medically trained people." It was stupid. The ordinances were simply wrong, that's all. She didn't say this, but her tone conveyed her thought.

"No doctors for the warriors, Stavia."

"You treat them when they catch diseases from the Gypsies!"

"We treat them if they have diseases we might get, yes. But they choose battle. They have to live with the consequences of battle."

"You give them water from the well," she argued. "That's not living with the consequences. . . ."

"The ordinances give mercy, Stavia. That's all. They're hard, but they're merciful."

They walked on, in silence. Tears were running down Morgot's face. Inside Stavia was merely a vacancy, a place too deep and empty for pain. She had given Chernon books. It was not merely a bit of rule breaking. She had broken the ordinances as well, and more than that, she disagreed with them. Maybe this was an ordinance that deserved to be broken.

She couldn't talk to Morgot, but she needed to talk to someone.

WHEN THE WARRIORS RETURNED it was almost midwinter. The whole city assembled on the walls and around the plaza. The air was crisp and cool with autumn's chill, and brown leaves from the parade ground maples blew in through the Defender's Gate when it was opened to bring in the dead. Row on row of them, the shrouds turned down to show their faces. Most of the dead, including all of those who had died early in the battle, had been buried on the battleground where they had fallen, and their litters held only their armor and their devices. At the head of each litter stood the T-staff which bore the warrior's honors. Beyond the wall, in the parade ground, the badly wounded lay on litters. Stavia and a dozen other maidens carried water from the Well of Surcease to the Council Chambers, where the Councillors mixed it with hemlock. Then the Councillors went out to the wounded warriors, offering the water to all in pain. Some warriors accepted it while others rejected it. Stavia went with Morgot on this duty, holding the cup while they drank.

"For release from pain," Morgot said, offering the flask.

"I do not need it, matron," said some. Some, those not too badly wounded, even grinned as they said it.

"Give it me, lady," said others, and then Stavia took the cup and held it to their lips. They drank and sank back upon their litters, silent. Some smiled. Some merely panted, begging for the flask with their eyes. Some were unconscious but so terribly wounded that their fellows begged it on their behalf. When it was over, someone came behind and pulled the shrouds up over their faces and carried them through the gate where their mothers and sisters waited.

There was no need of the cup for Barten. He was dead when they brought him back, speared from behind. Spearing from behind was what they always did to those who fled, or, sometimes, to those who were merely unpopular. His sister placed a red ribbon of honor on his chest; his mother wept; Myra threw herself upon his litter screaming, "So they've killed him, too, killed him, too," over and over again. When others tried to pry her away from the corpse, Myra clung to it more tenaciously.

"Let her be," Morgot said to them. "She will come home after dark when there is no one here to see her." And she did, creeping into the house and up to her room when it was dark and chill. In the morning she went back to the plaza again, but Barten's mother and sisters had taken his body outside the walls to their family plot and buried him there. They had not sent word inviting Myra to accompany them. Custom dictated dignity at times like these, and her grief had been too self-consciously dramatic, too shrill, too unwomanly to draw their sympathetic feeling.

"Who won?" Stavia asked, wondering why no one had told her.

"We did, of course. Susantown has given up any idea they may have had of attacking us." Morgot sighed and pushed the hair back from her forehead.

"How many did they lose?"

"As many as we."

"How many is that?"

"About six hundred," said Morgot. "Most of them were buried on the battlefield. Another hundred or so will die from their wounds."

"Mother! That's more than a quarter of the garrison. Almost a third!"

"I know. War is dreadful, daughter. It always has been. Comfort yourself with the knowledge that in preconvulsion times it was worse! More died, and most of them were women, children, and old people. Also, wars were allowed to create devastations. Under our ordinances, no children are slain. No women are slain. Only men who choose to be warriors go to battle. There is no devastation."

Stavia heard and was somewhat comforted, but Myra was inconsolable. Her cries of grief filled the house for days, and she would not be helped by anyone.

"Can't you do anything for her?" Stavia asked. "Give her some drug or something?"

"Better let her get it out," Morgot sighed. "She'll go on like this for a time, but eventually it'll stop. Grief is actually easier to live with than a host of other feelings, Stavia. Jealousy, for example. Or guilt. If Barten had lived, Myra would have learned a lot about both of those. As it is, Myra has nothing to reproach herself with."

In the weeks that followed, others of the wounded warriors died and there were other ceremonies of honor in the plaza. For a time it seemed there was no day without the rattle of drum and the cry of the trumpet, then the customary quiet came again.

Morgot summoned them all to the supper table one night and introduced a new member of the family.

"This is Donal," she said, putting her hand on the shoulder of the stocky, stern-faced young man with the iron-colored hair. "He is just sixteen. He has elected to return to Women's Country, and we have received him very gladly from Tabithatown in the north, where he has just completed the first stage of his education. Donal is enrolled in the servitors' school here in Marthatown."

Myra rose without a word and left the table. Morgot shook her head, meaning they should take no notice and let her go.

Donal murmured to Joshua.

"She was much enamored of a warrior," Joshua answered in a measured, formal tone which Stavia found unfamiliar. "He was not strictly honorable in his observance of the ordinances. He was successful in getting several girls to leave the city and live in the Gypsy encampment for his pleasure. Myra did not go that far, but she did entertain his ideas. He was recently slain."

Donal flushed and looked down at his plate.

"I suggest you simply ignore her," Morgot said. "She'll come around."

"Or make yourself indispensable with the baby," Stavia suggested. "Myra would like that."

It was Joshua who suggested that Stavia help Donal with his studies. "It's hard for him," he told her. "I know. Books simply aren't that important in the garrison. Reading isn't encouraged. One never gets into the habit. . . ."

So Stavia became a tutor, in math, in history, in composition, reminding herself of half a hundred things she had almost forgotten she knew.

"Councilwomen are not elected by the people," she told him in answer to a question. "They are chosen by other members of the Council."

"Your mother, that is, Morgot is a Council member. How long has she been on the Council?"

"Some years now. Since she was thirtyish," Stavia told him.

"Isn't that very young?"

"Rather. There aren't many that young."

"Why did they choose her?"

"I don't know. She doesn't say. None of them say. There's no specific number for the Council, and some women get put on and some women don't, that's all. Most of those on the Council are medically trained, I do know that. I think that's because the Council has to maintain the health of the city. . . ."

"That's probably it," agreed Donal. "Servitors never get on the Council, do they?"

The idea shocked Stavia into silence. Joshua spoke from the doorway. "Servitors have one or more fraternities in each city. The Council in each city often seeks the opinion of the fraternities, if they have opinions worth seeking. And the fraternities have opinions worth seeking in proportion to the amount of studying and thinking the individual servitors do."

Stavia stared at him, mouth open. "I knew about the servitors' fraternities, but I didn't know that."

"No one speaks of it from the steps of the Council Chambers, Stavvy. It wouldn't sit at all well with the warriors, would it? Still, don't you think it's reasonable? After all, none of you women have ever had to make such a choice as we have made. Most of you accept your way of life without much judgment of it. Donal and I have chosen your way as our own. Wouldn't you find that interesting, if you were on the Council?"

"I can't imagine caring what—oh, let's say Minsning thinks about anything."

"Minsning is Sylvia's servitor, a sweet little fellow," Joshua explained to

Donal with a straight face. "He has not a mean bone in his little body; he's as cheery as a sandpiper; and he's an excellent cook. I can't imagine anyone asking Minsning anything about anything except how to make a sauce, perhaps."

"So there are servitors and servitors?" Stavia mused. This distinction was important, terribly important, though she could not quite grasp where the implications were leading her.

Joshua laughed at her, showing his strong, slightly yellowish teeth in a wide grin. "There are women and women, aren't there? There's Morgot and there's Myra, for example. . . .

"Well, I have to take Donal away from you. He's due at the servitors' school, and I need to show him the way."

When he got to the door, however, Joshua paused and gave Stavia a strange, intent look. "When I get back, there is something I must talk to you about."

JOSHUA TALKED TO HER in the courtyard, beside the fountain, his hands at work on his forehead where the flesh wrinkled between his eyes. "Stavia, I have this strong, very troubling feeling there is something improper between you and Chernon."

She started to deny it, thinking he meant something sexual, then realized that, though it had nothing to do with sex, there was something improper going on. For a moment she could not speak, but his eyes were on hers, compelling.

"I gave him books," she whispered. "The ordinances say you can't give books to warriors, but he wasn't a warrior yet." She kept her eyes on her hands, twisting in her lap, not daring to look into his face.

"That's specious," he said. "You know that's a rationalization, Stavvy. Warrior or not, you know what the ordinances mean." He got the familiar, pained look on his face and began to rub his forehead as though it hurt badly. "I can't . . . can't," he murmured to himself. "So murky . . . Does he still have these books?"

"One book. I never gave him more than one at a time. He still has the last one I gave him, before I told him I couldn't give him any more."

"Do you meet him, talk with him regularly?"

She shook her head. "Sometimes I see him when Beneda and I go to the wall. Sometimes he's there. He hasn't really talked to me, not since that last time, the time he told me he was choosing to stay in the garrison."

"Unlike Habby . . ."

"Habby? Has he chosen to come home!"

"He will choose to return. There are about five of his century who will."

Stavia wept, the tears dripping soundlessly into her lap. She could not tell if they were tears of happiness for Habby or tears of angry grief for Chernon. "Morgot was worried he'd feel as Chernon did. . . ."

"No. Morgot should have known better."

"Where will Habby go?"

"He's agreed to go to Tabithatown. In exchange for Donal. All the towns try to keep things balanced, you know? Which doesn't help us right now with this problem." He shut his eyes, squinting, as though seeking something in the dark. "What did books mean to him, Stavia? Huh? Did he really want books, or was it something else?"

"I don't know what you mean."

"I feel . . . I feel him wanting something from you, but it isn't a book. Books. Not sex. A link of some kind. He feels some sense of attachment to you, but it isn't the usual youthfully romantic kind of thing."

"We're friends," she offered with some dignity.

He quit rubbing his forehead. "You may well be, Stavvy. Despite that—or, perhaps, because of that, it's important to return yourself to compliance with the ordinances. The book probably isn't very important, but we should take some steps to get it back. What I think you can do is this. Chernon is fifteen. Old enough for assignations. You can arrange to meet him in the assignation house at midwinter carnival."

"I'm not old enough," she blurted, shocked.

Joshua shook his head. "I don't mean you should attempt to have sex with him, child. I mean you can have a quiet time to talk with him, and that's the only one you're likely to get. He probably won't go home, not if he intends to stay in the garrison. Since the ritual of choosing hasn't actually happened yet, he could come home, one last time, but I'll wager he won't. The taverns and eating houses will all be jammed with drunken warriors and giggling women. The market swarms with them. You know that."

"What shall I say to him, Joshua?"

"Stavia, I don't know. I can't feel it clearly. . . ."

"I don't understand what you mean, you can't feel it clearly!"

"I can't comprehend what he intends to do! Or why!"

She stared at Joshua, trying to figure out what he meant. "If we knew that, we wouldn't need to talk to him."

"Of course. Quite right. Well, if I were you, I would tell him that your conscience is bothering you. It is, whether you knew it or not, or I wouldn't have picked up that something is wrong. Tell him you must either get the book back or report to the Council what you have done."

"What will they do to me?"

"If they find out." He reached out for her. Joshua had never reached out for her before, but he did, pulling her to him and crushing her against his hard chest. For a moment she was frightened, old stories of mad servitors darting through her mind like crazed swallows, but then she felt his hand on her back, patting her, as though she had been one of the donkeys, patting her, and she smelled him, the leathery, smoky smell of him, his sweet breath on her face as he turned up her face to him. "Oh, Stavia, Stavia. If the Council finds out about it, they'll be honor bound to punish you somehow. They're not going to find out from me. I think you've punished yourself enough already. I don't think you'll break any of the ordinances soon again. But it's not you I'm worried about. It's something to do with Chernon that bothers me. If the warriors caught him with womanly books, they'd punish him severely. Why isn't he worried about that? Stavia? Hmm? Think about it. Why isn't he worried about that?"

She went to the wall, day on day, finally managing a meeting which was unlikely to be overheard. He whispered to her to bring books to the secret hole, but she shook her head. "I'll meet you in the assignation house, Chernon. At midwinter. Bring that last book I gave you. We'll talk about it then. . . ."

He was stubborn and resentful, but she felt she had already yielded too much. She would not yield again.

"Child, you're not old enough," the assignation mistress said, a quirk at the corner of her mouth saying clearer than words could, "Oh, look at this precocious little miss, thinks she's in love with some warrior."

Joshua had told her what to say. "It isn't sex, ma'am, if you please. He's almost like my brother, just turned fifteen, and wants to talk to me. You know how it is—there's no place quiet he can go now. . . ."

A flipping of records, and the woman nodded. "I see. That's Sylvia's son, Chernon. You're neighbors."

"Yes, ma'am."

"I'll give you the end room nearest the plaza, first day of carnival, at six in the morning. That's an hour before we open for the lovers, so you'll have a chance for a quiet chat." She had a different expression now, a yearning, as though she had had a brother once, or a dear friend, she had wanted a quiet time with. "I wish you luck, child. Bring him home if you can."

Stavia flushed. It was a secret they all shared. Someone to be brought home; someone who could not come.

As it seemed he could not.

"You have to give me the book, Chernon." They were sitting side by side on the wide couch, not touching, embarrassed by the place, by the time.

"In exchange for one, Stavia. Just like always," he said stubbornly, lower lip clenched and angry. He had truly expected her to come to him before now, offering to put everything back as it had been before she refused him. Michael had thought she would.

"Not in exchange for anything. Oh, Chernon, don't you care about me at all? Or yourself?"

What was this? He was shifty, biting his cheeks, eyes darting this way and that as though she were trying to trap him. "Yes. You're my friend."

"Then don't risk our lives, Chernon."

His jaw sagged. "What do you mean?"

"If I don't get it back, I must tell the Council, Chernon. I broke the ordinances. Now that you're really going to be a warrior, I can't go on breaking them. If you won't give it back, I'll have to. . . ."

"Don't," he said hastily, too hastily. Michael wouldn't want that. Michael wouldn't want the Council knowing anything about Chernon at all, about Chernon and Stavia!

"Besides, you should be worried about what the warriors might do to you."

He had to detour her, distract her. He put out his hand to touch her face, the soft tips of his fingers making gentle trails down her cheeks to her jaw, his mouth like one on a tragic mask, drooping. "You were really worried about me. I didn't know. I thought you were just being . . . trying. . . ."

She had been *being, trying*. She was still *trying*, but none of that got through to him at all.

"I'll . . . I'll bring it back to you this afternoon," he said. "I'll put it through the hole." They had widened the hole. It was almost a window, now, suitable for the passage of books. When she leaned tight into the wall on the inside, and he on the outside, they could touch hands in the dark depth of the stone while the tree sifted the light onto his face. He could never see her, but she could see him. She felt he was closer to her then, separated by all that thickness of wall, than he was now.

Now he started to go and she stopped him. "Stay, Chernon. We have this room for an hour."

"No, no," he said, sounding trapped again. "I can't. Can't stay. Oh, Stavia. . . ."

And then he was kneeling before her, his head in her lap, weeping while she tried frantically to comfort him.

"I don't know what to do!" he wept, surprising himself by this flood of honest, uncalculated tears. "I think I've got it picked, and then I'm not sure, and then I think I'll do something else, but that's worse. I couldn't do anything that would make them hate me, Stavvy. I want him to, Michael to. . . . I just couldn't. You know that. I shouldn't have to. There should be something else I can do. . . ."

She held him. She didn't ask what he meant. There was nothing she could say. If she told him she loved him, it would only trap him more! She couldn't beg him to come home to her—she had already done that. It was all in the ordinances, ordinances she had already broken. All she could hear, inside her head, were Myra's words when she saw Barten's body. "So they've killed him, too!" It was as though she had killed Chernon, too. If she had not given him the first book, perhaps he would not be weeping now. She had wronged him, hurt him. She was guilty. Somehow, she would have to make it up to him. She swore to herself she would make it up to him. Somehow.

She held him, rocking back and forth, her face frozen. They stayed there until the attendant knocked on the door, telling them their time was up.

Joshua was waiting for her at home. He saw her face and his own changed. "Do you have the book?"

"He said he'll probably bring it. This afternoon." She was numb from emotion, pain, guilt.

"Tell me, Stavia!"

She temporized. "He's confused, Joshua, that's all. I don't think he knew how much danger he was in."

"I'll come with you this afternoon."

"You're not supposed. . . ."

"By the Lady, Stavia, you've already got me in over my head."

All his willingness to bend the customs did no good. When they went to the hole in the wall, the book was there, but Chernon was not. Joshua, after a long, calculating look at Stavia's stricken face, decided that something drastic had to be done.

13

REHEARSAL of *Iphigenia at Ilium:* Councilwoman Stavia in the part of Iphigenia.

———

CASSANDRA I have seen blood. . . .

HECUBA Cassandra, do sit down. *(To Polyxena)* Odysseus had Andromache's child thrown to his death from high atop the walls.

POLYXENA A pity, though no more than one might guess would happen with these disputatious Greeks.

IPHIGENIA For all the joy they take in getting sons, they take as great a joy in killing them. There's not a warrior but would have his sons be warriors in their time. *(To Andromache)* If Hector lived would he not teach this baby how to kill and how to die?

ANDROMACHE He would have, yes, if he'd lived long enough. He would have felt dishonored if his son had not espoused the sword.

IPHIGENIA *(Jiggling the baby)* It's just as well, then, that he didn't live.

ANDROMACHE Do you speak of my husband or my child?

IPHIGENIA What difference? I speak of either one.

POLYXENA Who are you to have cared for Hector's son?

IPHIGENIA Iphigenia, Agamemnon's child. I came to Ilium to avenge myself on him who murdered me.

CASSANDRA I have seen blood.

HECUBA Hush, dear, please.

CASSANDRA Blood and bodies broken.

HECUBA Shh, Cassandra. We know, dear. We have seen blood enough to last our lives. Blood and dead children and the bones of men. I cannot understand how warriors live among so many slain. They seem to take their strength from dying men as do the Holy Gods from sacrifice!

CASSANDRA White altars red with blood. With heart's blood shed. With blood and bodies broken.

HECUBA Shh.

14

FOR FIFTY DAYS after the war with Susantown, Casimur, warrior of
the thirty-one, had waited on death's landing for death to open the door—
waited and stank and screamed until everyone in the Old Warriors' Home
stuffed wool in their ears and drank themselves into insensibility. It would
have been a courtesy to kill him, a courtesy for him to take the Well Water
the women offered him, but he wouldn't. Even now that he was sure he
was dying, Casimur was very set on his honor. He screamed about it again
and again, until his throat was raw from screaming and he could only make
a hoarse, ratcheting sound, like a ladle rattling in an empty wooden bucket.

Chernon sat beside Casimur to serve him. He had to wait by Casimur's
bed, ready to receive the last words or the spirit or the instructions or
whatever it was Casimur might want to give him. There was always a boy
set beside a dying man, a boy to carry on the honor. Fifty days he had been
there, changing bandages and cleaning up when Casimur dirtied himself
and trying to spoon soup down his throat.

When Casimur was not screaming, Chernon tried to sleep. In the deep of
night, Chernon struggled with his pillow, searching for a way out, away

from wherever he was in the dream country. Where he was was bloody. He walked in gore, lifting clotted hands, gagging at the smell of it. He waded through the swamps of the sleep country, bellowing into the very mouth of the black cave he had tracked his dream guide into. "Is the way out through there?" No matter how sweetly he had called, it was never sweetly enough to evoke an answer. Sometimes in the dream he was horned and mighty. Sometimes in the dream, no walls or chains could hold him, and yet he could not find the way out. No maps were drawn in his dark dreaming, or, if they were, they were not written on his pillow when he awoke.

He turned in sleep, sweating, peering behind the pillars of the cave, hoping to see a road, a signpost, a pointing finger, but everywhere was only Casimur's agonized face, Casimur's voice screaming about honor.

Chernon believed in honor, as he understood it, as Michael and the others had explained it to him. It was honorable to protect women because warriors needed them to breed sons and—so dogma had it—they were incapable of protecting themselves, though there might be some doubt about that now, with this rumored weapon or power of theirs. Michael said women weren't strong enough to trust with power or weapons and that if it turned out they had any such thing, it would be perfectly honorable to conquer them and take the power away from them. Women didn't have the right kind of minds to use such things properly, so it would be most honorable to remove the danger from them. Michael had explained about Besset, too. How sometimes it was necessary to do unpleasant things for the greater good. Like turning Besset loose to join a bandit pack so he could bring back information. Even though the bandits sometimes killed people, the information was more important than worrying about their lives.

Everyone agreed that it was dishonorable to return through the Gate to Women's Country. Only cowards did it. Cowards and physical weaklings, though even they could be put to work in the garrison kitchens or doing maintenance of some kind if they confessed their weakness to the Commander. Beyond being the butt of a bit of rough teasing or donkey play, they got on well enough.

It was dishonorable to make a Gypsy of a young girl as it unfitted her for breeding, or to make a whore of a boy as it unfitted him for a warrior's life. Everyone agreed it was dishonorable, but sometimes the men did it anyhow. It was dishonorable, but it wasn't hateful. Going back through the gate, that was hateful. Getting some girl out to the camps—well, nobody would hiss you for that.

It was dishonorable to drink so much during carnival that you couldn't remember what women you'd been with, though most of the men had been guilty of that. More than one man had received a printed card from the assignation mistress after carnival, signed by some woman the warrior couldn't really remember. The cards always said the same thing. "If it is a boy, I will bring him to his warrior father when he is five." The cards went into the men's files at headquarters. A man might not exactly remember, but no man with a card filed for the proper date would care to say the son wasn't his when it showed up almost six years later. It would be the same as admitting lack of manhood! Of course, some warriors had grown too old for sex and some simply preferred the Gypsies as less trouble, and said so, and there was nothing held against them for that.

The conventional wisdom in the garrison was that it didn't matter if a man remembered clearly or not. Even though everybody knew that women cheated about other things, it was generally agreed that they were honest and sensible about warriors' sons because it was in their own best interest to do so. Women knew the warriors protected them only because women bore them sons, so it was in the women's interest to see that sons were produced and brought to the appropriate father. Though Chernon had serious doubts about this, it was true that almost every warrior had at least one son. Very few warriors got slighted during carnival. Very few of the men who wanted sex did without, even though some of them didn't re-member much about it afterward. Sons were the single most important thing in life to a warrior, and the women knew that. "In bearing a son for a warrior, a woman earns her life." That's the way the indoctrination for boys went. "Your mother earned her life so." Another saying was, "There's no use or excuse for a childless woman." Though, of course, everyone realized there really were many excuses. Without all the old women doing the weaving and preserving fish and shearing sheep, food and fabric would both be scarce. Everyone really knew that. When the centurions nicked off part of the grain allotment to make beer, someone always toasted "the grandmas" who grew the grain.

All of these things had something to do with honor, but nowhere in all that tangle of honor and dishonor, as Chernon understood it, was there anything about rotting away on a bed for fifty days before you finally died. Casimur should have taken the Well Water. Morgot herself had come to him and offered it three times. Each time, Chernon had hidden himself, not wanting to see her, not wanting to think about her or her family. Not wanting to think about Stavia.

It had all gone wrong with Stavia. He had done exactly what Michael told him to do, but it had gone wrong. Instead of becoming Chernon's willing informant, Stavia had gone away. One afternoon she was there, holding him in her lap while he cried, inexcusable, babyish tears. Five days later when he tried to find her to tell her the tears hadn't meant anything, she was gone. She had been sent to Abbyville to the Medical Institute, Beneda told him. Gone two years earlier than expected. Gone for nine years, and she would only be able to come home to visit once or twice, if at all. It made him angry, not so much that she had gone but that she had never said a word to him about the fact that she might go. It did not occur to him that she might not have mentioned it because she hadn't wanted to go.

No, he told himself, he had simply been wrong to think Stavia would behave differently from other women. All women cheated. His mother cheated, and Beneda, and so Stavia did, as well.

There had been the time that crazy Vinsas had been alive. Vinsas had told Chernon to go home at carnival time and say these things to Chernon's mother, not nice things exactly, but interesting things. "I cut her with my knife at the tip of her breast," Vinsas had said. When he talked like this, his lips wobbled loosely and the spit ran out onto his chin. "It made a scar. I bit her in a certain place. I left my teeth marks on her. Make her show you. . . ." Chernon found it interesting to imagine what she would say when he quoted Vinsas to her. That very first time she could have told him she wouldn't discuss it, but instead she'd tried to explain about Vinsas. If she hadn't intended to talk about it, she should have said so the first time. But she did say some things. Things about women and how men looked at women and what some men wanted. He didn't really want her to cry, but it was interesting that she did. Having her talk to him that way made him feel older and stronger. He had wanted to talk about it again, but after the second time she hadn't let him talk about it at all. Instead, she had sent him away, to his Aunt Erica's house.

And Stavia. It was the same with Stavia. "You've got to get them to break the rules, boy," Michael had said. "They think they're safe so long as they keep the rules. It's like their silly ordinances are a kind of protection for them. You get them to break the rules, all of a sudden they don't have that protection anymore. Then the only protection they've got is you, and they have to please you to get it, right?"

So he got Stavia to break the rules, but she had twisted on him. She had threatened to go to the Council.

"Give her the book back," Stephon had said. "Keep her quiet. Wait a few months and we'll try her again."

But there had been no opportunity to try again. She had gone. Would be gone. For years.

You couldn't trust them. That's what Michael said. You couldn't trust them. He was right. Even Beneda. Sometimes when he used to visit at home during carnival she'd ask him what he wanted to eat and fix it for him, then the next time she'd say she was too busy. Women had no right to do a thing and then not do it, to say yes and then no. The warriors said sometimes a woman would be with them at one carnival and the next carnival she'd say, no, she wanted to be with someone else! Even Barten had said that once about some girl. How she had said she'd stay at the Gypsy camp for him, but she didn't. Women had no right to do that. Once a woman consented to something, that was it, no saying no later or running away.

The worst part of Stavia's being gone was that Chernon's usefulness to Michael seemed to be over. Now there was only this waiting! Waiting until Stavia came back, if she came back. Waiting until Michael found something else exciting for him to do. Which would not be soon. Michael had decided that now was not the time to do anything.

"I've got this philosophy," Michael had said in his smooth, lazy voice. "You can plan all you want to. Plan and plan, and maybe something will happen and maybe it won't. Life's like the city. There's a wall around it with a gate in it. A Warriors' Gate. Once in a while that gate is going to open, and if you're ready, you can get through it before it shuts again. The thing we have to do is be ready. Someday the gate is going to open for us, for you, too, Chernon. If you're ready when it does, then you go through and there's all kinds of glory on the other side. Pushing that gate before it's ready to open—that's just stupid. Pushing that gate before it's ready can give you a hernia." He laughed then, throwing his head back, showing his strong white teeth. "I'll get in, but I won't strain myself!"

Stephon growled in his impatience to be doing something, but Michael just laughed at him.

"You're too itchy, Steph. Too itchy. Go on out to the Gypsy camp and get it out of your system. Just be ready, that's all. It doesn't matter whether it's now or later. Just be ready."

So they waited.

Even if he wasn't doing anything useful at the moment, Chernon was determined that when the gate opened, when the opportunity was there, he would be a part of it. He would learn whatever secrets there were that made the women powerful.

For there were secrets! The more Chernon thought about it, the surer he was of it. Otherwise, why had they sent Stavia away? Because they were afraid she'd tell him, that's why. For a time he had thought he might find secrets in the books Stavia had given him, but there were no mysteries there. Just numbers and names for things and stories about how people had lived long ago—not even powerful people, just ordinary shepherds and weavers and people who grew crops. They might have had reindeer instead of sheep or cotton instead of wool, but there was nothing useful in that. No mysterious knowledge. Nothing about the wonderful weapons. Nothing of the stuff he knew had to be there, somewhere. Stavia hadn't given him the right books. Probably those books, the powerful books, were secret. Perhaps Stavia herself hadn't even seen the secret books yet. Maybe only the older women saw them. But whether she had seen them or not, Stavia had been taught something about them. Michael thought so; Chernon believed it.

"She'll be back eventually," Michael said to Chernon. "Maybe it won't matter. Everything may have busted loose by then and we may not need what she knows, but if not, you can find out then. When she comes back, Chernon, you'll have to figure out a way to get her off by herself. As long as Stavia's in tight with Morgot and that bunch, you won't be able to do anything with her."

So he dreamed of getting Stavia off by herself. A journey of discovery, perhaps. That was something a warrior could do honorably. The Sagas were full of exciting journeys, dangerous quests. In the Odysseus Saga there was that long journey when old Odysseus fought to get back to his own garrison after the great war with Troy! In a favorite fantasy, Chernon imagined himself as Odysseus, leaving the battlefield after the victory. He was wounded, just enough that his bloodstained bandages showed everyone he had been in the battle. Then, as he started the journey home with the garrison, there was a great storm. Everyone got separated, and when the storm was over, he found himself alone, journeying, finding things out.

At first this idea of a quest, a journey, was only a recurrent fantasy, something to while away the long hours in garrison while others played games or carved new gables or doorposts for the barracks, activities that bored Chernon to gaping somnolence. Later it became an obsession. He would take Stavia along as a witness, as a scribe. Someone to record his adventures, someone to see that life need not be usual to be honorable. She would regret, then, that she had not given him books. She would see that he was not merely another warrior. And then he could find out what she knew, really.

Whenever garrison life became boring or sickening or frightening, he lost himself in daydreams of the other places he would go. He could ignore the garrison annoyances. The garrison was only the place he was, a place he would leave very soon, in the blink of an eye, whenever he chose. For now, he would not choose. For now, he would do what the garrison required, but the day would come when it was no longer necessary. Besides, just now he could not leave the wounded ones; he could not leave Casimur.

And then Casimur died at last, releasing Chernon to go back to the dormitory with the other fifteen-year-olds, where he went on tossing as restlessly upon his pillow as he had before. Even though it was the time to think of honor, he was not thinking of Casimur's honor or his own. His dream took him to places beyond honor, places dark and mysterious at the end of the journey he had not yet begun. In dream he went in search of that place, down dank tunnels and into echoing caverns, sometimes almost finding it. "Secrets?" he whispered in dream, begging the faceless darkness to explain why he was still here, still in the garrison when there was that other place waiting for him.

From the roof of the armory, a trumpet blew. Get-em-up, get-em-up, get-em-up. Ta-ta-da, ta-ta-da, ta-ta-da.

Morning noises. It was quieter than usual in the dormitory because today was the day of choice, and some of the fifteen-year-olds were going to go through the Women's Gate. Everyone in the century knew it and had known it for some time. Not that anyone said anything. The ones who were thinking of going could change their minds. Right up until the last minute, they could choose to step forward and do the honorable thing, provided they hadn't been pushed into a corner. So, no one said anything at all.

Chernon sat up, swinging his legs over the edge of his cot, not looking at Habby in the left-hand cot. Habby was going through the Gate to Women's County. And Breten, and Garret and Dorf. And Corrig, of course. Which was a good thing!

"Chernon." It was only a murmur, but it brought his eyes up. Habby was offering his hand. "Chernon, I won't have another chance to say good-bye."

Chernon ignored the hand. He didn't want to be seen shaking hands with Habby. Still, Habby was Stavia's brother and he didn't want tales carried back to Women's Country, either. Michael said they might still need Stavia. That's why Chernon had given the book back, because he might still need her. Better leave Habby with something Stavia would appreciate.

"Wills and that lot may try to beat you to a bloody mess," he said with calculated candor. This wasn't really taking sides. He'd promised himself he wouldn't do that.

"I know. But there's five of us, and we're going to stick together. Do you have any message for Stavia?"

Chernon shook his head, keeping his voice neutral. Any message he might have for Stavia, he could not send by Stavia's brother. "I told her why I was staying."

"The war's over, Chernon."

"It would seem cowardly to go back now." This was rote. This was what he had said before. It was what warriors said, and no one could fault him for saying it.

"They'll always find a way to make it seem cowardly. No matter when you do it." Habby was looking at him oddly, rubbing his forehead as though it hurt.

"It's a matter of honor," he said stiffly. "Doing what's honorable." Though he had fantasized leaving the garrison a thousand times, he had never seen himself going through the Gate to Women's Country. His departure had always been different from that. A stroke of fate. Some occurrence that was totally unavoidable. Something that just happened, like storm, like winter. Something he couldn't be blamed for. "A matter of honor," he repeated.

Habby shrugged. "That's only what the garrison calls it, Chernon. I don't call it that, so I can't argue with you."

Chernon turned away, trying to hide his anger. Stavia had said the same thing. And Beneda.

And his mother. "Honor is only a label they use for what they want you to do, Chernon. They want you to stay, so they call staying honorable."

"You want me to come back?! You call that honorable?"

"No," his mother, Sylvia, had said. "We try very hard not to call it anything, Chernon. We just tell you that we love you and would be glad of your return."

And Stavia had been the same. No books. "You have to make your own choices, Chernon. I can't go on breaking the rules and expect you to make proper choices. I must choose now to confess and be punished for what I did. You have to choose one way of life or the other. Not both."

He had cried then, mostly out of anger. He had regretted those tears since. When you cried, you gave them power over you. You couldn't ever cry. He had tried to see Stavia again, tried to tell her the tears hadn't meant anything, but she had gone. Gone away. For a long time. Years.

He got up and started to dress himself, not speaking to Habby again. There was no point in complicating his own life. Wills didn't care who he beat on, and if Wills couldn't get Habby, he'd be happy to settle for Chernon. Wills was a little like Barten had been. A trumpet-mouthed bully. Always blaring "Attack," even when there was no reason for it. Always calling someone a servitor-lover, or a tit-sucker, or a weird. Now, Corrig was really a weird, a wild man. Corrig was going to go back through the gate, too, and nobody would care. Him and his strange eyes that saw things no one else saw; him and his knowing things you didn't want him to know. Everyone would be more comfortable without Corrig.

It was a cold morning, a wet, mawky morning, with the wind blowing from the sea. Chernon put on his long cloak and drew on his thigh-length wool socks before stamping his feet into his boots. The socks tied to his cincture, and he struggled with the laces. Around him everyone else was doing the same except for Habby, and Corrig and the other three. They'd clumped themselves together at the end of the room, waiting for assembly to blow, barefooted, nothing on but their tunics. Habby was smart. Habby must have planned that. A tunic came off fast. Nothing to untie or unbutton. No excuse to knock a man down to take his boots if he was already barefooted. The closer to naked you were when you made the choice, the quicker you could strip. The less excuse for somebody to beat on you while they ripped off your clothes.

"Naked you came from your mother's womb, and naked you shall return to Women's Country!" The officers would say that when they got them into the ceremonial room under the wall. "Bloody you came, and bloody you shall go!" some others might say, enforcing the saying with flung stones.

Then the hissing from the century.

Chernon considered the hissing. In a way, it was what Vinsas had tried to do to Sylvia, a kind of hissing. To hurt. To wound. Something in the thought was teasingly distasteful, like a food one couldn't decide if one liked or not, and he set it aside, pulling his cloak tight against the wind. Habby and the others didn't seem to notice the cold. They stood quietly, ready for anything. Outside in the hall Wills was trying to agitate some of his cronies, getting no commitment from them. Habby was a very good fighter, and of course Corrig was insane. Corrig could damn near kill you. Even Wills, stupid as he was, knew that.

Assembly! The time in which Wills might have done his worst was lost. Outside the barracks door they formed up the square, ten by ten. The fifteen century. All of them in it were fifteen years old, more or less. A full century of one hundred boys. Not to be full for long. An hour from now they'd be five short.

"There was a time," Casimur had cried in one of his lucid intervals, "there was a time when a century might not have a single vacant space. Less than five men in a hundred went back, you know that? Less than five! And now—now, it's all come to rot and dishonor. Twenty in a hundred. That's how many go these days. Twenty in a hundred. . . ."

"When was that," Chernon had asked, "when was it only five in a hundred?"

"In my grandfather's time," Casimur had said. "He told me himself. In my grandfather's time."

When they formed up on the parade ground, the wind slashing at their long cloaks, turning their noses red, and bringing tears to their eyes, Chernon thought of what Casimur had said, as he waited for the twenty-four century to march around, keeping his eyes front, away from Habby at his side. When the twenty-fours went by, he blinked back the wind-whipped tears and counted. Twenty-one spaces in the ranks. Seventy-nine men. Casimur had been right. Say that five left at age fifteen, then another one or two each year thereafter until the century came of fighting age. It would be century twenty-five next year, and there would be fewer than eighty of them left.

"But it will be the best men who stay," Chernon assured himself, repeating what the centurion had told him. "The best warriors. Better have eighty good men than a hundred where twenty are cowards. . . ."

"STAND FORWARD," cried the centurion. "THOSE WHO CHOOSE HONOR, STAND FORWARD!"

"Good-bye," whispered Habby from his place beside Chernon.

Together with ninety-four other fifteen-year-olds, Chernon marched forward, leaving the five to strip off their tunics and stand naked in the chill wind. By the time the century had marched once around, eyes front, the five naked boys were gone, escorted into the gatehouse by the ceremonial company.

No one took any notice. No one would ever mention their names again. The fifteen century wheeled and marched, coming up before the reviewing stand where the Commander stood, his bearers on either side of him holding tall poles streaming with honors.

"Century Fifteen," the Commander roared, his voice cutting through the wind like a knife through soft cheese. "Honorable warriors of the garrison of Marthatown. We welcome you to the ranks of duty, discipline, and danger. We welcome you to the company of glory. We welcome you as companions in honor, and to you we award the first honor of many, the blue knots of honorable choice!"

Then all the centuries drawn up around the parade ground were cheering and the bearers were coming down the ranks, pinning the blue knots onto every man of the fifteen, holding the cup of honeyed wine to their lips. Chernon felt tears on his cheeks and was ashamed until he saw that both the men on either side of him were crying, too. Poor Habby. Poor Habby, not to have realized what he was giving up. And for what?

Then they wheeled to one side. The drums began the funeral beat. Casimur had died yesterday, and they paraded Casimur's century, the thirty-one. Forty-five men missing: twenty holes left by tit-suckers, and twenty-four honorable deaths filled by boys carrying the honor ribbons of the slain.

"The honorable Chernon," the Commander bellowed. "Chernon to parade the honors of Casimur!"

And there it was, thrust into Chernon's hands, Casimur's tall staff with the carved crossbar, bright ribbons dangling from it, so many they were like a fringe, lashing like cats' tails in the wind, and Chernon himself filling that empty place in the thirty-one like a reserve warrior into a hole left by a man fallen. Trumpets then, and drums, and the thirty-one parading before the army, up to strength again, those alive and those dead marching along together, the only holes in it the ones the tit-sucking Women's Gaters had left.

The assembled centuries cheered, their voices rising in a cyclone of sound. Bells rang. Trumpeters cried to the heavens. The ribbons whipped in Chernon's face like little hands, slapping him, saying, "Pay attention." Blood boiled out from the center of him to simmer in his veins. The music of the trumpets filled him. The hammer of the drums became the hammer of his own heart. The feet of the men falling in unison, the whip and snap of the banners, the ribbons, the plumes, and the drums, the drums. Honor, the trumpets cried. Honor, the drums beat home. Power, the garrison cried. And it was Casimur's honor that was evident at last as Casimur marched with honor, his place honorably filled. He had not sought the Women's Cup or the Women's Gate!

It was as though Chernon's veins had been filled with fire. This was the reason he was still here! He was here to learn of this, this mighty fabric of motion and sound, this tapestry with Chernon moving as a thread within it, bright as gold, the threads of all the garrison around him, the centurions, the fifteens, the twenty-fours, the thirty-ones, all of them up to the seventies, one old man by himself and all the rest living in bright ribbons which would never fade. . . .

It was a thundering glory and he was part of it. Now he was suddenly part of it.

If he could have been in the ceremonial room at that moment, he would have stripped Habby and spit on him and hissed him and then helped to beat him, too, and he would not have cared what stories were carried back to Women's Country.

IN HIS sixty-somethingth year, Septemius Bird had entered Marthatown through the itinerants' gate, showing his passbook, which was stamped and countersigned by the gate guards of a dozen cities. He had no idea at the time that he had come to stay.

"Septemius Bird?" The guardswoman had been only slightly incredulous.

"The late Septemius Bird," he said with a quirk, finger laid along his nose as though to stop a sneeze, eyebrows tilted up and outward in a Mephistophelian mask, showing his dark side, the one he favored for usages like these.

"Late?"

"Always, inevitably!" He had sighed. "Looking upon your beauty, I should have been here a week ago, a month, perhaps I should have been here always."

"Not on an intinerant's pass," the guardswoman had grinned, showing herself unimpressed by these theatrics. "Here for carnival, I suppose?"

"Also inevitably," he laughed, showing teeth white and pointed as fangs at the corners of his smile, like a vampire, licking them quickly as though to get the last taste of blood off. Not really fangs, no, merely teeth that were longer and narrower than most, the guardswoman had told herself with a half pleasurable shiver. "Magician?"

"Say showman. Bits of this and bits of that," he admitted. "It is my profession."

"Alone?"

"Who would be alone?" he said with a dramatic gesture. "Lonely, yes, madam, as are we all in these latter days when the desolation gathers around us like so many clustered pockmarks on the face of nature, but alone, no. I have some pretense of a troupe. An assistant, as it were, or two."

"Your first stop . . ." the guardswoman began.

"Must be at the quarantine house," interrupted Septemius. "We quite understand. Believe me, madam, we have no wish to distribute infection in these altogether admirable purlieus. Without Women's Country, we would have no custom, therefore we attend to your custom, do we not?" A quirk again, as though an announcement of laughter which was only assumed, not heard.

From the brightly painted wagon a touseled head emerged. "Bird, are we here, have we arrived?" A gray-headed oldster, face scruffily obscured behind a ten-day beard, coughing as he spoke.

Two other heads above and below, identical to one another, down to the copper locks falling in studied disarray before the ears. Women's voices from these girl's faces, two blended into one, like a voice holding its own echo close to its heart, "Septemius?" A vibration, like that of a tuning fork, dwindling into silence. From the cage atop the wagon came a muffled "whuff," as one of the dancing dogs turned over in his sleep.

"The elderly gentleman is Bowough Bird. The young women are my nieces." He presented their books and she took her time leafing through them, tracing back their travels. They had covered Women's Country. Bird's passbook was numbered eighteen, and it was almost full. Eighteen books he had filled! The old man had filled twenty-seven!

"Well, madam?" Bird bowed extravagantly, one foot well back, an arm bent across his chest, holding a broad-brimmed and plume-decked hat, his other arm sweeping the red-lined cloak into a wide wing at his side. "Well?"

"Get on with you, all four of you. Considerin' how polite you are, I won't make you use the outside entrance. You don't need to go back outside the gates. Quarantine house is down this road to your left. There's a medic there now."

The wagon rocked off down Wallside Road, leaving the guardswoman to shake her head. Carnival brought strange folk to Women's Country. Magicians, fire painters, dance troupes, animal trainers. And the likes of Septemius Bird. She sneaked a look at herself in the mirror hung behind the door while considering that she was looking rather well that evening despite this really regrettable tabard she had to wear to identify her status.

At the quarantine house they found a young medic on duty, more or less, a woman with a thick mop of tawny hair, eyes green as grass—though full of sleep—and a wide, tender mouth.

"Health cards," she demanded with a bright, wide-eyed stare, as though she was suspicious of them all or covering up the fact she had been drowsing when they entered. She hunched over the proferred cards making noises, hm and ah, to show she knew what the chicken tracks on them meant. "Seven days ago in Mollyburg, a clean record there. Any contact since?"

"If by that, madam, you mean any lascivious conduct, lecherous behavior, lubricious or priapic pauses in our days' endeavors, no. I am unsuited to such by mere inclination. Bowough, there nodding his gray head, is unsuited by age. My nieces, precocious though they are, are unsuited by aesthetic preference, which time will, no doubt, reverse."

Stavia, for it was Stavia, gave the girls a quick look. Prepubertal, surely, though it would not be the first time some huckster had tried to sell his female companions, over and over again, as virgin nymphs. She had learned of such in the academy at Abbyville, of such and of half a hundred other suches she would as soon not have known of. These girls had not that look about them, though. There was none of that Gypsy-camp lewdness in their eyes, though there was other sorts of wisdom there, the Lady wot. A certain knowledge of the world, perhaps. They returned her hard look with calm ones of their own, blue eyes like clear tidewater pools, reflecting the measureless sky.

She fought her way out of those pools, examining the books again. No! These women were the same age as she. Twenty-two years in the bodies of sylphs? Surely not. "They assist you?"

"A moment's thought will assure you of the value of identical twins to a magician, particularly twins who look like mere children." He flashed his teeth at her, a fox's smile. "May I introduce you to Kostia and Tonia. They are my sister's daughters, and I had the deepest affection for my sister." This time he did not smile, and Stavia believed him.

"For their sakes, showman, you'd do better to let them live in Women's Country."

He shook his head, evidently accustomed to this suggestion, placing his hands on the edge of her desk, poised on their fingertips, each hand like some five-legged creature pressing up and down, up and down. "I have considered that, from time to time. My sister thought not, however. There are advantages to our life, madam."

"If you can stay clear of bandits, no doubt." She sighed, and he heard the sigh. Something there that made her sympathetic to a wandering life. He gave no sign of having heard or understood that sigh.

"Thus far we have been lucky."

Stavia went through the motions with them, though both instinct and experience told her they were clean. The oldster—who sat beneath her ministrations almost unmoving, more than half asleep—had more than a little congestion in his chest, a bit of cold, perhaps, not helped by sleeping on the ground or in the unheated wagon. That should be watched. Pneumonia was no joke these days, for the drugs that cured it were the same that cured sexual diseases. Women's Country had only the one pharmaceutical manufactury, and production of drugs always lagged behind demand. The girls bloomed with health and showed no signs of sexual use. All four wore the seal of Mollyburg on their left cheeks still, so she stamped them on the right. "Will you be staying in the entertainers' hostel? Or in the wagon park?"

Bird cast a quick glance at old Bowough and shook his head. "My old friend could use a soft bed, if the hostel has such."

Her heart warmed toward him. "I was about to suggest as much. I'm giving you a supplemental ration card for him, as well, which will entitle him to extra foodstuffs while you are here. He will be the better for some cream and eggs."

Bird bowed, his extravagant bow, and said, "This is generous of you, Medic."

"Not really," she laughed. "All of Women's Country seems to be going to have an exceptional harvest this year. All the warehouses will be full to overflowing. All the ewes have had twin lambs and the fishermen have never seen such weight of silver in their nets. We can spare some cream and eggs for someone who has devoted his life to amusing us."

He bowed again, this time seriously, and she aped him, laughing. "Where will you be performing, magician?"

"Arriving early in this way, shouldn't I be able to secure a place in the plaza?" It was a question, accompanied by a quirked eyebrow and widened nostrils.

"You are among the first." She nodded. "I'll stop by tomorrow and take a look at your kinsman. Have you been together long?"

"Some might say long enough, madam. He is my father."

She handed them their ration cards, then stood staring after them as they took themselves off, the wagon rattling on the cobbles as it climbed the winding street toward the marketplace.

Septemius, on the wagon seat, held the reins in his left hand and put his right hand on the seat, balanced on its fingertips, each finger finding a rounded depression, five in all. "By five," he mumbled to himself, pressing his fingers down, his lean, agile hand doing five quick pushups on the wooden seat. Five was Septemius's mandala, his secret key. As a tiny child he had had a blanket with five embroidered bees upon it. The fingers of his hands had fit upon those bees as upon a spread glove. He had learned to count on that blanket. As a boy, he had sought five as a sign, a symbol of guidance. As a man, no less. Sometimes he mocked himself, denying it, while at the same moment seeking some configuration of stars or holes in the wall or trees growing in a meadow which fit his predetermined pattern. Five, done always the same way, one-two, one-two-three. Tip-tap, tip-tap-tap. If this pattern was then followed by another tip-tap, it was a signal of the most urgent kind, seven syllabled, tokening his name. He had learned that sept meant seven in some old language. Fives and sevens were his signposts, his omens, his prayers for protection.

He had never told anyone about this. Even to himself, it sounded silly, babyish, an attempt to attribute order in a world where there was little enough. Septemius had been reared to the belief there was no order, even when there seemed to be.

He had been the only child in the troupe. There had been Bowough, his father, and Genettia, his mama. There had been Old Brack and Old Brick —Bowough's parents—and Aunt Ambioise, Uncle Chapper, Cousin Bysell, as well as Aunt Netta, who was not really an aunt at all, and her sons and daughters, five of them, all grown up. All of them were animal trainers or magicians or acrobats or knife throwers or whatever else they chose to be at the time. All of them were very strong-willed. No two of them agreed about anything.

The earliest memory Septemius had of this peculiarity of the Troupe Bird had been the matter of the dishes. He could not have been more than five or six, just learning to help with campish chores. Mama had set him on a stool at the tailgate of the wagon with a towel in his hands as she washed the plates and handed them to him. Old Brick had come in and moved the stool to the other side, saying something about fools and mountebanks washing from right to left when every reasonable person knew it was done from left to right. Then Papa had said either way was wrong, that dishes were to be soaked in the soapy water then rinsed all at once with boiling water. Then someone, Mama probably, though it might have been Aunt

Ambioise, had screamed a name at him, and they were off, seething like a pot on the fire, with Septemius huddled down upon the stool as each of them boiled up at him at intervals, "Isn't that so, boy? Isn't that so?"

That was the first time he remembered, but after that, he remembered little else. Everything Septemius tried to do partook of the same quality of uncertainty. Whether it was feeding donkeys or training dogs or hauling water from the stream; whether it was driving the wagon or washing his own socks. If Mama did it, everyone let her alone. If Papa did it, no one said anything. Any adult member of the troupe could do what he or she chose with no more than a few carping remarks from observers. If Septemius did it, everyone in camp insisted on showing him how, none of them agreeing, each of them claiming to have the correct and only acceptable way, and the whole troupe demanding he openly approve of one or the other. "Isn't that right, Septemius? Isn't that right?" If he seemed to lean one way or the other, there were tears and protestations. The wonder was that anything got done at all and that he was not torn into pieces.

Septemius came to think of himself as a clot of flotsam on a restless channel full of sucks and eddies, each as unforeseeable and reasonless as the next. After a time, he learned simply to float on this turbulent flow of demands, sometimes touching this shore or that, not fighting them as he was wrenched away and twirled around and dipped and sucked at before being thrust toward another bank or tree or bed of reeds. He did not learn this, however, until after Octobra came, and she came too late to save him.

He had been about ten. Just outside Abbyville, a tall, wordless man had brought a little girl to their wagons and had delivered her to Genettia with a note. The girl was Octobra. The child of an old friend. Parentless now, and homeless unless Genettia would take her in. Of course Genettia did take her in. The troupe took her in, called her Octobra Bird. Another child for them to badger.

And they tried. They caught her up in their net of confusion and demanded of her, too. "Isn't that right, Octy? Don't you agree with me?"

She never answered. Never seemed to notice. Melted away from them like snow. After a time, they stopped, as though they stopped seeing she was there. Not Septemius, of course. From the moment she arrived, she with her bottomless eyes and hair like sunset, he never lost sight of her for an instant.

He remembered lying face to face with her in the back of a painted wagon, the moon falling in slender arrows through the shuttered window, touching fingertips. Thumb to thumb, finger to finger, pubescent children making magic.

"Don't ever change," he had begged her. "Don't ever let them catch you. Without you, I'd go crazy. Don't ever change, Octy."

"I never will," she had promised him, pressing her fingers five times against his own to signify an oath. His adopted sister. His lover. The only steady shore in a sea of molten disorder. And in the end, she, too. . . .

He had never learned what solid ground was like.

It hadn't been only the chaos of the conflicting emotional demands on him but the rootlessness of constant travel as well. Nothing to hold to. No one to cling to. As time went by, various of them left the troupe or died, but those who were left had gone on badgering him until the very end. Even when Bowough and Aunt Ambioise had been the only ones left, they had still kept him in the unquiet middle of things, "Isn't that right, Septemius? Don't you agree with me? Tell him he's crazy, Septemius."

Only now that Old Bowough was the last had the appeals for his approval stopped. Now his approval didn't seem to matter anymore.

Septemius had learned to navigate the inconstant sea of his life by intuition and indirection. By signs and omens. By never saying either yes or no. He still avoided definite answers to anything. Even though Women's Country now sometimes seemed very solid to him, with observable permanencies about it, he still stayed alert, sensing hidden currents, a fluid flow, with trickery and deceit swimming beneath the surface. If he settled, begged admission, would everything stay the way he thought it was? Or would it change, suddenly, leaving him awash, circling once more, like a chip in a gutter.

Until this very hour, it had seemed wisest not to take the chance, wisest to use charm and evasion whenever permanence was suggested, keeping free, just in case. It had seemed foolish to attempt assurances. "By five," he had always told himself. "Don't you fall for their blandishments, Septemius!"

He drove the wagon down from the market to the warren of alleys which extended eastward from the plaza, toward the hostel he remembered, built around an extensive yard, with capacious stables for the animals. He drove silently, scratching at his cheek where the drying ink made a small itch, lost in old memories.

"She was very distressed about something," Kostia said. "Tonia and I both felt it."

"Who, girlies?" He had lost track of the immediate past. Who? Not his sister, not Mama or Grandma? No. "The medic back there? Now what could a pretty woman of that age have to be distressed about. What is she, twenty? Twenty-two?"

"That, about," Kostia affirmed. "There is a man in her mind, Septemius. A warrior."

"Oh, by the Lady of the Cities. Is she worried he will not keep an assignation, perhaps?" Septemius knew it was more than that. He merely wanted his own perceptions confirmed.

"More than that," said Kostia. "Something interesting, Septemius. Something very interesting. All complex and knotted together, like some tapestry where the pictures are only half drawn, yet. . . ."

He gave her a quizzical look but did not pursue the matter. Kostia and Tonia found many things interesting, and they would undoubtedly enlighten him if the time proved propitious. As for him, he spent a good deal of time forcing himself not to think of them as if they were Octobra, come back to him again, never mind they were as like her as twins. They were, he reminded himself, themselves. He prayed he had built a strong enough island for them that they could live on or around it, never feeling like flotsam, driven by unknown eddies. If so, he had done all he could expect of himself. All Octy could have asked of him if she had lived long enough to ask.

At the hostel he obtained stable space for the donkeys as well as two adjoining rooms for his family, paying for a week in advance because he knew this made it less likely they would have someone else quartered with them when the city began to get crowded. The dogs, after a spell of freedom to sniff and pee, came pattering after them as they carried their gear upstairs, or at least that part of it which was irreplaceable and light enough to carry. Women's Country was notable for honesty, but at carnival time there were others about who had been reared in other systems of ethics.

The rooms were on the second floor, one of them at the corner of the hostel overlooking the street. It had a warm stove, two narrow beds, and a wide, lamp-lit table. Septemius grunted as he dropped his bag on the table, taking possession of it. Old Bowough fell onto the nearest bed with a sigh and was asleep within moments, a white dog on each side. Septemius stood looking down at him, his face drawn into vertical grooves, like the wall of a gully. "It gets harder on him all the time," he said to no one in particular.

"We should settle," said Tonia. "The medic girl at the quarantine house was right, Septemius." She lit a candle and wandered through the connecting door, approving the cleanliness behind it, the wood-paneled walls, the wide, quilted bed, the swept hearth before the tile stove in which a small fire was already alight. The other three dogs, they gray ones, were circling the hearth, their black ears and muzzles seeking appropriate smells, fuzzy tails cocked high over their rumps as they tried to agree on space and precedence.

Kostia jounced the bed once or twice, then moved to hang her clothing in the armoire, taking, by habit, the left-hand drawer and set of hooks. "We should settle down."

"Would you settle?" he asked from the doorway, examining the room for himself, seeing to the lock on the shutters, the bolt on the door, eyes glittering like so many shards of cutting glass, sharp as bright needles, wet from unshed tears. Memory did this to him, sometimes. "Would you?"

"Perhaps not yet," Kostia laughed. "Though we would if Grandpa Bowough needed." She took the candle and went to the door, drifting along the hall to locate the sanitary arrangements—individual little rooms with composting toilets of the variety used in many of the Women's Cities —and the shower room with its capacious and well-stoked boiler. She drifted back, well pleased. The facilities were as clean and well kept as the rooms.

"We could have a little house in the itinerants' quarter, outside the walls," Septemius mused, "for the old one and me. You would be accepted within the walls, no doubt. Their own citizens attend school when they are much older than you. You could go to the schools of Women's Country. There is no doubt work you could do."

"Perhaps not quite yet," Tonia said again, with good cheer. "Remember, Uncle, you are a historian by profession. There are still things we need to know about the lands outside the walls."

It was a device of theirs, this assignment of profession to him who had none except mountebank and traveler. His nieces made him over in their heads, dressing him up in scholar's robes, like the women at the academy in Abbyville, calling him a historian when he was only a wanderer who had seen what there was left of the world. And he had seen it all, many times over. The towering forests of the northwest, green with ferns and dripping with fog, misty and marvelous as a perilous faery-land; the rock-shattered coasts with the waves coming in during storm; the farmlands of the interior, hills or plain, with the surrounding fields laid out square-cornered and full of root crops or grain or flax fields so blue they seemed a reflection of the sky. And the cities strung all through there, Women's Country cities. As alike as one dog to another and as different as one dog from another. This place, Marthatown, now, it had its own flavor, partly sea-mist, partly smoke from the ovens where the cured fish hung, partly sheep manure and wool and rawhides—its own particular smell which set it apart from the other cities.

But it was not unlike the others. They all had warehouses where the food from the communal fields and flocks was stored and from which those stores were allotted, so much to each family, so much to the garrison, so much to trade with other towns. In Marthatown they stored wool and hides, grain and dried fish and some root crops. In Susantown they stored apples and smoked meat, flax fiber and linseed oil. Up at Tabithatown they stored dried mushrooms and cut lumber. The town always smelled of sawdust and pitch and rang with the scream of the saw at the watermill. All of them had a market section full of little shops and booths. They all had craftsmen's alleys where the weavers and quilt makers and candle makers and seamsters lived; every city had its candle shops and herb shops and scrap reclamation centers and streets lined with square, courtyarded houses where grandmothers lived with their daughters and granddaughters and baby boys and servitors.

All the cities had a Council Hall where the medical officers worked and the scarce commodities were allocated—drugs and glass, raw and worked metal. They all had plazas with gates that led out to the garrison ground. They all had streets where the provisioners of the garrison worked, and they all had carnivals, though not all at once.

"We did well in Mollyburg," he said, apropos of nothing. "We could live out the winter on what we made there. I think the people here would give us a license for temporary residence."

"Grandpa Bowough would probably like that," said Kostia, clicking her thumbnail across her teeth. "He's been very tired lately."

"Shall I see if we can rent a small house in Wandertown? Hoboville? Journeyburg?"

"Let's think on it," Tonia said. "For a day or two."

Conversing with Kostia and Tonia was like conversing with one person. They picked up each other's words, leaving off in midsentence to have the other complete the sense of it. One would ask and the other comment. If one closed one's eyes, it would be impossible to know there were two. So now Septemius Bird nodded at both, willing to wait a few days before making the decision. Things would come as they would, decide or no. Even the towns agreed on that. One said, "Woman proposes, the Lady disposes," another said, "The one sure part of every plan is that it will be set awry."

"When we were here last, you told us, did you not," said Kostia, "that Marthatown was the first town of Women's Country."

Septemius nodded, trying to remember when they had been here last. Four years ago, at least. Typical of himself, he did not say "Yes," but, "So it is believed in all Women's Country. Marthatown begat Susantown, and Susantown begat Melissaville, and so on and so on. Though I believe, personally, that Annville was there before the convulsions along with its power plant and most of its factories."

"Why do they split off? I should think life would be easier if the cities were larger."

Septemius shook his head, gesturing a great wide motion to include the surrounding fields and sea. "Food, fuel, and trade goods, nieces. They grow what they can within an hour or so's travel of the town. They cut wood within the day's travel, too. All the women come behind the walls at night, for fear of bandits. Though the warriors have scoured the land over and over again between wars, there are enough bandits left over—or perhaps they are new ones—to make a nasty slaughter. Some may be foolhardy, but as for me, I prefer being behind walls at night, and I suppose the women are no more fool than I."

"How many of them are there, Uncle? In Marthatown?" asked Tonia.

"Some fourteen or fifteen thousand, perhaps. Many of them are children, and there must be two or three thousand servitors."

"And in the garrison?"

"Four thousand, I should say, including the boys. There were more when I was here last, but their latest war killed six or seven hundred of them. It is middling in size as garrisons go."

"And when their croplands are stretched so far they cannot get behind the walls at night, they will set up a new town?" Tonia asked.

Kostia shook her head. "I should think the woodlands limit them more than croplands do. Crops grow every year, but it takes time to grow trees, and they must have wood to heat their houses."

"There was a time people heated with electricity," Septemius said. "My own grandmother told me. Now there is only one place in all Women's County to make electricity, and they use it all up on making glass and medicine and one thing and another." He sighed, thinking of the wonders which once had been made with electricity. Septemius was a great one for wonders. "They're prolific in Women's Country," he went on. "Scarce a woman among them has fewer than three or four. When they have expanded as far as they can, they must set up a new town. I saw it done, once, far northwest of here, in the forest country. Women and warriors marching out to set up a new wall and a new garrison."

"There is still space then?"

"They're pushing at the desolations. Some of the new towns are close to the edge. There is much empty land, true, but little of it is good for farming."

"We came through a stretch of that," Kostia nodded. "As we came north to the road from Susantown. All brush and gray trees and land the color of a donkey's hide."

"They'll have trouble finding more space very soon, I should say." He returned to his own room, settling down before the table to spread his journals out and his day's notes, preparing to enter the one in the other. Behind him a sigh.

"Septemius?"

"Father?"

"That was a kind young woman at the quarantine."

"She certainly seemed to be."

"She said I was to have eggs."

"I seem to remember her mentioning eggs."

"And cream. I'd like a nog, Septemius. Could I have a nog?"

"And what is a nog, Father?"

"Oh, before your time, Septemius. The yolk and white of egg whipped up, separately, you understand, and then the yolk mixed with sugar and cream and flavoring and oh, brandy, I think, Septemius, then the white folded in to make it fluffy and soft, like a coverlet."

"That would blanket your gullet right enough, old man."

"Most gently, Septemius. Most gently."

There was no further word, merely a quiet snore from the corner, a bubbling rasp beneath it, like something sharp sawing away at the old man's lungs. Septemius pulled one of the books toward him and opened it, searching for the word *nog,* which led him to *eggnog,* which led in turn to searches for the words *brandy* and *rum.* Lost arts, whatever they had been. Gone, along with nutmeg and cloves. Along with pepper and turmeric. All the spices were merely words now. Chocolate was a word. And coffee. Septemius would have given his back teeth for a taste of some of those. Now how had the old man known about brandy? From his own father, perhaps, or his grandfather? Brandy led to *distilled* which led to *still,* and he perused the picture of the device with interest. If they had wine, why could they not have brandy?

Likely because the women's Councils forbade it, and Septemius Bird was too old a coyote to arbitrarily question the actions of a Council. Likely they had reason. Septemius had seen men drunk enough on mild beer, and if brandy were stronger than that. . . .

He began to enter today's notes in his journal, making a marginal notation about *nog.* The old dictionary, among his most prized possessions, had said it could be flavored with wine. Wine was available. If the cream and eggs were truly forthcoming, tomorrow he would make a *nog* for old Bowough.

REHEARSAL:

CASSANDRA   I have seen the land laid waste and burned with brands, and
desolation bled from fiery wombs.

POLYXENA   So have we all, sister. Look around you. See what is lost. You
may weep for the walls of Troy, I would weep for the dances I will not
step again. You weep for the dead. I would weep for honey cakes. You
may weep for Troy's children slain. I would weep for the wine spilt from
the jar, never drunk. Oh, I pray the Gods had given me power to strike
those warriors down! I would have used it well!

HECUBA   Polyxena! How can you? To shed your tears for cakes!

POLYXENA   What tears? The dead have no tears. I can not weep. If I
could cry, then I would cry for cakes—sweet cakes, gay dances, and
bright flowing wine. You grieve your losses and I'll grieve for mine.

CASSANDRA   (*Shaking her head and crying*) No one hears me! I have seen
blood, not this blood here today. I have seen bodies broken, but not
these! I see a desolation yet to come! In time! At the end of time.

145

ANDROMACHE   She's at it still, I see.

HECUBA   *(Motioning toward her head)* Poor thing.

CASSANDRA   *(Weeping)* Apollo said you wouldn't believe me.

HECUBA   *(Cuddling her)* Well old Apollo can go scratch himself, of course
Mother believes her little girl. . . .

17

SEPTEMIUS AND HIS PEOPLE were in the street when they saw
Stavia next, she coming along the walk with her marketing bag on her
shoulder, brow furrowed with concentration over something or other, so
she almost bumped them before hearing Kostia and Tonia's greeting, a
vibrating "hello, Medic," which hung on the air like the reverberation of a
gong.

"Ahum," she said conversationally, trying to remember where she was
and who these were. "The magician's troupe!"

"Madam," he bowed. Bowough nodded, mistily, hardly seeing her.
Though he had slept very well, it was one of his mostly off days, one of
those times when he wandered more in memory than in reality. Kostia and
Tonia reached out to take her hands, ostentatiously not seeing the warning
glance Septemius gave them. Kostia and Tonia always found out about
people. Septemius did not know how they did it, but it seemed to work
better when they touched the person in question.

"Stavia," they murmured in unison. "Well met."

She remembered them now, and, remembering also she had not told them her name, she regarded them with some alarm.

"May we return your courtesy of last evening by offering you a cup of tea?" Septemius, his usual florid manner banked like coals kept for the morning, hands fingertipped together.

They were on the sidewalk before a teahouse, just half a block from the Well of Surcease. Inside the windows they could see women and servitors gathered around the tables. There were a few itinerants there as well. "Why not?" She smiled. "Actually, I was coming to see you later today. I have some medicine for your father."

"Medicine?" They went into the teahouse and took a table near the wall. The servitor set five cups before them, tip-tap, tip-tap-tap, and Septemius smiled. An omen.

"Something that may help his chest. I'd forgotten we had it, until Morgot—the chief medical officer, my mother—reminded me. An oil made from the eucalyptus trees, useful in boiling water to make a cleansing vapor for the lungs." Stavia nodded her thanks to the servitor who brought them the steaming pot of the tea she had suggested. "Put a kettle of it on the stove in your room and pull his bed nearby, with a sheet over his head and the spout so he breathes it."

"Ah. Something you have not used yourself?"

Stavia flushed. "As you can no doubt tell, Septemius Bird, I am newly assigned to the quarantine house, my first medical post after seven years at the medical academy in Abbyville and a two-year internship there. The quarantine house is a junior post, given to new graduates. I am told that in preconvulsion times, medical training would begin where I have already left off, and the extent of my ignorance oppresses me. So, we do what we can with herbary since our production of pharmaceuticals is so limited, but Abbyville taught little herbary and I have still very much to learn. Learning must come bit by piece, catch as catch can, on the job. If this stuff does your father good, I will be glad to learn of that."

"I see." And he did see. Ah, these girls of Women's Country! Often given their first postings at seventeen or eighteen, expected to continue their education meantime as well as having babies every year or two. And, of course, to take part in the arts and crafts of the community. "Your science is medicine then."

"Yes. My art is drama, and my craft is gardening. Is your work a science, a craft, or an art, Septemius Bird?"

"My magic? If it has no science, it fails, Stavia. If it has no craft, it bores, and if it has no art, it offends."

"You are fortunate to wrap everything up so neatly," she said, a pinch at the corner of her lips betraying that she meant more than the words said.

"It must be difficult to be a talented young woman in Women's Country," he replied sympathetically. "I don't know how you can get everything done."

"Oh, if it were only just Women's Country," she burst out, then, horrified, put her fingers over her mouth. "Forgive me."

"Would it help to talk about it?" he asked.

"To an intinerant?" she blurted, surprise making her sound rude, even to herself. "Why would I?"

"Because," said Kostia placidly, "he is a very wise man . . .

"An outsider," said Tonia, "who has been everywhere there is to be . . .

"And has seen bits and pieces of everything . . .

"And can be objective about things . . .

"Which others of us are unlikely to be."

Stavia flushed. "I didn't mean to be offensive."

"I took no offense," Septemius assured her. "My nieces are partly right. I make no claim to wisdom, but I am a fairly objective observer. My family has been in this business for generations, you know? Even before the convulsion, I am told, there were Birds traveling the wider world with carnivals and traveling shows. It came down at last to Bowough Bird and his Dancing Dogs, my father's troupe of mountebanks, and then to me. I am the last male of my line, but these two vixens may continue the work of the Birds, if they choose." He was talking to cover the awkwardness, to get a distance from it. He should not have suggested she confide in him. It had slipped out from habit, from being so much with Kostia and Tonia, from trying so hard to remedy the confusion of chaotic generations with a sneaky discipline of his own. Musing on this, he went on, "If there is art in our work, it comes from understanding human nature. There are several old words which were once used to describe what we magicians do. One such is legerdemain, meaning 'deftness of hand,' but the hand can only misdirect when the mind understands what is to be misdirected. . . ." He allowed his voice to trail off into his teacup.

Old Bowough said, "This is a very good tea, miss. Kind of you to suggest it."

"Kind of you to have offered it," said Stavia, giving him a close look. The tea had brought color to his face and a gleam into his eyes. He was older than she had first thought. Ninety, perhaps. A great age for a man in these times, but she did not like the crepitant sound of his breathing. Septemius himself looked well into his fifties, while yet hale and athletic in all his movements. The mother of the girls must have been younger. She became conscious that she was staring. "I was searching for a family resemblance," she murmured self-consciously. "But the girls do not look much like you, Septemius."

He shook his head. "Their mother was not related to me genetically. She was a foster child of my mother, the daughter of an old friend. We were reared together. She married late—you are aware of the custom of marriage?—and died in childbirth."

"Yes, I know of the custom," she said, being careful not to show on her face what she thought of such barbarism. "You should have brought her into a city of Women's Country," Stavia murmured, aghast at the thought of any woman dying in childbirth.

"Uncle Septemius would have done," said Kostia.

"He has high regard for your sciences," said Tonia.

"But our father would not permit it."

"More fool your father, then," Stavia blurted, outraged.

There was a strained silence, broken, strangely, by Bowough. "He was a fool, yes. We have a saying, we travelers: 'For a man's business, go to your troupe leader; for a woman's business, go to Women's Country. For a fool's business, go to the warriors.'"

"He was a warrior?" Stavia's face was suddenly ashen.

Septemius nodded. "Much decorated. Much honored. Retired from active duty, so he said, by his garrison. Allowed to travel as he would."

"I have heard that warriors sometimes decide to travel," she said with an oddly furtive expression, "but they are never retired from active duty. Not even when they go to the Old Warriors' Home."

"So I believe," said Septemius. "So you know. So these nieces of mine believe and know. But my sister—well, she wished not to believe it." Seeing the look in Stavia's eyes, he changed the subject. His nieces had been right. There was something eating away at this girl, and it was more than mere romantic wondering whether some young warrior would keep an assignation.

On the following day, they moved the wagon to the edge of the plaza and set up the stage under the interested gaze of the plaza guards, afterward returning to the hostel with the donkeys. Bowough seemed to be profiting from the rest, and from the extra food. The cook at the hostel had made him his nog, and he had profited from that, as well. They had all tasted it. To Septemius it seemed that something was lacking. It was what was always lacking, some mysterious dimension of taste which his imagination could evoke but which his tongue or nose could not fulfill, some spice or flavoring that did not exist any longer—vanilla in this case, said the cook, referring to her ancient recipe books. "A tropical product, no doubt," she commented, sighing. "We have nothing from the tropics in this age."

"Are all the tropics then dead?" Kostia asked, intrigued by Septemius's annoyance concerning the lack of spices and flavorings.

"Who knows?" Septemius replied, moderating his tone somewhat. "We cannot reach them, if they are yet alive, nor they us. Who knows if they are dead or not?"

"Have you ever tried to go there?" Tonia asked. "Has anyone?"

"To go south? I remember a journey, long ago, when I was young. The troupe went along the coast, circling inland to avoid the gray devastations which lie along the water. My grandfather had heard rumors of inhabited lands there that are not part of Women's Country." He said nothing more about the inhabited lands. They were not lands he would want to travel to again, nor would he want Kostia or Tonia to come there, even in flight for their lives. "Our southernmost journey ended in a place where three monstrous devastations came together, a plain of glass beside a huge bay with twisted remnants of great bridges thrust up out of the stone. We could find no way around it."

"Perhaps farther inland," murmured Kostia.

"Perhaps if you had had a ship," murmured Tonia.

"Well, perhaps," he said. "That was a quarter century ago. It is getting time for Women's Country to send their exploration teams. They do it every now and then, to see what has changed in that time. Perhaps they will find spices again."

"We do not miss them," said Kostia.

"Because we have never had them," said Tonia. "They are little things, after all."

"A little spice may outweigh whole generations of potatoes," growled Septemius Bird. "None of us have ever had them. But some of us would weep over not having them just the same."

Rehearsal:

Cassandra *(Weeping)* Apollo said you wouldn't believe me.

Hecuba *(Cuddling her)* Well, old Apollo can go scratch himself, of course Mother believes her little girl. . . .

Andromache Cassandra. What difference does it make if they believe? Perhaps it's better not if all you see is blood and splintered bone.

Cassandra You don't understand.

Andromache Well, stop crying and explain it to me.

Cassandra I am Cassandra! To be Cassandra is to prophesy! But if they will not hear me when I speak, then who am I but some poor fleshless thing, a ghost that no one sees!

Hecuba Shh, daughter. You are no less than Andromache. You are no less than I. At least the name 'Cassandra' is your own! One time I had the name of Priam's Queen. Once Priam died there was no Priam's Queen. Andromache was known as Hector's wife, but when her Hector died, whose wife was she? Our place was here at many-towered Troy, and when it fell, what place was ours to hold? All that we were, we were by others' strength; all that we had, we had because of place. Place gone, strength gone, we are nothing today. At least the name Cassandra means yourself.

CASSANDRA *(Thoughtful)* There are worse things than having one's own name.

19

AFTER HER nine-year's absence at the academy at Abbyville, Stavia had found it difficult to come back to her old place in Morgot's house and think of it as home. The idea of "home" summoned up the room she had occupied at the academy, scarcely more than a closet and yet a place very much her own, with only her own things about her. Once back at Marthatown, returned to the room she had occupied since she was a child, she saw it with new eyes as a cluttered, other-peopled space with too many things in it. Bits and pieces left over from herself as she had once been. Perhaps things left over from other parts of herself which she was not sure existed any longer or things other people had thrust upon her. Books she no longer wanted. Toys she could not remember ever having played with. Ornaments and oddities that had always been there, that could have belonged to unknown people long ago. After a week or two of discomfort, during which she circled, constantly, like a dog trying to find a place to lie down, she asked the new servitor who had taken Donal's place to find some crates and bring them to her room.

"Is this enough?" he asked, thrusting a stack of empty boxes through the door. "I figured a lot of small ones would be easier to move than one big one, and the storeroom had lots of them."

"I don't know," she said rather helplessly, looking at the room around her. "What was your name, again?"

"Corrig. I came back through the gate with Habby."

"Did you?! I left for the academy shortly before that." She turned to give him a closer look. Tall, slender, yet roped with long muscles; strange, light eyes almost like Morgot's and her own; thick, dark hair drawn up into the servitor's plait except for locks around his forehead and ears which had escaped; a wide, mobile mouth with the upper lip turned under so that one could only see the fullness of the lower one; huge, beautifully shaped hands. And a deep, vibrant voice which had already brought him to the attention of the choir director. "Where did you go? You didn't come here right away. Donal was still here when I left."

"I was assigned to the house of a Council member who lived over by the eastern gate. I was there three years, until she died. Donal was being sent out of the city for some special kind of education, and I felt I already knew the family because of Habby, so I asked to be assigned here in Donal's place. It seems like home to me now. Does it seem strange to you?"

"There have been changes in Marthatown," she said musingly. "People grown up. People gone. Commander Sandom dead."

Corrig nodded. "With his Vice-Commander and several other officers, too."

"Several of the older Councilwomen are gone."

"I meant did the house seem strange?"

"It's odd, but the house is wholly familiar. It's only this room that seems weird to me. Foreign, somehow. Do you like the place? Have you been contented?"

"Your mother is strong and interesting. I enjoy Joshua enormously. The fraternity is supportive and understanding. Your sister was very upset at my coming. I think Morgot asked her to leave soon after that."

"Yes," mused Stavia. "I heard."

Stavia had run into Myra one day at the grain warehouse.

"I didn't know you were back," Myra said rather coldly. "From your education."

"Oh yes. Some time ago as a matter of fact."

"I must say you've changed." Myra gave her a critical look. "You're a raving beauty. I suppose you know that."

"No. I didn't. Don't. Nice of you to say so, though. How do you like where you're living?"

"Better than Morgot's," Myra smirked unpleasantly. "No servitors, for one thing. Aunt Margaret is much more sympathetic than Morgot ever was. She understands how a person feels."

"Well, I'm sure Morgot tried. . . ."

"She did not. I'll never forgive her for sending me away. Never!"

"But you didn't like living with servitors, Myra."

"Morgot had her choice who she got rid of," she said darkly. "And she chose to keep him and let me go. Never mind her. I've got my own life to live. Marcus has gone down to the garrison. Baby Barten goes soon, and there'll be only one left at home. . . ."

"You'll have others."

"No. I can't. I had an infection after the last one. The doctors had to do a hysterectomy. . . ."

"I'm sorry," Stavia mumbled. "Truly sorry."

"I'm not. Three boys is enough. Even Morgot says that. Now I can do what I want to do."

Stavia did not ask what that was. The wounded expression on Myra's face reminded her too vividly of someone else. She did not want to know what it was that Myra wanted to do. She found it hard to think of Myra as a sister anymore.

Now Stavia asked Corrig, "Does Myra ever come here to visit?"

"Once in a while, yes. Once in a while she leaves the little boys here while she's doing something else. I like that, even though they're spoiled rotten."

"Poor Myra."

"Myra should have been born a man. She could have joined the garrison and been perfectly happy. She's like the warriors, living from carnival to carnival, game to game, and war to war, telling herself romances about honor and glory in between. She even watches the sports events from the top of the wall, cheering the century that Barten belonged to."

Stavia nodded, saddened. "I don't know what she'll do when all the boys have gone down to the garrison."

Corrig put his hand upon her shoulder, all at once in a familiar way as though he had known her forever. "She'll dance. I gather it's all she's ever wanted to do."

It was true. Dance was the only thing Myra truly loved, and if she had been allowed to do nothing but dance, she might have done a lot with it. The ordinances required that she have a science and a craft to bring along with it, however, and Myra had found nothing to suit her even though Morgot had done everything she could to help her. Pottery, carpentry, gardening, construction skills, Myra had rejected them all along with medicine and engineering and chemistry. She had wanted to do nothing but dance. But what good would a woman be who could only dance? When she was old, what use would she be? So, Myra wove and halfheartedly studied mathematics, enough of the one to make simple blankets and enough of the other to teach kindergarten girls, hating every minute that she could not spend in the practice room.

Perhaps if they had let her dance only, she would not have turned to Barten as she had. So hungrily. As though she were nothing on her own. As though she needed him to be anything. Perhaps if the ordinances had not been so demanding, Myra could have been happier with herself. It wasn't the first time Stavia had had these thoughts.

"Myra is so—oh, I don't know. She got all those ideas in her head from Barten. It's strange how they stuck. Morgot and I always hoped she'd outgrow them, but she hasn't. Is she still being rude to Joshua? And to you?"

He shrugged, smiling. "We ignore her, Stavia, which offends her sense of importance. Now, are there enough crates here for what you want?"

"We'll see," she said, moving speculatively along the line of shelves as she began to take things down: an ugly ornament made of seashells; a bear, badly carved out of a chunk of driftwood; alphabet books printed on heavy cloth and obviously used by generations of children. Wordlessly, he opened the sack of straw he had brought along and began to pack the things she gave him.

An hour later, the room was much emptier. She had kept a few books, the mirror in its carved frame, the fantastic dolls Joshua had whittled for her when she was little and the cushions Morgot had worked in multicolored wool. Everything else had been cleared away to leave the essentials of bed and chair, bare shelves, and a work table as naked as the walls.

"Better," Corrig approved. "It looks like there's room for you in here now."

She gave him a surprised look, meeting his eyes, letting her own drop away. My, oh my, but this was an unexpected man, here in her own house. Imagine his having read her need and intention so easily. She cleared her throat. "All the outgrown clothes and shoes should be taken to the salvage house," she instructed, as Corrig nodded, making a note on the crate. "The quilt makers will find some good material there. The books should go over to the main library. Most of them are in pretty good shape, and we haven't so many that any should be wasted. The other odds and ends should probably go down in Morgot's storage room. Label the boxes so she can tell what's in there. Some of this stuff must have belonged to women in the Rentes or Thalia lines, Morgot's mother's or sister's or even her grandmother's, and Morgot may want them someday."

"Except for the curtains, it looks a bit like a cell in the quarantine house." He pointed at a strangely shaped stone she had left on the window-sill. "What's that?"

"A boy gave it to me," she said, picking it up, running her fingers over and through it, smooth and weird, outside becoming inside, inside becoming outside. The shape had a name which she could not, at that moment, remember. Chernon had found it on the beach and had given it to her during a carnival. It was the only thing he had ever given her.

"Are you going to leave the room as bare as this?" he asked in an interested tone.

"Not exactly," she said, dragging in another crate which had been standing in the hallway. "I brought some things from Abbyville. Can you open this box for me?"

The crate contained more books, bulkier and more densely printed than the ones she had put aside, a thickly woven blanket in sunset stripes of blue and mauve and salmon, two paintings of misty landscapes with ethereal towers looming in the remote distance, and several bowls with a deep, sky-blue glaze on terra-cotta clay.

"The blanket was a gift from a colleague at the academy. Her craft is weaving. The bowls are from another friend. They've both gone back to Melissaville. I'll miss them." She arranged the blanket as a bedcover, then set the bowls on the shelves and hung the paintings on the hooks where others had hung before. "The paintings were done by my surgical instruc-tor." When she was through, the room seemed lit with color, though still restfully bare.

Corrig took a wad of straw to dust off the stove. "If you'd like, I'll dye some willow that color," he said, pointing at the deep blue glaze on the bowls, "and weave you a wood basket."

"Do you do that? Weave baskets?"

"I taught myself while I was with the garrison. There's a great deal of waste time in garrison. Every minute not spent on drill or housekeeping is supposed to be spent on sports, but some of the men take up one craft or another, just to keep their hands busy. Carving's a favorite, of course. The barracks are one solid mass of carved beams and carved wall panels and gables and doorposts. Basket making's acceptable, and weaving. I've seen some decent pots made by old warriors, too."

She sat on the edge of her bed and waved him toward the only chair in the room. There was something she was trying desperately to understand. "Corrig, tell me about garrison life."

He, with an odd smile, seated himself, folded his great, graceful hands in his lap, and complied.

CHERNON, now a member of the twenty-four century and within a few months of the twenty-five, learned of Stavia's return from Michael, though when Beneda repeated the news he pretended he hadn't known about it. He had made it a habit to come to the armory roof to meet his sister every week or so. It would have been considered undignified for a mother to come, but warrior mythology expected sisters to be almost as sentimental as lovers were, and it was a way of keeping in touch.

"How long has she been back?" he asked, trying to sound offhand about it and dismayed by his inability to do so.

"You still care about her!" exclaimed Beneda.

"I was always fond of Stavia," he returned stiffly. "I never made any secret of it."

"You certainly didn't act fond, telling her to leave you alone just because she didn't want to break the ordinances anymore."

"It was best for both of us. She was only a child."

"She was twelve, almost thirteen, and when she went away, she was still mourning over you. She's twenty-two now. Do you want to see her?"

He didn't answer this. He didn't know what his own feelings were in the matter, but he was quite sure what Michael wanted. Michael wanted Chernon to meet with Stavia. Michael wanted it very much. Commander Sandom had been dead for over a year. He and his cronies had been coming back from the Gypsy camp when they had been set upon by bandits. Only one of the armorers had escaped to tell the story. Michael was now Commander.

Michael was now Commander and his agents said the other nearby garrisons would either take over their own cities when Marthatown garrison did or turn a blind eye on the whole thing. This year could possibly have the best harvest anyone could remember. The warehouses would be bulging.

"Things," Michael had said, "seem to be coming together! We may be taking over very soon. So what happened with that letter you wrote to Stavia, Chernon? Did she ever answer?"

Almost a year before, Michael had instructed Chernon to send a letter to Stavia in Abbyville, a letter begging her to go away with him when she returned to Marthatown, not away to the Gypsy camps but on some romantic, memorable escapade. She had never answered—a fact which Chernon had found embarrassing.

"Not so irresistible as we thought he was, our Chernon," Stephon had chuckled.

After that Chernon had decided for a time that he hated her, but hating her had seemed pointless since she was not there to notice it. He didn't even hate Habby anymore, and he never thought of his mother at all. Time had passed, and the trumpets and drums no longer evoked quite the emotional frenzy they had done at the ceremonial when he was fifteen. Though his heart still surged when the centuries were paraded, and though he still carried Casimur's ribbons, plus the ribbons of another dead warrior from the fifty-five—honors he would carry for fifteen years until they were retired to the repository with the rest of the seventy century—the splendor of it was spasmodic, brief orgasms of emotion separated by long periods of calm, almost of depression, relieved only when Michael or Stephon or Patras involved him in the plans for the upcoming rebellion.

Michael said three other garrisons planned to move against their cities at the same time—Mollyburg, Peggytown, and Agathaville, away in the east—though he didn't sound as sure about the details as Chernon thought he should.

"We'll attack after harvest," Michael said. "Late fall or early winter. After the grain is in the warehouses, and the year's fish have been smoked and put away, and the fall trading is over. That way, there'll be stocks of everything right here, where they're needed. Once we decide to move, we'll only need a few days to let the other garrisons know and get our own men worked up and properly enthusiastic! One night the women will all go to bed in their own houses, and when they wake up, every house will have a warrior in it!"

"Then there's no real point in my getting Stavia away before then," Chernon had objected.

"Every point, boy. We still don't know about that weapon Besset claims he saw. Stavia's older now. She's more likely to know the women's secrets now than when she was a kid."

"If there are any secrets, I'll bet nobody but the Council knows them," Chernon had sulked. "Besides, we haven't heard a word about that weapon since. I think Besset was drunk."

"Possibly. Just in case, however, we've got men courting every Councilwoman young enough to be courted," snorted Patras, "and every Councilwoman's daughter as well. Don't worry about Besset. Your assignment is that girl."

It was true that Chernon still dreamed of journeying, of adventure and heroism. However, she had not answered his letter. . . .

Now he said to Beneda, "I don't know whether I want to see Stavia," knowing perfectly well he would have to see her, but toying with the illusion of independent decision. "Maybe I want to see her. I'll let you know next time."

"Make up your mind," said Beneda. "There's some talk she's going to go away again soon as part of an exploration team."

He was down the stairs and halfway across the parade ground before the sense of her words hit him. Beneda said there was talk of Stavia's going away as part of an exploration team.

His mouth dropped open and he stopped in his tracks. *Exploration team!* He had heard it without understanding it. Perhaps *this* was her response to his letter! But, if so, why hadn't she told him? Cursing, Chernon scuffed his foot in the dust for a moment, making angular, angry incisions in the soil before turning back the way he had come. Beneda was still standing on the wall, staring down at him. He crossed the parade ground and climbed the stairs again to stand beneath her, hands on hips.

"Tell her I want to see her," he said. "Tell her to come to the hole in the wall. This afternoon, if she can. Tomorrow at sunset otherwise."

He didn't wait for Beneda's joshing answer. When he had been fifteen, it hadn't seemed too undignified. Now that he was twenty-four, her little-girl teasing grated on him. Down in the parade ground once more, he walked across it to the northernmost barracks building, then onto the shady lawn of officers' country. Michael saw him coming and came out onto the porch, a mug of beer in his hand.

"I just found out," Chernon said. "Stavia may be going out with an exploration team."

"Well, well, well," said Michael, leaning back through the door to speak to someone. "Did you hear?"

"I heard." Stephon came out onto the porch, shutting the door carefully behind him. Through the crack between door and jamb, Chernon saw two strange men sitting at their ease inside. More conspirators from other garrisons. "I'd forgotten it was time for exploring again."

"They seldom find anything," commented Michael. "Last time all they came back with was two new kinds of bugs and some plant they could make tea from."

"She could be planning to let me go along," Chernon said doubtfully. "Maybe."

"Be damn sure she does, grub," Stephon directed. "Make yourself irresistible."

"You still think this is the year?"

"Looks like it, boy. Some of the other garrisons are just as sure as we are. But we've still got this one little, tiny, nagging bother. That weapon old Besset thinks he saw. We've been after him, now and then. He still swears to it. Not that it matters greatly. Just that it could make trouble for us."

"I know."

"Well, don't know it out loud," instructed Michael.

"Not if you don't want to vanish, just like your old buddy Vinsas did."

Chernon, not liking this thought, changed the subject. "You really think Stavia knows anything?"

Michael raised his eyes in Stephon's direction, as though in question.

Stephon frowned, then nodded. "We've got a man courting Stavia's sister, Myra. Myra moved out of Morgot's house a few years back, but she still spends a lot of time bitching about Morgot and her sister. How Stavia was always the favorite, how Stavia always got to do the interesting things. One of the interesting things Stavia got to do was to go on a trip over toward Susantown with Morgot, and that servitor of theirs."

"So?"

"Well, the interesting thing is that Myra can remember exactly when it was. It was just before the Susantown war. Before Barten died. Myra remembers that. She's not ever going to forget that. It was about the same time that Besset and his bunch saw that wagon coming back from Susantown."

Chernon cast back in memory. "You think Stavia was in that wagon? You think she knows what happened?"

Stephon shrugged. "Likely. Could be."

"I think Besset made it up. Or he was so drunk he didn't see anything."

Michael smiled a particularly menacing smile. "Pretend you believe it, boy. Give her a try. Make yourself pretty and try it."

There was no point in making himself pretty to talk to Stavia through a hole in the wall, so he didn't bother. The big old tree at the edge of the parade ground still hid the hole through the wall. It also hid the oiled paper package Chernon had kept hidden there for four years. A book he had stolen from Beneda.

He worked his way into the hollow behind the tree where he could hear if anyone came into the room at the other end of the hole. The package was there, in a crevice in the bark of the tree. One red book. Even though he knew every word of it by heart, even though he found nothing in it of significance, having it was forbidden. The significance lay there, in his defiance of rules, in his contempt for the ordinances. He was not allowed to read, but he would read!

The pages opened almost of themselves. "Migratory societies, the Laplanders." Sticking his fingers in his ears to shut out the distant sound of cheering from the game fields, Chernon began his ritual of contempt for the ordinances of the women.

———

STAVIA CAME AGAIN to treat old Bowough Bird, and then yet again, but his condition did not improve. If anything, it worsened. His breathing grew more labored. His mind seemed to wander. Septemius fretted, jittering, gnawing his knuckles and engaging in frivolous, irrelevant expostulation whenever Stavia appeared.

"Hush, man," she said, drawing him into the adjacent room where the three gray dogs curled on the hearth, raising their black muzzled heads to stare at her, licking their black lips with quick, pink tongues. "You're worried about him. How old is he, really?"

"Old," admitted Septemius. "You know as much as I how old. He doesn't remember now, if he ever did. I know how old I am, which is sixty something, but how old he was when I was born, I haven't the least idea."

"Somewhere between eighty and ninety, at least," she mused. "I've got some stuff that will clear up his lungs, pretty surely, but it's not on the open list for use on itinerants. Which means, Septemius Bird, that I must either withhold it from you or steal it from Women's Country."

He fumbled for words, not sure what she was leading up to, though certain she was leading up to something.

"She wants something," Kostia had said an evening or two before. "That medic wants something from us, Septemius."

"Something she can't get otherwise," Tonia confirmed. "She's a very troubled woman. Something strange going on there."

"One thing," Kostia murmured, "she doesn't have a child yet, and her in her twenties."

"Some of them don't," Septemius objected.

"A few don't," Tonia agreed. "But damn few."

"She's been several years at the medical academy at Abbyville. She hasn't had time for childbearing," Septemius objected.

"Even so. There's more to it than that, Septemius. She wants something from us. We can both feel it."

How many times had she run into them on the street? How many times had she invited them to tea? How many times had she questioned them?

"Tell me about your travels south of here," she had demanded.

"Not a pleasant subject," Septemius answered, trying to be politely evasive.

"I have a reason for asking," she had said, as politely but firmly. "I'd appreciate it."

Shrugging, he had complied. "South of here are two smallish Women's Country towns, both fairly new, one on either side of the desolation, Emmaburg near the shore, and Peggytown inland. Neither are in any way remarkable. You probably know more about them than I do."

"South of that?"

"I have heard there is a fortified sheep camp south of Emmaburg now. It was not there when I traveled south, once, long, long ago when I was a child. As I remember, one comes first to broken country and badlands, a fantasy land of pillars and carved towers, of wind that sings endlessly among the stones. This is a stretch of this, a mile or so wide, then there is a range of mountains that runs all along on the east and south. If one keeps along the coast, one comes to several great desolations. But if one goes along the foot of the mountains—which one would not normally do, because the land is very broken and full of little canyons—one finds people living back in the valleys, just the way they did before the time of convulsion, I suppose."

"Unfriendly, from your tone."

"Stavia, the population there is sparse, suspicious, and unprofitable. The river courses tend to be more like canyons than valleys, with precipitous sides of unscalable stone and no way in or out except at the northern ends or deep to the south where the watercourses fall from the heights. We didn't go into the valleys by choice. We were driven to take shelter in one of those sheer-sided traps because of a great storm. It was many years ago. At the time we had my cousin Hepwell's acrobatic troupe traveling with us, and there were a dozen strong men along. If it hadn't been for that, we'd be there still, for the natives were strangely disinclined to let us be on our way. However, most of their older menfolk—their elders—were off at some kind of religious observance, so they hadn't quite the force they needed to keep us against our will."

"Fertile land, though?"

"Amazingly, from what I remember. Flat fields along the streams. Green pastures. Wooded along the streams, but not many trees elsewhere except upon the heights. They had sheep and goats and chickens, I remember that, and gardens. Fruit trees. I don't remember it well, but then it was thirty or forty years ago, Medic. I can't say I remember it rightly."

"But sparsely populated?"

"As I remember, yes," he had said, wondering both at her persistence and at her dissatisfied expression.

"She wants something from us," Kostia commented later.

"Something to do with the places we've been," said Tonia. "Or places you've been, Uncle Septemius, before we were born."

So now he asked Stavia, "What is it you want, Medic? Is there a price for the medicine for old Bowough? Something you've a mind to trade?"

She shook her head. "I don't know at this moment, Septemius Bird. Perhaps. But, whatever I might want, I wouldn't like to say I'd trade the

old man's life for it. More, I'd like you to think that if I do you a favor now
—and not an inconsiderable one, either—you might do me one later on."

"So?"

"We'll talk more on it again." He could not pin her down. She was as
slippery as one of those rare fishes that were showing up every now and
then in the streams. However, that evening she appeared with a syringe
and gave old Bowough an injection which seemed, by morning, to have
made his breathing easier.

WHEREVER SHE HAPPENED to be working during the day, Stavia took her
breakfast and supper at home with her family, Morgot, Joshua, Corrig, and
very occasionally Myra and her little boy. The toddler was usually enough
distraction to keep Myra from being rude to the servitors or from recalling
old injustices and dissatisfactions.

Tonight there was, however, a new source for annoyance.

"I don't see why it is that Stavia gets to do everything," Myra complained, wiping applesauce from the little boy's chin. "As she does,
Morgot. You do have two daughters, you know?"

"I did not nominate Stavia for the exploration team," Morgot responded
calmly. "The nomination came about largely because she is medically
trained."

"Surely they're not sending just people who are medically trained!"

"No, of course not. But they aren't sending any mothers of young children, either. They prefer young people, without children, trained in some
useful field. There won't be a lot of people involved. The team going south
will be only two people, one woman, one servitor, and a pack animal or
two. It will have two purposes; finding botanical specimens and spying out
the land south of there which we have reason to believe is occupied. We
don't want a large team that might stir up a lot of attention or trouble, just a
small one that can sneak along the hills and find out how far north the
strangers come."

"There are other teams!"

"Yes. Two middle-sized teams will go east and north, the eastern one to
see whether the desolations there have shrunk any and the northern one to
explore the limits of the ice. Those, too, will search for botanical or zoolog-
ical specimens of interest. One quite sizable group will go westward by
boat and then down the shore to see whether there is any sign of useful life.
All will be strenuous trips, not something you would much enjoy, Myra."

"I would simply enjoy getting out of the house and away from babies for
a while!"

Morgot shook her head and remained silent. Myra had chosen to have three children, Marcus first, then baby Barten when Marcus was five, now this one. All suggestions that she might take the babies to the crèche for a few hours a day in order to focus on her education met with tears and stubborn incomprehension. "They're all boys! I'll only have them for a little while, Morgot! I want to spend all the time with them I can!" Only to exclaim in the next moment that she would lose her mind if she didn't get away from children! Motherhood had not changed Myra appreciably. Well, the second boy would be going to his warrior father within the month.

"Have you decided whether you will accept the nomination?" Morgot asked Stavia. "You've been very dilatory about making a decision."

Stavia, who had already planned to go, who was considering breaking the ordinances once more but putting it off as long as possible, tried to avoid making a commitment just yet. "Thinking, Morgot. You said the trip might take as much as six months. That's a chunk out of my life right now."

"It has compensations. My mother went on one, thirty years ago it would be. Her art was poetry, and she wrote some very good things afterward."

"My art is drama, Morgot. What do you expect me to do? Do mimes about it?"

"No, I thought more about your science and your craft, quite frankly. They're short of medical attention at the sheep camp. And you have more information about botanical things than most of our candidates. Collecting plant specimens isn't exactly a mindless activity."

Stavia fell silent, embarrassed. She hadn't even thought about it. "Hasn't a systematic collection been done?"

"No, only sporadic bits and pieces. A new grain crop or root crop could more than pay for your time. Or some new herb with therapeutic properties. Even some new garden flower would be welcome."

"Well"—she fell silent, thinking—thinking, as it happened, about a good deal more than the periodic journey of exploration—"since you recommend it so highly, Morgot. If they will assign me to the southern exploration, I'll go. After four years in close quarters in Abbyville, I'd rather not join any of the larger groups."

"IT'S AS I SAID in my letter," Chernon muttered through the hole in the wall. If she only knew what it had cost him to get that letter secretly delivered! "I've looked it up in the ordinances. There's nothing there about taking a leave of absence."

"I know that's what you said in your letter," said Stavia, patiently. "But there's nothing that says you can." She shut her eyes, listening to his voice, summoning up the Chernon of ten, eleven years ago. He sounded different, looked different, but that boy was still there, inside somewhere.

"There's nothing that says I can't," he persisted, unable to tell her about Michael's assurances. "If I just go, when I return I'll tell them I thought it was permitted. They'll yell at me. They might even discipline me, but they won't execute me for cowardice or anything because I'm not yet twenty-five. In a few months, I will be twenty-five; then it will be too late."

Stavia shrugged, unobserved, torn between argument and good sense. She had read his eloquent letter over a dozen times with different responses each time, responses varying from anger to pain, from laughter to longing. He had begged her to go away with him, just for a time. Begged her for something to remember in later years, something to make his life seem worthwhile. "Why do you want to do this, Chernon? You chose to stay with the warriors. If you're not contented, you could still come back through the Women's Gate. Why this!"

"Because going off on a trip with you this way isn't dishonorable," he said, half angrily. "They may call it foolish or wrongheaded or even child-ish, but they won't call it dishonorable."

"It matters that much to you what they call it?"

He chose not to answer the question. "Stavia, you owe me this." Another of Michael's ploys, perhaps it would work.

"I?"

"If you hadn't given me books, you wouldn't have started my mind boiling about things. I'm not satisfied with the only choice I had. I want to know more about life than that. You got me started on this, and it's up to you to let me satisfy it honorably!"

She mumbled something he could not hear.

"What did you say?"

"I said, what makes you think this will satisfy it?"

"You have my word."

She did not really believe his word. "Why drag me into it?"

Stung, Chernon said something that was almost the truth. He had seen Stavia on the wall with Beneda. She had been a pretty little girl when he had seen her last. Now she was a stunningly beautiful woman, and the thought of having her to himself stirred him in ways he had not known were possible. "Because I can't give you up. Because I can't forget you. Because I love you," he cried. "The whole point is to be with you, Stavia. Isn't it? Isn't that what we both want?" In the instant he said it, he knew this is what he should have said all along.

She sat stunned. Was it what they both wanted? If he had asked that question years ago, before she left for the academy, she would have said yes. Yes, at once and without thinking about it. She had ached for him, longed for him. Even now, parts of her went all wet-crotched at his words.

She could feel some inner part of her breaking loose, panting against the thick wall between them, ready to dig through it to him, some frantic bitch part with hard little tits and all four feet flailing. "Yes, I want to be with you, Chernon," she said, being honest, almost apalled at the longing in her words. "At least part of me does. But I think I could wait until carnival."

"No!" It was almost a shout. "Not carnival. Not orgy time, with everybody in the city falling in and out of bed with everyone else. . . ."

She was angered at this. "I didn't say I intended to fall in and out of bed with anyone!"

"I don't mean that! I mean I don't want what I feel for you to be . . ." he reached for loftier words than those that first came to mind. "I don't want it to be part of some general . . . some ritual indulgence. I don't want us surrounded by a thousand drunken warriors and giggling women. I want it to be . . . something finer than that." These were Michael's words, and Stephon's, cynically composed and now offered out of desperation.

"Simeles," she said, her lips quirking, half amused.

"What?"

"Your warrior poet Simeles. Doesn't he have a song about being in paradise alone with the beloved."

Silence. Then, "I don't care if it's paradise or not. But I do want it alone, with you. Without some assignation mistress tapping on the door saying time's up."

She couldn't answer him. The observer Stavia was paralyzed, bitten by some viper of indecision, unable to say yes, no, perhaps later, let's think about it. She didn't want this conspiracy, this subterfuge. She felt herself standing aside, felt that other Stavia taking over. The actor. The actor who made it all seem so easy, right or wrong, so easy.

"All right," she said, not letting herself feel anything except that this was Chernon, and that her heart turned over when he spoke to her. She had wakened in the night sometimes in Abbyville, dreaming of him. He was not merely another warrior, not one like Barten, not a loudmouthed braggart. He was Chernon. Beneda's own brother. He was in her marrow. She had tried exorcising him, and she couldn't.

"I'll be leaving shortly for an exploration trip to the south," she told him. "I'll arrange for you to have transportation to a place well south of Emmaburg, and I'll meet you there. You'll have to cover your brand and shave off your beard—not that you've got much—and plait your hair like a servitor."

Stubborn silence. "I don't want to. . . ."

The actor Stavia could deal easily with this. "Chernon, it's that or nothing. I can't be seen wandering around with a warrior down there. You may not be seen, but if you are, so far as anyone knows you'll be a servitor named Brand from Agathaville. No one knows you, you don't know anyone. I'm the only team member from Marthatown, so there won't be any questions asked. Unless we're alone, you'll take orders from me, politely. You'll call me ma'am."

"What about the real servitor, the one who was supposed to go with you?"

"I'll have to figure something out. Some way to send a message telling him not to come. You and I will do the exploration I would have done anyhow, then we'll return separately. I'll come back to the town; you'll come back to the garrison. According to you, that will satisfy you." Her voice gave no indication of the turmoil inside. She wondered at that, finding it inconceivable that she could sound so cool and feel so hot.

He had to agree to what she wanted. His visions of quest had always concluded with his return to the garrison, his return to honor and glory. That there was something unsatisfying about the plan Stavia laid forth, he perceived only dimly without in any way recognizing what it was. If he had been capable of analyzing it, he would have been astonished and shocked to find he did not really like the idea of returning.

"I'VE BROUGHT MORE MEDICINE for Bowough." She was drinking tea in the room Septemius shared with old Bowough. "That's the favor I'm doing you. As for the favor you can do for me. . . ."

"Yes," he asked, interested, conscious of the quiet in the next room where Kostia and Tonia were hanging upon every word.

"I want you to travel south from here, as soon as Bowough is able to travel. Once you're a mile or so outside the city, someone will hail you by name and ask for a ride farther south. I hope you'll be sympathetic to that request."

"Where might this person want to go?"

"South. Almost to the sheep camp you mentioned to me before. There should be no trouble taking him there. The roads that far should be quite safe. It would be very helpful to me."

Septemius didn't say anything.

Tonia, who had overheard this with a pang of apprehension, came in from the neighboring room. "Do you believe in fortune-telling?" she asked Stavia.

Stavia looked up abstractedly. "Fortune-telling?"

"Kostia and I are very good at it. We'd like to lay the cards for you, Stavia. Would you mind?"

Stavia gave Septemius a suspicious look.

"Let them," he sighed. "They are good at it, and it won't hurt anything."

Bonelessly, Tonia sank to the rug before the stove, pulling over the bench that stood beside it. The deck was in her right hand, and she passed it to Kostia who shuffled the cards before passing them on to Stavia. "Shuffle," she said. "Any way you like."

Almost angrily, Stavia shuffled the deck, knocking it into alignment with a sharp tap. "So?"

"Cut it."

She split the deck into two.

"Now choose which half is your future, Stavia."

Still angrily, she tapped the left-hand stack. Tonia picked it up, turning it in her hands.

"How old were you when your trouble began?"

"What trouble?!" Stavia demanded, now really angry.

"Oh shhh," urged Septemius. "Let us have no hypocrisy. You are in some difficulty, Stavia, or you would not be asking our help. How old were you when it began?"

"Ten," she said sulkily. "I was ten."

Tonia counted cards onto the bench, turning the tenth one faceup. A black-cloaked woman spred her cape across the chill stars on a field of snow. "The Winter Queen," she said. "Lady of Darkness. Bringer of cold. Nothing will grow begun under this sign, Stavia. How old were you when he sent you away?"

"How did you know he sent me away?"

"We know things. How old?"

"Thirteen."

Tonia counted three more cards, turning the third one faceup. A man in motley leaned against a tree, his head turned to one side. On the back of his head, he wore a mask so that a face looked in each direction. One side of the tree was alight with blossoms. On the other, snow covered the branches. "The Spring Magician," she said. "The two-faced one. Who says yes and means no, or t'other way round. How old are you now, Stavia?"

"Twenty-two."

Nine more cards. And the one turned faceup was of a warrior standing over his recumbent foe, leaning on the sword that had killed him. "The Autumn Warrior," Kostia said. "Death, Stavia. Not for you, though. For someone else."

"What are you telling me?" she demanded.

It was Septemius who answered. "This journey will not profit you,

Stavia. It will be full of lies or misdirection. And it may be full of death, as well."

"But not mine?"

"Not necessarily. Someone's."

"You're refusing to do me the favor I've asked?"

He shook his head, sighing. "No. Why should I? What business is it of mine? Are we family that I should thrust unwanted advice upon you? Are we friends? I am only an intinerant performer, an oldish sort of man, with an ancient father and two weird nieces, four donkeys, and five dancing dogs. If I am reluctant, it is only out of memory of my sister. She, also, heard the blandishments of a warrior. . . ."

"She went with him," said Kostia.

"She got pregnant with us," said Tonia.

"He was typical of his class. He wanted sons. And then, when he saw we were girls, he left her," said Kostia.

"And she died," said Septemius. "I always thought it was from a broken heart, though the midwife said not."

"Unlikely," Stavia commented, drily. "Broken hearts are more common in romances than in life." She had told herself this for several years and had not yet had any evidence to the contrary.

"And yet you are listening to the blandishments of a warrior. . . ."

"Not exactly," she said, trying for the hundredth time to explain herself to herself. "And not blandishments. I made someone unhappy, without meaning to. Perhaps I tried to buy his affection by doing something I knew was wrong. Even if I was not wholly responsible for his unhappiness, I still contributed to his misery. It's my responsibility. I must do whatever I can to set it right. Perhaps to give him something else in place of what I cannot give him. Even though it may cost me a great deal."

Septemius said nothing more, although he shook his head at intervals all through the evening and spent the night turning restlessly upon his bed.

STAVIA SLEPT SOUNDLY, though not so soundly she did not hear her door open in the night and the voice that spoke her name.

"What is it?" she asked him, not yet quite awake.

"A dream I had," Corrig said, sounding disturbed. "A dream I had, Stavia."

"Is it part of normal servitor's behavior, Corrig, to walk about the house involving the women of it in his dreams?"

"It was about you. No, it was partly about you."

"Ah."

"Don't do it. Whatever it is you plan, don't do it. There's trouble there. Danger and pain. I've seen it."

"You sound like Kostia and Tonia, Corrig! Do you see the Winter Queen in my future? Or the Spring Magician or the Autumn Warrior?"

"I see pain."

"Again, I ask, is this normal servitor behavior?" She was awake enough now to be slightly angry, though she was more interested than annoyed.

"It is . . . it is servitor behavior to see things, Stavia. I have seen, and I've told you. Don't do it." He turned and left the room.

She lay back on her pillow, thinking she might have dreamed the exchange. She didn't believe him, any more than she had believed the twins. Perhaps it was better not to believe.

"Perhaps it's better not, if all you see is blood and splintered bone," she quoted to herself, her mind running on among the lines of the old play.

How strange of him to have come to her in that way. Evidently he shared Joshua's strange gift. "It is servitor behavior to see things." To see what things, in what way? Was he claiming some extrasensory ability? Clairvoyance, perhaps?

She snorted. It was a subject for fairy tales. Still, he had sounded very sure.

Suddenly she remembered the trip made years ago with Morgot and Joshua. Joshua, too, had been very sure. Afterward, Stavia had wondered who he was, what he was.

Now she wondered about Corrig, again taking a line from the play to ask herself, "But if they do not hear him when he speaks . . . then who is he?"

20

FROM THE DEEP-WELL, which was at the bend of the valley, Thirdwife Susannah Brome could look both south, to the slope where Elder Jepson had established his family manor, and northeast, to the grassy hill where Elder Brome's wife-houses surrounded the Father-house in a similar clutter of sun-faded wood. Susannah's own house was there, a small, peak-roofed cottage half hidden behind the hay barn. The dozen or so other elders were established farther south or over the passes in the adjacent valleys of the Holyland, and except in times when All Father punished his sons with desperate drought, their womenfolk did not frequent the deep-well. The shallower wells of the upper valley were quite sufficient at most times, and the bachelors made do with water from the intermittent spring behind their quarters down at the mouth of the valley, toward the north. Thus there was little excuse for Susannah to linger at the deep-well, since the best she might hope for would be a quick word exchanged with one of Elder Jepson's wives, and them so terrified of him they hardly dared say boo.

"Mama?" whispered Chastity, tugging at Susannah's sleeve. "Oughtn't we be getting back? Papa'll be angry with us if we're not diligent."

"I thought we might see Charity or Hope," Susannah said, honestly enough. "Charity wasn't feeling well last time I saw her, and I wanted to inquire after her health." Which was a perfectly sound reason for lingering, having no lack of diligence connected with it. Womenfolk were expected to take care of one another since no man would lower himself to do it, and it was well recognized that some women, Susannah among them, had more nursing skills than others.

"Besides," Susannah went on, "you know Papa pays very little attention to us when we're unclean."

"He still watches," the girl said, her voice shaking a little. "He might not say anything today, but he will later."

Poor chick, Susannah thought, reaching out to pat her daughter's face after a quick look to see no one was watching this unseemly expression of affection. Chastity took everything so hard, so much to heart, as though any amount of diligence or duty could prevent Father bellowing at her if he felt like it.

"We'll get ourselves back, then," she said, raising the yoke and settling it onto her shoulder pads. Chastity raised her own yoke and buckets, only slightly smaller. At thirteen, she was just come to her uncleanliness and not yet to her full growth. No use praying to All Father to let her have a year or two yet before setting her to breed. Someone would be after Chastity before fall, even though it was hard on the very young ones, and there was just no excuse for it but black lechery, no matter what the elders said about it. She remembered her own initiation at fourteen, and no one could convince her that all that puffing and grunting had been divine duty. She'd never seen a man doing his duty so outlandish pleased with himself and so eager to do it all over again.

Susannah led the way back up the hill, taking each turn of the path in one surge of effort, then resting before going on to the next. While it was meritorious of her to have had three sons before spawning a girl, she sometimes wished for the help another older daughter or two might have given. Preferably plain ones, with crooked teeth and crossed eyes, like Charity's daughter Perseverance. Maybe they'd let Perseverance stay home and be a help to her mother until they both died of old age. At least none of the elders had made an offer for her yet.

Chastity, though—well, Chastity Brome wouldn't last long. That pale yellow hair and that sweet skin, like a baby's bottom, drew men's eyes like honey drew ants. If Elder Jepson didn't make her his sixth, then Elder Demoin, over in the next valley, would make her his fourth. And meantime all the boys down in the bachelor's house would keep on hiding behind the bushes to have a look at her, every time she went down for water.

The worst thing about it, if Chastity went to Elder Jepson, likely she'd be a widow before she got much older. He was only seventy, but he was a tottery seventy. If Chastity had a baby by the time he died or soon after, they'd send her back to Susannah to live out her life, and there were worse things than that. If she hadn't been pregnant or had miscarried, though, they'd say there hadn't been any true marriage and give her to some boy just starting out who'd work her to death before she was thirty. None of the old men would take her after another had had her. It was like the older a man was, the surer he had to be that a woman couldn't compare him to anybody else.

"There's Elder Jepson," Chastity whispered from behind Susannah on the trail. "Just coming out of Papa's house."

"Take no notice," Susannah murmured. "Remember we're unclean and just keep on right into our own place." She trudged up the last few feet of the trail to the path which led to her own wife-house, its tiny, sun-grayed porch facing away from Papa Brome's house with Chastity's faded red kerchief hanging on the latch to show there was a menstruating woman in the place. They set the buckets on the splintery floor of the porch, wiped their feet on the braided rag mat, then took the buckets into the kitchen to fill the reservoir. Early that morning, Susannah had made the daily extra trip needed to bring water to Papa's house. First trip in the morning was always to Papa's house for Papa and the little boys who studied there.

A thready wail greeted them as they poured the last bucket into the wooden tank, turning into a full-fledged howl as Baby heard their voices.

"Faith?" Susannah called, then again. At her third call, an answering voice came from outside.

"Mama. Sorry. I had to go to the privy, and I thought Baby was asleep." The eight-year-old who came in had obviously been crying and her bodice was soaked and smelly.

"Honey, love. What is it?"

"Elder Jepson told me I was a slovenly slut."

"You're not. Of course you're not. Why would he say such a thing."

"Baby threw up all over me. I wouldn't have gone out where he could see me if I'd known he was there, but I didn't."

"Shh, now. Never mind. You didn't talk back, did you?"

The little girl only wept, shaking her head.

"Chastity, you help her clean herself up. I'll see to Baby." She took off her headscarf, scratched her bald scalp where the hair was beginning to sprout in an itchy silver brush after the last shaving, then moved into the room where Baby slept.

Baby had no name. If he lived to be a year old, Papa would give him a name. If he lived to be six, he would go over to Papa's house every day and attend school. Boys had to be able to read and write so they could discuss the Scriptures. They had to be able to calculate some, as well, in order to be efficient shepherds for All Father, who wouldn't tolerate lack of discipline or diligence. Until the first year was over, however, babies were only "Baby." "Sweet'ums," sometimes. "Honey child." Not when Papa could hear, of course. Baby names and displays of affection were trivial things, unworthy of All Father. Anytime during the first year, a baby could disappear, just up and vanish, with nobody knowing a thing about it. That's what had happened to the two girl babies between Faith and Baby. Most always, it happened to girls. Hardly ever to boys unless there was something wrong with them. Though, sometimes, an Elder might sell a boy baby to some other Elder desperate for sons. Not that anybody would ever let on.

Susannah unbuttoned her bodice and put Baby to the breast. She wouldn't wean him until she had to. As long as he wasn't weaned, she wouldn't get her uncleanliness, and as long as she didn't get it, she probably wouldn't get pregnant. She couldn't bear to be pregnant again right away. Maybe not ever. She'd been pregnant almost all the time since she was fourteen. She'd had eleven pregnancies and had six living children, not counting the two girls who had just disappeared. If she got pregnant again, she thought she'd kill herself. It would be easier to die than to go through it again. Let Papa get some more babies on the sister wives, Matilda and Cheerfulness and Plentitude and Rejoice. No, Rejoice was too old, but Plentitude only had one at home, almost five years old. Let her have another one. Cheerfulness only had four and she hadn't had one for three years. Let her. Let Matilda get up out of that bed she'd been in for five years and get pregnant. Having three dead babies and coughing up blood now and then wasn't any reason to escape duty. If that's all it took, maybe Susannah could manage to cough up some, too.

Susannah's eyes filled. All these thoughts were wicked and uncharitable and unkind, and she knew they were but she kept having them anyhow. Everything was just so . . . so wearisome. It got so you looked forward to your daughter being unclean just so Papa wouldn't come to the house. And Chastity had long, unclean times, too. Seven or eight days, sometimes. It meant Papa had to leave Susannah alone for a whole week at a time. She wished it was forever. Let him take some other girl, a really young one, and spend all his time and energy on her. Susannah was too old for this. She was almost thirty—much, much too old for this.

INSIDE THE FATHER-HOUSE, Elder Resolution Brome sat in his comfortable chair before the window, drinking hot mint tea one of the grannies had prepared, and considering Elder Jepson's offer for Chastity. Elder Jepson had a son, Thankful, almost thirty-five now, who'd cleared himself around forty acres in the third valley over, dug him a well, built him a fairly good log house, accumulated about a hundred sheep, and was ready to enter into the community of Elders and Fathers—if he could find a woman. Women were a might sparse right now, and Elder Brome silently brought to the attention of All Father the shortsightedness of Elders who had killed off all their infant daughters twelve and thirteen years ago. There'd been a drought then, which was all the excuse anyone needed, but where did they think their sons were going to get wives twelve and fifteen years later if they put all the infant girls out on the side of the mountain for the coyotes?

Resolution considered his own foresight in keeping Chastity. Of course, he'd laid out a few infant girls himself—later, after Faith was named—but he'd had good reason. Susannah hadn't seemed to be able to produce anything but girls there for a while. She'd had Chastity, then two girls stillborn, then Faith. Resolution had decided to leave Faith alone, even though she was a sickly little thing, because a woman needed a baby in the house to keep her working right. Then Susannah'd had two more weakling girls born early before she finally came out with Baby. And the worst of it was, if he wanted Susannah to be around to raise Baby, he'd better leave her alone. Everybody knew when they started dropping babies before their time, it wouldn't be long before the mama dropped, too, if you didn't leave her alone. Ewe sheep and women, both of 'em worked the same. And that was a pity because Susannah was the one it was easiest to do his duty with. She wasn't the best-looking, but there was something about her body just heated him right up. Something about the way she went all stiff and shivering under him made him just want to pound away at her.

Well, he'd have to do his duty on somebody else. Cheerfulness, maybe. There would be one good thing about giving Chastity to Elder Jepson for Thankful Jepson, because Elder Jepson had a thirteen-year-old girl named Perseverance he was willing to give in trade. Ugly little thing if you looked at her face, but Elder Jepson said he'd had a look at her through a hole in the bathhouse wall recently and she had a suitable body. Besides, if Resolution didn't want her himself, he could give her to one of his boys. Both Retribution and Vengeance were getting ready to settle down, though Retribution was oldest. Perseverance wouldn't be what Ret would pick for himself, but a man could always throw her nightgown up over her head.

Most women liked it better that way anyhow, not that you could say they liked it. Not if they were decent.

And not that he'd decided yet. Retribution was barely thirty-five. He could wait a while longer. But if Resolution Brome himself took another wife, he'd have to fix up that old wife-house that was half falling down where Resolution himself had been born, where his own mama had lived right up until she died. He hadn't put anybody in there since his own father had died and he had taken over the farm.

He wasn't sure he wanted anybody in Mama's house. Maybe he could lay off a wife. Send one back to her mother or over to the granny house. Retribution's ma, Plentitude, was no damn good for anything, maybe he could move her over to the granny house. Not that she was quite old enough to be a granny. Close to fifty, though. One boy born to her when she was still a girl and then nothing until that other one five years ago, which was his own damn fault for takin' too much of the sacrament at the observance. If he'd been sober he'd of known which wife-house he was headed into even if it was dark, and it sure wouldn't have been Plentitude, who always smelled like sour milk and something moldy and had a duty place like wet sandpaper. But if he did move her into the granny house and put Perseverance in her place, it might give some of the other Elders ideas. Pretty soon he could move Rejoice, though. She was a granny, sure enough. Every time he saw her he thought of the smell of chicken soup. Woman always smelled like chicken soup. Hadn't been a red scarf on her doorlatch for two years now, but it wasn't usual to move a woman out of her wife-house until her youngest was gone. Rejoice still had one girl at home. Modesty, ten years old.

Then there was Matilda. Thirty-two years old, three dead babies, and her lying there coughing blood and taking up space. Nicest-lookin' woman Resolution had ever seen, even now. Matilda was a Demoin. Maybe he'd do some sheep tradin' and send her back to the Demoins. No point keepin a wife who couldn't produce.

He counted on his fingers. Seven from Rejoice, all grown but one. Four from Cheerfulness, the oldest was only nine, and two from Plentitude. Six from Susannah, not counting the ones he'd disposed of. Nineteen, all together, fourteen of them boys. Could be that was just enough. . . .

Damn Susannah, anyhow, he told himself. Any other wife a man could do his duty on for most of a year if he was minded to without her getting pregnant. It was like she did it just to vex him.

AT THE BACHELOR HOUSE, Retribution Brome was sharpening a scythe and preaching sedition to his brothers.

"Well, I say they're not of a mind to let us have any wives at all, no matter how many acres we get cleared. You look at the home manor, now. You've got Susannah's two girls, Chastity's thirteen and Faith's eight, and I'll bet Chastity's spoken for already. Cheerfulness has a seven-year-old who looks all right, her other girl's a baby.

"That ten-year-old of old Rejoice's has sniffles and a squint. Meantime, there's only one of us Brome sons married off, and eight of us here in the bachelor house, and five more with their mamas. That's a total of thirteen boys left unmarried and only five girls to trade off. Now you can bet the Jepson manor is just about the same, and so is the Gavin manor, and the rest of 'em on up the valley. Every family has three or four girls and a dozen or more sons. Papa's getting on for seventy-five, and he won't last forever. And when he goes he'll leave Susannah, she's younger than me, and Cheerfulness, she's younger, and Matilda, she's younger, but they'll all of 'em be widows with kids, so nobody else can have 'em. What it amounts to is the Elders using up six or seven women apiece, some of 'em more than that, and killin' off baby girls whenever they care to, and the rest of us can go hang! There's about one girl for every four of us."

"What you goin' to do, Ret? Run off and join the devil women up north?"

"Figure I might catch one and bring her back."

"You think she'd stay? You're talkin' just plain silly."

"Figure if I break her leg, likely she'd stay." Retribution continued stroking the edge of the scythe with the stone, glaring across the room at his half brothers, Diligence and Vengeance, Rejoice's sons.

"Wouldn't be any good to you. Those are city females, Ret. Wouldn't know how to make a cheese, even."

"One thing she'd know how to do," he said darkly. "All she'd have to do about it is lie still."

"I don't know what you're in such a sweat about," Diligence observed. "Firstborn didn't get him a wife until last year and he was almost forty."

"And what did he get? Humility Gavin, from over the hill. She was half bald."

"She had to have her head shaved when she got married anyhow, Ret. What the hell difference did it make?"

"Big difference between a woman with her hair shaved off and a woman without any. Like she'll probably have half-bald kids, and Firstborn'll be walkin' around with his head down and these skin-headed kids trailin' after him."

"Way I hear it," Vengeance observed, "Elder Jepson's wants Chastity for Thankful, so he's goin' to trade Perseverance, and likely you'll get her."

"Perseverance, shit. Her eyes are so crossed you think she's lookin' past both sides of you!"

"What'll you care in the dark?"

"Same's I'd care about a bald wife. Makes it harder to do your duty, and besides, she'll have ugly kids. And if you've looked around some lately, you'll notice how many ugly kids there are. You notice that? You take a look at all the grannies and the old men. Not bad-lookin', most of 'em. A few ugly ones, but not many. Then you look at folks the age of Plentitude and Rejoice and younger, down to about our age. There's more ugly ones. Then you look at the young ones, the age of Chastity, and you'll see what I mean. Lots of babies bein' put away because they've got split lips or their feet are wrong, somehow. Lots of crossed eyes and crazy teeth and funny, squinty-up faces. Like something went wrong somewhere."

Vengeance got a peculiar look on his face, but he didn't say anything. What he was thinking was that Papa had married first when he was twenty-five years old. And Grandpapa had been less than that. Now here Firstborn was, almost forty, and Retribution was thirty-five, Vengeance himself was thirty-four, and the only females around were seven or eight years old!

"Not much point in you goin' off and catchin' one of those Women's Country females," he said with a deep and abiding anger. "Likely Papa would only take her away from you if you did."

AT THE WIFE-HOUSE of Rejoice Brome, Firstborn Brome, forty years of age, sat in the half dark of the kitchen talking with his fifty-five-year-old mother. His brothers, Vengeance, Diligence, Determination, and Preserved by the Lord were all down at the bachelor house. His sister, ten-year-old Modesty was carding wool in the shed out back. His other sister, Gratitude Brome, now thirty-two, had been married off at age fourteen to Elder Gavin, over the mountain, and her mother had not seen her for several years, though Firstborn had. He had ostensibly come, as was considered reasonable, to bring his mother what news there was about her daughter.

"She just had her twelfth," he told his mother. "Eight of 'em livin'. She said to tell you somethin' broke this time, but she's not too miserable over it. Said you'd know what she meant."

Rejoice nodded, making no comment. She thought she knew what Gratitude was trying to say. "Next time you see her," she murmured, "you might suggest she ask for your Aunt Susannah. Susannah's mama or grandma—I forget which it was—was caught out there in the outside and brought into the Holyland. She knew quite a bit about female kinds of things, and she taught Susannah."

"I didn't know that," Firstborn said in a tone of wonder. "Who caught her? Susannah's mama or grandma, I mean."

"I think it was Elder Demoin, when he was just a young man livin' in the bachelor house. Anyhow, it could be Elder Brome would let Susannah go do some nursin', if Elder Gavin would allow it. Only other woman I heard of with any healin' skill is clear over four valleys. She's a Simpson, I think. She'd be real old now."

"I'll tell Sister," he said, staring at the floor between his feet. "Mama . . . ?"

"Yes, Firstborn?"

"What I really did was I come to ask you about somethin'."

"I'm sure Papa could answer anythin' you want to know."

The middle-aged man flushed, red showing darkly at the edge of his beard. "Don' want to ask Papa. Want to ask you!"

"All right, son. Just so long's you remember I'm only a woman and don't know much about things." Rejoice kept her face calm and quiet, just as she always did. It was easiest just not to show anything, not to seem to want anything. Then, pretty soon, if you lived long enough, you got to be a granny and life got to be pretty good for a little while before it ended.

"I got me a wife," he said.

"I know you do, son. All your Aunts and me, we was at your marrying. You got Humility Gavin for a wife."

"She cries," he said. "She cries."

Rejoice thought this over very carefully. There was things a woman could say and there was things a woman couldn't say. Questions a woman couldn't ask. "She cry all the time, or just some time?"

"Some time." He flushed again.

She decided to risk it. "Like, when you got your duty to do?"

"Like then."

"She cry like . . . like's she's hurt?"

"Like that, yeah. She's got no business crying, and I chastised her for it, but it's like she can't help it, and it puts me off doin' what I got to do."

Rejoice sighed. Oh, she thought, I wish there was some female in heaven a woman could pray to. I wish there was somethin' a woman could look forward to. "I tell you what, son. You tell Humility to boil a fat chicken. Don't let her put any salt in, or anything but just the chicken. You have her skim off the fat and put it in a pot someplace cool. When you got to do your duty, you smear that fat all around the duty place, you know, and likely she won't get hurt so bad."

He thought for a moment. "Like a wagon axle, huh?"

Rejoice nodded, unable to trust the voice inside her which was screaming, "Yes, you stupid, cruel ramsheep of a man. Like a wagon axle, only you'd care more about the wagon." Instead, keeping her voice very quiet, she said, "You see, Humility's only fourteen years old. She's not quite grown yet. She's not . . . she's not really big enough yet."

"Well, that could be," he said. "But she's the only one I got."

"Well then, maybe you'd like to bring her down from your place to visit with your Aunt Susannah. Maybe she knows somethin' that could help some."

"I don't hold with visitin' around," he said stubbornly. "Women visitin' around breeds mischief. That's what the Elders always say. You womenfolk get together at Holydays and Thanksgivin' time and at birthin' time. And you sister-wives are all the time chatterin' about somethin'." Though he did not realize it, he sounded exactly like his father, even to the intonation of individual words.

"I just meant she might be lonesome," Rejoice offered. "Since she's got no sister-wives yet to be company with."

"That's woman's lot," he said indifferently. "Because she's the spout and wellspring of error and sin, that's woman's lot."

There was a short silence. "Have another piece of bread and preserves," said Rejoice. "The bees and the sugar beets both did real well last year. I made more preserves than I think we'll need. I'll send a jar home with you, for your . . . for Humility."

21

$\mathcal{S}$ EPTEMIUS BIRD sat at ease on the wagon seat, letting Chernon drive the donkeys, which by this, the fourth day of their travel, he was doing rather well. Old Bowough Bird lay on a mattress in the wagon behind them, Kostia and Tonia beside him, stubbornly present despite Septemius's repeated insistence that they remain in Marthatown. He had remembered his former trip to the south, and he had been of no mind to risk the twins even to what little he remembered of that place. Women had been in short supply, as he recalled. By now, if things had gone on as it seemed they would, the situation might be growing somewhat desperate. He had intended to say something of this to young Stavia, but had not had the opportunity. He was still debating whether to try and warn her through this callow youth at his side. Septemius was slightly ashamed of himself, but he could not bring himself to much like young Chernon, though the boy was polite enough, within his rather self-engrossed limits.

No, he decided, better to tell Stavia herself when they met. "Where will Stavia meet you?" he asked now, a question he realized came tardily. "You never said."

Chernon roused from his musing. "Oh, we've agreed on a signal. I'll drop off before you get to the camp. When you arrive, you tell her how far back you left me, and she'll be able to find me." Stavia had started on the trip days before Bowough Bird had been well enough to travel, and by the time Chernon arrived, she would already have spent some time in the fortified sheep camp toward which they were traveling. She had assured Chernon that she had put off the servitor who was to have been with her, and that she would be alone. What good to her a servitor might have been, Chernon could not imagine. It was widely supposed in the garrison that returnees through the gate were gelded by the women doctors, and Chernon more than half believed it. At least, they got no sons, for every boy in Women's Country came to a warrior father. Some said the servitors were used to beget girls, but Chernon doubted it. His unauthorized reading had taught him enough elementary biology to make him question that supposition.

Well, whatever use the servitors were, there wouldn't be one with Stavia.

As though reading his mind, the older man said, "She didn't travel alone down here, did she?"

"She told me she would be perfectly safe."

"And you accepted her assurances?"

"In Women's Country it is usual to do so," Chernon said, only slightly sarcastically.

"But she'll be at this sheep camp we're headed for?"

"That's what she planned."

Septemius fretted. He didn't like this, not any of it. If only the twins had consented to stay where they were. They could have lived a time in the itinerants' quarters outside the eastern wall and attended the Women's Country schools. The Councils of the various towns encouraged such participation on the part of female itinerants, and did not even mind if the women passed on their learning to itinerant menfolk, though they did not allow the copying of books. Nonetheless, the girls had insisted upon coming, and he would not risk them by staying near the badlands for any length of time.

"It may not be as safe as Stavia believed," he said at last. "When you are traveling together, take great care." He could not keep himself from sounding worried, at which the boy seemed to bridle, resenting it. They rode along for some time in virtual silence and increasing discomfort.

"Would you like us to tell your fortune, Chernon?" Kostia called. "Can we lay out the cards for you?"

"What cards are these?" he asked, drawn away from a continuing daydream in which he and Stavia were the central figures, glad of any excuse not to let Septemius's anxiety infect him with similar concerns. He had been uncomfortable since he left the garrison, but he did not really want to examine the causes of this vexing agitation. Thinking about it led him down roads he preferred not to travel. It had occurred to him, very briefly, that his manipulation of Stavia might be rather like things Barten used to do, but he had set the notion hastily aside as a fault which he could not possibly be guilty of. He was not tricking Stavia out of the city entirely for his own purposes; she had been going anyhow. He was not risking her life or health for his own gratification; he had no diseases, and had no intention of acquiring any. Michael had promised that when the time came that the warriors took over Marthatown, Stavia would belong to Chernon, if he still wanted her. Chernon supposed that he would still want her, and this assumption made his conscience clear. He was doing nothing, planning nothing which would not continue in the future time. In the end, she would be glad of it. Michael had assured him of that.

That nine tenths of his conscious thought was occupied with lustful anticipation, he did not deny, nor did he make any effort—once darkness came and the physical effects of his imaginings were not so obvious—to curb fantasies which were inventive, expectant, and extremely pleasurable. Oh yes, he wanted her, wanted her for himself, to himself, with no interruptions and no preoccupations. He could hardly wait until the miles had rolled away between here, where he was, and there, where it would all happen. Until that time, he would prefer not to be worried unnecessarily with side issues and ethical nitpicking. "What cards are you talking about?" he repeated in a voice hoarse with tumescent longings.

Tonia thrust her head through the open door at the front of the wagon, just behind the seat, and showed him the deck of cards, faceup upon her hand. "The cards of fortune, Chernon. Haven't you seen them before?"

"I'll tell you about them," said Kostia, peering over Tonia's shoulder. "There are four sets in the deck, one for each season. Each set has a King and a Queen and one other as the Royal Triad." She handed Septemius a wine bottle and four cups, watching carefully to assure an equitable distribution. There was another bottle behind her. She and Tonia had decided to get Chernon slightly drunk.

"In the spring set," Tonia said, "the King bears a flowered scepter and the Queen is heavy with child, while the Spring Magician looks both forward to fruitfulness and warmth and back toward the cold."

"In the summer the King drives a pair of oxen," Kostia continued, handing Chernon a filled cup. She pointed to a card. "That's what these are, oxen. A kind of cattle. We don't have them anymore. The Queen carries a harvest cornucopia full of grain and vegetables and fruit. The Summer

Priestess is naked within her thin robes. She wears a wreath of ivy and carries an incense burner before her. The smoke hides her face."

Tonia took up the story. "The Autumn King has a gray beard and carries an oaken staff with red leaves upon it; the Queen holds out her hands and rain falls from them upon the fields. The Autumn Warrior leans upon his sword."

"Finally," Kostia concluded, "in winter you see the King being drawn in his sled by reindeer. We don't have them anymore, either. . . ."

"I know about reindeer," mumbled Chernon, half draining his wine cup.

"The King has a white beard and a blood-red robe. Then there's the Queen with her dark cloak spread before the stars, and the Winter Princess, clad all in furs, with eyes of fire which can freeze or burn, as she chooses. She has a knife in one hand and a sheaf of grain in the other, to feed the animals. The signet of spring is the fruit blossom, of summer the headed grain, of autumn the red oak leaf, and of winter the holly leaf. There are ten numbered cards in each set." She refilled Chernon's cup.

Chernon handed the reins to Septemius and took the cards the girl offered him, leafing through them. They were beautifully hand painted and varnished, with only the edges slightly worn. He turned two of them out on the wagon seat. The five of holly, the one of grain. Kostia sighed.

"That was a heavy sigh," Chernon jibed at her. "Did I pick unlucky cards?"

"The one of grain is a card of destruction," she answered.

"Why?" It showed a man with a sickle at his belt, holding a single sheaf of grain. The man's head was back so one could not see his eyes, but his mouth was open and the cords of his neck stood out as though he had just shouted or screamed. "It looks like a harvest to me."

"He has cut all the grain, but he has replanted none," Tonia said. "The five of holly shows a five-branched tree weighted with snow against a gray sky. It is midway in the set, not early, not late. It has no people on it. It is a waiting card. A card betokening the passage of time."

"You cannot stop with two cards," Kostia intervened. "You must lay out at least one more."

"Why?" he asked again, stubbornly.

"Three, five, seven, eleven, or thirteen," Kostia said. "Numbers which cannot be separated into even parts."

"Odd and prime," Septemius offered. "Numbers divisible only by themselves. Evidently they have always been considered to have occult significance."

"Oh, all right," Chernon said, laughing to show he did not believe or care. He pulled out another card and set it next to the two already on the seat. Kostia drew in her breath between her teeth and took the cards from him. "Well, you have chosen the Winter Princess, Chernon."

"And what does that mean?" He drained his cup again and took the reins back from Septemius. "Something dreadful, no doubt."

"No," she said. "Only that she is a woman and can be either loving or angry."

"Crap," he said rudely. "This sort of thing. Of course time will pass, destruction will happen, and all women are either loving or angry, sometimes both. You have told me only simple truths and inevitabilities."

Kostia gave him an offended look and shut the door between them, silently, leaving the bottle on the wagon seat.

Chernon laughed as he poured his cup full again. So much for fortune-tellers. He gave Septemius a sidelong look, surprising a troubled expression on his face. "You don't believe in this stuff, do you, Magician? You, particularly? You make your living fooling people, don't you?" Chernon had long since decided that he need not worry about what Septemius might think or say or do. No one would give any credence to a traveling showman, and when the warriors took over, the old man and his girls would do what they were told.

"Oh yes," the old man admitted. "I do. Making people think they see what they do not see. Making people believe I have done what I have not done. I know all the lies people tell themselves. I help them lie to themselves; it is my craft. And I, Septemius Bird, say to you, Chernon, that when Kostia and Tonia lay out the cards, they often tell more of the truth than I care to know."

"Lucky for me, then, that I laid them out for myself," Chernon replied, clucking to the donkeys. He wanted to get where they were going. "Well, the cards are true enough, Septemius. Time will pass. I may have to cut some wood along the way, for our campfire, and this will no doubt fulfill the prediction of destruction. I should have turned up the Summer Priestess though, you know that? The one with the hidden face. When I meet Stavia, I will see her body"—he laughed, a crapulent, lubricious sound which betrayed much more than he meant it to—"but maybe not her face. None of them in Women's Country show us their real faces, do you know that?"

"It surprises me that you do." There was more asperity in Septemius's response than he had meant to allow. This time he refilled Chernon's cup.

"Oh, we're not stupid, Magician. I've thought about it a lot, you know? I had books there for a while, before Stavia decided to play me false by not letting me have any more. I managed to get away with one for myself. It belonged to my sister Beneda, and I swiped it from her. She didn't miss it. Beneda is not much for reading, anyhow."

"Do you still have it?" Septemius asked, curiously.

"Oh yes. I have it with me. It tells all about animals and people, before the convulsions. I have read of elephants and crocodiles, of Laplanders, tropical islanders, and people who lived on boats on great rivers. At one time, life was varied, Magician. It was not all alike as it is now."

"It may still be varied," the older man replied. "Across the desolations, who knows what may exist?"

"Who cares, if we can't reach them? Here it is all the same. Women's Country inside the walls. Garrisons outside the walls. Gypsies and bandits moving among us like the jackals I read of in those books. And itinerants, of course, like you. Showmen. Magicians. Actors and acrobats. And scavengers who dig metal out of the ruins of old cities and wagoneers who seem to spend most of their time transporting things from place to place." He clucked again to the donkeys and smiled, a cynical smile. "I've thought about it. It seems very simple on the surface, but there's more here than we can see, Magician, though we've no way to get at it."

Septemius shivered, without letting it show. When Chernon said "we," was he referring to the warriors? "I don't understand what you mean."

Chernon smiled again, disagreeably, Septemius thought. "Well, there's this, for example. The women depend upon us to defend them, don't they?"

The old man nodded, unwilling to trust his voice.

"So, they should be interested in our keeping the garrisons up to strength, right? I mean, we're their shield. Without us, they'd be overrun by the garrison of some other city, or chipped away at by bandits." He stared at Septemius, waiting for the answering nod before going on.

"Well, they should be most concerned about keeping us strong, but they aren't interested in that. All they're interested in is getting us to come home. Whenever I think about it, I think of two wheels, turning in opposite directions. These big, big wheels, one inside the other, whirling, making a kind of deep, humming sound. Sometimes I can almost hear it."

Septemius cleared his throat. "Isn't what you're seeing the inevitable conflict between personal and societal needs and desires? The society of women needs you to defend them, yes. But the individual mothers and sisters in that society want their own sons and brothers home, where they'll be safe. So, they do the best they can with both. They honor the warriors, but they do everything they can to urge their own loved ones to come home. It seems perfectly understandable to me. As a system, it doesn't work badly, does it?"

"It weeds out the ones who wouldn't be much use on the battlefield," the boy agreed. "Or most of them, anyhow. And that gives the women in the cities some men to work for them. I suppose they need that. I remember Minsning, my mother's servitor, from when I was a kid. He made me cookies and played horsie and I can't imagine him being any good at fighting. But that's not what I meant. I mean, there's more to the system than we know about." He hiccuped slightly, unaware that the wine was making him say more than he should. "The whole garrison thinks so. Michael . . . Stephon . . . they say the women have these secret meetings all the time, Council meetings."

Septemius laughed, sincerely and convincingly. "It seems to me I've heard of secret meetings in garrisons! Isn't there some kind of secret society, some group of initiates? The Brotherhood of the Ram? Haven't I heard about oath taking at the foot of the monument on the parade grounds?"

Chernon flushed. "That's different. That's very much like the women going to temple. More . . . more religious."

"Well, maybe the Councilwomen are religious, too, but I don't think that's why they have secret meetings. The reason is simple enough, I'd guess. It's the Council that has to allocate the food and scarce supplies, Chernon. They try to do it fairly, so far as I can see, and that probably takes a good deal of discussion which is better held in private so that people don't get upset. It isn't unlike the meetings your officers hold. Your Commander makes his decisions in private, too. He doesn't ask the centuries what they think before he decides how he'll go into battle."

Chernon thought this over, wrinkling his nose and upper lip. It sounded plausible, but then many womanish things sounded plausible. He was of no mind to accept it. "If you say so," he said, not believing it. If it were that simple, Michael would have known it. One thing all the warriors were agreed upon and most of them resented: The women did things and knew things that were secrets. Powerful secrets.

Septemius watched the boy's face, his heart sinking within him. He had expected . . . well, what had he expected? A youthful romance? An infatuation fueled by separation and imagination into something transcendent? A joyous fling?

None of the above. Something calculated and chill, though powered by lust which was probably honest enough.

Septemius sighed. Oh, he did not want to be involved in this at all.

It was a three-day ride southwest along the shore to Emmaburg, under the best conditions. The fortified sheep camp which Stavia had specified as the end of their southern journey was two days' farther south and east. At that point, they would be south of the desolation, and a four-day trip toward the northeast would take them around it to Peggytown. Fortuitously, Peggytown would be having carnival shortly after they arrived. The shore route was very little longer than the more usual route—east from Marthatown to the Travelers' Rest, east and a little south to Mollyburg, and then southwest to Peggytown. All roads in this part of Women's Country made a circle around the desolation, with Tabithatown and Abbyville away in the north and Melissaville and the other cities more toward the east.

Septemius had no real worries concerning the route as far south as the sheep camp. He did not like the idea of the four days from there to Peggytown. There was a road, but it was one not much traveled. There were forests and hills and broken lands. To the north was the desolation, and to the south were people he remembered as unpleasant. So he fretted as he drove, wondering if this were not one of those times when any bargain was a bad one, a time of no good choices. From time to time he had to look into the back of the wagon, at old Bowough's rosy cheeks, to convince himself he had behaved even halfway ethically.

AT THE SHEEP CAMP—where she would have met the servitor
from Tabithatown if she had not sent him word not to come—Stavia spent
her spare time treating several of the women and servitors for various
conditions either brought about or exacerbated by their daily occupations.
She told one rash-pied woman to return to Emmaburg and stay away from
sheep in the future because she was allergic to the oil in the wool. She
treated abrasions and cuts received from thorn and rough stone. She had a
look at the animals, as well—though there were medics better trained than
she in animal troubles, none of them had been south recently—and suggested salves for eye infections and treatments for insect bites. Then, when
that was done, she inspected the gardens and fortifications and wrote a
generally laudatory report to be sent back to the Council at Emmaburg.
The Emmaburg Council had set up the camp, and if all went well the camp
would expand and grow into a daughter-town.

"Any trouble with bandits?" she asked.

"Somebody spying on us," the camp manager told her, rubbing the
wrinkles on her forehead as though she might rub them away, then taking a

swipe at her graying head where unruly locks broke out of the sensible braid. "South of us. We catch sight of them now and then, shadows sneaking around behind the bushes, mostly around about dusk. A few sheep have disappeared, too, maybe a few more than we can account for. I think we can say definitely more than we can account for. Most of them have been young rams."

"Could be coyotes?"

"We see coyotes every now and then. They don't bother the flocks too much in the daytime. They'd prefer to be night raiders, but we bring the sheep back into the folds when it gets dark. No, the sheep that vanish are the ones that graze at the edge of the flock, wander off a bit, then suddenly they aren't there anymore." She didn't sound disturbed by this.

"Ah," said Stavia unhelpfully.

"Way I figure it is, the ones that get picked off are the ones that don't stay tight, which are the ones we want to be rid of anyhow."

"Ah," Stavia said again, in sudden comprehension, half remembering something she had read, years ago. "Selection! You're selecting for herding instinct."

"I'm selecting for sheep that get very uncomfortable if they aren't jammed up against about four more of their kind," the manager admitted, still rubbing away at her forehead. Speaking of which, I've got something to show you." She opened the door at her side and went through into a yard Stavia had not yet seen. Against the wall was a pen, and in the pen were some strangely shaped sheep.

"Dogs," the manager said, giving her a sidelong look.

"What?" Stavia stared at them in disbelief. They were dirty white, wooly, with the convex noses and loppy ears of the sheep she had been staring at for days.

"Dogs. I don't know where they came from, but one of the herders came in the other day and here were the three of them, mixed right in with the sheep."

"I thought they were sheep!" Stavia leaned over the pen and the animals stared at her, tails wagging slowly.

"Look almost like sheep, don't they? Let me tell you. I got real curious, so I kept one female and the male here and let the other female go out with the flock. Told the shepherds to keep an eye on her. Long about dark, they were coming back and a coyote ran out of the bushes, trying to grab off a lamb. That dog was right there, between him and the lamb. Couldn't budge her. Every time he shifted, there was this dog between him and the lamb."

"They're not herders?"

"Didn't try to do any herding. Nope."

"Up north they've got some herder dogs. I've heard about those."

"Me, too. Lots of times wished I had some."

"But these are something else? Sheep protectors, sort of. Strange."

"Before the convulsion there were sheep here, we all know that. Otherwise we wouldn't have them now. So maybe before the convulsions there were different kinds of sheepdogs here, too. Herding dogs and this other kind. They look all soft and babyish, like puppies!"

"You think they survived all that time back in the mountains?"

"The deer did. The bear did. Foxes, too."

"Two females and one male isn't much to breed from."

"I've told all the shepherds to keep their eyes open. If they see any more of them, they're to let me know."

Stavia shook her head, reaching a tentative hand into the pen. A pink tongue came out and licked her fingers. Dark eyes completely surrounded by white woolliness blinked at her. "Tame," she said. "Completely tame."

"Which argues people close by, don't you agree, Stavia? That's what we all think. We don't think they're wild survivals. We think they belong to people. Not bandits. Not Gypsies. Settled people, somewhere."

"There was a showman came to do carnival in Marthatown, Septemius Bird. He'd traveled down this way years and years ago. He told me there were settled people south of here. In the valleys, beyond the badlands. But that would be quite a long way south. They shouldn't be within miles of you."

"I was told to stay out of there and keep the flocks out of there, but no one ever said. . . ."

"According to Septemius, the people living there are not the kind of people we'd want to . . . well . . . take in."

"Ah. From the way you sound, not the kind we'd like to take over, either."

Stavia nodded. "I gathered their way of life wouldn't be anything we could either change or much approve of. I'm trying to remember what Septemius said. Something like 'sparse and unprofitable.' Whatever he meant by that."

"It tells me where the spies are probably from."

Stavia nodded, thinking hard. If people from the south were within spying distance of the sheep camp, it would be foolish for her to make a two-man foray in that direction. An immediate report on the spies should go to Emmaburg, for the Town Council, and to Marthatown, for the Joint Council. Probably the dogs should be sent as well. Women's Country couldn't lose this chance to add other animals to the limited number available to them. Septemius would be arriving within the next few days, and she could probably get him to carry both reports and dogs.

Chernon would leave the wagon before it came within sight of the camp, go east and make a smoke to guide her to him. She had told those at the camp she was meeting her co-explorer elsewhere. Even though he would be disguised as a servitor, it would be better if no one from the camp actually saw him. She didn't want his name mentioned in some future report, or for someone to be so put off by his manner that it would cause problems later—when she was back in Marthatown and he in the garrison.

Or, later, when he'd returned to them through the gate. He might. It was possible. After the few weeks or months of traveling together, he might stop this garrison-but-no-garrison flailing about and come back. As for her, it wasn't really a breach of trust. She'd be doing the job she'd been sent to do. No guilt, she assured herself. No one cheated. The exploration would get done, just as she'd promised. Her mind ran over this well-worn track without convincing herself. If she were being honest, she'd admit the whole thing was a risky, possibly dangerous bit of foolishness.

Meantime, however, since it would probably be several days before Septemius would arrive, she could spend a day or two reconnoitering the lands south, edging up on the badlands, getting some ideas. Something was going on here. Something the Council would need to know about.

23

SUSANNAH'S THREE TEENAGED BOYS, Capable, Dutiful, and Reliable—known to themselves as Cappy, Doots, and Rel—were committing one of the major sins known to the Holylanders, that of going out into the devil's country on a bit of exploration and pillage. Though, as they had pretty much convinced themselves, they might well be doing All Father's work of justice and recovery. Three of the dogs were gone and it was likely the devil-spawn women had taken them for demonish reasons of their own.

Their determination covered no small amount of guilt. It was they who had taken the dogs with them in a previous foray, which had included spying on a sizable herd of sheep and making off with one good little he-lamb, not even weaned yet. They'd been milking one of their own mama sheep for the critter ever since, though they'd about got him onto grass by now. Hard though it had been for the Elders to accept, Holyland ewes bred by the rams from devil's country had healthier lambs than they did when dutifully served by Holyland rams. Everyone just had to admit it because it was true. Just the last five or ten years there'd been all these sterile ewes or ewes dropping dead lambs. Then Retribution had found a young ram wandering around in the badlands. He'd brought it back, there'd been this big yelling match among the Elders about whether they could use it or not, and finally they'd put it in a pen with just a few of Elder Brome's ewes to see what happened. What happened was healthy lambs, and another yelling match about whether the devil was trying to trick the Holylanders or not.

Well, Elder Brome won that one. Since then it'd got to the point the Elders didn't even fuss about using outside rams anymore. Whoever brought one in got rewarded; the Elders did a service over the ram to make it fit and dedicate it to All Father's purposes. Evidently the devil's country rams hadn't caught any demonish diseases, because they got the job done. The general opinion among the Elders now was that all animals were made divinely immune to devilishness because they couldn't sin anyhow.

Which wouldn't help the boys any if the Elders found out the dogs were gone. The dogs might be immune from wickedness, but the boys weren't; the scars on their backs attested to that fact. Trouble was, they hadn't even known the dogs were gone until the three of them got back. Cappy thought Rel had them. Rel thought Doots had them. Doots hadn't even thought about them, and nobody saw where they went.

"I'll bet they got into that flock," Cappy had admitted at last, after they'd spent most of one evening denying it could have happened. "I'll bet they did."

"We wasn't supposed to take 'em," said Doots. "We wasn't supposed to go ourselfs and we sure wasn't supposed to take those dogs. Papa's gonna chastise us half to death."

"Well I wasn't exactly gonna tell Papa what we done," Cappy said. "I may be wicked, but I ain't dumb."

"Everybody's wicked," Rel announced. "Everybody's got the devil in him, specially women. We ain't no wickeder than anybody else. Specially not if we get 'em back."

They lay now behind a long ridge of wind-gnawed stone at the northern edge of the badlands, observing the sheep which moved on the grasslands below. There were three flocks, each guarded by three or four shepherds with horns hung around their necks for sounding alarms, spindles twirling constantly in their hands. The flocks were tight as a virgin's duty place. The dogs might be right down there in the middle of a flock, but from here nobody could tell. All they could see from where they were were the flowing blots of dirty white and the dark figures of the guards, robed down to their feet and with their hoods up over their heads, hiding their faces. Could be devil women. Could be some of their captives—cursed men bound as servitors to the devil forever. Nothing to do with one of those but kill him, if you caught one and had the chance. Devil women, though, you could tie them down and tame them after a while. Drive the devil out with duty and chastisement, so the Elders said.

A motion to the west, toward the fortified camp, drew their attention, and they saw a woman striding toward the flocks, leading a donkey along behind. No question about this one being a woman. Hair halfway down her back, uncovered, little light shirt on her showing her shape, no decency to her at all. Decent women didn't permit themselves to do anything that'd stir a man, and they sure didn't do it on purpose. Decent women hid themselves and shaved their heads and walked kind of bent over. Not this one. She stopped at the westernmost flock and spoke for a time with one of the shepherds, then moved eastward to stop at each of the others before leading her pack animal on toward the east and north.

"Holy All Father," breathed Cappy. "Wouldn't you like to have the chastisement of that one?"

"Have to keep her hid," whispered Doots. "Papa'd have her in a wife-house before you'd even got your cock up."

"Would not," Cappy snarled, pointing at himself. "Got it up already, just watchin' her walk across there."

"That's wickedness in you comin' out," Rel commented, adding hopefully, "you think she's comin' back?"

"Probly. I think if she's around, she's probly lookin' for somethin' out there. Probly be lookin' for whatever it is tomorrow. Next day maybe. Maybe for days. We could get out there, ahet of her."

Doots shifted uncomfortably. "Have to keep her hid!"

"Well, sure," Cappy acknowledged breathlessly. "I may be wicked, but I ain't dumb."

Stavia felt eyes on her. It was a prickling, unpleasant feeling, and she wanted to turn and scan the stony ridge to the south of her to see who might be watching from there. However, if she did so, particularly if she used her field glasses (for exploration use only, and heaven help the woman who broke a pair), whoever it was would know that she knew. Better pretend she was unaware, scout off away from them, circle to the north and reenter the camp well before dark. She moved purposefully on, eyes on the ground, stopping here and there to dig up things that looked either collectible or totally unfamiliar. There was a particular weed the shepherds had recommended as a possible insecticide, and another one that sick sheep seemed to seek out. A vermifuge, perhaps? These she took with plenty of soil, wrapping the entire plant in oiled paper to retain moisture. She'd pot them up when she got back to camp and have the next wagon transfer them to the botanical officer in Emmaburg, if any. If not, they could go on to Marthatown.

Morgot had told her to keep her eyes open for something called "costimy." Triangular leaf, yellow cinquefoil blossom, trailing habit, reputed to be an excellent treatment for lung congestion. It was also, from what she had been able to find so far, invisible and possibly nonexistent. Or it bloomed in the early spring or late fall when no one was around looking for it.

She still felt eyes. Resolutely, not looking behind her, she moved toward the north. Away from them. She had gone a full mile before her skin stopped prickling. Either they couldn't see her at this distance or they had gone away. She turned, casually, scanning the horizon. Nothing there. She moved behind a bush and used her glasses. Still nothing. No movement. There could have been an army up there in those pinnacles, completely unobserved. Canyons, towers, boulders—everything wind-smoothed and carved into fantastic shapes. She tucked the glasses away and went back to the donkey.

Enough for today. She'd head back to the camp and confirm the manager's opinion that somebody . . . somebodies were watching.

I T WAS TWO DAYS LATER that Septemius Bird arrived at the sheep camp, Kostia and Tonia on either side of him on the seat of the wagon, the doors open to allow Bowough a view of the passing countryside, and Septemius himself more cheerful than at any time in the past several days. He had, as a matter of fact, brightened up considerably when Chernon left them, half a day's travel back.

"You don't like him, do you?" Kostia asked, nodding her head to show him she already knew the answer. They were passing through the tall wooden gate which closed the fortification against the world outside, the servitor-guard looking them over carefully and seeming reassured at the sight of the young women and the aged man. "You don't like him one bit."

"He's a . . . well, he's a difficult lad to get to know."

"Oh piss," Tonia announced in a no-nonsense voice. "Piss and sour milk and sheep-shit. You knew him half an hour after we picked him up, Septemius Bird. You had him all figured out. Him with that wounded child look, those pouting lips, those heavy eyes. Did get hurt some as a child, probably. Found out it made people feel guilty, so he kept right on getting wounded, here and there, now and then. A little obvious suffering to make mama and sister pay attention. Stavia saw that and took to him, mothering as much as sex, I'd say. There's lots of the Great Mother in Stavia."

"I agree," said Kostia. "So then he grew up, refusing to heal, keeping the pitiable parts of him foremost, where they'd draw his mama's attention, and his sister's, and probably Stavia's as well. Good mind, behind all that, and he knows she's not stupid, so he begged books. That makes her guilty for it's against the ordinances, and her guilt means she's going to hurt him again, and that gives him a hold on her."

"But he won't do anything dishonorable, despite what he's already done and is about to do," Tonia drawled. "Brave, pitiable boy, no he won't. So there she is, caught in the middle, feeling she's been the one to hurt him most, all her fault. Oh, sheep-shit, Septemius, you know all about it."

"At your age," he announced, "it would be considerate to be less wise. I take some comfort from the fact that you will both undoubtedly be driven to ill-considered and reproachable behavior by some future romantic attachment."

"At your age," Kostia said, "you might as well stop mincing words. There's something about him puts me off. A kind of destructive audacity about him."

"Or behind him," Septemius agreed. "For all he'd like us to think this is an illicit trip, I'd bet anything you'd like that his officers know all about it. Maybe they even sent him."

They were silent a time, exchanging significant glances. "I feel you're probably right, Uncle. But it's Stavia I'm concerned about," mused Tonia. "I'm worried about her."

"And there she is," said Kostia, gesturing down the narrow, dusty alley they were on toward an equally dusty square compassed about with wool sheds and sheep pens. Stavia stood at one corner of the earthern plaza, talking with a middle-aged woman dressed in leather trousers and a loosely woven woolen cape. Both looked up at their approach, Stavia at first frowning, then smiling, as though she was glad to see them but had not expected them quite so soon.

"Septemius," she called, drawing the woman with her. "I'd like you to meet the camp manager, Marietta. Septemius Bird, his nieces, Tonia and Kostia. The gentleman in the back of the wagon is the elder Bird." She leaned through the door. "How are you, Bowough? You're looking better than when last I saw you!"

"It's the medical miss, isn't it? Come in, my dear, come in." He reached for her hand, tugging her over the seat and into the wagon where she crouched beside him, taking note of his improved health while Septemius conferred with the manager about the possibility of doing a little show for the camp residents. Marietta was delighted and willing to pay. Keeping up morale in this isolated place was one of her major concerns.

"You picked him up?" Stavia whispered to Tonia, who had come back into the wagon with her. "Chernon?"

"Oh yes. He left us half a day out, Stavia. He's gone eastward to make some signal for you. That is, if you're still sure you're going off with him this way. Kostia and I don't recommend it."

"Still telling my fortune?" Stavia asked, not really upset. "Come, now. He's a dear old friend, brother of a dear old friend, and he's counting on me."

The young women shook their heads at her but didn't say anything more. Stavia had that bland and unresponsive face which often masked with an appearance of politeness the most implacable sort of obstinacy. No point in wasting one's voice. "What have you been doing here?" Tonia asked instead, detouring the boggy place in their relationship. "It seems very remote."

"I've been collecting plants, inspecting the camp, treating the people and the animals, writing reports, and I'm about to go off to collect a few more plants and explore to the east before returning home again," Stavia said in a carefully cheerful and totally uninterested voice that said, better than words could have done, "Don't talk to me about not going, because my mind is completely made up." Then she smiled, a Stavia smile, more herself. "Before I do that, though, I'll treat you and the family to dinner. How does roast lamb sound?"

"If it didn't sound good, what?"

"You could have a nice dish of local greens," Stavia laughed. "Which would probably smell like sheep. Everything does."

The lamb was roasted over an open fire. It was tender and delicious, oozing with succulent fat which ran down their fingers to their wrists and dripped off their chins. They had the dish of local greens as well, which smelled of sun and herbage and not at all of sheep, as well as porridge flavored with drippings and onions and garlic. When they were done, Septemius opened out the stage from the side of the wagon. As an overture, Bowough played a reedy accompaniment upon a squeeze organ while the gray dogs danced soberly on all fours and the white ones hopped about on either their front or back legs, laughing the while with lolloping tongues. Then Septemius ascended to the platform, cut Tonia in half and restored her, made her disappear in several different ways, from his empty hat drew doves, and from the shepherds' ears plucked coins, which he then poured into the hat and caused to vanish once more. Tonia and Kostia,

Kostia in a veil so as not to reveal that they were twins—which would have explained a good deal about her recent disappearances—did a mind-reading act which involved answering questions sealed in envelopes, without opening the envelopes until after the question was answered. Everyone had beer, a treat, since grain was always short, and went to bed feeling jolly. The guards on the walls sang their alls-wells into the star-pricked sky, and the camp settled down.

"When are you going to meet him?" Septemius asked from the fireside.

"Tomorrow," said Stavia, looking up from the paper she was holding down on a flat board before her, squinting in the flickering light. "I've got to ask another favor, Septemius."

"I've done entirely too much already," he said, trying not to sound as annoyed as he felt. It was annoyance mostly with himself. He had done too much, too much harm. He wanted to dissuade her.

"I want you to deliver this report and three strange dogs we've found."

"Dogs?" he asked, suddenly interested.

"I know you probably planned to go on over to Peggytown, but it would be better if you didn't travel on that road. Not alone. Besides, the dogs and my report, both, should get back to Marthatown as soon as possible. There are people spying on the camp here, people from somewhere south, maybe those same people you told me about. The Joint Women's Country Council should know about all this as soon as possible. I think we need a garrison down here. Know it in my gut, mostly." She frowned, remembering the itchy feeling of being observed she had had when she wandered away from the camp.

"I've written a letter to Morgot. In it, I've asked her to pay you for your time. I'd pay you now if I had any exchange money with me, but I don't."

He shifted uncomfortably. "You don't want us to travel that road, but you're going to be out there, you and Chernon, alone?"

"We won't be alone! We'll have the donkey." She grinned at him. "And no, I'm teasing you. I've decided the itinerary as laid out by the Joint Council isn't appropriate. I don't need to explore south to find out if there are people there, we already know that. So, I'll just do a very brief and sneaky reconnaissance toward the east, mostly to collect botanicals. No sense wasting this journey entirely, even though I won't do all of what was planned. I was out there on the prairie today and I could feel eyes all over me, like a swarm of bees. I'm not going to show myself again. Exploration south of here should be done in strength, including warriors, not by one or two."

"I worry about you," he said impotently. "I do, Stavia."

"Tss," she teased him. "Worry about your own family, old Bird. Worry about those twins. Better settle down near Women's Country and let them live in a civilized manner."

"I've thought that," he replied. "Yes."

"Well, speak to Morgot about it when you get back to Marthatown. Tell her I begged your assistance and promised our best efforts in return. She'll get you an itinerent's permit to settle."

"And how would I earn a living, girl? You seem not to think of that."

"Thought of it long since," she grinned at him. "You could do messenger and freight service for the Council. They use wagoneers and show people all the time to carry messages and material from one city to another, and they pay for it. Or, if you'd rather stay close, they'd probably give you a grandsir job."

"A grandsir job?" It was not a term he had heard before.

"A sinecure, Septemius. Some small thing that needs doing a few hours a day and leaves a man time free to do other arty-crafty things to suit himself. Additionally, you could have a garden. . . ."

"Oh good," said Kostia. "I'd like that."

"And if your nieces chose to attend school, they'd get a grain and cheese allotment. . . ."

"Really?" Tonia seemed impressed by this.

"And, once you'd lived in the itinerants' quarters a year or two, you could petition to come inside the walls on the basis that your status is essentially the same as servitor, that Tonia and Kostia wish to establish residence, and that you've been stable long enough to indicate sincerity in wanting to stop this endless flitting about."

"You women think of everything, don't you?" he said, somewhat cynically.

"No," she sighed. "But we've learned enough to know that we don't get stronger by setting arbitrary impediments in the way of good people joining us. Kostia and Tonia would be assets, and we're not fool enough to think they'd come inside and leave you out."

Septemius found his eyes suspiciously damp. "So there are ways for men to get inside your walls besides the Gate to Women's Country."

"Old men," she said. "Grayheads. Yes. Usually only if they have younger female family members. Though not always."

"Not always?"

"Only five years or so ago, we took in an old man who'd traveled far north beyond Tabithatown. He had no family at all, but he had maps, good ones. We figured the maps paid his way."

"And the dancing dogs?"

"Maybe the dogs will pay yours! I suppose they can dance as well inside the walls as out. We're not about to decrease the number of species available, though we'd have to work out some kind of ration for them. What do you feed them?"

"Rabbits, mostly," answered Tonia. "And mice. And little furry short-tailed things that come out at night. Septemius sets snares, and the dogs catch a lot for themselves. They eat grass sometimes, too, and berries, and bugs. And they're not very big. . . ." She was looking at Stavia anxiously.

"Don't worry about it, girl. Breed them, let them have puppies if they will. We'll try them as mousers in the grain warehouses. We've had no dogs in Marthatown since the convulsion, but there's no ordinance against it. I've heard there are a few dogs up at Tabithatown, and the Gypsies have some. Very civilized, dogs, so perhaps it's time we civilized ourselves again. Besides, I'm giving you these three strange ones to take back, along with rations to feed them. Dried meat, I think, and enough grain to make some kind of cooked-up mess they'll eat." She went on telling them about the strange dogs, as she lit a lantern and led them through the alleyway to the pen so they could see for themselves. Bowough creaked along behind on his cane, vocal as a magpie about the strangeness of them.

"I think you'd better keep them penned or tied," Stavia told Septemius. "If you pass flocks, likely they'd try to join the sheep. I want them well away from here before their owners come looking for them."

Septemius gave her another worried look. "I told you about those people who live south of here, Stavia."

"I remember. Don't worry. You sound like Joshua."

When morning came, she was gone. Septemius spent half a day with a helper from the camp building a cage for the new dogs, another half day getting a few stores together, one night safe behind walls, and then they started back the way they had come.

"I don't like her being out there," he said for the dozenth time, to no one in particular.

"I know," replied Kostia. "And when we deliver the message and animals to Morgot, we ought to tell her so."

R EHEARSAL:

(Achilles approaches the group of women purposefully)

ACHILLES   This then is Polyxena.

POLYXENA   *(Yawning)* Yes, I'm Polyxena.

ACHILLES   My slave, Polyxena.

POLYXENA   No one's slave, Polyxena.

(Achilles attempts to grab her and finds he cannot hold her)

ACHILLES   She sifted through my arms, like rays of sun, like moonlit
smoke, like mist, like. . . .

IPHIGENIA   Like a ghost.

ACHILLES   Like a ghost. Yes.

POLYXENA   *(Pleased)* Somehow I was not surprised.

ACHILLES   How can I force obedience on this? In other times I've used
the fear of death to make a woman bow herself to me. If not the fear of

her own death, then fear for someone else, a husband or a child. How can I bend this woman to my will?!

POLYXENA   I think I will not bend.

IPHIGENIA   You see, it's as we've tried to tell you, Great Achilles. Women are no good to you dead.

AFTER LEAVING Septemius, Chernon hiked out of the flatlands onto a moderate height, camped on it, spent a virtually sleepless night, and then lit a smoky fire at dawn. Stavia rose early, watched for the smoke, and was already out the northern gate of the sheep camp by the time Chernon buried the fire, which he did very shortly after lighting it. All was precisely according to plan. She traveled toward him in a mood of fatalistic expectancy, not precisely joyous, but with more contentment in her than she had felt in some time, her feeling of guilt toward him eased.

It took her several hours to reach him. Though he kept himself well concealed in forest as she had instructed, he watched for her from the high edge of a ridge, growing more impatient and heated with each passing moment. When she arrived he had no words to greet her with. Imaginings had kept him awake for most of the night; his restless body had done the rest. He took hold of her as she approached the camp, pulling her away from the donkey, dragging her toward his spread blankets, covering her mouth with his own so that she had no time to speak. He gave her no time, no word, nothing but a frenzied and almost forcible ravishment which, while it did not totally surprise her, left her, when he rolled away, completely unfulfilled and trembling in a state of pain and half-aroused anger. He was tangled into his blankets, eyes closed, breathing like surf in deep, liquid heavings. If it had not been precisely rape, it had been close to it.

She drew her clothes together and rose, crouching away from him, as she might have done from some normally tame animal which had turned dangerous. He sank deeper into sleep, and she retreated farther into the woods where her pack animal waited patiently, reins dragging on the ground. She lifted the pack off, pegged the animal to a line, searched until she found a trickle of water down a nearby wooded gully, then stripped and washed herself, pouring the water over herself again and again from cupped hands, all very quietly, trying to keep from screaming or striking out or going back where he lay and killing him. There was blood on her thighs, but she had more or less expected that. She had received more hurt than pleasure from the encounter, but she knew that was not unusual. She had started women's studies at ten; she had had classes in physiology and sexual skills; at her age she was far older than almost all of her acquaintances in gaining her first actual experience, but she was no less prepared than they had been. Chernon had simply given her no time or opportunity to do or be anything except a receptacle for his hasty passion. She was not terrified or greatly hurt, but she was angry.

He had said nothing! Nothing loving, nothing sentimental. He had done no wooing. He had taken her as though she had been one of the Gypsies. . . .

"You could have stopped him," the actor Stavia remarked from some dim and cavernous mental recess. "You could have laid him out, Stavia."

"It wasn't stopping him that mattered. I wanted something else from him, not something else from me." That wasn't the real reason. It wasn't. She tried again. "I was so surprised, I couldn't figure out what to do, and then it was all over." And still again. "This wasn't what I thought he wanted."

"Better let me handle it."

"All right." Certainly she couldn't handle it herself. She would kill him if she did. Let the actor Stavia do it.

She put on her clothes, fastening them tightly, went back to the place she had met him, and kicked him sharply in the ribs.

He woke with a whoof, staring wildly about him.

"If you ever do that again," she told him, "it will be the last time you ever see me."

"Do . . ." he mumbled, gradually focusing on her. "Do . . . what did you expect me to do?"

"I expected you to act civilized. I did not expect to be attacked. Is that kind of behavior considered honorable in the garrison?"

He couldn't answer her. Certainly it was. It wasn't acceptable in Women's Country, he knew that, but in the garrison? Of course it was. With . . . with . . . certain kinds of women. Women who came out to the camp for you. . . .

She saw the way he looked at her, looked away, the quick darting of those suddenly guileful eyes. "So, Chernon," the actor Stavia demanded, "is this your idea of getting even?"

He blushed. Maybe. A little. It had been.

"Did you expect me to like it? Accept it?"

He shook his head, searching for an acceptable reply, remembering too late that he had been sent to woo information from her. "I didn't think at all. I've been . . . I've been waiting for you for weeks. I've been . . . I've been thinking about you. I just couldn't . . . I couldn't wait, that's all." He flushed again, got to his feet. "I'm sorry, Stavia. I wasn't even . . . I wasn't even here, I guess."

"Shall we get some things straight?"

He nodded, giving a crafty appearance of willingness though he was beginning to feel aggrieved. Saying it once had been quite enough. She could let it go. It wasn't anything they needed to go over and over.

"We're supposed to be companions on this trip. I agreed to this whole thing at least partly to make up to you for having misled you when we were just kids. Well, when I was a kid—what was I, ten, eleven years old?—we agreed to make this a kind of adventure. Fulfillment of some kind of fantasy for both of us. Right so far?"

He nodded. Of course that is what they'd said, what he'd said, mostly. Did she think he had forgotten?

"I'm not some girl you've seduced out to a Gypsy camp for your pleasure. The pleasure is supposed to be mutual. That means we both work at it and are careful of one another's feelings."

He couldn't think of any suitable response. Certain things about the encounter had just struck him, and he was trying to figure them out.

After waiting for a time she said, "I'm hungry," in a neutral voice which hid a mild nausea. She got the necessary supplies out of the donkey pack and set about putting together a meal of bread and cheese, lighting a tiny, smokeless fire to heat water for tea. "I left very early," she went on, still in that neutral, impersonal voice. "Before breakfast."

They ate together, silently on the whole, though Chernon managed one or two comments on his trip with Septemius. Stavia thought the remarks were unnecessarily carping, but said nothing. He might merely be trying to be funny.

Finally he found a source of his discomfort and blurted, "That was the first time you ever . . . ? Wasn't it?"

"Yes."

"I thought you all started when you were real young. Beneda did."

"Beneda may have been teasing you. She certainly had not had any assignations when I left for Abbyville."

"You were gone nine years," he said in a hostile voice, as though she had somehow offended him by being a virgin.

"I know."

"Eighteen carnivals," he asserted. "I . . ."

"I'm sure you took part in carnival, Chernon. I didn't expect you not to. But, except for a little drinking and singing at the one just past, I didn't. I didn't have time." She gave him a look which he did not return. What was it that bothered him? She could not find an explanation for his reasonless hostility. "Look, we were never 'lovers.' I loved you, I think. The way a kid does. Infatuation, maybe. For you—well, I was your little sister's friend and you used me to get books. Then I realized what I was doing and stopped it, and you got angry at me. And then I went away. That's all there really was between us. Let's not pretend there was something more than that."

She said nothing about all that time in Abbyville, the carnivals there that she had avoided, always thinking of him, of Chernon, of that boy with the wheat-colored hair and the wary, hurt look in his eyes. She wanted him to listen to her, to hear her. She wanted him to say something that told her he saw her. "This adventure—this is my way of saying, 'I'm sorry I hurt you when we were young."

My way of saying I love you, Chernon.

"But it can't go on unless it's enjoyable for both of us. . . ." She was not really seeing him there before her, the man's body, the man's face. She was seeing the boy, still, wanting the boy, still. The boy wasn't in there. The boy was gone. Somewhere in there, Chernon had metamorphosed into something different, not merely grown up but changed in kind. ". . . that wouldn't be fair to either of us," her voice went on.

Trite. What was fair? Was anything fair? This whole thing was a cliché. He wasn't answering her at all.

Inside, she wept. It had all been a stupid idea. Septemius had tried to tell her. Kostia had known. Tonia had known. Her own ten-year-old self would have known. What was it Stavia herself had said about Myra's infatuation for Barten? "She doesn't have any sense at all."

"No," Morgot had yawned. "None of them do. Neither did I, when I was that age."

"I refuse to be that age!" Stavia had asserted.

"I wish you luck," Morgot had replied.

Meaning, we all do it, daughter. All of us. We know what's sensible and right, and we do foolishness instead.

And here she was. Actor Stavia, trying to make the best of it. While inside the silly, sentimental, loving part of her howled for her own lost childhood.

And then he smiled, like the sun rising, suddenly, without warning. She saw it on his face: capitulation, a decision not to be angry. What she saw was not an emotional need to reconcile himself to her but a conscious decision that anger would do nothing for him. She could not see to the reasons behind that decision; she saw the mind at work, however. "You're right, Stavia. I behaved like . . . like one of those ancient peoples in Beneda's book. Like a barbarian. Let's start over." And smiled again.

She perceived the coldbloodedness of it, the chill manipulation of it, but decided to ignore it. They were new to one another after all. She let everything within her melt and flow and reform again in a new and softened shape.

Actor Stavia was waved off into the wings.

"Oh, Chernon," she said, opening her arms.

STAVIA HAD NEVER had a lover before, so she had no one to compare their lovemaking with. She did compare him with other men she knew, however. With Joshua. With Corrig. With her surgical instructor in Abbyville.

Chernon seemed anxious, rather than eager, to give her pleasure and sometimes succeeded, though it happened more often by accident than it did through Chernon's understanding of what he was doing. He was so engrossed in his own feelings that he wasn't able to pay much attention to her. She was soon adept at pleasing him, which was not very complicated. He needed little arousal and did not tolerate long delays. He reminded her a little of the ram lambs she had seen in the meadows around the camp, suddenly hungry, butting at their mothers' udders with fierce determination, only to become as suddenly satiated. Everything was now. Nothing was later. She remembered what Beneda had said about him, years ago: "When he comes home, he eats all the time, everything, just gulps it down and doesn't even bother to taste it. . . ."

Which, she reminded herself, her studies had informed her was a frequent state of sexual affairs among very young men. Chernon was twenty-four, but that was still very young in garrison country, where a man counted for little until they had been tested in battle, even though he might have fathered sons before then. In Women's Country one was adult at sixteen or seventeen. Stavia thought about this, between times, bemused and a little sore from the unaccustomed lovemaking, though Chernon did not call it that. In Women's Country it was generally thought that the best lovers were older men who had given up being carnival cocks and who enjoyed intracarnival wooing—letters, verses, gifts—to stir up their own passions, and their partner's affections. Stavia thought that some between-fuck wooing might be rather nice, but she did not suggest it. She had come to the conclusion that just meeting Chernon's demands would take more of her energy than she had expected. She would have enough left over to complete the task at hand only if everything was kept as simple as possible. Sentiment, too, took energy. She had no extra energy. Sentiment would have to wait. She made this decision coldbloodedly, almost in retaliation for what she had seen in his face, without recognizing that a large part of their emotion toward one another was hostile.

They worked their way east, and then south, making each night's camp in late afternoon, leaving it in midmorning. The collection of herbs grew, notations on Stavia's maps became denser. Chernon was only mildly interested in what she was doing, mildly interested in the collection.

"I should think you'd be very interested," she chided him tiredly at the end of a long day's travel. "You told me once you thought wounded warriors deserved better care. Some of these herbs may be excellent wound dressings."

"How would I know?" he shrugged.

"You'd test them. Surely men get minor injuries in weapons practice? You could test different herbs to see which ones had healing properties."

"We do well enough with moldy bread poultices," he said offhandedly. "Bread is always available. Some of these herbs might not be growing when we needed them."

She gave him a tired half-smile and dropped the subject. His desire for books had probably been more a desire for dominance than a lust for learning, so much was clear. Perhaps forcing her to bring them to him had been more important than what was in them.

Though he still carried the book he had stolen from Beneda. What did books mean to him?

"You once wanted to borrow my biology books," she ventured.

"I wanted to know the secrets," he blurted. "The ones you women know, that's all." He had been wondering for several days how to approach the subject; now it popped out of his mouth like a frog into a pool.

Leaning across their evening fire, she struggled with this. Did he think that what was in the books was somehow magical? That the same information, discovered for himself, would not have the same efficacy? Perhaps it wasn't knowledge he wanted. It was magic he coveted. Magic and the power it would bring.

"You know," she ventured, "the books were written by people. Just people."

"Preconvulsion people," he averred. "They knew things we don't." His tone was dogmatic, vibrating with the power of prophecy. "They knew about . . . about weapons. And things." He waited for her to say something, extend the conversation, make it possible for them to discuss weapons, and things.

She said nothing. She wasn't thinking of weapons at all. She thought he was partly right, of course. Preconvulsion peoples had known things the women didn't. But he was partly wrong, too. Many books were newly written, newly printed, and they contained information that preconvulsion people hadn't known of or thought important enough to record. She wondered whether it would be wise to try to convince him of this, realized that doing so would take hours, and decided on silence. Whatever words she gave him, he changed them, as though by sorcery, into something else. She gave him assurances, and he twisted them into things to be aggrieved or angry over. The way he had done with Sylvia, all those years before, over the subject of Vinsas. No point in endless argument. Better give him the least possible material to misunderstand. Or pretend to misunderstand, observer Stavia noted. Much of the misunderstanding was willful, and she would have to have been completely besotted not to see it.

The fire burned down and they settled into their blankets, reaching for one another like well-practiced raiders, stealing familiar treasure, grabbing it all by huge handfuls, not bothering to sort it. Nothing between them seemed to carry the implication of "later," as though this was all there ever was to be. There were lovers in Marthatown who were together every carnival for decades, as faithful as though they had been "married" to one another, but nothing in Chernon's words or behavior said that he intended them to be lovers again. She said to him once, "Next carnival," and he had turned on her angrily. "Not carnival," he had said. "Not then." Now, their assault on one another left them gasping, and she cried out, a muted howl that lost itself in the tree-waving wind.

"You'll bring me a son, won't you!" he demanded, lying with all his weight upon her, growing flaccid within her, his teeth at her ear. "A son."

"Perhaps, someday," she said without thinking, witlessly, hate-loving him, both at once.

"Now!" he demanded. "Soon."

"I can't," she murmured, still carelessly. "Not on this trip, Chernon. I've got an implant to prevent it."

He rolled off of her, sat up, glaring at her. "What do you mean?"

"I mean I have an implant to prevent my getting pregnant on this journey," she said, suddenly aware of what she'd said. These things were not discussed with warriors. She remembered that now. They couldn't be expected to understand.

"And who, may I ask, did you expect to protect yourself from? Your 'servitor'?" He made the word an obscenity.

"No," she said honestly. "Of course not. I've never even met the man. But there are bandits about, and Gypsies, and women have been captured or raped. Don't be silly, Chernon."

"What's his name," he growled at her. "The one you were supposed to be with."

She stared at him, at his face, reddened both by anger and firelight. "His name was Brand, I believe. He'd made quite a study of botany, up in Tabithatown, and it was thought he'd be a considerable help in collecting plant material."

"How old is he?"

"I haven't any idea. I never asked." She hadn't. She had assumed he would be one of the rather special servitors, someone like Joshua, with some of Joshua's strange and unspecified talents. Morgot would hardly have let her go off with him alone, otherwise.

"And you've never seen him," he jeered at her.

"No, I never have. And if you don't stop this behavior, Chernon, I may not see you anymore, either. What are you angry about?" Stavia felt fury beginning to boil in herself.

"It's one of the reasons I wanted to come," he said between tight teeth. "To have a son. One I was sure was mine."

"One you were sure was yours?" She shook her head at him incredulously.

"Yes, damn it. One I was sure was mine. Not one you'd send to me when he was five that might be mine and might be anybody's. Oh, don't pretend you don't know what I'm saying. Everybody in the garrison knows that you women do it with everybody. Sometimes three or four different men during a carnival. How do you know who the father is?"

She smiled, a tight-lipped smile. "You've given a blood sample to the clinic, haven't you, Chernon? Yes, you have, and so has every other warrior. That's all we need. We take blood from the baby, from its cord, as soon as it's born, and we can tell who the father is. That's why sometimes we bring boys to the garrison whose fathers have died, and we say this is the son of so-and-so, even though he's dead. By my Gracious Lady, Chernon, but you men are sometimes impossible."

She rose, her naked skin glowing like a ghost light among the dark trees. She dressed herself and took her blankets, leaving him alone.

"Where are you going?" he demanded in a tone of anger blended with pain. "Where!"

"Where I can get some sleep," she replied. "I'm tired."

He bit his tongue, so angry he could hardly speak, remembering Michael and what Michael would want to know. "I'm sorry, Stavia."

"So am I," she said, thinking that he did not sound sorry enough. "But I'm still tired, and I don't care to discuss it anymore." As she moved away, Stavia realized that the movement was both actual and symbolic, that she was leaving Chernon, the Chernon she had thought she knew. In that same moment she realized she had broken the ordinances for no good reason and wondered, with a surge of deep, nauseating guilt, whether Morgot would ever forgive her for it—whether she would ever forgive herself. Only one thing was certain. She had parted from Chernon and would not return. So far as she was concerned, he was dead.

STAVIA HAD STARTED their venture determined to stay well away from the badlands to the south and equally well away from the observers who lurked there. She had worked toward the east, following this fold of hills and that valley as the days went by, tallying those days in her notebook each evening when she wrote up the day's discoveries or lack thereof. On the morning following what she thought of as her coming to her senses, the fifteenth day of their travel, she told Chernon they had to start back. She was not sorry to say so. She would have ended their journey immediately if there had been a short route by which they could have returned.

He did not want to go.

"We have food enough if we leave now," she said in a quietly reasonable voice without any hint of anger. "I'll get more in the sheep camp and bring it out to you for your trip back to the garrison. I'm expecting a message from Marthatown, and it will have arrived by the time we return."

He stared southward. "It's necessary," she said. He mumbled something. She turned and began packing the donkey.

"When we planned this, you said months," he complained.

"Originally, that's what I thought. However, there's another team exploring eastward, so we needn't go farther in that direction. It's clear that going farther south would be dangerous. That needs a large force, not just two people."

"You'd planned to travel months with him."

"I didn't plan anything, Chernon. I did not plan this trip. It was planned before anybody even considered my doing it. It was planned before I talked to the women in the sheep camp. It was planned before I heard about the people spying on the camp." She said all this patiently, knowing by now that any display of anger or impatience on her part would only make him dig in his heels. "I had to change the plans when we found out about that."

"One or two more days."

"We have food enough if we leave now," she repeated. "This is not country we can live off of, Chernon. I recognize only a few things that are edible, and you would not relish them." She realized how much she sounded like Morgot, as Morgot had used to talk to her when she was very young.

He folded his blankets, punishing her by not talking. She snarled silently to herself in exasperation. He was like a small child. Like Jerby had sometimes been. Like Myra's oldest. All sulks and silences, pretences and games. It didn't matter. No longer. Simply let there be an end.

They started back, down a hooked valley which led them slightly southward and into another which led them farther southward still. When they stopped for a midday meal, she climbed to the top of a hill, spying out the way they would go. The fold would lead them too far south to suit her, but the ridges to their right were too precipitous to climb. "No fire tonight," she advised Chernon when she returned. "We're too far south." She had warned him repeatedly about the dangers of the south, but did not do so again because of his moodiness.

They ate a cold supper and slept. Deep in the night she awoke, smelling smoke. A fire glimmered in the shade of the trees. "Chernon!" she demanded, outraged.

"I wanted some tea," he said defiantly. "I'm putting it out right now."

The glimmer had been enough to guide Cappy, Doots, and Rel to the right area. They had been searching the folded hills for some days, several times just missing Stavia and Chernon by passing before them or behind them.

"There," breathed Cappy, pointing to the starlike gleam in the shadowed ripple of trees. "Got 'em."

"You goin' to kill him?" asked Doots.

"Maybe not right away," Cappy replied. "Maybe ask him some stuff first. He didn't come out of that place, you know? She met up with him somewhere else. Could be he's a different kind than those down there at the town."

"Devil men," Doots cautioned. "That's what Papa says."

"Wouldn't hurt just to ask him some things," Rel offered in Cappy's support. Leave it up to Doots and nobody'd ever do anything at all.

The three of them worked their way silently through the trees at first dawn, when the sky was still so dim that stars glimmered weakly through the gathering light. They found Chernon and Stavia lying side by side under blankets. Stavia was facedown, Chernon faceup. After a whispered conference, Cappy threw himself onto Stavia, holding her down while the other two dealt with Chernon.

Reliable was a skinny, wiry boy, strong but not heavy. Doots, on the other hand, was what the Elder Brome called "pure stove wood." All in all, the two who had attacked Chernon had an easier time of it than Cappy did.

In the open, Cappy would not have occupied Stavia for long. She had learned how to fight, as all girls did in Women's Country: how to wrestle and kick-fight and disarm or disable an opponent. She had never learned how to do so when covered and entangled in a blanket. In the end it was the blanket which conquered her. She tripped and fell, knocking the breath out of herself, and Cappy, bruised and breathless, managed to get a rope around her wrists and force her to her knees.

"Y'got some bruised," remarked Doots. Cappy was fingering his left eye which was already beginning to discolor and swell.

"Devils can really fight," Cappy offered.

"Devils!" Stavia spat. "Are you calling me a devil?"

"Not a decent woman, that's for sure. Hair hangin' down. No clothes." Cappy was having some trouble with the fact that Stavia was largely unclothed. Among the three brothers, he was not alone in this regard.

"She belongs to me," said Chernon very clearly. "Do you understand that?"

"Whyn't you keep her decent then?" Reliable asked.

"You let her loose and she'll get decent quick enough," Chernon said. "Don't want to have to chase her."

"She won't run. You won't run, will you Stavia?" he asked, nodding at her.

She thought about this. There were three of them, two holding Chernon, one ready to jump her again. "No. Not if he'll let me get dressed."

It wasn't what Cappy wanted to do, but he had not thought this far in his plans. Doots and Rel were looking at him, waiting for a signal. If Cappy did what he wanted to, right now, then the others would want to do it, too. That way, they'd have to kill the man first, to keep him from interfering. Also, he wasn't sure he wanted them watching him. His object was to take the woman back—to maybe ask the man some questions then probably kill him, but to take the woman back. The best way to do that might be to get past this spot he was in. "Get dressed," he demanded throatily, loosening the loop that held her hands and picking up a stout branch which lay nearby. "And move real slow or I'll bash you with this."

She dressed herself. It had not been correct for them to say that she had no clothes on. She had been wearing a long shirt and knitted socks. She pulled on her trousers, slipped her feet into her boots, then put on her padded vest, a voluminous garment which effectively hid her torso. She braided her hair and tucked the ends in. "Even your mothers," she offered, "get undressed sometimes."

"In the bathhouse," said Doots. "And that's all. Never in bed. That's not decent."

She cast a horrified look at Chernon to find him staring at the three with the most perfect focus of concentration she had ever seen upon his face. It had occurred to Chernon that the adventure he had so long sought had come upon him. "What do you want with us?" he asked, his voice calm and interested. "You've been following us, haven't you?"

"Saw your fire," Doots mumbled, at which Chernon quivered, only slightly, realizing the indictment without acknowledging it. "We saw her and decided to take her. These devil women, you tame 'em down and they're pretty good wives."

"Tame them down?" asked Chernon, still in that interested voice.

"Tie 'em up," said Cappy. "Break their legs, maybe. They heal crooked and they can't run."

Stavia could not believe what she was hearing. What she was hearing was not as bad as what she was seeing, however—an expression on Chernon's face which was frankly collusive. He understood these animals. He understood them from a place inside himself which empathized with them. In that instant she comprehended much that had been unclear to her before.

"She's already a wife," Chernon said, still in that calm, interested voice. "Mine. She's carrying my baby right now."

"Oh shit," said Cappy, throwing the thick branch to the ground in a frenzy of frustrated purpose. "Oh shit."

"We're goin' to take her back anyhow," said Rel. "We're goin' to take you, too. If'n she has a baby, well, maybe the Elders'll say she 'uz married and maybe they won't. Maybe she'll drop it afore time. Women doesn't have a baby isn't really married, that's what they say."

"And if she does?"

"Maybe they'll say you wan't no real man to have a wife nohow. Widow woman with a baby, nobody else can have her. But maybe she ain't a widow and maybe she won't have a baby, neither one."

Cappy nodded, bending to pick up the stick again. "And the devil women know things," he said. "Secrets. Like healin'. Things like that."

"Oh, this one knows secrets, all right," Chernon said. "But she's got a little magic thing in her arm that keeps her from telling. That's all right, though. I can cut it out if you want to know anything."

"Chernon!" she gasped, shocked and surprised by this, though not at all disbelieving.

"Stavia," he mimicked. "Better let me do it now." He wrestled his way closer to her, dragging his two captors along, reaching out to rip away the sleeve of her shirt. "There," he said. "See that lump on her shoulder?"

They stared at one another. After a time, Cappy nodded, and they handed Chernon a knife, holding fast to him the whole time. When he cut her shoulder, the surprise of it broke a scream from deep in her lungs. It was surprise more than pain. Blood ran down her arm and dripped from her elbow through the fabric of the shirt.

"See there?" Chernon crowed. He was holding up the implant, a tiny sliver of translucent material, the size of a matchstick.

Stavia shivered, holding herself tightly together, refusing to speak or scream. It was Rel who ripped off the sleeve of her shirt and bound it untidily around her upper arm, stopping the flow of blood. It was Cappy who took the implant from Chernon and buried it in a pocket, Cappy who urged her to her feet.

"We're goin' back," he said.

"We takin' him?" Doots asked.

"For now," Cappy replied. "We'll see what Papa says."

Stavia went haltered, a rope around her neck. Chernon's hands were tied behind him, as though he represented a greater threat. Despite the fact that Stavia had injured Cappy in the initial encounter, none of the brothers could think of her as a real threat, simply because she was a woman. Stavia realized this, took note, set the fact aside for use at some later time.

She set aside Chernon's complicity until later, as well. She told herself she would not feel what she knew she felt; she would not venge herself upon him, not yet. He had probably saved his own life by assaulting her, and he might have saved hers as well, though this had not been his intention. Aside from the small wound on her shoulder, he had not really hurt her. All in all, considering it coldly, it might be best to go along with him for the moment. Real Stavia hid in a deep, horrid cavern of hate and let actor Stavia go on with it.

The men, including Chernon, wanted her secrets. Secrets she didn't know, didn't have. Were there secrets she could pretend to have? Her life might depend on that. And since Chernon was already convinced that she had them. . . .

She walked, lost in furious thought, devising a strategy for her own survival, setting her anger aside, refusing to feel it. The best bet might be to agree with Chernon. Claim to be his "wife." Claim to be carrying his child. Seemingly, the customs of these barbarians did not permit them to take the wife of another man—and wifehood was demonstrated by production of offspring.

Well, in fact, she thought in dismay, she might be able to demonstrate just that. Sperm could live for several days in the reproductive tract. Abrupt removal of the implant could prompt ovulation. Or, depend upon it, Chernon would try to get at her soon again.

"Secrets," she stormed to herself. What did she have that she could hold out to these men as secrets?

IT TOOK FOUR DAYS for them to arrive at the Holyland. Rel went on ahead to inform Elder Brome that they were coming. When they arrived, the full complement of wives, children, and sons was arrayed on the porches of the wife-houses or Father-house.

Carefully and bit by bit over the four days, Stavia had changed her garb. When they arrived she was clad in her felted coat, with the hood drawn over her head. Under the hood, a wide sash was wrapped around her hair. Under the coat were her thickest trousers and shirt, covered by a long, quilted tunic. She had made no effort to keep her face clean. She was as unattractive as it was possible to appear, under the circumstances.

Cappy told his story. Just as Stavia had changed her appearance for her own benefit, so had he changed the history of the brothers' expedition for their benefit. There was nothing in it of their desires for a woman, nothing in it of their original intention of keeping the woman hidden. Now it was all about duty to the family. They had gone out looking for sheep. They had happened upon the woman. Then it had seemed a good idea to get the woman for the family, to learn the secrets the woman had. There was a problem they hadn't counted on. The woman had a man with her, and he claimed to be her husband. He claimed the woman was carrying his child. He had cut out a magic thing the woman had in her.

Elder Resolution Brome held out his hand and Capable put the tiny implant in it.

"What is this?" Resolution demanded of Chernon.

"He doesn't know," said Stavia before Chernon could speak. "It isn't even magic." This was a calculated risk. She expected to be hit, and was, but it was a not ungentle cuff from Doots.

Chernon had been ready to speak, but now he subsided angrily. She had already cast doubt on what he intended to say.

"What is it, then?" Resolution demanded of her.

"It's a kind of medicine to keep me from dropping babies before their time," she said. "Now he's cut it out, I'll probably lose this one." She patted her stomach. It suited her to pretend pregnancy. She dropped her eyes, pretending modesty as well.

"How come he didn't know?" Retribution demanded. When Rel had arrived with the story, Retribution had been filled with a sudden and irrational hope. Maybe the foreign woman could be his! That hope now died squirming. "How come?"

"It's a woman's thing," she said, eyes down. "We don't bother the men with women's things."

"He says you've got secrets!"

"Just women's things," she said again. "About healing and childbirth. Things like that. Nothing men want to know about." She risked an upward glance, intercepting a hot and angry look shared by most of the older males in this family. The father, his older sons. There seemed to be eight of them, counting the three who had captured them. And only one adolescent girl! She read it all in that, inferred it all. They had learned about it in history class. Female infanticide or female sacrifice, one or both. But not polyandry, which could have solved the situation. She risked another glance, meeting the eyes of the worn, middle-aged woman who stood beside the girl. The girl's mother. Holding a baby. Perhaps not middle aged then. Perhaps younger.

"What've you got on that donkey?" Again this was addressed to Chernon, but Stavia answered for him.

"Herbs for healing," she told him. "That's what I was doing. Collecting herbs for healing."

"I'll think on this," declaimed Resolution. "I'll think and I'll pray. Meantime, take the woman into your house, Susannah."

"Papa," cried Doots. "She'll run off."

"Not with you watchin' the house," the old man said. "You or some of the others. And you take this man down to the bachelor house and keep him there. I'll want some time to think this out." He looked at the implant lying in the palm of his horny hand, eyebrows drawn together to make a deep, vertical furrow. "Think it out."

Stavia turned and went up the two splintery steps to where the woman and girl were standing. Another girl, younger, was hiding behind the open door. "Susannah," Stavia said quietly. "My name is Stavia."

"This here's Chastity," Susannah murmured. "Inside's Faith. She's eight."

"What's the baby's name?"

"Babies don't have names," whispered Chastity. "That'd be right wasteful."

OUTSIDE THE WIFE-HOUSE, Doots and Retribution watched until midnight, at which point Vengeance and Diligence took over. Stavia made one trip to the privy under their voracious gaze. She decided to use something for a chamber pot if she had to go again, rather than submit to these stares.

The supplies from the donkey were stacked on Susannah's porch, including the emergency medical kit that Stavia always carried. She laid out its contents for Susannah's scrutiny. "You're the healer, here?" she asked, already sure of the answer from things the boys had said.

"I'm what they've got," the woman agreed. "All I know's what my mama taught me, and all she knew was what her mama told her."

"I'll leave this kit with you when I go," said Stavia.

"You're not goin' nowhere," Susannah said. "It'll take that old man some time to figure out, but he'll figure a way. Either he'll get you hisself or he'll give you to one of the boys. Retribution, most likely."

"I've already got a husband," Stavia claimed, not liking the sound of the word.

"Maybe. You have a live baby, maybe Papa'll let you be. If that man's still alive, maybe."

"Still alive?"

"Likely they'll kill him. Maybe not, but likely."

"And you don't think they'll let me go."

"Not likely. If I was you, I wouldn't try. Better to have two good legs than two crooked legs. That's what they did to my grandma. She come from out there, too, y'know. Women's Country. That's what she called it, Mama said."

"What do you think your . . . husband is going to do?"

Susannah shook her head. "Somethin' that makes it dutiful to do whatever he wants."

She wouldn't say anything more. Stavia was too tired to ask anything more. She fell onto the hard, straw-filled mattress in the attic room with a sense of fatality. Let happen what would. She couldn't do anything about it until morning.

She was considerably surprised at what she was asked to do about it first thing in the morning on the steps of Susannah's house.

"You take this thing," Resolution Brome told her, handing her the implant, "and put it in Susannah."

"Susannah!" she blurted in disbelief.

"She's had babies afore their time. There was two dropped early afore this last one. You put this thing in Susannah."

Susannah had been watching and listening. When they were inside the house, she began to keen, a little moaning sound in her throat building into a low, hideous howling, "Oh, ahh, ahh, ahh. I can't. I just can't. Oh, don't make me. Oh I can't."

"Shhh," Stavia said automatically, as though Susannah had been a patient in the quarantine center. "Hush. You can't what?"

"I can't have another one. I get so sick. I can't have another one. I'm so tired."

"How old are you?" Stavia asked.

"Twenty-nine," she replied. "I'm too old. Oh I can't. I can't."

Stavia wanted to laugh. Oh, by the Great Lady but this was a mockery, a comedy. "Susannah! Hush. Can you keep a secret from that man out there?"

The keening faded into sniveling, then into silence. "What?"

"I lied about what this thing is for."

"What?" Dazed. Uncertain.

"It actually prevents pregnancy, Susannah. That's why I had it. So I wouldn't get pregnant on this trip. If you don't want another pregnancy, let me go ahead. If I can figure out some way to sterilize the damn thing. . . ."

"How long?" the woman begged. "How long is it good for?"

"Years. Four years. Five. Maybe longer."

"You got another one?"

"Why would I . . . ? No. Just this one."

"Ahh," the woman cried. "Oh, let me think a little. Just a little."

Uncertainly, Stavia filled the kettle and set it on the stove. There was good herbal tea among her supplies, better than anything Susannah had yet offered her. By the time the kettle had boiled and the tea steeped, Susannah had stopped crying. She was gasping now, in a fashion somehow resolute, as though deeply frightened but determined to meet whatever it was with courage.

"Stavia. You do something for me, I'll try to do something for you. You do something for me, I'll try to help you get away from here."

"What? What is it?"

"You make some kind of wound on me to make him think you did what he told you. Then you put that thing in my little girl."

"In Faith! She's only a child!"

"No, no. You put it in Chastity. They're goin' to marry her off, maybe soon. It's so hard on the young ones. If she had four or five years to grow up a little. . . ."

"I see. And what are you going to do?"

"You'll have to tell him it doesn't always work. Or maybe it got ruined, bein' taken out that way. Probly I'll drop another baby or two then he'll let up on me. I wish he'd do it to somebody else. Oh, I do!"

"Me, for instance," Stavia said cynically.

"Anybody but me," Susannah admitted. "But I'll help you get away. I swear I will."

Stavia stared at the woman through the steam from her teacup. How many times had she sat across a table, staring at someone through the steam. Morgot. Myra. Septemius. Trying to understand why people were as they were. Here was no need for much analysis. Susannah was simply beaten down, worn down, worked down. "I could use it on you and come back with one for Chastity," Stavia whispered. "We could arrange to meet out in the woods somewhere. I could bring you a dozen of them, if you like."

Susannah shook her head. "They might catch you again. Besides, there's no need. It's comin' to an end, can't you see? More'n more babies born dead or put out to die because there's somethin' wrong with 'em. It's all comin' to an end, and I'm glad. It's just . . . you know, you get to love your girl children. . . ."

"If that's what you want."

"That's what I want. What d'you need to do it with?"

"I suppose the men drink? Beer? Something stronger than that?"

"Somethin'. Yes."

"I need a little of whatever that is to sterilize this thing as best we can. I need something like—like an awl?"

"I got one I use to make shoes. Is it goin' to hurt her a lot?"

"I think we'd better be sure we don't hurt her at all," Stavia said. Susannah might be able to keep a secret. She wouldn't bet her life on Chastity, however. The girl looked as though she would fade away if anyone said boo.

There were ampoules of local anesthetic in the medical kit, hidden in the lining along with a few other supplies which were, more or less, "secret." Susannah's obvious wound was inflicted painlessly. After Chastity had drunk a strong barbituate and while she slept, Stavia inserted the implant—

after soaking it in something alcoholic, since she dared not boil it—deep in Chastity's buttock, a place which, according to Susannah, no man would ever see.

"Might be he'd feel it in her arm," she said. "But not back there."

"It'll hurt when she wakes up."

"I'll tell her I kilt a big old spider in her bed. Must've bit her somethin' awful."

Susannah reported to Resolution Brome that she had the medicine in her arm. What she actually had in her arm was an injection of beeswax, which was all either she or Stavia could think of to make a raised lump of the proper size and shape. It had been heated enough to sterilize it, or so Stavia hoped.

That night Elder Brome came to the wife-house, and Stavia lay awake listening to the sounds from below, like blows, then later, when he had gone, to Susannah's weeping. Damn it, there were other contraceptives, ancient ones, not totally effective but better than nothing. When morning came, she explained them to Susannah. The woman seemed scarcely to hear. It was as though she wanted to die, wanted to be already dead.

Days passed. Susannah hung her kerchief upon the door latch, then Chastity did so. Weeks went by, then Susannah again.

"You haven't had your uncleanness," Susannah said to her.

Stavia had been thinking the same thing. "Why no," she said. "I told you. I'm pregnant."

"They thought you 'uz lying," the woman said. "Papa did. I'll tell him you wasn't."

The following day they sent her to the old tumbledown wife-house at the edge of the compound where she found Chernon awaiting her. "Well, wife," he said, with an expression that was almost a sneer. "So you're going to give me a son after all."

"Perhaps," she said.

He shook her angrily. "Perhaps?"

"It could be a daughter," she whispered. "Had you thought of that?"

He turned away with an expression of disgust. "Can't you tell? You women? You can tell everything else!"

"I think there were tests, back before the convulsions. They aren't done now. We haven't the equipment."

"Then I'll just have to wait to find out," he said. "Assuming they decide to let me live." He was looking out the window of the rickety house, and she followed his gaze. Under a small tree Vengeance was sitting, whittling at a stick. She walked through the other room of the house to look in the opposite direction. Cappy. So. They were still being watched.

"What do they want from us?" she asked carefully. "I can't do much healing for them without medicines and equipment. Don't they understand that?"

He laughed, a short burst of laughter. "They want you to lose the baby, Stavia. Then you won't be pregnant. Then, if they kill me, you'll be a childless widow, and they can give you to one of the boys. It's a two-way race between Vengeance and Retribution. Poor Cappy's out of it."

"They could kill you anyway."

"But if you have a baby, nobody else can have you."

"Ownership," she said with heavy irony. "Whoever impregnates me, owns me, is that it?"

"That's it!" he blurted, his face angry. "Yes. That's it. And no cheating. No saying yes then no. You have my child and you belong to me, and that's it. Once you've had the child, there'll be no point in killing me, either. If they can't have you, they might as well let me. I can help them get more women."

"From the sheep camp."

"Exactly," he sneered. "I've already told them about that. It's what Michael and Stephon are planning to do anyhow, take over the city and the women. And not just Marthatown. Peggytown and Emmaburg, too. And Agathaville. And if it works there, there are other warriors ready to do it from their garrisons, too."

"Why?" she gasped, horror-struck. "Why, Chernon?"

"Because . . ." for a moment he could not think why.

"Don't you have a good life in the garrison? Plenty of food? Plenty of clothing? Amusements? Do you really want to grub away as shepherds and farmers?"

"You'll do that," he said uncertainly, seeing the look in her eye. "You'll go on doing that."

"Will we?"

"You will or else. They know about that here. The women do it or else."

"What was it you used to tell me about honor?" she asked.

"I haven't done anything dishonorable." He turned to stare out the window once more. "I'll go back to the garrison. In time."

"With or without me, Chernon?"

"With my son," he said. "You can depend on that."

IT WAS OLD REJOICE who pointed out that having Stavia and Chernon living together in the compound was an evil thing. Plentitude agreed with her.

"Her head's not shaved," Rejoice advised her son. "None of the proper things 've been done, so far's we know.

"How do we know whether they was really married or not," Plentitude harangued. "If she wasn't proper married, then she can't be a proper widow, can she?"

Vengeance and Retribution carried this word to Papa, and after due thought, Papa agreed that Stavia and Chernon should be married according to Holyland custom.

Chernon was taken away by the men, Vengeance and Retribution staying behind only long enough to tie Stavia down on the ancient bed frame in the derelict wife-house.

Plentitude, Cheerfulness, Rejoice, and Susannah saw to the rites. Plentitude shaved Stavia's head. Then Rejoice, Cheerfulness, and Susannah beat her. They were using whips of willow, whips which cut the skin, leaving long, ugly welts. Rejoice would have gone on doing it for some time, but Susannah stopped her.

"She's carryin'," Susannah said in an exhausted voice. "Don't do it no more, Rejoice. Let her go."

"You did me worse than that," Cheerfulness said.

"I know. But you wasn't carryin'."

"So. She loses it. That's what they want, isn't it?"

"Maybe it'd kill her, too."

Silence then for a time before the ropes were loosened. Three of them went away. Stavia was silent, immobile, so consumed by fury and a sense of violation that she could not speak, would not move.

"Reason they do it," Susannah was saying in her weary voice, "is that you should know ahead of time. That's what your husband will do to you if you fail in duty to him. You should know how it feels, so's not to provoke him."

"And my head," grated Stavia. "What's the reason for that."

"So's you don't look like anything to stir up lust. Man's got to do his duty, but he's got to do it as duty, not because he likes it."

"Besides," Stavia said, turning on one side with a yelp of pain. "It violates the woman, doesn't it? It diminishes her. It makes her feel shame. Which is what they really want."

"Hush," cried Susannah. "Oh, Stavia, hush. I kept them from doin' it too hard. I did what I could."

"Get my kit," Stavia instructed. "There's some salve in there. . . ."

"They took it," Susannah said. "You can't have it anymore unless your husband says so. He'll tell you can you use it or not."

Chernon was having his own induction into Holyland society and was not available to give permission. The wounds on her back became infected.

Two days later, made stupid and slow by pain and fever, Stavia tried to get away. Cappy was asleep. She had almost reached the woods when he woke and saw her. In his frustration, he picked up the only weapon at hand and went after her, bringing the edge of the shovel down upon her head with a solid, chunking sound. Intent upon her escape, Stavia had not even heard him coming up behind her and she felt the blow only as a silent, hideous explosion which dropped her into darkness.

When Chernon returned and saw her, he exploded in fury and would have killed Cappy if they had not held him back. He was very angry, but he did not cry.

29

REHEARSAL:

IPHIGENIA You see, it's as we've tried to tell you, Great Achilles. Women are no good to you dead.

ACHILLES Then I . . . I, too. . . .

IPHIGENIA Are but a ghost. Your killing and raping done. Your battles over. A wanderer among the shades, like us.

ACHILLES But I—I am an immortal! The poets say I am. Destined to walk among the Gods!

IPHIGENIA Are the Gods then dead?

ACHILLES They live!

IPHIGENIA And when you lived, you walked among them.

ACHILLES I did?

POLYXENA We all did.

ACHILLES What did the poets mean?

IPHIGENIA That you would be immortal while you lived, and may still be

well remembered now you're dead. Men like to think well of them-
selves . . .
POLYXENA   . . . and the poets help them do it.
ACHILLES   *(Weeps)*
POLYXENA   He cries like a child. Poor boy.

"Stop," called the director. "Stavia, when you do the next line, 'Did the
men cry?' bend over and touch his face.

"Touch his face?" asked Stavia. "Achilles?"

"Yes. Touch his face to see if the tears are real. And then again, right at
the end, lay your face alongside his when you say the last line."

"Right," said Stavia, bending, reaching out a hand to touch Joshua's
face.

IPHIGENIA   *(To Polyxena)* Tell me. Did the men cry when they slit your
throat?

Stavia's hand was wet and she looked at it in amazement, and at the tears
coursing down Joshua's face as he looked at her.

"No, no they did not," Polyxena cried.

"They didn't cry when they were slitting mine, either," Stavia said,
through the rasping dryness memory had made of her throat.

30

M ORGOT WAS IN A COUNCIL MEETING when one of the women came to tell her there was a servitor waiting. If it had been Joshua, the woman would have said so, and Morgot bit down an expression of annoyance at being disturbed only to swallow it when she saw that it was Corrig, white-faced and trembling.

"What?" she asked. "Who? Stavia?"

"Yes, ma'am. Joshua felt it, too. Both of us, just a few minutes ago."

"Hurt? Badly hurt?" Morgot fought down a shriek. "Dead?"

"Not dead. No. Joshua says we should go at once. I think so, too."

"How far?"

"We can't tell. A long way. Too far to locate with any certainty from here."

"You'll need a wagon to carry . . . tools and things."

"Joshua says we'll get Septemius Bird to take us. Septemius knows something, Joshua thinks. Joshua is on his way to Septemius now."

"Do you want help?"

233

"Yes, ma'am. Joshua said to ask you if the Councilwomen would approve Jeremiah and the two new men."

"Councilwoman Jessie's Jeremiah? Councilwoman Carol's men?"

He nodded, seeing her puzzlement. "Joshua says they can see up close clearer than any of us."

"Go get them," she said. "I'll fix it with the women."

"Morgot," he said, forgetting himself. "Ma'am."

"Yes, Corrig."

"Joshua said to be sure and tell you it's all part of the other thing."

"The garrison? Is something going to happen right away, Corrig?"

"Not right away, ma'am. But be careful."

31

Stavia was the winter princess. She had a sheaf of grain in one hand and a knife in the other. The Council was sending her out to find the deer. "Cow," they had said, pointing to the picture in the book. "This is a cow deer." It had antlers which curved like the new moon, one point coming forward over the animal's brow and the other extending back in an enormous, weighty curve laden with branches and juttings of horn. "About this big," they said, indicating something which would be about the height of a donkey. The cows had white fur down their chests, muzzles spattered with foam and long, grasping tongues. Perhaps they told her this or perhaps she had read it somewhere else.

She did not know why they were sending her. Surely one of the others would be better fitted for the job. They already knew what cows were and how they should be handled. Why pick on her, a stranger? She asked them this.

"Your dowry," they said. "The cows will be your dowry." Why she needed a dowry, or even what one was, she couldn't remember. There was a sense of urgency about it all, however, something she could not merely ignore. Urgency and inevitability. It had to be done.

Somehow, she had lost her own clothes. They lent her boots and a heavy, quilted coat and a cap with earflaps which tied under her chin. She was naked under the coat. She could feel the cold at her crotch, a wind blowing there. It wouldn't be so cold if she could only get her legs together, but something prevented that.

It was better simply to ignore the cold at her crotch and go out into the snow. Someone had pointed out the way she should go, over there, where the fold in the hills opened up and the trees showed dark against the snowfield. Someone else had pointed out the tracks the cows had left, a cloven, vaguely triangular mark. . . .

"She may die," a woman said.

Whoever it was who was speaking tied the bandage more securely on her head and wiped blood from her face. Stavia ignored it.

"You shouldn't have hit her." The same woman's voice.

"She was tryin' to get away!" A boy's voice, a young man, uncertain but defiant.

"What good is she to you with her head bashed in?" The woman asked. "What were you going to do, kill her and then do your duty on her dead body? Cover her up for decency's sake!"

The sound of a slap, a cry.

"Mind your words, woman. That was disrespectful of your son." A man's voice, heavy, ponderous with something lubricious and inflexible about it.

Stavia decided she had listened long enough. It was time to go search for the reindeer cows. The trail led into the darkness, into the trees, the forest, where the wind soughed in the branches and all voices were stilled. Even in the dark she could see the footprints. They shone like little fiery hearts in the shadows. She followed them.

"You'll heal her, Susannah," the man's heavy voice demanded.

"I'll do what I can." A kind of stubborn dignity there.

"You'll heal her."

"Husband, I'll do what I can. I've got no magic to heal wounds like this. Maybe if you'd of given her time to teach me the things she knew, I could do something. There's things in her medical bag, but I don't know what they are. Capable chops wood real good. He does skulls real good, too. You got to face it, Resolution Brome. He maybe killed this girl."

"This devil."

"Doesn't look like a devil to me," she retorted with that same perverse integrity, tears bubbling through it. Stavia wanted to laugh, but she couldn't. "Looks like any woman's been abused bad. Looks like any wife. Beat and shaved and left hungry."

Slap again. Cry again. Not a surprised sound, more a ritual one. Slap; ahh. Slap; ahh. The one following the other like an acknowledgment.

"You'll heal her." It was a command. There was a promise of pain in it.

Silence. Then, "I done all I can do with what I have here. I got to get some things from my wife-house." Some new emotion in that statement. More than the words. An ultimate sadness. A finality. Whoever the woman was, she went away, into a distance too far to follow.

It was not Stavia's concern. Stavia went back to tracking the footprints. They led down a long, winding pathway among the trees. Ahead of her was moonlight, come from somewhere. Not the sky. The earth, perhaps. Light from the snow itself. And there were the cows, their antlers curved twigs against the trunks of huge trees, standing like gray statues, as still as though carved from stone. Only their breath told her they were alive, little puffs of steam coming from their black muzzles, now, and again, and again. All she had to do was offer them the grain she carried in her left hand and drive them back.

The bellow came from behind her. She turned, seeing it all at once, the source of the light, the reason that the reindeer cows were here. They hadn't run off. They had been stolen away and brought here, by him. His antlers swept back and upward like the edge of a breaking wave, foaming forward into a dozen lesser points of white bone. Over his forehead other points protruded, bright fringes of ivory. His muzzle pointed up as he called to her, telling her why he was here. The cows belonged to him. Now that she had come, she belonged to him, too. There would be no rounding up, no taking back. The white mane around his shoulders and down his chest was a royal robe, his kingship made manifest.

"Go find that fool woman," the man's heavy voice said. "She's been gone long enough to cook a meal. Chastity, go find your maw."

"Yes, Papa." A girl. There was a girl there, somewhere.

It wasn't important.

The bull deer bellowed once more. "Mine," he said. "Mine."

"I need them," she said in a reasonable tone. "Don't you see, I need them."

"Mine." He lowered his antlers. They pointed at her head, her chest. He scraped with his feet, finding solidity from which an attack could be launched. "They are mine."

"You don't even use them for anything," she said. "You just own them. If they have bull calves, you fight them and kill them. You say they're yours, but they aren't useful to you at all!"

"Mine," he said again.

The girl's voice came back, frightened. "Papa, Papa, she's dead. Ma's dead!"

"What do you mean dead?"

"She's hanging from the ridgebeam, Papa. On a rope. I can't reach her to get her down. . . ."

There was confusion. Stavia ignored it. The knife was in her right hand. Over her shoulder was a rope. "Will you let me have them?" she asked the bull deer. "I need them. More important than that, they need themselves. They have names, you know. Names of their own!"

"Mine," he trumpeted. "Mine the power! Mine the glory! Mine the females! Mine the young!"

She threw the rope. It moved as though it could think its way through the air, a serpent which knew how to go where it had to go, looping around the mighty antlers and around the tree, a great slithering of purpose. She made it fast while the bull struggled and screamed. Then, miraculously, there was another rope in her hand to hold the bull's back legs and another tree to tie them to. She had a knife. It was ready in her hand and she moved close against that hot, musk-smelling, muscle-throbbing beast, thrusting herself against it, her blade out to cut, cut, letting the parts fall on the snow where they steamed hotly while the great deer screamed and screamed and she said . . . something. What was it she said? A line from a play. Something about crying. . . .

When she had done, she drove the cows back the way she had come. Behind her, the magical rope loosened and the animal went away. She could not hear it anymore. There was no bellowing but only the soft breath of the cows around her, the light reflecting from their eyes as they stared at her, the steam from their muzzles rising. "I did it for you, too," she said.

"I brought them," she said when she came where people were again. "See, here they are. All of them."

"You'll need them," they told her. "If you live, they will be your dowry."

She heard a man's heavy voice, full of baffled fury. "Put her in that little back room and lock her in."

Chernon objecting to this. "She's dying. She can't move. There must be someone else with some healing skill. . . ."

"Susannah was the only one here. Not goin' to waste time an' trouble goin' over the mountain for anybody else. Let her die if she dies. It's All Father's will, either way."

Chernon's voice again, and the sound of a blow, and then nothing but quiet and jostling dark with the cows all around her, their rank, animal smelling filling her nostrils.

"If you live," the cows told her, "you'll need us." They stayed with her, leading her through the dank darkness which went on and on until she supposed it would simply go on forever.

DILIGENCE, the twenty-eight-year-old son of Rejoice Brome, had been rounding up a recalcitrant sheep that had seemed possessed of a demon. It was one of the ram lambs lately captured from the devil women, which probably explained the animal's orneriness, but it also made the animal valuable, which meant Diligence couldn't just consign it to the netherworld and leave it to be eaten by coyotes—though he fervently hoped that's what would happen someday, when he wasn't the one responsible. He didn't dare cross Papa at the moment. Nobody dared cross Papa right now, not even a little. It was only yesterday Susannah had hung herself up on that old rope, only yesterday that the demon woman got shut up in the back room of Papa's house to live or die. Not even a day yet since that fella from outside had that set-to with Papa and got hisself knocked down. No time to be causin' trouble was the way Diligence had it figured out, so he'd kept after that ram lamb until he found it even though it had taken all day.

He had just shut the sheep in the fold in the falling dark, fighting it every step of the way, and was about to go up the path to the bachelor house when something stepped out of the trees in his path.

It had teeth, and the teeth glowed. He saw that much. It had a face that was way too big for anything he knew of. His mind shut down in panic and he tried to dodge it by jumping into the trees along the path, but something invisible caught hold of him and the next thing he knew he was lying on his belly with his head pulled up by the hair by the invisible thing sitting on him while the glowing teeth and the glowing eyes moved around like there was maybe one and maybe three or four things coming at him in the night.

"Chernon?" asked a horrible, echoing voice. "Where is our friend Chernon?"

Diligence couldn't think. He didn't know what a Chernon was. He gargled, spit filling up his throat as the thing on his back did something cruel to one of his hands. "Arghhah," he gurgled around a half scream. "Don't know. What is it?"

The thing let up on him a little. "You people brought a man and a woman from out there. The man's name is Chernon. He's not really a man. He's a demon. He's a friend of ours, and we want to know where he is."

"Up t'Papa's house," Diligence howled. "He was up t'Papa's house with the woman. Cappy hit her with the shovel and she ain't been able to talk since then. . . .''

"Ahh," said the deep voice, who had already known that Stavia had been badly hurt. "There's an angel coming to get that woman. You shouldn't have hurt her. That's something you shouldn't have done!" Later on, remembering, Diligence had the strange idea that the voice had had pain in it, but at the moment he didn't think anything because something hit him behind the ear with a kind of lightning flash and he didn't know anything else.

"Cappy," said one of the invisible creatures. "That would be one of the young ones up at their barracks. I'll take care of that one."

"We'll take the masks and go create a little more demonology," the deep voice said. "Papa's house would be the one up the hill there?"

"Take you about an hour?"

"About that."

"Who's got the feathers?"

"I have. I'll bring them."

As luck would have it, Cappy Brome was leaving the bachelor house for the privy when the invisible thing caught him, threw him down with his face in the dirt, and then pounced on him.

"Cappy?" a voice whispered to him. "You're Cappy?"

Though almost paralyzed with fright, Cappy managed to nod. The thing that was sitting on him seemed satisfied with this. "That woman you hit with the shovel, that was a holy woman," the voice said. "She's a healer."

Cappy convulsed as he tried to throw off his attacker. "She 'uz a whore," he cried. "Walkin' around with her hair hangin' and her body showin'. She 'uz no better'n a whore of Babylon. She 'uz tryin' to get away. . . .''

"Umm," said the voice. "Well, it's obvious that disputation is not going to change your mind. I will, therefore, simply make my point in blood." And with that Cappy felt his shirt ripped away and a knife moving on his back. "An angel is coming to rescue her," the voice said, punctuating the remark with a whole series of jabs and slices of the blade. "Remember that!" Then something hit Cappy on the head and the thing went away.

From up the valley came confused sounds of people yelling. Fire bloomed from the location of Elder Jepson's barn.

"Good idea," said the invisible thing, moving toward the bachelor house. After a brief interval, fire glimmered at the base of the bachelor house and was fed into rampageous life with handfuls of straw.

INSIDE THE TINY, STUFFY ROOM in Elder Brome's house, Stavia lay in stupefied darkness. From time to time, the darkness wavered and broke, leaving a gray space at its center in which there was sometimes a sound. This time there was a tapping at the window, a soft, almost random knocking, as a twig might tap in a light wind. Even through her pain, through the gray blanket of mist which wrapped her around, stifling her, she told herself there was no wind, there was no tree, there could be no twig tapping. In her mind the twig wavered, becoming a tree, a forest, blackness once more, full of great, horned beasts which bellowed at the sky. "Come, Stavia," they cried.

"Stavia," someone whispered, evoking the grayness again.

She could only moan. It was what was needed, an imperative moan, voiced so that the twig, the forest, the darkness would know where she was. Still, she did it softly. Then again. There was no shout from the other rooms of the place, no threat. She moaned again. Worth the risk of more pain to be able to express pain. Hurt *some*thing. Hurt somewhere. She was in the middle of a seeking whirlpool of pain, like a chip in an eddy, whipped around and around by it.

Perhaps there was a whisper outside the window. She couldn't be sure. It didn't matter. The moaning had taken too much energy. She had no more to wonder with. The bellowing blackness came again.

Far away, outside, over a hill, perhaps, or across some unmeasured gulf of shadowed night, there was a great deal of unshaped noise. A blot of noise, running off in all directions, with clangor in it and voices and jagged edges of agony.

Above her in the house someone stirred, cursed, shouted. Heavy feet stamped their way downstairs. Voices banged together. Doors uttered. A confusion of noise here; another one there; and then the two moving toward one another, mixing, like ugly colors in water, swirling. Dark yellow and sullied wine, in saw-toothed patterns.

Near the head of her bed something snapped.

Cold air on her face. Hurting air.

"Ahhhh," she said, not aware she'd said anything.

"Here," said someone. "She's tied up. By all that's holy those bastards. . . ." There was light on her face, very dim, as from a dark lantern. Even the light hurt. When the pressure on her shoulders stopped and someone's arms raised her, it hurt even more and she began to scream—began only. There were soft things in her mouth keeping her from screaming. Fingers. She bit the fingers and someone cursed.

"Stavia!" voice in her ear. "It's Joshua. Be still, love. We're getting you out." She felt a prick in her arm, something sharp to hold against the wall-wide agony of all the other hurt. "For the pain," Joshua's voice said. "Be still."

"Out," her mind said. "Be quiet or they can't get you out." She stopped fighting the hurt and let it be. The blackness came back as she thought, "That's good. I won't be around to care."

"Get every piece of rope," Joshua's voice said. "Spread the bed back up neatly. Put the feathers around the bed. Remember to make those footprints down the wall under the window. . . ." They were carrying her out through the door, through the house, out the front door, then away into the trees. She was cradled in Joshua's arms. There was someone else, whispering. She knew that voice.

"It's Corrig, Stavia," someone whispered. "It's all right. Be still."

Then there wasn't anything else at all as the pain went somewhere else and left her alone with the loving, comfortable darkness.

ELDER JEPSON'S BARN burned to the ground. Elder Brome's bachelor house was only partly burned, though the whole front of it would need to be replaced whenever people could get to it. That much they could see by lantern light. By that same light they could see the words carved on Capable's back as well. "She is a holy woman." It was not until Capable came around that they were able to ask him who "she" was, and it was only then that they went looking for Stavia.

The room was untouched, as though no one had ever been in it. There was no sign of the woman, or of the ropes which had bound her to the bed. There were footprints leading vertically down the wall from the high window. There were several great white feathers lying by the bed, feathers larger than any they had ever seen.

"The thing said an angel was comin' to get her," Diligence cried. "He said it. An' Susannah said we shouldn't have hurt her. Susannah said it wuz a mistake."

Elder Brome struck his son across the mouth without changing expression. He did not wish to be reminded of Susannah. As for the idea that any woman might have had anything sensible to say about the whole matter, that smacked pretty much of heresy. However, the feathers and the footprints and what the boys had to say about the faces made bile rise in his throat and burn there until he spat and spat again. He was frightened. Something had gone wrong somewhere. Something needed thinking out.

Elder Jepson brought several of his grown sons to talk it over, and Diligence repeated to this group what he had seen and heard. "The devil said Chernon was their friend," he claimed over and over again, and this information was supported by others. Several of the younger men had seen and heard the demon or demons. They had chased Chernon in the night but had lost him. They were sent to track him, find him if he could be found, and bring him in.

"Hear Susannah kilt herself," Elder Jepson remarked. "Why'd she go and do that?"

Elder Brome affected not to have heard. Unwisely, Vengeance said, "She left a note. Said she was tired of bein' hit."

"Chastised," corrected Elder Jepson.

"She said hit," Vengeance insisted. "Said it 'uz better bein' dead because he couldn't do nothin' to her dead. Said she'd rather die than have Papa do his duty on her again."

This time Resolution Brome knocked his son to the floor.

Cappy, meantime, was harboring a deep and abiding suspicion that when he had used the shovel on the devil . . . on the holy woman, he had done something very, very wrong, something wronger than Papa would ever admit to. He looked up and caught the swollen eye of his half brother, Vengeance Brome, finding in that glance a gleam of something hard and implacable. Vengeance, Cappy realized, hated Papa.

It was a revelation which Cappy was to ruminate over for some time, a revelation which would eventually be shared with others before spreading like a cancer through the Holyland. It gave them all someone on whom to blame the ultimate Armageddon.

THE NEXT TIME Stavia woke, the vague grayness in which she was submerged included movement, a bumpy rocking. Someone was doing something to her head.

"It's all right," said Joshua. I'm cleaning this cut on your head, sweetheart. Be still. I'm sorry if it hurts."

"Doesn't hurt," she tried to say, through swollen lips.

"Luckily," he went on in a soothing voice, "your head is already shaved. That means I didn't have to shave it. You've got a nasty gash here."

"Hit me," she explained. "When I got away from there, one of them hit me with something." None of the consonants sounded right. Evidently she couldn't quite move her lips.

"Ah," he said. "Well, that explains it."

"Where Chernon?" she asked. It seemed important to know that he was not here.

"Mumble?" asked someone.

"She wants to know where Chernon is."

"The last time I saw him, he was running for his life with about six Holylanders after him." A stranger's voice. ". . . angel coming to rescue her."

"Angel?" she asked, fading into darkness once more.

"Angel," affirmed Joshua. "We left angel feathers in that room you were in, just to prove it."

There was nothing after that for a long time, then a cessation of movement, firelight, someone spooning something warm into her mouth. Four or five shadows, people moving.

"They'll find us," she said, clearly.

Corrig leaned over her, smoothing her forehead. "No chance, love. They aren't even looking. They're all huddled in their houses hoping the devils don't come back and finish them off."

"Devils?"

He started to explain, but she was gone again.

When the light came back, she asked, "Angel . . . feathers?"

"Septemius gave us a whole bunch of his stagy stuff. . . ."

"Why did you do that?" she wondered.

Several voices, including Septemius's, offered explanation: ". . . credulous and superstitious. . . ." ". . . inbred to the point they'll only last a few more generations . . ." ". . . spread confusion and general dismay. . . ."

She didn't hear the rest.

SHE KEPT FADING AWAY. It was only slowly, over a long period of time, that she began to understand and remember anything that they told her. There was something about her eyes being different sizes that Joshua was worried about. She was in Septemius's wagon. They were almost back at Marthatown. She was in the wagon, alive, because Joshua and Corrig had sensed her capture, felt it when Chernon had hurt her. Over all those miles, they had simply known. They had known when Cappy hit her, too, which had brought them running. In her delirium, this did not seem impossible. It did not even seem unlikely. They had known, that was all, and like the good servitors they were, they had come to get her.

Septemius was there, and nobody was trying to keep secrets from Septemius because he already knew about it. Whatever it was that Joshua and Corrig could do, Kostia and Tonia could do as well. It was a secret, but some people knew about it.

So much Stavia understood. Knowing certain things about Joshua that she did, it didn't take much understanding. The only thing that really surprised her was that Corrig was part of it.

From the time Chernon had cut her, it had taken almost forty days to track her down. According to Corrig, that part had been simple though time consuming. They could feel where she was, but not how far. And, at first, she had not stayed in one place. From some directions, they could not feel her at all. The new men had been invaluable, as they seemed to have a unique sense of distance that the others lacked. It had taken longer than they liked, but they had located her at last, luckily only a day after she had been struck down by Cappy.

On their way, in Septemius's wagon, driving relays of donkeys all day and all night, they had discussed what they would do, and how, thoroughly betraying themselves to the old man in the process and completely destroying any illusions he might have had about the nature of servitors. In the end, it was Septemius who suggested that they raid the Holyland in the guise of devils, leaving ambiguous evidence of the supernatural behind them wherever possible.

"They're superstitious," he had said. "I remember that. They're self-righteous and superstitious and fearful and vengeful as all get out. If you just go in and get her, they're likely to think in terms of retaliation, and that will put your sheep-camp women at risk. If devils and angels and whatnot go in and get her, the Holylanders won't know what to think or who to retaliate against. A good demonic raid could keep them confused for several generations!"

Joshua found this sensible. He thought it was particularly sensible after Septemius told him about Chernon.

"That boy didn't think this up by himself," Joshua said.

"That's what my nieces and I decided," Septemius agreed. "I thought he'd been put up to it, and they agreed. Not that it wasn't his own nature to go along. He's a smooth-talking little weasel, too. Both of the girls commented on that."

"Then just in case he's been up to smooth talk down there among the barbarians, we'd best do what we can to discredit him." Claiming Chernon as a friend of demons, they decided, would be useful in destroying any credibility Chernon might have established. Joshua did not want to report to Morgot that Chernon had been left alive among the Holylanders to fulminate more trouble, later on.

Once they had located her, they had waited only until dark to mount their rescue attempt.

"You almost waited too long," she murmured to Corrig and Joshua. The other three servitors had left them to travel north at speed in order to arrive home long before Stavia, Joshua, or Corrig came there. As far as Marthatown was concerned, Stavia had had an accident while on her exploration trip and the family servitors had gone to fetch her. That other servitors had been absent simultaneously was purely coincidental. Servitors were always coming and going on one kind of business or another.

"I don't know if I'd have lasted much longer," she murmured again.

"Sorry, love," said Joshua, raising her on his shoulder to feed her more soup. "We didn't know you were going to try to escape."

"Couldn't stand it," she mumbled through the mouthful of vegetables and broth. "Couldn't stand him."

"Yes," said Corrig. "That's easy to understand."

Sometimes it was Septemius who raised her head and fed her broth. It was to him that she whispered the terrible secret, the one she had forgotten until that moment and forgot again a moment afterward.

They entered Marthatown at night, driving the creaking wagon through dark streets to the small hospital where Morgot and a quiet little room awaited. Morgot took one look at Stavia and turned away, her voice coming oddly, as though from a distance. "Janine, Winny, will you attend to this, please?" Then she went away, not to return for a little, by which time Janine and Winny had Stavia bathed and gowned and stretched out on the clean, unmoving bed with her head on a proper pillow.

Morgot came back then, with her eyes red but her voice perfectly calm. "It's going to take you a while to heal, child. I suggest you go right off to sleep and start doing it."

32

CHERNON ACCUSED US of knowing secrets," Stavia said, rolling her head upon the pillow. She had tried to sleep, as Morgot had suggested, but she couldn't. She was feverish, restless. All through the night her eyes had popped open at every movement, every sound. Now that it was daylight again and Morgot was there, Stavia needed to tell her things. "He said the women had secrets. Things he wanted to know. To be powerful."

There was a long, pregnant silence, one so reminiscent of other silences which had fallen from time to time when she had been very young (silences older people had imposed when they became aware she was listening) that she opened her eyes, almost expecting to find herself a child again. Morgot was looking at her intently. "We do have secrets," she said. "Of course."

"I know," Stavia said. In the wakeful night hours she had thought about that, about the things she had said to Chernon, all unwitting. "I'm afraid I told Chernon a few of them."

"Like?"

"Like how we know who a baby's father is—the blood test."

Morgot didn't say anything for a moment. "Well, that's really no secret,

247

Stavia. Chernon may never return here. If he does, and if he tells the warriors everything you told him about that, it doesn't really matter."

"Like the contraceptive implants."

"We would have preferred they didn't know, but it doesn't cause any major emergency. We use implants for many things besides contraception. That can be managed, I think." The expectant silence came again. "You are pregnant, you know?"

"I thought I might be. Chernon cut the implant out some time ago."

"It was the shock and pain of that which Joshua and Corrig felt," Morgot said. "I saw the wound. Not a neat job."

"I don't think Chernon cared."

"No, possibly not. The question is, do you want to have the child?"

Stavia turned her head wearily away. Did she want to have this child? Was there any reason not to want a child, except for her fury at Chernon, this blistering feeling she had when she thought of him, as though he were a wound that needed cautery, a boil to be lanced, something requiring an immediate, terrible pain so that healing could start. "Is there some reason of health that I shouldn't?" she asked, begging for an excuse.

"We're not sure yet. The wounds on your back are fairly superficial. Painful, because they're infected. Unless there's something else, something unforeseen, you could probably manage the pregnancy without any physical damage."

"Well then. What was it Myra said that time? I've got to start sometime." It wasn't what she felt, but she was too sick to feel what she felt. If she gave in to her anger, it would overwhelm her, wash her away, and she would never find herself again. Somehow, though she was conscious for longer periods each day, she felt no stronger, no more able to cope. She did not want to feel anything, decide anything.

"There are at least two differences between you and Myra."

"I don't understand."

"You were forced and she wasn't. And you're carrying a warrior's child."

"Well so was Myra. . . ." Stavia's voice faded away into aching quiet.

Morgot was shaking her head. No. To and fro like the pendulum of a clock. No.

The silence became deeper, more vibrant with meaning, things that were not said suddenly more important than anything she had ever been told. Something she should have known, should have guessed.

"Myra's first child . . . little Marcus. He wasn't Barten's child." She didn't say it as a question. It wasn't a question. "Not Barten's child. Not any warrior's child. The warriors father no children. Not for any of us."

Stavia shut her eyes and the dizziness came again, washing over her in a series of little quivering perceptions, as though the room shook to a strong wind, now, again, again. Something was wrong inside. Something broken that she hadn't known about, that Morgot hadn't known about, something wrong in there, like a fire burning at her from inside. A hairline crack in some essential part which was now growing wider, letting the fiery darkness out.

When she spoke it was so softly that she didn't know if Morgot would even hear her. "Reindeer," she said as consciousness fled away. "Reindeer."

33

STAVIA AS IPHIGENIA and Joshua as Achilles and all the rest of the cast—including the director, who had finally decided what it was she wanted from the performance—were walking through a final, afternoon rehearsal. The performance would be given that evening. The summer theater was gay with banners, and the food kiosks were already steaming with flavorful things to be sold when dusk came. The small cast was going through the play in costume and makeup, a final run-through to get used to the just-completed set, speaking their lines over the sound of the chorus practicing across the grass. The walls of Troy tumbled in wreckage about them. Hecuba huddled with Andromache. Halfway up the walls of Troy, Achilles knelt, weeping. Stavia as Iphigenia leaned down to him as directed, her hand on his cheek.

IPHIGENIA   Achilles, why are you crying?

ACHILLES   It's gone, all gone. My honors and my glory. Thetis, my mother, said my name would be immortal as the name of Jove himself, yet here I am beside these broken walls, alone, alone. . . .

IPHIGENIA   I'd not have said alone.

ACHILLES   Who's here? Is my friend Patroclus here? Is Ajax here? Where are those of the Argive host who died? All my brave Myrmidons, where are they?

HECUBA   What is he saying, Agamemnon's child?

IPHIGENIA   He cries for heroes, Hecuba. He cries for his friends or any other dead Greek to keep him company.

HECUBA   Lonely, is he? With us here to attend him?

POLYXENA   Ungrateful of him, isn't it? Achilles! We are here to keep you company? Tss, why should you be lonely?

ACHILLES   *(Passionately)* What have women to say to a warrior?

CASSANDRA   Oh, a woman might say much, if he would listen. Men do not listen, though. They disregard the things we say as though we were caged birds, singing our songs by rote. For instance, I've told Agamemnon what fate awaits him, but he laughs. . . .

IPHIGENIA   *(Tittering)* He never listened to good counsel before. Why should he now?

ACHILLES   *(Continuing, as though there had been no interruption)* Yes, what have women to say to a warrior? And what has a warrior to say to women?!

ANDROMACHE   Why, you might tell us how you made us love you. I had a father once in goodly Thebe, the city of the Cilicians. You came there, warrior. You sacked the place, slaying my father and his seven sons. What fame you brought my brothers, great Achilles, slain by such a man as you. You could speak of that.

IPHIGENIA   Or speak of your wooing. Tell how you killed the menfolk of Briseis. Tell how you raped her there inside your tent while calling her a "fruitling of your spear." Warriors have much that they could say to women if they would use their tongues. . . .

ACHILLES   It's not my fault she longed for my embrace. She threw herself before my sandaled feet, reaching with ivory arms to feel my thighs. What you call rape was only that sweet violence the trees well know when, lashed by summer storm, they crash together in the wilderness. . . .

IPHIGENIA   What storms these were in which so many died! What summer tempests leaving all those dead! So many husbands, fathers, brothers slain! No doubt they were struck down all tenderly, caressed by loving blades.

POLYXENA   If Briseis threw herself at your feet, she might have been pleading for mercy. Had you considered that?

ACHILLES   *(Sulkily)* If Patroclus were here, he'd understand. We men understand one another.

IPHIGENIA   Well, Patroclus has gone on down to Hades along with all the rest of the dead Greeks.

HECUBA   And Trojans. . . .

IPHIGENIA   And Trojans. You'll have company enough when you come there. I've been there and I know.

POLYXENA   That's true! For you were slain ten years ago.

IPHIGENIA   Ten years, such little time. But long enough to learn the way to Hell and back again.

———

"Stavia," said the director uncertainly, seeing her stagger. "Are you all right?"

"Of course," Stavia said, feeling the flood of momentary emotion depart. "Sorry. I didn't mean to interrupt."

It had been ten years from the time she had taken Dawid to the warriors until the night a few weeks ago that he had chosen to remain with the garrison. Time enough to learn the way to Hell and back again.

34

STAVIA'S HEAD INJURY had been worse than they thought. The chief surgical officer had drilled holes in her skull and lifted a piece out, like the lid of a teapot, removed the clot which pressed against her brain, then laid the bone back with the scalp neatly stitched across it and white bandages to cover it all. Through it all, Stavia dreamed again of the deer, over and over again.

There was a long time during which voices spoke in other rooms, a time when everything was far away and nothing was important enough to look at or listen to. She did not really hear the conversation between Septemius and Morgot as they sat by her bed, watching her breathe, breathing for her when she forgot to do so, though the substance of it entered her, as the dreams had done.

"How did you find out?" Morgot asked.

"Ah." Septemius thought about this. "I would say through the innocent eye, madam. Through untutored observation, in which we do not perceive the fabric of your lives, worked into the pattern you are accustomed to showing others. We are therefore free to make other patterns from the threads we see. We unraveled all your threads and from their substance rewove the truth. Our attention focused, for example, on the amount of medical attention given women before and after carnival. . . ."

"To prevent disease," Morgot said quietly.

"There was rather more to it than that. After all, we itinerants have had experience with what you do to prevent disease. We've been in the quarantine house, and it's no lengthy process. No, all this doctoring was to do something more, to prevent pregnancy during carnival, to assure pregnancy afterward. I assume the servitors chosen to father children provide the necessary . . . ah . . . wherewithal."

"Yes. They do. Willingly."

Stavia imagined his lips curving. "I did not think you took it by force. Then, too, madam, I am a magician. Magicians understand misdirection. We do it all the time. We say, watch my left hand, and then the right hand plays the trick. So it was easy for us to see the misdirection in what you were doing. You women were saying, 'Watch us bringing sons to their warrior fathers, watch us weeping,' and all the time the trick was going on somewhere else."

"Surely you weren't sure," Morgot said. "You're not supposed to know anything about it."

"There were other clues." Septemius nodded. "Firstly, everyone said that more men came back through the gates in each succeeding generation. That argued for something, didn't it? Selection, perhaps? Tonia and Kostia are attending classes in Women's Country, and they bring their books home. Remarkable how many books in Women's Country refer to selection. Even Chernon had a book with something in it of great importance to Women's Country. Put there as a clue, I'm sure. Put there, so that those with eyes will see it. Needless to say, he couldn't see it. He sought the secret of Women's Country, and it was there before his eyes. . . ."

"And then there's the matter of the servitors. Some of them, of course, are like Sylvia's Minsning, fluttery little fellows who are simply happier in Women's Country as cooks or tailors or what have you. For the most part, however, the servitors are more like Joshua or Corrig, highly competent, calm, judicious men, and they are highly respected, particularly by the most competent women. It argues that both their status and their skills exceed what is generally supposed."

"Skills?"

"You know what I'm talking about, Councilwoman. We need not play games with one another. I am too old for that. They have martial skills to be sure—I saw that in action down in the Holylands—but something other than that as well. My nieces have it, too. I've known a few others who have it. It's a valued trait among showmen, this ability to hear trouble at a distance, to know where people are, to know what's going to happen. The old words for it were telepathy, clairvoyance. They are very old words, from before the convulsions, though I think they were only theoretical then. Tell me, did you women plan it?"

She shook her head. "It just appeared. Like a gift. A surprisingly high number of the men who came back had it, that's all."

"Perhaps because they had it, they chose to come back."

"We've considered that."

"And, of course, you've bred that quality in."

"We've tried," she admitted. "We had hoped many women might turn up with it, but there are very few women with the talent. It does tend to breed true in sons. I am glad to know about your nieces. For a time we worried that it might be sex-linked." She rose to look out the window, turned to stare at Stavia's pale face, then sat down once more. "I suppose Kostia and Tonia know all about this."

"They do. And all three of us are as safe as any secret holder you may know, Morgot. We would not do anything to endanger you or Stavia or Women's Country. Believe me, we understand it far better than . . . well, than this poor child lying here on the bed. She had worked so hard all her young life, being good, being womanly, arguing every point of it with herself that she had not had time to understand the whole of it at all."

"She broke the ordinances," Morgot said, her voice very cold.

"She did not understand them. She did not see them as one thing but as many. She thought she could break one without touching the others. Also, I have a feeling that she did not so much break them as bend them, and it is likely you should be glad she did," he said. "She found out about the planned rebellion, something you otherwise might not have known until too late." He had told Morgot about Stavia's terrible secret almost as soon as they had arrived.

"As for the rebellion, we have known about it since it began. Women's Country has been here for three hundred years, Septemius. How long could we have survived if we had not known about rebellions? How many rebellions do you think there have been? Every decade, every score of years there is a rebellion. Some faction in a garrison begins to feel aggrieved. Some group of women begin to play the fool. Rebellions! They begin like a boil, swelling and pustulent, and we let them grow until they come to a head. Then we lance them, and there is pain, and the swelling goes down. Until next time. It is true, we didn't know precisely when it was planned this time, and that information is good to have. But the servitors knew about it, long before you told me. It was more difficult in the early years. Then we used spies. . . ."

"Stavia didn't do what she did out of any unworthy motive," he suggested.

"Out of ineptitude," Morgot suggested bleakly.

"Misplaced nurturing," Septemius corrected her. "The biggest chink in your female armor. The largest hole in your defences. The one thing you cannot and dare not absolutely guard against, for your nature must remain as it is for all your planning to come to fruition. You dare not change it. Still, it is hard when your own female nature betrays you into believing the ones who abuse you need you or love you or have some natural right to do what they do."

"There is also misplaced passion," Morgot said. "When we fix ourselves upon objects unworthy of us." She sighed, remembering.

"Maybe the selection ought to be working the other way as well," Septemius sighed. "Maybe you ought to be weeding some of the women out."

"There are a good number of sterilizations done every year," Morgot said. "Tubal ligations. Hysterectomies. It should not surprise you to learn that we do just that, does it, Septemius?"

"Little surprises me, madam. I do wonder, though, sometimes. . . ."

"Yes?"

"Whether you ever feel guilty over what you do? You few who do all the doing."

She sat for a time without answering. At last she shifted in her chair and said, "I'll tell you what we call ourselves, among ourselves. That will answer your question."

"Ah."

"We call ourselves the Damned Few. And if the Lady has a heaven for the merciful, we are not sure any of us will ever see it."

ONE MORNING Stavia opened her eyes to see Morgot still sitting by the window but wearing different clothes and with the light coming from a new direction. On the windowsill a glazed blue pot held bright flowers in a tight, self-conscious knot. Stavia looked at them with a half-conscious, musing gardener's eye. She had gone into the southlands in the spring when the wild iris bloomed in the dry meadows. These flowers were shaggy asters and bright buttons of chrysanthemums. The pot was her own, from her own room. Beside it was a tiny basket of blue-stained willow, filled with tiny cakes.

"I've been asleep a long time," she said with a dry mouth.

"We've been giving you various things to keep you asleep, but you're right. It's been a very long time, Stavvy. Corrig sent you the flowers and the cakes. And he says to tell you that the funny white dogs have had puppies."

"Ah." Puppies. Stavia had never seen puppies. That would be interesting. "Why was it so long?"

"It seems that bash on the head had caused some bleeding on the brain. And then you already had an infection in those wounds on your back. We've had quite a time bringing that under control. You've used up more than your share of antibiotics, Stavia. Your head is healing clean, however. There'll be a considerable scar, but your hair will cover it when it grows in again."

"They shave the women's heads," said Stavia, a bubble of screaming hysteria rising inexorably in her throat. "They . . . they . . ."

"Shhh." Morgot sat on the bed and gathered her up, holding her as softly and firmly as Corrig had done, as Joshua had done. "Shhh, love. We had to shave it all over again, and so it doesn't matter. Shhh, my Stavvy. It's all right."

Stavia calmed a little, recalling what had gone before. "Back there, with the Holylanders, I kept thinking, that was how it used to be, wasn't it? Before the convulsions. Before Women's Country, that's how it used to be for women. To be shorn like sheep, and bred whether they wanted to or not, and beaten if they didn't. . . ."

Morgot rocked, murmuring. "No, no. Not that bad as a general rule, I don't think. Love existed, after all. Some men and women have always loved one another. Not all cultures oppressed women. Some did shave heads. Some allowed beating. Other cultures were quite advanced, at least in principle. And we have to remember that many women did not resent their treatment because they'd been reared to expect it. Of course, it was even worse than that for individual women or in certain places. The Council keeps some old books in a locked room under the Council Chambers. I've read some of them. There's a phrase they used to use—'domestic violence.' "

Stavia raised her eyebrows, questioning.

Morgot responded. "I know. It has a funny sound. Like a wild animal, only partly tamed."

"What did it mean?"

"When a woman's husband beat her, sometimes to death, it was called 'domestic violence.' " She paused, breathing heavily. "In some parts of the world, they cut off women's external genitalia when they reached puberty —not the breasts, though they might have done if they hadn't been needed

to feed babies. Compared to ancient times, you got away virtually un-
scathed. Your hair will grow back. Your back will heal." Her voice was
shrill. She was talking just to make noise, to distract them both. Why was
she crying?

"Morgot. . . ."

"Yes, Stavvy."

"I was trying to be nice to him. Trying to make it up to him. I felt guilty
over what I'd done before. I was so stupid. As though making another
mistake could correct the first one. I was so dumb."

"Yes. All of us are. From time to time." Morgot rocked to and fro. "All
of us. We would be fools not to admit it. We try and we try, but we betray
ourselves."

"Sometimes I wanted him so! So terribly! And other times I almost hated
him. Did hate him!"

"I know." Morgot fell silent lost in memories, then shook her head
impatiently, wearied of that. "While you were sleeping, you kept mum-
bling about reindeer. Over and over. I couldn't figure out what you
meant."

"It was in Beneda's book about the Laplanders. Chernon stole it from
her. He had it with him. All about how they selected the bulls that were
herdable and castrated the others. . . ."

"Oh. So that was the book Chernon had. The Laplanders selected the
bulls that didn't fight. They selected the bulls that didn't try to own the
cows. They selected the bulls that were cooperative and gentle. They castrated the rest. We're kinder than that. We don't castrate anyone. We let
our warrior bulls believe they father sons."

"It's hard to accept that it's that important to them."

Morgot looked at her pityingly. "Remember Chernon and his knife,
Stavia. Then look at the monument on the parade ground. Then think of
the Holylanders. And believe. That's been your problem all along, child.
You saw. You had the proper information. You fed the proper language
back to your teachers, but you didn't understand! You couldn't believe."
She sighed. "No, we don't let the warriors know they don't impregnate us.
It's better so."

"And all the children that are born, all of them are fathered by . . . by
servitors?"

"Joshua is your father, Stavvy. He's Habby and Byram and Jerby's father
as well. And, of course, since there is only about one fertile servitor to
every three fertile women, and since there's only one of Joshua's quality for
every twenty, he's also fathered children for other women here in

Marthatown and in other cities. I am at considerable pains to make myself take pride in that fact. It does not come naturally."

"Does Myra know?"

"Of course not. As a matter of fact, Myra was born before I knew. That pregnancy was by artificial insemination, of course. Later, after I was on the Council and had been told, I took the trouble to find out who he was. Not anyone I'd ever met, and, as it later turned out, not a satisfactory sire. Almost none of his boy children return. We've stopped using him." She might have been discussing the breeding of sheep or the crossing of grain. Her voice was as unemotional as a wind on a distant ridge, her light eyes fixed on something Stavia could not see. "I believe, however, that he was Chernon's father as well."

"How many of the women know?"

"Very few, actually. The women on the Council, of course. Very few others. We put clues here and there, for those with the wits to see them. Most women don't know anything about it. We can't risk telling the ones who talk too much. Or the ones who drink a lot during carnival. Or those who are still young and silly. Who fall in love with warriors. . . ."

"How have you kept it a secret? How can you?"

"We medical officers work very hard, Stavia. It's all in our hands. Who bears, who doesn't. And when. And by whom. Haven't you noticed that almost all of the Council members are medically trained? Most of the women don't know what we're really doing. A very few figure it out for themselves. Some are told, but not usually when they're as young as you."

"But you're telling me."

"When I found out you were pregnant, I told the Council they had to allow me to tell you. I told them I would resign otherwise. They fussed about it, but in the end they said to tell you the truth and demand your oath to be quiet about it, just as we all do when we're told. You had given your oath once before, and kept it, so I knew we could risk your doing it again."

"And if I didn't?"

"You would never leave this room, Stavia. Because you've broken the ordinances and endangered us all." And those strange light eyes were fixed on her now, filled with so much pain Stavia could hardly bear it.

"You would let them kill me, wouldn't you?" she said.

"I wouldn't 'let.' " Morgot answered. "There would be nothing I could do. I might choose to go with you, but. . . . Oh, Stavvy, we've taken so long, worked so hard, sacrificed so much—our lovers, our sons. . . ."

"You have my oath," Stavia said quickly, without thinking about it, needing to get the words out if only to bring Morgot's pain to an end. Later this would seem strange and bewildering. Now, in this soft bed, with whatever drugs they had given her, it felt right. Dreamlike, but right. "On my citizenship in Women's Country, I swear. But why did they let you tell me?"

"They felt that since you had been forced and were carrying a warrior's child, you should have the right to know the truth in order to make a choice whether to abort or not. That was over a month ago, however, and we're afraid to do it now, even if you want to. It's this infection. . . . we're not really sure we have it stopped. I'd love to know what they beat you with. Something dipped in dung no doubt. . . ."

"Why does carrying a warrior's child make a difference?"

"One chance in twenty of a son returning if a warrior is his father. One chance in five if a servitor fathers him. Roughly. Given Chernon's heritage, probably less than that."

The dizziness came again, and understanding with it. Yes. She knew that. She had known that for a long, long time, without even realizing that she knew it. She had symbolized it, somewhere in that sick grayness, without realizing what it was she was doing. "We're selecting, aren't we?" she said. "And we'll keep doing it, on and on, and the years will go by, and eventually, all our sons will come home, is that it? No more penis worshipers? No more trumpets and drums and games. What will we do then, Morgot?"

"We won't have any more wars," Morgot said, holding her tightly. "Theoretically. No wars at all."

"Morgot . . . ?"

"Yes, Stavvy?"

"Am I still not allowed to ask about . . . about that time?"

"Not until or unless you're asked to serve on the Council, Stavvy. Despite what you've been through, you don't know anything at all. Remember that. Nothing at all. You didn't hint to Chernon, did you? You didn't tell him . . . ?"

"You had my oath," she said sleepily. "I didn't say anything at all. He said things to me. . . ."

"Well, don't worry about any of that. It will all be taken care of."

"BENEDA WANTS to visit you," said Joshua. "She and Sylvia."

Stavia's reply was a wordless cry of anguish.

"I know," said Joshua. "But I think you should."

"I'm supposed to make small talk with Chernon's mother? His sister?" she cried in protest. "What have they been told?"

"Just that Chernon sneaked off to meet you in the south, and that he left you there, and you were subsequently injured. In an accident. A fall, we told them, on a rocky slope. They think the servitor who was with you rescued you. I wasn't specific about who."

"They'll want to talk about Chernon. You know they will!"

"Oh yes, Stavvy. Yes they will. And you can tell them that the blow on your head gave you amnesia. You don't remember anything at all about your exploration."

"I don't remember anything?"

"No. You don't remember, for example, what Chernon said about the conspiracy. You don't remember telling Septemius about it. Because if you don't remember, then no one will worry about your knowing. . . ."

"Ah. I see." She thought about it and did see. No one must know that she knew, that any of them knew. She didn't have to make anything up. She could just say she didn't remember, didn't remember. She could just lie to Beneda her friend. Lie to her.

"All right," said the actor Stavia. "Let them come."

BENEDA AND SYLVIA CAME, and came again. They talked, among other things, of Stavia's baby. Chernon's baby. How wonderful that Stavia was having Chernon's baby. Beneda bubbled and giggled, as though she had planned it, as though she had prayed for it. Stavia smiled, when she could, and said she didn't remember.

Of course, Stavia's child could be a girl. A daughter, sharing some of the qualities of Beneda and herself, perhaps. Someone to be company. While Stavia gained strength over the slow weeks, she eased herself with this thought. Corrig was gentle with her, bringing her flowers and books, rubbing the marks on her back with ointment, tempting her to eat when she did not much seem to care. One night she found herself clinging to him, crying as she had not cried since she was a child, with him rocking her to and fro as Morgot once had done.

"Hush, my darling," he whispered. "Little bird, little fish, shhh." As though she had been a baby.

"I'm not a bird," she sobbed, trying to feel indignant.

"My bird," he lulled her. "My little bird, my little fish, something dear and loved and rockable."

"As big as a huge old jenny-ass," she cried. "Like I'd swallowed a melon."

"Or the moon, or the sun, or a bale of hay," he crooned, the chair creaking as it carried them back and forth, a pendulum swinging. "Or an ancient elephant or whale. Leviathan, behemoth, huge she is, like the spread of a tree or the girth of a watering trough. Big as the moon. Monstrous huge. . . ."

SHERI S. TEPPER

She could not stop the giggle which bubbled up unbidden. The tears dried and a wondering comfort replaced them.

"Corrig?"

"Hmmm?"

"When this is all over, will you still be here? With me?"

"Such is my intention," he said. "I have this consistent hunger for you, Stavia. Maybe it's because of all the things Habby used to tell me about you."

"What?" she demanded wonderingly. "What did he say?"

"Oh," he resumed rocking, chuckling to himself. "All kinds of very interesting things. . . ."

"And do you see what will happen to us?"

"Oh, and I do," he said. "There will be a girl child. Yours and mine. And we will name her Susannah."

"Poor woman. She did try her best for me."

"We will go into the southland, Joshua and I and others, and we will bring back all the young women there."

"Good," she sighed.

"And we will have another daughter. Her name will be—Spring."

"Ah. And what about this baby, Corrig?"

"This is a boy baby, Stavia."

He rocked her gently while she cried.

It was the next evening that Corrig told her—tentatively, as one might offer a bit of food to a possibly dangerous animal—that Chernon had returned to the garrison.

"Where has he been?" she asked in a sick whisper. "I thought he was dead."

"There was no point in upsetting you by talking about him. Actually, he's been traveling with a group of Gypsies, but he has been in touch with the garrison officers from time to time."

"Why did he come back!"

"You know why."

"Because it would have been dishonorable to do anything else?" she sneered.

"And because he knows you're carrying his child, perhaps."

Seemingly, that was not all.

Morgot came to Stavia's room that same evening and asked her to get dressed. "The Council wants to see you," she said. "Ask you some questions."

"About what?"

"Your brief sojourn with the Holylanders. They've been told all about it.

It's just that there's a big decision coming up, and they want to be quite sure they have all the facts.''

"It's Chernon, isn't it? He's come back full of information about how women can be enslaved. How their heads can be shaved and they can be beaten. He's talking to everyone in the garrison.''

"He is, yes. He's evidently heard that you 'can't remember anything,' so he's telling whatever story he pleases. He orates like something demented, but people are listening. He's been allowed to rejoin his century, the twenty-five. The servitors tell me the things he's saying are being widely accepted by a great many of the warriors.''

"Oh, by our most merciful Lady.''

"It may seem like a crisis to you, Stavia, but we've had worse. Now get your boots on.''

The meeting was a very short one, mostly questions about the Holy-landers and the beliefs they had held. Toward the end of it, they asked Stavia to join the Council, not so much because she had earned the responsibility as because it would be helpful to have her as a member. She was still too young by at least a decade they felt, but her unpleasant experiences had given her knowledge and insights that could be valuable to them. Besides, they wanted her under the Council oath for a whole variety of information. She, too weary even to argue, consented.

A MAN CAME to the garrison at Marthatown and knocked on Michael's door late at night, slipping inside like a shadow when the door was opened. He was, he said, from the garrison at Peggytown. Peggytown garrison was wavering. Her Commander wanted Michael and Stephon and Patras to meet him and help him out of a difficulty.

"What the hell?'' sneered Stephon.

"Shh,'' Michael directed. "What do you mean, they're wavering?''

"Some of the men think it's dishonorable. They may spoil the whole thing. Our Commander wants to talk to you about it.''

"We don't have time to. . . .'' Stephon began.

"Shh,'' said Michael again. "We need everything to hold together, Steph. We don't want a break.''

"That's what my Commander said. He doesn't think it's really serious, but he wants to know how you'd handle it. He thought you had the whole thing in your hand, sir. He said to tell you that. 'Michael's got it in his hand. Those men of his—Stephon and Patras—they know exactly how to talk to my men. He'll know what to do.' ''

"Where does he want to meet?''

"I brought a map. If you go straight south, he'll meet you on this line, here. Two day's travel, at most."

STAVIA LOOKED AT THE MAPS with an expression of wonder. "These are the maps they're giving to Michael? But the devastation isn't on this map. I mean, it's there, but it's in the wrong place."

"Yes," said Morgot.

"If they go on this trail that's marked, they'd go directly through it."

"Yes," Morgot replied. "They would. If they got that far."

THEY DID NOT GET THAT FAR. At the end of one day's travel, still north of the devastation and well away from the road which would have taken them to Emmaburg, in an isolated glen far from any human travel or habitation, the three settled into a spartan camp and drew lots for guard duty. Stephon had first watch. Michael took a whetstone from the donkey pack and set about sharpening his dagger. Patras amused himself with a bit of carving. He was making a daggergrip out of bone. Stephon drank the last of his tea and looked about for a good place to sit while on watch.

"How long do you think this will take?"

"A day or two. We've got time."

"I wish we'd found out about that weapon Besset saw."

"I think I've come to agree with Chernon. Besset was drunk. Seeing things. Stavia didn't know anything about a weapon." According to Chernon, Stavia had told him everything she knew about everything, none of which was important.

"Other people have heard. . . ."

"I know. But when you ask them if they've seen it, no one has."

"A myth?"

"Oh, probably not entirely. Probably truth in it."

"I heard about a weapon once, something called a gun. It could shoot daggers a long way." Stephon yawned.

"Not much good for what we want. We don't need to throw daggers a long way to take over the city," Patras grumbled.

"Anyhow, the dagger I have in mind is a lot closer," Stephon leered. "I'm planning on using it a lot."

"On what?" said a voice.

"On any of them I can catch," Stephon answered, laughing.

"Including that Morgot of yours, Michael, when you're tired of her."

Silence fell. It occurred to each of them in the same instant that the voice which had asked, "On what," had not been one of theirs. They rose, putting themselves back to back near the fire. Daggers and swords slipped from sheaths with a slithering sound, swords in right hands, daggers in left.

"Who's there?" asked Michael.

"I am," said the voice again. "Don't you know me, Michael?" She came out of the dark into the nearer shadows, dressed all in black. Morgot. There was a hood over her head, hiding her hair. "After all we've meant to one another, I should think you would have known my voice," she said gently.

"What are you doing here?"

"Come to ask you, what you are doing here, Commander of the garrison?" There was a stump near where she was standing and she sat upon it, crossing her legs, leaning slightly forward, as she had done time on time again in the taverns, listening to their songs and tales of battle. "Tell me."

"Garrison business," he blurted. "None of women's concern."

Stephon and Patras became aware of their martial stance, of their beweaponed selves. Somewhat ashamedly, they put the weapons away and stood a little aside. Whatever this was about, it was between the woman and Michael.

"Oh, Michael," she said. "Dishonor is always our concern."

"Dishonor," he grated. "What would you know about that! What would any woman know about that!"

"Much. You are sworn to protect us, Michael. Why are you conspiring against us now?"

The challenge caught him by surprise. It was a moment before he could summon the necessary bluster. "What nonsense are you talking, woman?"

"Let me tell you some history, Michael."

"We have no time to sit here while you tell stories," said Stephon, nastily. "Get yourself back to Marthatown, Morgot. You have no business here."

"Oh, you'll have time for this story," she said comfortably. "Sit or stand as you please. But I will tell it."

"Let her talk," said Michael, regaining his composure. In his lazy, half-jeering voice, he said, "So, tell your story, Morgot."

"Three hundred years ago almost everyone in the world had died in a great devastation brought about by men. It was men who made the weapons and men who were the diplomats and men who made the speeches about national pride and defense. And in the end it was men who did whatever they had to do, pushed the buttons or pulled the string to set the terrible things off. And we died, Michael. Almost all of us. Women. Children.

"Only a few were left. Some of them were women, and among them was a woman who called herself Martha Evesdaughter. Martha taught that the destruction had come about because of men's willingness—even eagerness —to fight, and she determined that this eagerness to fight must be bred out of our race, even though it might take a thousand years. She and the other women banded together and started a town, with a garrison outside. They had very few men with them, and none could be spared, so some of the women put on men's clothes and occupied the garrison outside the town, Michael. And when the boy children were five, they were given into the care of that garrison.''

"Women warriors?" scoffed Patras. "Do you expect us to believe that?"

"Do or not, as you choose. When enough years went by, it was no longer necessary for the women to play the part, and it was left to the men. Except for those few who chose to return to the city and live with the women. Some men have always preferred that."

"Cowards," snorted Stephon. "We know all about that."

"You don't know. Not really. No.

"In the first hundred years, the garrison twice tried to take over the city. But the women had not forgotten their years as warriors, Stephon, Michael. They fought back. Also, they greatly outnumbered the men. It is part of our governance to see that they always greatly outnumber the men."

Michael said nothing. He was beginning to have a horrible suspicion, a terrible surmise. His eyes sought the shadows behind her. Was there movement there?

"In the two hundred fifty years after that, warriors have tried to take over this city, or other cities, time after time. None of the rebellions have succeeded, Michael. What kind of fools would we be if we were not aware and prepared for such things? Would we be worthy to govern Women's Country?"

"Who's with you, Morgot!"

"We," said a voice from the darkness under the trees. "The humble. The lowly. Those who have left you."

"Show yourselves," cried Stephon. "Only cowards hide in the dark."

"Cowards do many things," said the voice. "Cowards kill their Commanders and make it look like a bandit attack. Cowards plot in secret. Cowards breed insurrection. Cowards plan the abuse of women." One of the shadows under the trees moved. It was a man, or at least of a man's height and bulk, dressed as Morgot was, all in black with a black hood over his head and only his eyes showing.

Behind him in the dark were other shadows. Michael counted six or eight. "I suppose it isn't cowardly to attack when you outnumber us."

"I see no outnumbering," said Morgot. "There are three of you. There is one of him. There is one of me."

"I am required to tell you," said the shadow confronting them, "what our code of behavior is. We never attack merely to wound or incapacitate. If we are driven to attack at all, there is no point in leaving our opponents alive. We never kill except in self-defense."

"Self-defense!" snorted Patras. "Sneaking up on us in the middle of the night!"

"Self-defense," repeated the shadow. "The defense of ourselves and our cities. The defense of Marthatown. The defense of Women's Country."

Patras did not delay. He had been waiting a chance, waiting a moment's inattention, and he thought he saw it now. He lunged toward the figure before him, but it was suddenly not there. He turned to find it facing him with something in its hands, a short stick. The stick moved, spun, became a silver wheel, and Patras looked down at where his sword hand had been.

"Never to wound," said the shadow. The silver wheel spun toward Patras's neck, and through it.

Michael grunted as though he had been kicked in the stomach. The man in black vanished into the darkness. Michael and Stephon held their breaths.

Morgot spoke again. "What you just saw? We call that one of our mysteries, Michael. Something the women warriors and the servitors learn and practice together. Martha Evesdaughter knew of these mysteries, and she taught them to her daughters. You have been asking our daughters about it. It and the other mysteries have their own honor. Never to be used for anything trifling. Never to be used for anything slight. For self-defense only, and always to rid Women's Country of those who are not and will not be part of it. . . ."

She rose from her place and came toward him. "Stephon, you think I am mad. I see you do. Pick up your shield, Stephon. Pick up your shield and come to me. See if you can use your dagger on me. See if you can catch me and stick your little dagger in me as you would have done with the helpless women of Marthatown."

Stephon stared at her. She was slight, small, shorter than he, obviously without the strength of arms he had. He did not bother with the shield. He was no longer surprised or afraid. He could counter the weapon he had seen by catching the wheel on his sword. He was in control of himself. He crouched to make a smaller target and lunged toward her, repeating the mistake Patras had made.

Something flashed across the distance between them and buried itself in his face. He screamed, dropping his weapons, his hands went up to push the blood out of his eyes. Through the dark curtain of blood he could see a silver glimmer as the wheel spun. He fell. He had no leg on that side.

"Never to wound," said Morgot sadly. "Always to kill. We try to be merciful." He did not even feel the blow which finished him.

Michael had seen, almost without believing. The thing that hit Stephon in the face was a toothed missile thrown from the hand. The silver wheel which cut off Patras's leg was a curved blade at the end of a chain, whirled by a short handle. A blade heavy in the middle, sharp at the edge. A blade that would whirl flat, with the sharp edge foremost. A blade that would need a shield to counter. . . .

"You wondered what weapons we had," Morgot said, stepping forward into the firelight. "You wondered, Michael. You set Barten on one of my daughters and Chernon on the other, trying to find out. Barten ruined one of my daughters and Chernon almost killed the other."

"Morgot. . . ."

"Yes. Morgot."

In the woods the other shadows stirred restlessly. Michael dropped his weapons. "I will not fight a woman." He licked dry lips. "I will not fight the mother of my sons."

"Michael, murderer of Sandom, conspirator with thieves and murderers, greedy, ambitious, destroyer, it was men like you who brought the devastations upon us. Do you think I would have had you as the father of my sons? You did not father any of them!"

He scarcely had time to comprehend what she had said, scarcely time for the rage these words created to fill him with bloody violence before there was another figure beside her. It, too, stripped its hood away. Michael didn't recognize the face, except that it was a servitor's face, with a servitor's braid. "We would not ask the mighty Michael to fight a woman," the servitor said. "But you may wish to fight the father of her sons. . . ."

They were the last words Michael heard. He moved as he had been taught to move. For a moment or two he thought he might prevail, except that the dark figure was never where he thought it would be. The blade that slit his throat came from a direction he was not even looking.

Silence fell.

Somewhere in the woods a bird made a sleepy sound. Far off on the plain a coyote yipped and was answered by a chorus of others. Beside the fire several black-clad figures moved, looking at the carnage three of them had made.

"Now," said Morgot softly. "Leave Patras here. The coyotes and the magpies will make meat of him. The other two still have their heads. Two will be enough to stir the garrison."

"I wish you had let me fight him," said Corrig.

"I needed to do it," said Joshua, as others came quietly out of the woods to pack the two corpses upon donkeys and lead them away. "In Women's Country we learn not to have jealousy, Corrig. They teach us and themselves to be calm, to take joy in the day, to set aside possessiveness. And yet, despite it all. . . ."

"Despite it all, you needed to kill him."

"Yes," said Joshua with a shamed face. "I did."

THE REST OF THAT NIGHT and a day and a night went by.

As chance would have it, it was Chernon who was first on the parade ground, near dawn of that next day. He had not slept well since he had returned to the garrison. All day, every day, men asked him about the Holylanders and how they lived. Chernon had seen Resolution Brome with half a dozen wives; he had not noticed how many men there were with none. He had not seen much of the women, and it was not his intention to tell the whole truth in any case. What he had seen was enough. It was proof, proof enough that men could do what they pleased, that men could have their own ordinances, run their own society, make the women do their will. This he said, over and over, speaking mostly of those he had seen who had many wives to wait on them, to do their pleasure.

He should have been elated, but he could not sleep well after he had finished talking. Whenever he drifted off, he saw Stavia's face, as it had been when he had first seen her, as it had been while they had been together, as it had been when he cut out that thing, whatever it was, as it had been when he had seen her last, white as bleached linen, bloodless, the eyes shadowed like skull eyes. Four faces. Excitement. Joy. Horror. Death. Those eyes seemed to follow him wherever he went, whatever he did. Interest. Delight. Anger. Death.

He had a good mind, as Tonia and Kostia had noted. It was not beyond him to draw inferences. Was what he had seen what he really wanted? In all his dreams of journeying, all his dreams of heroic quest, he had not seen faces like those last two faces, and yet there must have been many faces like that when Odysseus was finished with his quest. He had killed and ravished everywhere he went. It sounded well in the sagas. They did not talk about the women's faces. Why was it that the sagas never spoke of the women's faces? Odysseus said, "The wind took me first to Ismarus, which is the city of the Cicons. There I sacked the town and put the people to the sword. We took their wives. . . ."

"Put the people to the sword." That meant they'd killed the men, killed the children, too, likely. And then they took the women, but Odysseus didn't say anything about their faces. Nothing.

Why? Why didn't Odysseus say how the women felt? How they looked? Why didn't any of the sagas talk about that?

The questions plagued him, kept him awake at night, wakened him early in the morning to go out onto the parade ground and stalk about, trying to tire himself out so the faces would go away.

And as he strode by the victory monument, he saw another face, a bloody face, upside down, and thought for the moment he had dreamed it. But this was Michael's face. Michael's body, and Stephon's body, hung by the feet from the victory monument, dead.

His harsh scream, half shock, half stomach-wrenching panic, brought the men on guard duty, and within minutes every man in the garrison knew what had been found.

As for Chernon, he was in his dormitory, huddled under his covers, sick with fear. It had something to do with Stavia. He knew it did. And if it had something to do with Stavia, he would be next.

By noon, the Heads of Council requested audience with Centurion Hamnis, the next highest in command, and informed him that they had discovered who had committed the atrocity. Spies from Tabithatown had done it, to render Marthatown helpless against an attack, to destroy morale.

The garrison raged as it prepared itself for war.

IT WAS BENEDA who brought the news to Stavia.

Stavia's hair had grown out into a wavy crown, mostly hiding the scars where Cappy had hit her with the shovel and where the doctors had drilled holes in her skull. The lash marks on her back had faded, leaving only a few vague stripes to show where they had been. She had been able to leave the hospital and was back in her old room at Morgot's house.

Beneda was in and out of that room almost every day, bringing a few flowers, bringing freshly baked cookies. Sometimes Sylvia came. No matter how often Stavia tried to pick other topics of conversation, they always wanted to talk about Chernon. Now they wanted to talk about Chernon and war.

"Have you talked to him since he came back?" Stavia asked, wondering if he had told Beneda any part of the truth.

"Once," Beneda confided. "Just from the wall. I told him how you'd been hurt, and he got this strange expression on his face. I just know he was kicking himself for not staying with you and protecting you, Stavvy."

"I doubt he could have done anything," said Stavia through dry lips.

"Mother's pretty broken up over this whole thing," Beneda said. "I mean, she sent him away that time, and then he came back. And then he chose to stay in the garrison. And then he went after you and stayed away, and we thought he was dead, but he came back. And now he's going to battle. . . ."

"It must be very hard for her," said Morgot, who had come into the room during this confession. She laid her hand upon Stavia's shoulder, comfortingly, warningly. "Tell her she has my deepest sympathy, Beneda."

Beneda nodded, "Oh, I will." Then she launched herself at Stavia, hugging her close, cheeks together as she murmured, "It isn't just mother. It's me, too. It seems like I keep on mourning over him. . . . I don't know what I'd do without you, Stavvy. You're my best friend. Next to Mother and Chernon, I love you the best. . . ."

When she had gone, Stavia stared after her, her mouth working, tears welling.

"Stavvy?" Morgot put her hands on Stavia's shoulders again, shaking her.

"Let me alone!" She got up, turning away, dragging at her shoulders with her hands as though she would uproot her arms. "How in hell am I supposed to feel? I can't say anything I want to. Not to Beneda. I can't tell her things. I hear her going on and on about Chernon returning from battle, and I . . . I feel like a filthy hypocrite. Like a traitor. I hate myself."

"Sylvia is my friend, too, Stavia. Often I feel unworthy of her friendship. But what else can I do? Have friends only among Council members? Then people would think we're clannish, and if Council members appear to be clannish and not to have friends among others in the town, it would lead to a failure of confidence."

"It's like we were two people," Stavia said. "One who thinks. One who acts. Acts a part, as in a play."

"Yes," her mother nodded. "That's exactly what it's like."

THE MARTHATOWN GARRISON marched out two days later, at dawn, twelve hundred men, down to the last noncombatant foundryman and cook. Even the twenty-four century went along to serve as messengers and in other noncombatant roles. All night the Council members had kept vigil beside the Gate to Women's Country, praying for those who might yet return through the gate to Women's Country, praying that some would return. None had.

Morgot and Stavia stood among the other blue-robed Councilwomen, ranged at the easternmost end of the wall above the armory, to watch them depart. It was the first time Stavia had worn the robes. She felt self-conscious in them, and yet there was an inevitability about their substantial weight. She remembered thinking once long ago that she was a kind of Morgot, a younger copy. Now the copy was even closer than before.

At the far end of the wall, Sylvia and Beneda stood, both weeping and waving.

Down on the parade ground, many of the young men displayed devices or surcoats, or bright banners on their spears. Chernon wore a coat of green and blue which Beneda had made for him. He was not looking at Beneda, however. His eyes were searching the women, ranging across them again and again. When at last he found Stavia among the Council members, his eyes went wide and his nostrils flared. He had not thought to look for her there.

"Wave to him," instructed Morgot. "Sylvia and Beneda are watching him and you. Wave to him and smile."

Stavia waved and smiled at a point just above his head. She saw faces she knew, an amusing man she had spent parts of two days with during carnival just after she got back from the academy, another who had sung sagas in a tavern while the roisterers, she among them, had banged their cups upon the tables. She had enjoyed them both. She waved at them also, and smiled. Morgot was not looking at the men but at the women, searching the faces ranked along the wall, stopping to examine this one and then that one as they waved. Mothers of men in the garrison. Sisters. Lovers.

The trumpets blared. The drums banged. The numbered centuries, with their gaps where men had fallen or returned through the gate, consolidated with others until there were twelve full centuries for the march, the officers striding ahead, making a long column with guidons slapping and honors lashing in the wind, all the honors a garrison had been given in all its years of service.

Behind them, in the plaza, the women's band struck up its song, "Gone Away, Oh, Gone Away." Silently the words, as sung by the Councilwomen, ran in Stavia's mind.

> "Where has my lovely warrior gone,
>   the one who made me sigh?
>   the drums have beaten him away,
>   he's gone away to die,
>   he's gone to fight for honor,
>   he's gone to fear and pain,
>   Gone away, oh, gone away,
>   I'll not see him again."

Sylvia and Beneda were still there on the wall, their arms moving in endless farewell. Far down the road, almost as an afterthought, Chernon turned back, sought his mother and sister and lifted his hand. Beneda redoubled her efforts, arms blurring in an arc above her sturdy form.

On a hill to the west, Stavia could see several figures mounted on donkeys. There were more along the line of march. Outriders. Servitors. There to see that none of the warriors left the line of march and sneaked away to join the ranks of the lawless.

The women began to leave the walls. Stavia and Morgot delayed until they could delay no longer, but still Sylvia and Beneda waited for them in the plaza below, tears staining their faces. Sylvia threw herself into Morgot's arms.

"I can't bear it," she wailed. "I've mourned for him too many times. . . ."

"Shhh," said Morgot, her face as bleak as a winter cliff. "There, there."

"He'll be all right," Beneda said bravely. "Mama, come on. We thought Chernon was gone before, you know? And he came home perfectly safe. Come on, now. Morgot and Stavia have things to do. Come on." She hugged Stavia, her tears moistening Stavia's face and making a hard, hideous lump come into Stavia's throat.

They turned and went up the hill, two women supporting each other, among a hundred other such.

Morgot wiped her eyes as she looked after them. It was as though she had wiped all expression from her face, leaving it blank, like a manikin's. Like the face of Hecuba in the play. She and Stavia started up the hill, slowly, letting the mourners go on ahead.

"Exactly what was the agreement with Tabithatown Council?" Stavia asked. "You haven't told me."

Morgot's voice was as expressionless as her face. "We have been watching the messengers sent by Michael and Stephon for some little time, ever since the servitors warned us that rebellion was actually brewing. Michael had been in touch with three other garrisons. We have identified the troublemakers in each garrison, and members of the fraternity in each town have taken care of them."

"And?"

"Unfortunately, Michael's plans have pretty well permeated the Marthatown garrison during the last few months. And, of course, Chernon's propaganda swept through the warriors like wildfire." Her hand went to her eyes, pressing in, as though to keep captive some dangerous intention which threatened to break free. They went on a few steps in silence before she finished the thought.

"Yes," said Stavia.

"When our garrison reaches the battle site, they will find that the Tabithatown troops have been joined by the full garrisons from four other cities. We have met with representatives from all their Councils. Their massed garrisons will outnumber ours at least four to one."

"Ah!"

"Even with the good harvest, the Councils agree that all five of the garrisons arrayed against us need to be reduced in size."

"And?"

"And we have agreed that none of those from Marthatown are to return at all."

THE EVENING before summer carnival, in Stavia's thirty-seventh year.

During performances of *Iphigenia at Ilium,* the actors who stood upon the walls of Troy, Iphigenia herself, and Achilles, could look out across the gathered audience and the green of the park to the garrison ground, still echoing and empty-seeming, though it had been almost sixteen years since the Marthatown garrison had been lost. When the news of that loss had come, there had been shock and panic and hysteria in the city. There had been grieving, but no graves. There had been no warriors left to bring home the dead.

Among the boys and men under twenty-four, after the shock had passed, there had been a need to seek causes and lay blame. It was the Women's Council who told them that Michael and Stephon and Patras had betrayed their men for pay, that they had planned to lead them into a trap. Someone among their fellow conspirators had undoubtedly killed them in an argument over the spoils. Council had not said, not then, not since, how many garrisons from how many different cities had formed that trap. It was for-

bidden to parade the honors of any in that lost garrison since none knew—
so it was said—who had been among the conspirators.

Adding together Council members and servitors, there had been many
who knew the truth, but the truth had not been spoken. A myth was spoken
instead. In time, what was spoken became the truth. "The Lady," the Council had said, "will distinguish the guiltless and the honorable from the
traitors. Their honors will be paraded in heaven."

A song had been written about the lost garrison, a song about betrayal of
trust and broken ordinances and shame. It had been commissioned by the
Council, but it became popular and widely sung, despite that.

A few months after the disaster, Susantown had sent two centuries of
young men for Marthatown's defense. Later some of the other cities had
sent men of their own, enough to make up a small though respectable
garrison. Though they were all young men, they were tried men, men who
had no patience with deviation from the ordinances, and they had soon
whipped the fifteen- to twenty-three-year-olds into shape.

Beneda and Sylvia had never stopped talking about Chernon, any more
than hundreds of other lovers or sisters or mothers had stopped talking
about their lovers or brothers or sons. Stavia had learned to join in the talk,
as Morgot did, holding the center of herself quiet, letting the actor Stavia
do all the work.

And now the actor Stavia stood on the stage of the summer theater as
Iphigenia. In the morning, at dawn, summer carnival would start. There
would be drinking and laughter and sex. There would be jokes and singing. Before all that there had to be this, this reminder for those who could
see what was in it.

Such as those on the stage with Stavia, or those sitting in the first few
rows—the Councilwomen. Tonia. Kostia. Old Septemius. Behind them a
select group of servitors. Less than two hundred in all. What Morgot called
the "Damned Few." Those who kept things running. Those who did what
had to be done.

And behind them were all the other women of Marthatown. Beneda and
Sylvia were there, on the aisle, where Stavia could not help but see them.
During the early stages of the play there had been laughter and catcalls,
giggles and whispers in the audience. At the end, however, a hush had
fallen, the rattling of candy baskets had stopped, and the eyes of all the
audience were fixed upon them where they stood halfway up the walls of
Troy, Stavia and Joshua: Iphigenia and Achilles.

From the high plinth beside Iphigenia, Achilles asked the question.
"What's it like, this Hades?"

ACHILLES   What's it like, this Hades?

IPHIGENIA   Like shadow with no sun, like dark with no day. Like the mating of ghosts.

ACHILLES   Riddles! Only riddles!

POLYXENA   I think she means, Achilles, that in hell we need not damn ourselves by trying to defend ourselves.

IPHIGENIA   That's what I meant, yes.

ACHILLES   It makes no sense! What has defending yourself to do with it?

POLYXENA   I pled for my life, Achilles. When they said they would kill me, I wet myself. My bowels opened and the shit ran down my legs. I screamed and groveled. I hated what I was doing, but I did it. Achilles, I wanted to live! I wanted to live, but they killed me, stinking like a dung-covered animal. I was slender and still young, Achilles. I loved to dance, Achilles. But they killed me there in the mess with my skirts hiked up and blood and shit mixed like a stinking stew, damned to forever remember myself like that—like that. . . .

In Hades, perhaps I'll dance. I won't have to beg for my life, Achilles. I'll have no life to lose.

ANDROMACHE   I saw my father slain. The spear went into his chest where he'd cuddled me, sometimes, calling me his sweetheart. The blood came out and he grunted like a slaughtered pig, a kind of squeal. He was surprised, I think. My brothers came running, but you and your men slaughtered them. Now, here at Troy, you've done it again, hacked my husband to bits. I keep seeing it in my sleep, arms, legs, fingers, thighs, all mixed in this terrible clutter. I keep trying to sort them out, calling, "Daddy, Hector, where are the parts of you I loved. . . ."

And Hector's baby? My baby, his baby, our son. Thrown from the walls like rubbish. I heard him cry as he fell. He made a sound like a hunting bird, falling into the sea. . . . I can't think of anything else.

When the ship that takes me gets far enough from shore, I'll leap out into that sea. I'll be damned for taking my own life, but that's all that's left to do. I can't risk loving anything else to see it slain. In Hades there's no life and there's no pain. The dead are dead. They can't be killed again.

HECUBA   I had a knife in my skirt, Achilles. When Talthybius bent over me, I could have killed him. I wanted to. I had the knife just for that reason. Yet, at the last minute I thought, he's some mother's son just as Hector was, and aren't we women all sisters. If I killed him, I thought, wouldn't it be like killing family? Wouldn't it be making some other mother grieve? So I didn't kill him, but if I had, I might have saved the baby. I'm damned to think of that, that I might have saved Hector's child. Dead or damned, that's the choice we make. Either you men kill us and are honored for it, or we women kill you and are damned for it. Dead or damned. Women don't have to make choices like that in Hades. There's no love there, nothing to betray.

ACHILLES *(Shaking his head, still weeping)* I ask you yet again, Agamemnon's daugher. What's it like, this Hades!

IPHIGENIA   What's Hades like?

Like dream without waking. Like carrying water in a sieve. Like coming into harbor after storm. Barren harbor where the empty river runs through an endless desert into the sea. Where all the burdens have been taken away.

You'll understand when you come there at last, Achilles. . . .

Hades is Women's Country.

Stavia leaned over Joshua, putting her cheek against his own, her eyes fixed on the half-empty garrison ground, seeing in her mind the thousands who had marched away. Gone away, oh, gone away. Wetness ran between her face and his as he—servitor, warrior, citizen of Women's Country, father—as he wept.

Wept for them all.